THE THING ON THE SHORE

Tom Fletcher was born in 1984. He is married, and currently lives in Manchester. He blogs at www

Also by Tom Fletcher

The Leaping

THE THING ON THE SHORE

Tom Fletcher

Quercus

First published in 2011 by

Quercus
21 Bloomsbury Square
London
WC1A 2NS

A CIP catalogue record for this book is available
from the British Library

ISBN 978 1 84916 136 7

10 9 8 7 6 5 4 3 2 1

Typeset by Ellipsis Books Limited, Glasgow

Printed and bound in Great Britain by Clays Ltd, St Ives plc

For my parents

PART ONE

THE LIGHTHOUSE NIGHT

Arthur had been what, twelve years old. So this was, what, fourteen years ago. He had woken up, not knowing why, and had lain there in bed and listened out for whatever it was that had disturbed him. He had not long to wait.

Raised voices from downstairs: the words were unclear but the sentiments were not. Arthur's room was dark but for the moonlight coming in through the thin blue curtains. He got out of bed and went to look out of the window. No point, really, in trying to sleep now.

The moon hung fat and the stars also appeared extravagant; the sea was alive with the joyous shimmer of reflected light. Arthur looked at the sea and it looked like the perfect medium for life. It looked absolutely ideal. What if to be in the sea were to exist in a kind of luminous weightlessness? It sounded quite perfect. Of course you would not be surrounded by that light, not really, but what if?

Arthur was almost ignoring the shouting from downstairs, but not really ignoring it well enough. He shifted his gaze from the sea to the lighthouse. The lighthouse had a green light. He dimly remembered the lighthouse once having a white light, as most lighthouses in films and TV programmes and illustrations did, but at some point – he couldn't remember exactly when – the light of Whitehaven lighthouse had gone green. Sometimes, at night, Arthur liked to look at the lighthouse and lose himself in the rhythm of that light. It was not a very bright light, and there was no rotating beam extending from it. It did not flash suddenly; it was just a slow blinking. The light would subtly appear at the top of the red-and-white tower, and then disappear. A gleaming thing: less like a light and more like something green and precious that was reflecting some other light. Arthur liked the fact that it was green and that it was understated. He narrated the status of the light in his head: *on-off-on-off-on-off-on-off*. The words were stretched out in his head because the light was either on or off for what felt like a long time. A good three or four seconds, at least.

The front door slammed. Arthur tore his gaze away from the lighthouse and looked down at the floor. Some kind of continuous noise had suddenly stopped with that slamming. Then the front door opened again. He heard his dad calling from the doorway.

'Rebecca!'

But Rebecca, his mum, did not respond. She was running away. Why would she be running away? She was running across the grass towards the cliffs and the sea. Arthur could see her now, dressed all in white – thick

4

white pyjamas – hastening off. Harry, his dad, was out there too, although he was less prominent, wearing dark colours that did not stand out against the dark greens and browns of the scrubby ground. He wasn't moving very quickly. He was shouting but he was not moving very quickly.

He was not moving quickly enough.

Arthur started trying to open the window but fumbled with the catch.

What had they been fighting about, anyway?

Arthur's mum reached the cliffs and paused there. She turned back to look at Harry, who was now jerkily hopping and jumping towards her. He must not have had any shoes on. Arthur hammered on the window but neither parent looked up. He looked briefly at his mother standing there, luminous against the sea beyond; then, feeling some kind of desperate certainty about what was going to happen, he looked away. Looked at the lighthouse instead. From the corner of his eye he saw the shining figure of his mother slip away but, with some kind of world-shaking feat of mental strength, he concentrated on that flashing light instead. That *on-off-on*.

TRANSITION

The whale was young and injured. Something vicious and grasping and unseen had ensnared it from behind during its migration, squeezing it tightly in a tentacle grip. The young whale had only been released when its giant mother had turned back and ploughed into its attacker, mouth open wide, her pointed teeth tearing at squid flesh. Everything moved agonisingly slowly under water, though, and by the time the squid had let the young whale go, it already had several broken bones and ruptured internal organs. It spiralled downwards, keening, crying, singing in a doleful voice, its eyes swivelling to and fro, looking for its mother. It could see her floating up above, quite far away now, struggling as if herself in some creature's grip. But it could not see any sign of the squid.

The young whale felt different now. The element in which it moved felt unfamiliar. This was not the ocean that it knew.

It was no longer swimming through an ocean at all, but it could not know that.

The whale was not aware of its mother any more. Still quite far below it, there stretched a seemingly endless plain of pink and yellow and white and red and green organic matter – tendrils and shells and matted, hair-like material. Above it there appeared to be some kind of strange, closed-in sky. It was a creamy colour – not the familiar deep blue of hundreds of metres of brine – and it seemed to throb with some kind of energy. The whale did not think in such terms, but the sky was vibrating so violently and at such speed that it looked like there were two skies, one laid beneath the other and flickering in and out of existence.

In the distance there was a cluster of purple lights.

The whale stopped moaning as it drifted, and not long after that it died.

A Fantasy at the Lighthouse

Arthur had experienced one of his lighthouse days. Not a day spent at the lighthouse; rather a day spent longing to be at the lighthouse. It was getting dark by the time he finally got down there after work, and after tea.

Increasingly, Arthur found himself alone. There were always traces of the fishermen, but the fishermen themselves tended to have left by the time he arrived. Of course it was not actually true that he was always alone at the lighthouse; it was just that he had started to become more and more aware of the solitude.

He leant across the wall from which the fishermen fished, avoiding the smear of fish guts. The sea was relatively smooth and still. Not still – it was never still – but relatively flat. Nearly still. Arthur looked all the way out to the horizon and thought it was a bit weird, actually, the way that there seemed none of the usual peaks and troughs.

He pressed his cheek to the sandstone of the wall and closed his eyes.

Arthur was woken by cold water falling on his face. He stood up and saw that it was now dark. It was not raining, as he had first thought, but sea water was spraying up from the other side of the wall. The surface of the ocean appeared to be more agitated than it had been earlier. It looked like there was a disturbance of some kind – like in a film when a submarine was surfacing. Arthur watched raptly, hoping that something huge and monstrous would emerge, something that just kept coming and kept coming, more and more of it, some kind of shiny black tentacle, or a mass of shiny black tentacles . . . Or some kind of huge, blind, bulbous whale-like creature, grotesque in its enormity, pale-skinned and moaning, mouth open wide, the whole creature straining against its skin, somehow rising from the water even still, more and more of its flesh being revealed as the brine ran slickly back down the body of the beast, whatever it was, back into the liquid mass of the sea itself. Some kind of saucer-eyed, seal-faced titan with a blank expression and a gigantic mouth hanging open, an endless flood of water streaming from between its teeth as it rose up over Whitehaven, taller than the lighthouse, taller than any lighthouse, bigger than any building. Like Godzilla but just standing there, no apparent desire to destroy, no apparent anger, just a fucking horrible blankness, a terrible apathy, like this thing had just woken up and just wished it was dead.

Arthur looked out over the sea – now black under the night sky – and thought of a planet he had read about in the science bit of the newspaper. This was a planet that had been discovered outside our solar system, using a network of telescopes trained on a not-too-distant star. A water planet. One three times as large as the Earth and made almost entirely of water; a colossal spherical ocean wrapped around a ball of rock. That ocean was over fifteen thousand kilometres deep, which was a detail Arthur had not been able to forget. Fifteen thousand kilometres of water heading straight down. Fifteen metres seemed deep enough, to be honest. If you knew that the water beneath you was fifteen metres deep, that was enough to make you feel small; that was enough to make you feel like there was some serious depth below you. But fifteen thousand kilometres? That didn't really bear thinking about. Arthur thought about it quite a lot, though.

The same planet was believed to have a thick atmosphere that rendered it permanently dark. There was no visible light from the sun reaching that ocean. It was hot, being seventy-five times closer to its sun than the Earth was to our sun, and yet the ocean remained liquid because of the weight of the atmosphere. So the water could reach nearly three hundred degrees Celsius and still not evaporate.

Theoretically there could be islands floating on this planet. Not made of rock or soil, but a kind of ice formed after it was subjected to phenomenal atmospheric pressures. Crystalline structures forced into existence through the compaction of water.

When they got a chance, they would turn the Hubble Space Telescope on to this planet in order to analyse its atmosphere. They would look for oxygen: something that only exists on Earth because of the presence of life there. Oxygen in the atmosphere of the water world would indicate the presence of life there, too, which would not be as impossible as it might sound, given the way weird creatures thrived around volcanic vents at the bottom of the sea on Earth. And what kind of life might exist in an ocean fifteen thousand kilometres deep?

Imagining this planet with its heaving, bottomless ocean, an impossibly hot ocean, an ocean totally enveloped in darkness, orbiting a red dwarf star – a dying star – felt very sad and eerie. It was an eerie sadness that Arthur could enjoy, though. He liked to imagine himself swimming through those black waters, somehow immune to – but not unaware of – the hideous temperatures. In these fantasies, the sky would flash red or white as unearthly storms tore open the heavy clouds, and barbed threads of lightning skittered across the peaks of the mountainous waves.

He imagined the whales, or their equivalent, that might live in those depths. These creatures would be blind and they would also be gargantuan. They would be pale and they would have strange skin able to deal with the heat and the pressure. They might have some kind of rigid exoskeleton. Maybe those creatures would be more insect than mammal, or God knows what else. It probably wasn't even possible, though. The planet probably didn't even exist. How could anybody really know? Still, he often imagined himself swimming – flailing – across the surface of that orb, and waiting for something alive to brush against his feet.

He now imagined something alive, one of those monsters from that planet, rising directly up out of the sea in front of him, somehow here with him, somehow in the water just by virtue of being from other water, as if all water were somehow connected; as if the oceanic depths of one planet were connected to the oceanic depths of another.

The sea off the shore of Whitehaven would boil and the creature would thrash its way up above the surface and halfway on to the land and, without even knowing it, it would knock the lighthouse down.

ARTHUR AND HARRY

The next day, Arthur sat at the desk with his head in his hands, because it was somehow the most comfortable position. The chair he occupied was old and broken. His posture would be ruined for ever. He should do something about it. He grimaced as one of the recorded voices rattling out of his earpiece grew louder and angrier. He felt like he wasn't physically big enough to deal with the anger he was listening to. He wanted to expand and break and flow across his desk, until he was pressed into all the corners. He wanted to fill the small, perfectly square 'pod' with himself, with just his body. Completely. He wanted to be bigger, and he wanted to be made out of water.

The pod was not a real room, but a space partitioned off by walls that were actually more like windows. Each wall was made out of two large sheets of very strong glass with a blind fitted between them. These blinds could be lowered so that whatever happened inside the pod remained hidden. The walls only went halfway up to the ceiling, though, so the pod was never entirely private. Conversations could be overheard. The pod was one of many lining one wall of the call centre in which Arthur worked. He could hear the general murmur of hundreds of people talking on telephones on the other side of the glass, the insect buzz of typing, the hum of all those computers. He could smell dust and hot plastic.

Arthur had lowered the blinds of the pod he occupied, so he could now feel alone. His back was hunched. His longish black hair flopped down in front of his face. He wore black trousers secured high about the waist by a belt in which he'd punched new holes with a corkscrew, and a white shirt with a red tie. The trousers were too big for him. His mum always used to say he was too thin.

The angry voice that he was listening to had momentarily stopped shouting, and a second voice was now audible as it apologised. The second voice was weak, and its owner stammered.

'I'm . . . I'm sorry, Mr McCormick. I'm very, very sorry. Um . . . before I look into that, I just need to . . . um. Can . . . can I just ask, do you have a mobile number that, um, or any other . . . any other contact number that I could, um, take? Please?'

Arthur squeezed his eyes shut. He heard a sharp intake of breath from Mr McCormick.

'No!' shouted Mr McCormick. 'No, you cannot! You . . . you bloody people, you'll know more about me than I do myself!' His voice grew louder and Arthur could picture the spittle flying from his lips and sticking to the telephone receiver gripped in his fleshy hand. 'I've got a heart condition! I'm not a well man! And you . . . you won't even try to help me! It's bloody disgusting! I'm ill, I am! And you just keep asking questions!'

'I . . . I'm sorry, Mr McCormick.'

'Yeah, well, I'm sorry too. Sorry I'm not talking to somebody who knows what they're doing!'

'If—'

'Just forget about it! Don't even bother! All this nonsense'll kill me! Bloody idiots!'

Arthur heard Mr McCormick slam the phone down forcefully, missing the cradle, then swearing, before righting his error with the understated *click* of a call being disconnected. He bit his lip. The second voice continued.

'Mr . . . Mr McCormick? Are you there? Hello? Oh.'

That second voice – that weak, stammering sound that worried and fussed into one end of the dead telephone line – was the voice of Arthur's father, Harry, one of the many customer advisers working at the call centre.

Arthur stopped the recording and was about to close down the Random Call Recorder computer program when the door into the pod swung open. It banged into one of the glass walls with enough force to send a sharp cracking sound bouncing around the small, square space. Arthur spun around on his chair, his eyes and mouth wide open.

'Arthur,' said the pale, stocky man standing in the doorway. 'What are you still doing here?' He looked at his watch. 'You finished half an hour ago!'

15

'Yeah,' said Arthur. 'Yeah . . . Hi, Bracket. I was just catching up. Marking a few more calls. I don't want to claim overtime. Don't worry about it.'

'I wasn't,' said Bracket. He had a cracked kind of voice that always sounded tired.

'OK,' said Arthur.

'You all right?'

'Yeah,' said Arthur, shutting down the computer. 'I'm fine.'

'Good.'

Bracket stood awkwardly in the doorway for a moment. He had short, bristly grey hair and dark blue rings under his eyes. His shirt was creased and the sleeves were rolled up to the elbows. He wore a chunky watch that looked expensive but, Arthur reckoned, probably wasn't. Bracket held a small stack of paper in one hand as he chewed on his lower lip. He was Arthur's team manager, Arthur being on the Quality Assurance Team.

'Arthur,' Bracket continued at last. 'There's been some news. We're delivering team briefings, so I'm trying to round up all of the QPs who're still here. I wasn't expecting to find you but, well, seeing as you *are* still here, you'd better come too.'

'OK,' said Arthur.

'You're not in a rush to get home, are you?' asked Bracket.

'No,' said Arthur.

The QPs were the Quality Police, which was how Bracket referred to the Quality Assurance Team. It was his little joke.

16

'Then you'd best get yourself to the scrum sofas,' said Bracket. 'That's where the others are. Have you seen Tiffany anywhere?'

'No,' said Arthur. 'I haven't seen anybody since I finished. I've just been in here all the time.'

'I'll meet you over there,' said Bracket, 'once I've found Tiffany. That woman, I don't know.'

He turned and left the pod, shaking his head and muttering under his breath.

Arthur waited a few seconds longer, so that he would not have to walk alongside Bracket, then picked up his coat and made his way out on to the main floor of the call centre. This place always felt somehow green to him, but not in a healthy, fresh way – it was the sickly green of swallowed frustration, of exhausted arguments, of boredom, of well-thumbed £5 notes. This was probably partly because the carpet was green, reflected Arthur, but there was more to it than that.

The scrum sofas were beneath a long window on the opposite side of the room to the pods. Most of the QPs were already seated there. With his coat draped over his shoulder, Arthur threaded his way between semi-circular huddles of desks, each one assigned to a different team. When he finally reached the bright blue sofas, he put his coat down next to a boy called Dean, and then stood by the window and looked out over the sea towards Whitehaven lighthouse. The sea was a bitter grey colour and looked violently rough. Waves threw themselves high against the wall of the far harbour, which rose about six metres above the water at that point, and then crashed over the top of it. The spume rose even as high as the top of the lighthouse, which itself stood on the harbour wall, and a never-ending wind whipped it up into the sky, in bright white specks that stood out starkly against the glowering black clouds.

'Right then!' came Bracket's voice from behind him. 'Looks like we're all here now. Arthur, come and sit down. Is everybody actually here? Yes? Good.'

Arthur turned from the window and sat down next to Dean, in the spot where he'd left his coat. He saw that Bracket had found Tiffany. She was now squeezing on to one of the sofas, pushing everybody else along.

'Ooh, sorry I'm late,' said Tiffany. 'I didn't know! I didn't know there was a meeting!'

'Short notice,' said Bracket.

'I was just on the bog,' said Tiffany. 'Caught unawares, I was. But a girl's gotta do what a girl's gotta do!'

'Tiffany,' continued Bracket, and he looked at her hard.

'Sorry,' said Tiffany. 'Sorry, you know what I'm like with my mouth.'

Tiffany usually wore the strangest combinations of clothes. She made them all herself, and they were always covered with geometric patterns in strange, dysentery-hued colours. They were like the clothes that Arthur imagined older women used to wear in the seventies. She had long hair that might never have been washed or combed for as long as it had grown on her head. Her teeth were mostly black with rot, but her gums were a bright electric pink. All the younger girls said she was a witch, partly because of the way she looked and partly because she herself claimed to be a medium.

'I have to read this verbatim,' announced Bracket, holding up the thick document he was carrying, 'and I also have to give you each a copy of the brief. This is so that everybody working here receives exactly the same message as everybody else. Do you understand?'

'Yeah,' said somebody, quietly. Everybody else nodded half-heartedly. Arthur noticed that Diane, an empty-eyed girl on the team, was texting somebody while using her notebook to hide the fact from Bracket.

'That means that you will all take away these hand-outs,' said Bracket. 'You will recognise the importance of the message they deliver and keep hold of it, partly to refer to in your own spare time and partly to demonstrate your interest in the workings of this corporation, this workplace, and your employer.'

'Is this part of the brief?' asked Dean.

'No,' replied Bracket. 'Here, Dean, you distribute these.' He handed the stack of paper to Dean, who stood to receive it and then shuffled around the sofas, with his back slightly hunched. Dean had a significant overbite and bad skin, and he smiled genuinely at the rest of the team as he passed them their individual copies of the brief. His short brown hair had been shaped into greasy spikes with the help of some sort of gel. Once he'd finished, he turned to Bracket.

'Thank you,' he said.

'That's OK,' said Bracket, his forehead creasing slightly. 'OK then, at last. The brief is starting. I am beginning now. I am reading from the briefing note, so please listen.

'"It is with great sadness that I have gathered you here to inform you of some recent events. As you may be aware, certain contractual renegotiations have been ongoing between Outsourcing Unlimited and the parent company, Interext, with regard to the Northern Water contract. For three years now, Outsourcing Unlimited have provided Northern Water with an excellent customer-management service from the Whitehaven contact centre, and both Interext and Northern Water would like to express their unreserved gratitude to both the centre and all of the hardworking staff employed there."'

Arthur's eyes strayed once more to the window, and the elemental turmoil beyond it. Storms were not unusual in this part of the country, but they were invariably spectacular. He was gratified to see that the weather showed no sign of improving and, if anything, was growing increasingly lively. He could hear the entire roof of the building groaning. Maybe, with luck, it would be whipped away or there would be some catastrophic power failure that meant the place had to close down. Arthur fantasised about this kind of occurrence frequently.

'"However,"' continued Bracket, '"despite their best efforts, Outsourcing Unlimited have failed in one of their contractual obligations. This is of great regret to all concerned, but particularly to Northern Water, who have no other option but to terminate their contract with Outsourcing Unlimited."'

One of the older team members, Johnny, looked alarmed at that. He had been in the navy once upon a time, and sported a thick, grey handlebar moustache and tattoos all over his wrinkled hands. He now widened his bright blue eyes in a way that Arthur found over-dramatic, as if it were a deliberate action and not simply a reaction to what he had heard.

"This means that, as of the first of October, the arrangement between Outsourcing Unlimited and Northern Water will come to an end. Employees based at the Whitehaven contact centre will no longer be working for Outsourcing Unlimited. Instead, Interext are moving the operation in-house and will be your employer from that date on. This is the end result of several months of intense negotiations and renegotiations with Northern Water, whereby Interext have been granted the contract only on the basis that they will satisfy the contractual obligation that Outsourcing Unlimited previously failed to honour. That is, Interext have guaranteed that they will achieve the revenue targets set by Northern Water, and Interext will bring their unrivalled resources into play in order to do so."

That didn't sound good. Arthur thought about his dad's paltry cash-collection figures.

"If those revenue targets are not met, Northern Water will face serious difficulty in continuing to provide the northern counties with the level of service we are committed to providing. As you will all appreciate, the delivery of fresh clean water, on demand, and the removal and treatment of waste water, also on demand, are basic measures of a civilised society. We are fully committed to this task, and we are sure that all of you share that commitment."'

Arthur frowned at 'civilised society'.

'"The first major change will be the replacement of your current section manager, Jessica Stoats, by a senior Interext director – Mr Artemis Black. Mr Black will be joining you all at Whitehaven on the first of October. Thank you for listening."'

Bracket looked up at his team. They were looking around them as if they'd just woken up.

'Is that it?' said Diane, who was chewing some fruit-flavoured gum very loudly. Arthur could smell it distinctly from where he sat.

'Yes,' said Bracket, 'that's it.'

'Does this mean we'll be getting sacked?'

'No,' said Bracket. 'Erm . . .' He looked at the brief again, and then back to Diane. 'No,' he repeated.

'Good, good,' she said, standing up, and then everybody else was standing up too.

'Hang on,' said Bracket. 'Hang on! Nobody got any questions?'

'What's Interext?' asked Dean.

'It's the parent company of Outsourcing Unlimited,' answered Bracket, uncertainly.

'What's a parent company?' asked Diane.

'It's a company that owns another company,' said Bracket.

'Have *you* ever heard of Interext?' asked Arthur.

'Well,' said Bracket, shrugging. 'I must have. I mean, I don't really remember, but yes.'

'Jessica Stoat's that big lass up on t'pedestal?' asked Johnny.

'She's the manager of this whole operation,' said Bracket, 'so you should know who she is.'

'Aye, well,' said Johnny. 'Is she that big lass up on t'pedestal?'

'She sits on the command centre, yes,' said Bracket.

'Then I do know who she is!' Johnny sat up, straightening his back, his moustache bouncing up and down as he worked his mouth in exasperation.

'The important thing is that she's leaving,' said Bracket. He looked over at the command centre, which was a raised circular platform right in the middle of the room. Jessica wasn't there today, but usually her unseemly bulk could be seen firmly settled in behind one of the three desks overlooking the workspace.

'But *we're* not getting sacked?' asked Diane again.

'No,' said Bracket. He put the document down and clapped his hands together. 'Now. Before everybody rushes off to their desks – and I know you're all desperate to get back to work – don't forget our company values! Just because we're going to be working for somebody else doesn't mean we can't stick to the same values we work to at the moment: *faith*, *positivity*, *loyalty* and *team!*'

Nobody said anything. Heavy rain suddenly swept past

the window, battering the glass. All around them the call centre continued to vibrate.

'Team isn't a value,' said Arthur. 'A team is a thing. It's not a value. Just a thing.'

'Don't be smart.'

'I'm not,' said Arthur. 'It just doesn't make sense.'

'Look,' said Bracket, pointing at Arthur. He opened his mouth but didn't say anything. Instead his shoulders sagged and he lowered his arm. 'You get the idea, anyway,' he sighed. 'Now go on, all of you.'

The team dispersed, drifting away from the sofas, everybody but Arthur weaving their way in amongst the maze of desks. Arthur gravitated towards the window. He still held his briefing note in his hand. Everybody else had left theirs on the sofas. Diane had left her chewing gum there as well.

'Hey!' said Bracket, but not loudly, because you shouldn't speak or shout too loudly in case of disrupting phone calls. 'Come back and get your briefing notes!'

Nobody heard him or, if they did, they pretended not to. He turned to Arthur. 'Honestly,' said Bracket, 'this is big news. This is important. And it's as if they really don't give a shit.'

Arthur studied him silently. Why was Bracket saying this to him? Did Bracket think that he, Arthur, gave a shit either? He looked down at the briefing note in his hand.

'We need more people like you here,' said Bracket, slowly moving around and picking up all of the discarded notes.

'Properly committed. Less kids just after their drinking money.'

'Right,' said Arthur, thinking 'fewer, not less'. 'Well, I'm going to go now.'

'Yeah,' said Bracket. 'Get yourself home.'

Arthur jogged down the steps leading to the foyer. Sometimes he would take a pack of printer paper from the stock of boxes that were, for some reason, stored beneath the staircase. Not for himself, for Bony. But this time the security guard was not too busy to notice him, so he left it.

It had stopped raining, but the clouds were still heavy and full-looking. The air was like some sort of glass: everything looked crystal clear and all the colours were sharp and intense. He turned around and looked up at the massive white bulk of the call centre. The revolving doors were like a vertical mouth. Like some strange, intricate sea-creature mouth, both beaky and mechanical. He shook his head, took a few steps backwards, then turned and walked down North Shore Road towards the town's harbour. The wind was still strong. The air smelled salty.

On the left-hand side of the road was a huge supermarket with the obligatory car park. Beyond was the small train station. To the right was a new red-brick, barn-like building which had a small-scale replica of a ship's prow mounted above its giant doors, together with the words 'WHITEHAVEN SHIPYARD' spelled out in silver lettering. The ship's prow was made of cast-iron and it looked like a trophy – like the head of something that had been hunted down and killed.

Due to the bad weather, the harbour was not as busy as usual. Even the geese were huddled together against the buildings, instead of marauding thuggishly around like they did when the sun was out. Arthur turned right off the road, by the sculpture representing a shoal of fish that swam ever upwards in a spiral of verdigris, and set off along the harbour walk. He staggered like a drunk as the wind pushed him this way and that, and his hair blew out horizontally, first in one direction and then another. He kept his eyes focused downwards so that he didn't step in any of the goose shit or dog muck that littered the way. Although, thanks to the rain, whatever shit he did see looked quite vibrant and appealing, like big blobs of green and brown oil paint. And stopping to lean over the railings, which he did frequently, the water looked opaque and deeply coloured, like enamel. It was mildly rippled, but no doubt there were larger waves to be seen beyond the harbour walls. Filthy, rusted fishing boats floated beneath him, but the strange quality of the atmosphere meant he could trick himself into seeing them as resting on the top of something solid. Something restless maybe, but solid all the same.

Arthur continued along the harbour, past the big pink buildings that had once been warehouses and were now flats. He walked on past the pubs and the restaurants. The wind made him feel as if he were stripped to the waist. He headed towards the hill at the far end of the harbour. Walking past the empty shell of the derelict hotel, he took the steps up the hill two or three at a time. At the top he came to the housing estate on which he lived with his father. The sky resembled a thin, greenish membrane, through which heavy black clouds were trying to force their way.

Arthur opened the back door and the first thing he saw was his father's pair of spectacles left on the kitchen worktop, surrounded by crumbs and baked beans. The kitchen was a mess. Hearing his father's voice from the front room, Arthur paused and listened.

'But I don't want to do the shopping,' his father, Harry, was insisting. 'I mean, I'll do it if you really want me to, but I'm no good at it. You can go in there and keep a hold of whatever you need, but I get all in a flap. You think because you can do it, everybody else can do it, but I can't do it.'

Arthur listened for a response. There was nothing. Just a moment's silence. Then Harry continued.

'It's like I keep saying, Rebecca. We're all good at different things, that's all. Please, Rebecca—'

Harry stopped as Arthur opened the door into the front room.

'Who are you talking to, Dad?' asked Arthur.

'Your mother,' said Harry.

'Mum's not here,' said Arthur. 'I can see that she's not here.'

'I was talking on the telephone,' said Harry. 'That's the magic of the telephone. They don't have to be here at all.'

'Dad,' began Arthur.

'I know you don't believe me,' said Harry. 'I know you don't believe me, son. I'm not asking you to. Just – let me talk to her.'

'OK,' said Arthur, after a moment.

Harry was a small man, painfully thin, and he lived in a navy-blue fleece. His pointed face was red and flaky, his hair was grey and greasy, flecked with dandruff, and he always smelled faintly of old raw meat.

'Do . . . do you want some tea?' he asked, then he gave a little smile. 'I had beans on toast. I can make you some beans on toast if you like. I saved half the tin.'

'Go on, then,' said Arthur. 'I'll just go up and get changed.'

Later on, as Harry sat on the edge of the old grey sofa and shouted out the answers to *University Challenge*, Arthur went upstairs to use the toilet. The light on the landing was dim. The carpet was green and cheap and badly fitted. The walls were a dirty cream colour. Arthur stood there for a moment and listened to his father's voice carrying upstairs from the front room. Harry got most of the answers right when it came to *University Challenge*. It seemed that watching it was one of the highlights of his father's week. Second only to karaoke night in the Vine, maybe.

It was a shame, Arthur thought, that his father was not as good at his job as he was at *University Challenge*.

Arthur eventually went into the bathroom. There was

no window there, so he couldn't see anything much at first, but he couldn't really bear that so he tugged the light-switch cord. He urinated into the toilet bowl, fixing his eyes on the cistern. As he washed his hands, he noticed something move, out of the corner of his eye. He turned to look at it but couldn't see straight away what it was.

The walls above and around the bath were covered with small white tiles. The bath itself, despite Arthur's best efforts, was a little stained. He leant over it to look more closely at the wall. Something had definitely moved. A lot of the grout was rotten or missing, and it was into one of the black holes left by some missing grout that Arthur now peered. There was something in there.

He wasn't sure that it was what he had originally seen, but he could certainly see it now. It looked as if a small part of the remaining grout was somehow alive and wriggling. He shuddered involuntarily as he watched the soft, tiny piece of darkness squirm its way out from between the tiles and drop, silently, into the heavy glass soap dish that had once been his mother's. He saw then that it was a short black worm, maybe no more than a centimetre long. There was one already in the soap dish. That must have been what he'd spotted from the corner of his eye – the first worm falling. Together they made up an '=' symbol in the soap sludge.

Arthur's face twisted as he examined them. Then he tore off some toilet paper and rolled it into a ball, before using it to squash the two worms. Gathering them up with it, he flushed the toilet paper away. Arthur shuddered again as he washed his hands, and then he left the bathroom, turning off the light as he went.

The soap dish that had been his mother's was heavy because it was so thick. It was made out of blue glass, with a shallow cavity at the top to hold the soap in place. Inside the glass itself were lots of tiny mirrored squares that caught the light and reflected each other, or whatever else was there.

THE OMINOUS PASSENGER

Bony turned off his Walkman – he had been listening to whalesong – and put on his hi-vis jacket before jogging down the steps to close the level-crossing gates. He could smell cow muck and hear the cows themselves in the distance. Maybe, if he stood completely still, he could also hear the sea. And he could just about hear the train if he put his mind to it.

He closed one of the gates – the one on the far side of the line from his signalman's hut – and then stood between the rails and looked southwards, which was the direction from which the train approached. The level crossing was at about the halfway point of a particularly long stretch of straight track, and Bony stared all the way to the vanishing point of the rails. Beyond that rose the humped blue shadow of middle-distance mountains. If he were to turn around, he would be able to see the rails passing beneath a bridge and then disappearing towards the horizon that way too. The sky was growing dark, turning purple. The sky was big here in Drigg. There was nothing getting in the way of it.

The sound of the train was now definitely audible – a low, rhythmic rumble that sounded warm to Bony, warm and reassuring – although the train itself was not yet in sight. There were no cars or people around. There never were at this time of day.

Bony lay on his side across the tracks, facing south, with his ear to one of the rails. It was vibrating and he held his head up slightly, so that the vibrations didn't rattle his skull. He longed to lie face down along one of the tracks, and let the humming metal bring him to orgasm. The only reason he didn't was that somebody might catch him there and guess at his motivation. He didn't want anybody thinking that he was some sort of pervert. So he contented himself with lying there on his side just for a short while, while trying to enjoy the sensation. Normally he did. Normally it inspired a sense of belonging that he found difficult to explain: a sense of companionship emanating from the ground itself. This time, though, there was a spiky violence to the oscillations that was entirely unpleasant. It was almost like being run over by a ghost train, he thought. *It is almost like there is a ghost train here with me.*

Slightly unnerved, he got up after a moment and returned to the western side of the tracks, closed the second gate of the level crossing and ascended the steps to his hut. The train would still be passing through Ravenglass, so he had some time yet. He opened the door and did twenty pull-ups on the top edge of the doorframe. As he lowered himself the last time, he saw the light of the train had now appeared at the end of the straight. 'Well done, Bony,' he said.

It was getting dark now. Up above, the sky was a purplish black with a couple of big bright stars, but over the sea, to the west, it was still a pale blue. In that direction there lay nothing but fields and sand dunes and then the beach and the sea, with a few sheep scattered over both grass-land and dunes.

Bony watched the train get steadily nearer. The Cumbrian coastal line was not a busy route, and the trains running up and down it were old and slow, so, as ever, the thing seemed to be taking an age to arrive. Being so small, Drigg was a request-only stop, so Bony didn't know if this train would even stop. For some reason he hoped it wouldn't. He chewed the fingernails of his left hand absent-mindedly, running the right hand over his shorn skull. Something about this particular train was making him feel sick; he had known there was something wrong with it from the vibrations. It was moving with an agonising sluggishness, and he wanted it to be gone. He just wanted the train to have passed through, so he could open up the level crossing and then get back to his pull-ups, his press-ups, his *National Geographic* magazine.

He tapped his foot frantically, noticing that it had got dark very quickly. His hut looked on to the track at such an angle that he could now see all the train's lit-up windows, appearing as orange squares with rounded corners. He turned away then, because he didn't want to see inside. Instead, he picked up the telephone and rang the conductor of the approaching locomotive.

'Hello?' said the conductor in response.

'All right,' said Bony. 'It's Bony.'

'All right, marra,' said the conductor.

'You stopping?'

'No, not tonight,' said the conductor. 'Gotta go slow, though. Some bugger's reported a cow on t'line just past Seascale.'

'Oh, right.'

'You OK?'

'Yeah, good. Thanks.'

Bony hung up. A cow on the line? He should have received a call about that. They'd probably tried to call him while he'd been speaking to his mother. He kept telling her: 'Don't call me at work. It's very important that the phone line is always kept free. It's very important. Don't call me at work.' But she didn't seem to understand. He looked back out of the window: the train had slowed to a crawl. It was only fair, of course; you didn't have to be going that fast to burst a cow. It was typical, though. The one and only time a train feels somehow sinister, and a fucking cow appears, as if by magic, to slow it down.

Bony continued gazing out of the window and noticed the last of the light had drained away during that brief phone call. And there, right opposite him, but a little bit lower, was a train window, through which a passenger stared up at him. All sound slowly stopped.

Looking slightly too big to be human, the passenger was squeezed tightly into his seat, his knees pressing against the one in front. He was wearing a black suit with an open-necked white shirt. His huge, long head was perfectly bald and unusually pointed. His eyes were dark and deep, overshadowed by a pair of thick, heavy eyebrows that swept upwards like the feathers above an owl's eyes. His actual eyes, in fact, were just about invisible – all Bony could see of them were twin points of light. His nose was sharp and pointed. He had a neatly trimmed black goatee, and his lips were thin. His skin looked naturally tanned and, even though he sat folded up into a train seat too small for him, he gave an impression of physical fitness and coiled-up strength. Each of his hands could have encased Bony's entire head, and on his fingers he wore thick gold rings.

Bony quickly scanned all the other windows of the train, but there didn't appear to be any other passengers. He then stared back down at the massive man below him, whose mouth was now twisted in derision.

Stop looking at me, thought Bony. *Stop looking at me, you terrifying bastard.* But the deep glints that passed for the man's eyes didn't leave Bony's face until the train had edged further along the track, and the windows finally shifted out of alignment.

Once the big man had passed from view, everything started moving more quickly. Bony opened the cabin door and watched the train recede to the north. It appeared black against the inky blue of the landscape and the luminous purple-blue of the sky. The orange windows still stood out clearly, as if they were the only lit-up things in the world. Bony became aware of the sound again. The sound of the train as it grew quieter. He stood in the doorway and watched.

Soon he felt totally alone once more, standing in the doorway watching nothing, and listening to the Drigg cows bellow and moan in the darkness of night.

Artemis Approaches

The train's conductor was young and fat and sweaty, and his badly shaved head was covered in small cuts and spots. Every now and again, he would dash up and down the train as if he had something important to do. Artemis couldn't bear the sight of him, and wished he had a gun, even a knife, just to scare him. And why didn't this stupid fucking train have a first-class carriage, anyway? And where was the shop? Where was the wi-fi? He would have waited for the fucking monkeys at the garage to fix his car if only he'd known he would end up stuck here in one of these crappy tin cans. Pitiful things. Small and slow and old.

He stood up to stretch his legs. The dome of his head bounced against the carriage roof as the train swayed, so he hunched his back a little. It wasn't even as if there was anything of interest outside the window. Just the sea at night. He couldn't believe they were sending him to this no-place: this empty coastline with its small, grim excuses for towns and villages, its miserable little houses, grey stony beaches, the cold grey ocean, and the weird, unintelligible people. If the ice caps actually melted and angry water swamped this bleak shithole of a place then it would be no real loss. There wasn't even anybody else on the train, but then nobody in their right mind would come up here if they didn't have to. Artemis shook his head at his reflection in the window. Out there on the sea shone an orange light. Some sort of boat? It shone at him through the reflection of his shadowed eyes.

At Home

'I don't want to talk,' Bracket said. 'I don't want to talk about anything. I'm sorry. Just— I'm just going to go and sit down.'

He regretted saying that almost before he finished uttering the words. Isobel had been looking at him as if she were about to tell him something fantastic; a smile playing around the corners of her mouth, her eyes wide and bright with excitement. He hadn't read her face until it was too late. He felt a coldness settle in his stomach as he turned to hang his coat up on the back of the kitchen door. When he turned back, she was still looking at him. She wore a long black cardigan over a shirt and some jeans, and around her the cluttered yet tidy kitchen was glowing orange. Her rust-coloured hair was tied back, but a halo of loose strands floated about her head.

Yorkie raised his old, tired dachshund face above the edge of the dog basket in a kind of lazy greeting, and then let it fall back on to the cushion with a *humph*.

'I'll make you a drink,' said Isobel.

'Thank you,' said Bracket. 'I'm sorry.' He bit his lip and smiled to prevent himself from crying. 'I, um . . . It's just . . . I don't know.'

Isobel stepped around the kitchen table, piled high with newspapers and unopened envelopes, and ran both her hands down his arms. 'Go and sit down,' she murmured, and kissed him on the cheek. 'I'll be through in a minute.'

Before finishing work, Bracket had checked his emails and read one that had been sent out to all of the managers on site. There had been an attachment – the new organogram. The word 'organogram' itself made him feel a kind of nausea. He had pinched the bridge of his nose, then opened the attachment and scanned the slick PowerPoint slides which presented the new management structure. He had grimaced at the headshots which illustrated it. His photo in particular was a poor one – he looked like a condom stuffed full of bread dough. As he had expected, virtually nothing in the structure had changed – not yet, anyway – except the face and the name appearing at the top of it. Jessica Stoats, with her pursed lips and huge false eyelashes, had been replaced by Artemis Black, with his gleaming bald skull and sneering mouth. His eyes oozed contempt even through the photograph, through the desktop monitor, and it had taken an effort of will for Bracket not to smash his clenched fist into the screen. He had kept a lid on it, though, as he was surrounded by customer advisers taking calls from customers. It was on his personal development plan to always remain positive in the workplace. In his last performance review, Jessica had spoken to him at length about what she called 'the shadow of the leader'.

Now, though, sitting curled up on the sofa in his darkened living room, there was nobody to pretend for. At home he acknowledged the truth: he was a seam of coal being steadily mined. He was an ocean being emptied of fish. He was a field being slowly stripped of nutrients. He was giving everything away to people and things he felt nothing for. He had told Isobel that he didn't want to talk, but actually words were queuing up inside him. She would understand, if he explained. I am thirty-six, he imagined himself saying. I am thirty-six and I spend the majority of my waking hours pretending to be interested in what's going on around me. I pretend to like people. I pretend to care about what I'm doing. But everything I see and everything I hear and everything I have to do makes me angry. My anger is very deep and very distant. I keep it very deep and very distant. I am thirty-six years old and I hide myself. I hide myself so that I can keep my job. A job that I hate. I cannot explain how pathetic that makes me feel. If I keep myself hidden for much longer, I will disappear. I am thirty-six. I should not feel so pathetic. Nobody should feel pathetic. Nobody should feel as pathetic as I do. And now everything will change. The routines that have allowed me to survive will be broken. The surfaces that I skate over will collapse. The new site manager is coming, and he will expect things of me. He will expect more of me than I can bear to give. And I want to use myself for something good. I want to give you more of myself, Isobel, so I am going to leave. I know you'll understand. I am going to write my letter of resignation tonight and hand it in tomorrow. It will be OK. It will be OK. Is it normal to be so angry and to be so far away?

Isobel nudged open the living-room door with her foot, a mug in each hand, and turned on the light with her forehead. Yorkie dragged himself in after her.

'Look at you,' she said, 'sitting in the dark.'

'How was work?' asked Bracket.

'Oh, you know,' said Isobel, rolling her eyes. 'The usual.'

'Yeah.' Bracket smiled.

Isobel worked in an office at Sellafield nuclear power station. She would meet any jokes made about her glowing in the dark with a long, cold, hard stare, and would maintain a healthy lack of respect for the perpetrator's sense of humour for months afterwards, if not years. She sat down on the far end of the sofa and looked at him keenly. That excited smile was back on her lips.

'I've got some news,' she said.

'Good,' said Bracket. 'I want some news. I want something that will change everything.'

'It will change everything,' said Isobel, and she laughed suddenly and brightly. 'It will. Bracket, I'm pregnant. We're pregnant.'

Bracket laughed too. He reached out and held her close to him. 'Isobel,' he said. 'Oh, Isobel.'

He closed his eyes and stroked her hair. He allowed himself to believe that the entire world was completely silent.

He clipped the lead on to Yorkie's collar, filled his coat pockets with carrier bags and slipped out the back door, into the still night. Inside the house, Isobel was getting ready for bed, and before he could join her he had to take the dog out for its evening walk. Yorkie was an old, ugly little dog that was quite short-bodied for a dachshund. Bracket had suggested 'Meatball' as a name when they'd first acquired him as a puppy.

Beneath the streetlights the tarmac shone a wet yellow colour, still slick with the rain from earlier in the day. The sandstone terraces lining the street contained large, comfortable townhouses that implied a certain understated wealth. They spoke of a more prosperous era, having been built when Whitehaven was an important trading port. Nowadays they were mostly bought and paid for by Sellafield wages. Cosy light shone from the gaps around or between heavy, expensive-looking curtains. Bracket could hear the constant traffic travelling along the nearby A595, and the ever-present seagulls yammering on. He headed down the road towards the Tesco supermarket, which he passed at least twice a day on his way to work and back. There he bought some cigarettes at the petrol station, and made his way on to the harbour. He stroked Yorkie's head, let him off the lead, and watched as the dog ambled off to piss against the railings which prevented unwary people from falling into the oily water. He didn't often talk to his dog, like some people did, but he was concerned about the decrepit little creature dying on him. He liked having a non-verbal relationship and could spend hours with the dog, just thinking. He worried that after the dog died he wouldn't be able to think at all.

The clouds were being torn into blue-edged tatters by some high-up wind, and between them the crescent moon was visible. Bracket walked a little way along the harbour and sat down on one of the big wooden benches, where he lit his first cigarette in six years. He narrowed his eyes against the smoke and scratched his nose with his thumbnail. His parka was closely bunched around him, as the cold always headed in from the sea at night. He gazed at the masts and rigging of the old fishing boats and yachts moored in the marina, and then beyond them towards a row of tiny lights far out to sea. Only visible sometimes, they were the lights of a town or village on the Isle of Man.

He finished his cigarette. *A baby! Good God.* He laughed a little and then stood up – then saw Yorkie and grimaced. Yorkie was crouching, further along the side of the harbour, and unloading what looked like about half his body weight in loose faeces. Bracket fished a carrier bag from his parka pocket.

Just beyond where Yorkie was defecating was 'The Wave'. It was a sculpture installed as part of the harbour's Millennium regeneration, and took the form of a long, curvy, white metal bar supported on white metal legs. It ran the entire length of the Lime Tongue, the jetty on to which ships had once unloaded their cargoes of limes. The Wave had neon lights embedded along its structure, so that blue neon shone on one side and green neon on the other. At least half of the time one of the neon bulbs had blown so the whole thing was switched off, but tonight it was fully operational.

Bracket studied it as he waited for Yorkie to finish his massive job and, as he admired the bright blue and green ripples in the water on either side of it, he suddenly became aware of somebody else standing on the harbour, near the far end of The Wave. Not just another dog-walker, which would not have been unusual, but a strikingly large man dressed in a black suit. He kept scraping one foot backwards across the ground, like a cartoon bull about to charge. A sizeable black suitcase rested beside him. The blue neon gleamed off his bald head and it took Bracket a few seconds to work out why he looked familiar, but then it clicked. *Artemis Black.* The man was Artemis Black.

Bracket's heart scuttled out of its shell and right down through his body, to seek refuge in his shoe. He turned away and was all set to scuttle off himself, but then realised that Yorkie, incredibly, still hadn't finished shitting. What the fuck was wrong with that dog? Internally it must have been just a pea-sized brain packed in amongst a maze of intestines. Nothing but stomach and guts. Stupid fucking meatball.

And then Artemis was walking towards him. Not walking but *striding* – marching, almost – bearing down like one of those minotaur things from the old *Doom* games that Bracket still played sometimes when alone in the house. He didn't look happy. As he got close Bracket saw that he looked distinctly unhappy, in fact.

'I've got dog shit on my shoe,' declared Artemis. 'It's disgusting. This is the first time I've ever set foot in this town, if you can even call it that, and on my way to the hotel, on the very first journey I make, I tread in a pile of dog shit.'

'It wasn't me,' said Bracket.

'No,' replied Artemis. 'Glad to hear it. But was it your *dog*?' He was speaking through gritted teeth, and slowly, like he was trying to tell off a three-year-old child while suffering from a terrible headache.

'No,' said Bracket. He raised his right hand, which was holding an orange carrier bag already inside out. 'I pick his up. I mean, when he's finished. He hasn't even finished yet.'

Artemis gazed down at Yorkie with such a sneer of disgust that Bracket flinched. Yorkie looked up, made a last explosive moist sound, and wagged his tail. 'He stinks,' said Artemis.

'He's an old dog,' said Bracket.

'What's this thing, anyway?' Artemis pointed over his shoulder with his thumb towards The Wave.

'It's a sculpture,' said Bracket.

'It's fucking bollocks, is what it is,' said Artemis. There was a silence as if he expected a response. Bracket just let his eyes slide from Artemis's face towards the neon lights, and didn't say anything. Beyond The Wave, the harbour continued on down to the burnt-out hotel, and the hill with that rough residential estate at the top of it.

'Have you been crying?' asked Artemis, after it became evident that Bracket wasn't about to agree with him.

'No,' said Bracket.

'You have,' said Artemis, leaning forward and peering into Bracket's face. 'You've been crying.'

'Look,' said Bracket. 'It's been a heavy night. I just— I just need to pick up this crap and then go home. Please. I don't really want to have to pick it up in front of my new boss.'

'What?'

'I saw you on the organogram,' said Bracket. 'I work at the call centre. I'm a team manager there.'

'What's your name?'

'Bracket.'

'What the fuck kind of name is that?'

'Oh . . . Oh, sorry. I mean that's just a nickname. Hackett is my real name. Not really any better than Bracket, is it?'

'No, not at all.' Artemis sighed deeply and looked past Bracket, over his head, in the direction of the call centre. 'So why were you crying, then? You can tell me all about it, you know. I think you'll find me quite approachable. And if it's something major, then I should probably know anyway. If it might affect your work.'

'My wife is pregnant,' said Bracket. 'I just found out tonight.'

Artemis's eyes suddenly focused back on Bracket's. 'Then

47

you're crying because you're happy?' he asked. His expression was severe.

'Oh,' said Bracket. 'Yeah. Yeah, of course.'

'Good,' said Artemis. He clapped a heavy hand on Bracket's shoulder. 'I guess you'll be wanting some overtime, then, eh?'

Bracket bit his lip and looked down at Yorkie. Yorkie gazed back at him with an expression that said nothing at all.

'Yeah,' he said, eventually. 'I guess I will.'

'Ha!' barked Artemis. 'Excellent! I have a couple of projects that I want to kick off, so you can be my right-hand man.'

'Sounds good,' said Bracket.

'I'll talk to you some more on Monday.'

'Great,' said Bracket. He was still looking at Yorkie.

'I'm going to go and find my hotel now,' said Artemis. 'You go home.'

'Yeah,' said Bracket. 'I was just about to, anyway, actually. Which hotel is it?'

'The Waverley.'

'Down there,' said Bracket, pointing along a pedestrianised street that ran from the harbour straight into the town. 'Down there and to the left.'

'See you on Monday, then,' said Artemis, and strode away again, back towards his suitcase.

Bracket just looked at Yorkie for a while, who sat there looking back up. Then he bent down and picked up the still-warm faeces. He could feel the heat and the wetness of it through the thin plastic of the carrier bag. Once he'd gathered most of it he reversed the bag the right way round again and tied it closed.

'Come on, then,' he said to the dog. 'Come on, old man.'

SWANS

Artemis walked on past his suitcase towards what looked like a ramp for getting boats into or out of the water, just beyond the piece-of-crap 'sculpture' that was The Wave. Behind him, he could hear Bracket scraping up the dog shit and he shook his head. How could anybody lower themselves to that? He then sat down on the ramp, just above the water level, and took off the shoe that was smeared with muck. He dipped the sole of it into the water. The liquid was an inky black, except where the ripples caught the moonlight or the neon, shining their reflections silver and bright blue respectively. He paused momentarily as he thought he saw a ghost emerging, head first, from the water, but then realised that it was just a sleeping swan tinged with a blue luminescence from The Wave. It was one of many bobbing gently on the surface, their heads tucked beneath their wings so that they appeared almost spherical.

Once his shoe was clean, Artemis put it back on and just sat there with his head in his hands.

He'd loved his wife. They'd first met in the zoo; he'd gone to look at the big cats and she'd been on her way to the aquarium. Artemis had loved her dearly.

Bathroom Dream

In the early hours of Saturday morning, Arthur dreamed that he stood looking at the toilet. Small black worms were overflowing from beneath the lid of the cistern, which shifted slightly due to the tumultuous mass heaving beneath it. He knew the cistern was full of them. He knew they were hidden inside all of the walls, all of the pipes. Even as he watched, more and more of them tumbled down the bright white sides of the cistern. He could hear the wind outside, just the wind and nothing else, and he imagined that there was nothing else, just a flat, empty landscape, as flat as a still sea.

PART TWO

PART TWO

Victorian Gothic

Bony had a very impressive 32-inch flatscreen monitor, together with a brand-new, cutting-edge graphics card, and Arthur kept getting so absorbed in watching the mist drift across the screen that he neglected to play the game itself. Bony was sitting next to him, slurping from a fresh cup of tea, but that didn't really detract from the atmosphere created by the surround-sound set-up and the dim lighting in the room.

'I am blown away by the mist all over again,' said Arthur.

'It's good, isn't it?' said Bony. 'It makes the game seem almost worthwhile.'

'Don't mock that which you don't understand.'

'You'll start playing it for yourself next.'

'I do play it for myself, really,' said Arthur. 'I mean, I don't know how playing it for myself would be any different.'

'I don't understand it. I mean, I understand why *you* do it but I don't understand Tiffany's motivation.'

Arthur paused the game and sipped from his own mug meditatively. The curtains were closed and the only light came from numerous candles spaced around the small room. The squawking of seagulls came from outside, but apart from that the only thing to be heard was the game's soundtrack – vaguely spooky piano music evocative of its nineteenth-century setting.

'I can't say I really understand it either,' said Arthur, tipping back on the two rear legs of his chair, 'but people earn a living doing this full time, you know. You have, like, *offices* full of people doing it in Japan.'

'What? Playing multi-player online games for other people?'

'Yeah. So, like, you have some rich businessman who wants a super-high-powered character, but he can't be bothered playing as a low-powered character in order to gain the experience points he needs. Like, he can't be bothered trotting around the sewers killing giant rats, or whatever. So he pays somebody else to play all the early stages of the game for him. Then, once the character is powerful enough – say the businessman has specified that he wants a level-thirty character or whatever – the person who's been playing it so far just tells the businessman that the character's ready whenever he wants to log in, and that's it.'

'And people do that for a living?'

'Yeah, but it's illegal. So if you're doing it for that businessman, you have to pretend to *be* that businessman. Like, you have to pretend you're that same businessman playing the game as his allotted character.'

'And that's what you're doing for Tiffany?'

'Yeah, kind of.'

'Playing the game as her because she wants to play it but can't be bothered playing it?'

'You finally understand,' said Arthur. 'I couldn't have put it better myself.' He unpaused the game and gestured at the screen. 'Currently, my character – I mean, Tiffany's character – and her delightful companion, Miss Lynch, are exploring the backstreets of Whitechapel, looking for a drunk who may have some information regarding Jack the Ripper.'

'I prefer proper games,' said Bony, 'like *Fallout 3* or *Command and Conquer*. Games with nuclear weapons.'

'You would,' replied Arthur. 'Anyway, I think that will have to do for now.' He opened a dialogue box on screen and typed a short message addressed to Miss Lynch.

I have to go now, Yasmin, he wrote. *Be in the Vagabond tonight. You out?*

Will be if you lot are, replied Yasmin. *See you later!*

He logged out and closed down the game, and the misty world of *Victorian Gothic Online* dissolved from the screen. He realised that Bony was eyeing him and frowning.

'What?' said Arthur.

'She knows who you are,' said Bony.

'Yeah,' said Arthur, 'but that's OK, because I know who she is, too. Yasmin won't go to the game police.'

There was a moment's silence.

'Can I blow these stupid candles out now?' asked Bony.

'You can stick them up your arse. What time's the train?'

'It's in ten minutes. We'd better get ready.' Bony started opening all the curtains.

He lived in a tiny bungalow in Drigg, a couple of minutes' walk from the level crossing at which he worked. If you didn't know him properly you would be surprised at how pretty his house and garden were, given his cadaverous appearance and his devotion to all things technological.

Arthur opened the front door and squinted up at the grey clouds. It was Saturday afternoon, not late at all, but the sky was dark with the approaching storm. 'I hope we don't miss the best of it,' he said.

'We won't,' said Bony. 'It's going to be another big one, I think.'

EARS

Yasmin wanted elf ears. She spent hours looking at photo galleries on the internet, studying photos of people with elf ears, people who'd had cosmetic surgery to make their ears look like the ears of elves. Or those of Vulcans, sometimes, but mostly elves. The surgery was expensive but she reckoned she could afford it if she started doing some overtime at the call centre. She tucked her long blonde hair behind her current ears and inhaled deeply on her gentle spliff. As she exhaled, the smoke curled beautifully in the draught from the open window. The windows on either side of her desk looked directly out over the harbour and the marina and the sea.

Yasmin lived in a first-floor flat in a harbourside building that had once been a warehouse for storing sugar and limes and rum, and possibly – probably – slaves. Tonight, black clouds were gathering on the horizon and turning the sea slate-coloured. She preferred the view as the sun was melting into the sea, when it looked like the whole world was swaddled in the yolk of a bloody, broken egg.

Ultimately she would like to live on a riverboat somewhere. With friends, though. On an impossibly huge riverboat big enough for her and all of her friends and all of her books and CDs and video games. She finished the spliff and turned her PC off, then lit an incense stick and put Fleetwood Mac on and started getting ready to go out. Spectral fingers, reaching down out of the sky, approached from across the sea. They were composed of rain.

THE GHOST SHIP

Artemis stood on the raised platform in the middle of the call centre floor and looked out over the rows of deserted desks. Six o' clock on a Saturday evening and the place had closed at five. No fucker around. The windows looked out over the darkening sea, and a rising wind was starting to make the roof creak. The telephones were still and silent, though they were never turned off, only ever sleeping. Artemis stroked the black receiver of the unit on his own desk. If he deliberately listened for it he could hear the insistent hum of electricity. He smiled to himself. This building felt like a ship, and he was the captain. It felt like an empty ship. A beached ship. A ghost ship.

He sat down and turned on his computer. Then he stood up again and paced his way from one end of the huge, empty room to the other, keeping to the west-facing side and looking out of the window. Next he walked down the southern wall, until he found himself inside the glass labyrinth of the pods. He opened all of the shutters and raised them till he was surrounded just by sheets of glass that reflected each other and reflected his bulk between them, although his reflections seemed ethereal and lost amongst the shining panes. He left the shutters up, and weaved his way through semi-circular huddles of desks back to the raised platform, the command centre. He was a giant stalking through streets at night and the desks were houses. He was the Beast of Bodmin and the desks were just little lambs. When he got back to his desk the computer was fully awake and waiting for him. He logged on using his employee number and password – L1SA – and pursed his lips when the Outsourcing Unlimited logo appeared as his desktop wallpaper. That would have to be changed. In fact, the whole site would require complete re-branding, starting with the logo displayed on the outside wall. He'd get on to the Comms team about it on Monday – and Facilities Management too. Still, at least he'd been able to bring in his own night-watchmen. They'd worked with him in the past, at previous sites, and they had developed certain understandings.

Artemis bent down and retrieved an unmarked CD from his briefcase. It was contained in a thin, transparent, plastic jewel case. The CD itself was a couple of years old, and he had not listened to it before. He had never had the courage to, but now it seemed right. Now it seemed fitting. This was the key, really, to whether his most ambitious project for the call centre would happen or not. He held it between the forefingers of both hands, each one supporting diametrically opposite corners of the case. Like that, he spun it around and around. He meanwhile felt sick. After about five minutes of just spinning it and trying to keep his mind blank, he leant forward and opened the CD drive of the computer. He placed the CD on the tray and closed the drive again. The media-player programme opened automatically and started playing the first audio file. A warm female voice whispered out to him from the shitty PC speakers.

Do you have a water meter? it said.

Is your property domestic or commercial? it said.

How many people live at your property? it said.

Artemis's lips curved into a kind of smile, and his eyes narrowed as if he was remembering something. He *was* remembering something. His eyes filled with tears. The voice continued, asking more and more questions. The rain suddenly hit the call centre, and the harbour and all of the town of Whitehaven, and it was so heavy it sounded like falling stones. The wind started to howl. Artemis's chest heaved as he sobbed, and the choking sound of his grief was loud in that empty space, but still not as loud as the wind and the rain outside. He picked up an empty folder and threw it as far away as he could. That done, he squeezed at his erection through the thin black fabric of his trousers. He clicked the pause button on the PC screen and shouted out: just a sound, but no words. He dried his eyes and then started playing the recording again. He unzipped his trousers and pulled them down, together with his purple boxer shorts. He was the captain and the ship was sinking.

He kneeled and started to masturbate into the waste-paper bin, and imagined waves towering like skyscrapers around him, growing ever larger, their dark green flanks terrifyingly translucent beneath the lightning-cracked sky. He was kneeling on the deck and high above his head, strong grey sharks swam past inside those walls of water. He saw one of the waves grow white at the top and it started to break, and it looked like a mountain in winter and, as it started to rush towards him, he grabbed hold of the tiller with both hands and the wave crashed over him and he came and he beat his forehead against the edge of the desk as he did so. After he was done he collapsed and lay on the floor, conscious but completely silent. Salt water ran from his body. The sound of the waves echoed around inside his skull. Above him the recorded voice continued.

Do you have an outstanding balance?

Would you like to pay in full?

Would you like any plumbing and drainage insurance?

The voice of his wife.

What he really missed, though, was her body.

WITH THE ANIMALS

Isobel opened up the hand-held games console and turned it on. She never tired of this beautiful object, was constantly delighted by the perfect tactility of its buttons and its plastic gleam and its pale, chalky-blue colour. It was small and rectangular and she opened it like a book. Two screens welcomed her in.

She was sitting on the sofa in the living room while Bracket was doing the washing up in the kitchen. Yorkie humphed around in between. Outside it was raining again, another reason not to go out. Sometimes she felt guilty for staying in on a Saturday night. Like she was wasting her life. But really, after being out all week at work, all she wanted to do was curl up somewhere warm, like a cat, and rest. God, another week of it. Sometimes she felt sick at the length of time she spent at work. But best not to dwell on it. After all, everybody else did the same, didn't they? Everybody hated their job, it went without saying. Bracket probably didn't want to hear about it, so best just for her to get on with it and shut up. And when the weekend came, she would use it however the fuck she wanted to. Which, more and more frequently, meant disappearing off to visit her friends in the video game *Animal Crossing*.

In *Animal Crossing* you play a character who moves into a small town populated by animals. Except all of the animals behave like humans: living in houses, going to shops, talking, that kind of thing. The town is idyllic: all grass and fruit trees and irregularly shaped buildings and crystal-clear streams and butterflies. You take out a mortgage and have to pay it off, except, instead of getting some kind of boring, realistic job, you do things like dig up fossils and sell them to the museum. You could spend any spare money you had on decorating your house, buying new clothes for your character, or maybe buying presents for other characters. You could design and make things: clothes or ornaments or images. As the game progressed, more and more shops would open up in the town, selling a vast array of different virtual objects. You could go round to the other animals' houses and talk to them, or meet up in the local pub for a drink. You could write them little letters, too, or send greeting cards.

If you connected to the internet, then you could visit other towns and meet up with other people playing the same game – real people, that was, not the computer-controlled characters who lived in your own town. Isobel had tried that once, after seeing a hot-air balloon float through the distance in the rich blue digital sky of her screen. The most exciting thing she'd found was an incredible range of things for her character to buy; the number and variety of objects that had been created for buying and selling seemed limited only by the collective imagination of all of those worldwide players and, of course, the filters that blocked out any content that might make the world unsafe for children.

But the downside of this wider exploration was that the real people she'd met in various communal online areas were not as interesting as the fictional animals populating her small town. Their lives were not as interesting. They communicated in typing errors and bad spelling and the ugly, lazy elisions of 'txt spk'. Their comments and opinions were not as surprising or insightful as those of the AI animals with which she had made friends. Or maybe they were, and she had simply mistaken any articulate players for in-game creations; either way she had been uncomfortable. That was the primary reason for her discomfort, actually – the fact that she frequently felt unsure whether she was simply communicating with the console or with real people elsewhere within the human world. She could have asked, she supposed, but that would have felt wrong. She didn't want to break the sense of immersion either for herself or for others.

Isobel had started playing *Animal Crossing* after asking a young girl at work what its attraction was. The girl had told her a story, then, about a woman with cancer. This woman had had a son, her only child, who lived with her.

The boy's father had gone – he'd left, or died, it didn't really matter. As a distraction for his terminally ill mother, the boy had bought one of these little consoles and a copy of *Animal Crossing*, reckoning it a game she could play while he was away at work. And she'd fallen in love with it. As the illness wore her down and she became less and less able-bodied, she would play the game more and more. She spent hours and hours of each and every day picking fruit and planting flowers, or fishing on the virtual beach. The friends she made in *Animal Crossing* – the foxes, owls, hedgehogs, badgers, turtles, parrots, dogs, pandas – they were with her almost until the end. She played right up until a day or two before she died, leaving the little console and the game to her only son.

After the funeral, he switched the console on to see what her in-game house might be like. He found that she had created a character representing himself, so he logged in and started playing to find out more. His character woke up in a small, plain bedroom, which is how the game always starts. He walked his character downstairs and found himself in a room so large that he could not even see the walls of it. The floor was covered in gift-wrapped presents and there were so many that it must have taken all of the hours she spent playing to earn enough in-game currency to buy them all. Directly in front of his character lay a small note carefully placed on the floor. It was from his mother's character, addressed to him:

Thank you so much for all of your love, and for all of my friends. I loved you so very much. I hope you like all of your presents. They are all for you. All of my love forever – Mum xxx

The boy spent hours unwrapping all of these virtual presents and with each and every one an animation showed his character holding the new gift up towards the screen, smiling delightedly. He loved them all.

Isobel had been so touched by this that she borrowed the girl's console so that she could understand the story fully. She thus found a game that enabled her to live in a world almost identical to that which she had fantasised about as a child. And that was it: she was hooked.

'How did you know about that woman and her son?' she'd asked the girl at the time.

'I was at the funeral,' the girl had replied. 'Not the real one, obviously. But they had one online.'

She'd waved her little pink console in the air.

So now Isobel was curled up on the sofa, playing *Animal Crossing*, wishing furiously that she could make a living by selling seashells in real life. She found herself holding her stomach and smiled at the thought of the child inside her, and all of the worlds that the child would have to discover. She was excited at the thought of them exploring together.

Somewhere in the background, Bracket turned on the radio. He didn't seem to understand the appeal of *Animal*

Crossing at all. Never mind, though. Everybody had their own hobbies. Isobel slowly became completely oblivious to the growing storm.

At the Lighthouse

Arthur wore an old waterproof coat that wasn't really waterproof any longer; it had rips under the arms from being a bit too small, and the rain burrowed its way in through those holes. The raindrops came down like ball bearings. Like bullets. Arthur stood there on the harbour, near The Wave (currently deactivated), and imagined the height from which the water was falling. He imagined the force of the wind behind it. If Yasmin had glanced down from her living-room window, she would have been able to see him. He kept his head down and his hair hung around his face like black pondweed. If she were still alive, his father's mother would have said the rain was coming down like stair-rods. And she would have been right. These weren't raindrops – they were solid bars connecting the earth to the tops of the cumulonimbus clouds, piercing his body and pinning him to the spot in the process. Arthur could feel them running right through him. His hands were pushed deep into the pockets of his thin black trousers. His ears were so cold that they felt skinless, but he didn't mind. The thin layer of water dancing across the pale stones and small metal fish adorning the harbour promenade looked like boiling oil.

Bony spotted Arthur standing there from a short distance away, but he couldn't attract his attention through the noise of the downpour and the voice of the wind. He wore his hi-vis jacket and some blue waterproof trousers that he occasionally used for fishing. He jogged towards Arthur and slapped him on the back.

'You ready?' shouted Bony.

'Yeah!' shouted Arthur. 'Been here for bloody ages!'

'Why didn't you give Yasmin a buzz? Could've waited up there!'

'No answer!'

'Come on, then!' shouted Bony.

They turned and ran past the end of the Sugar Tongue, then past the end of the Lime Tongue, occasionally skidding and waving their arms about in an effort not to fall over. They ran past the Zest Harbourside restaurant, and at the end of the promenade turned right on to the long stone harbour wall. They ran along it, past the green hull of an upturned rowing boat. They ran on past the Sea Cadets' building. The sky was something between black and green, and seemed alive and pulsating. Arthur and Bony ran until they reached the warning sign.

WARNING
The surface beyond this point is uneven.

They stopped running here and started to walk instead. The sign marked the point at which the harbour wall really struck out into the sea, because it was here that the land fell away to the left-hand side as well as to the right. The sign indicated the point at which it became the West Pier.

It was a two-tiered structure: one a wide, uneven surface with huge rusty lumps of metal sticking out of it, to which tall ships had once been moored, and the other a high, narrow wall, running alongside the left-hand edge, which had protected sailors from the sea while they were working in bad weather. You could walk along either, but Bony and Arthur now chose the lower path. The smell of salt water filled their heads like a corrosive vapour. The sea down to their right was in a constant state of violent motion as the rain hit it with enough force to smack the water straight back up into the air again, turning it white and soft. When the pair looked up and ahead of them to where the West Pier began curving round to the north, they saw the crests of waves breaking against the barrier wall and showering foam down on to the path that the two of them intended to follow. The pier was so big, so strong and wide and deep and old-looking, that they were both – unknown to each other – reminded of the architecture in that video game, *Shadow of the Colossus*. They hurried onwards.

As they came to the very end, they slowed down. The structure widened out here, like the clenched fist at the end of an arm, and rising from the centre of the bulge was Whitehaven lighthouse. The lighthouse entrance was at the level of the lower tier, but some steps led up around it to enable access to the upper tier. Here, at the end, was an additional low wall protecting the edge of the higher level also. The lighthouse was white with a red door and a red balcony around the top of it, and it looked bright and vibrant against the angry sky. Water pooled in the dips and hollows of the stone surface on which Bony and Arthur stood. The broken remnants of mammoth waves surged around beneath the structure, indicative of the peaks and troughs of the ocean still hidden by the higher levels of the West Pier.

'Ready?' shouted Arthur.

Bony nodded in response, despite Arthur's words being snatched away by the wind as soon as they'd left his mouth. They lowered their heads and slowly approached the base of the steps. There was a rusted yet sturdy metal railing which they held on to as they ascended, and they kept their heads bowed beneath the weight of the weather. To their left, the lighthouse seemed like some kind of magical monument, glowing white and streaming with liquid. They eventually reached the upper level on all fours, with waves constantly collapsing over the low wall that separated them from the sea. They crawled towards the wall, the lighthouse behind them now, their hands and knees submerged in the restless water hissing across the stonework. When they got to the wall, they turned and sat with their backs resting against it. This was the same spot where, on friendlier days, fishermen would stand with their rods and eat their sandwiches and gut fish and leave the entrails lying around to stink in the sun.

Bony and Arthur glanced at each other, then turned so that both were on their knees facing the wall. Slowly they gripped the top of the wall with their hands and raised their heads above it to look out to sea.

They saw a landscape, not a seascape. They saw mountains and valleys, as if they were looking at an aerial photograph of the central Lake District. Except everything was moving. The mountains were rolling along and then subsiding and then leaping up again, and in between them were cavernous hollows that deepened and deepened, like there was no limit to the depth they might achieve. The peaks would roll in and smash against the fortress-like structure of the West Pier, spraying the exhilarated pair's faces with their shattered remnants. And already there would be replacement peaks spawning a long way out, growing impossibly huge, racing with fantastic speed towards the shore, towards the town, towards the land, towards Arthur and Bony with their little wet faces like two smiling, stupid peaches just waiting to be swallowed up. The heights and depths of the water were astounding and terrifying, and this turbulence stretched for as far as their eyes could see, before being obscured by veils of sheeting rain. Somewhere above the clouds, thunder roared as some forgotten god stamped its feet. And the sky would flash as lightning lit up the clouds from the inside. Arthur and Bony looked at each other, nodded, and raised themselves a little higher. They wormed themselves forward so that they were looking directly down into the water, each bent over at the waist to ninety degrees.

Arthur studied the green hell beneath him. He blew a kiss downwards. He felt as if his mother were closer to him when the weather was like this. He had this idea that she would be nearer the surface, though he knew this was ridiculous. He knew that wasn't how it worked. The ocean broke bodies down into nothing and spread them out across the Earth. He knew that. But he still couldn't help looking for her.

He let himself slip backwards, back towards the relative shelter of the wall, and raised his head so that he could see further. If this was *Shadow of the Colossus*, then he was the Wanderer. He was exploring an abandoned world, discovering architecture built for giants, and every now and again one of those giants would rise up from the surrounding environment and look down at him with glowing eyes. He wanted it to happen now. He wanted some huge creature to emerge.

Bony slipped back alongside him and gave a jerk of his head backwards towards the town. Arthur nodded.

The Vagabond

Yasmin was drinking white wine and Dean was drinking some kind of blue alcopop. They were sitting in a corner of the Vagabond, which was a pub occupying a part of the same building – the old converted warehouse – as Yasmin's flat. They were near the door but in an alcove. The floor was old black stone but the wooden tables and benches were new. Pictures of Jack Kerouac and Mohammed Ali and Joni Mitchell and Bob Dylan covered the walls. The place seemed quite full, but only because it was relatively small. Small and warm and dry. Dry, that is, until Arthur and Bony blew in.

'That was a good one,' said Bony.

'It was,' said Arthur.

'Neither of you are sitting next to me,' said Yasmin. She shook her head. 'No way.'

'Have . . . have you been in the sea?' asked Dean, mystified.

'Not quite,' said Bony.

'They go out to the lighthouse during storms,' explained Yasmin. 'Mental.'

'Why do you do that?' said Dean. 'I . . . I thought it was dangerous?'

'I suppose it is, really,' said Arthur.

'It's like you're plugging in,' said Bony. 'It's like you're engaging with everything. You should come with us next time, Dean. Honest to fucking God. It's like the world is talking to you alone.'

'Are you OK for drinks?' said Arthur, standing up again. He left a puddle behind on the stool. There was some early Jimi Hendrix playing in the background, and the smell of grilled Cumberland sausage wafted through from the kitchen.

Later, despite the warmth, Bony was still wearing his pair of soggy gloves. They were now covered in yellow crumbs.

'Bony,' said Yasmin, 'please take your gloves off to eat your crisps. It's making me feel sick.'

'Don't look, then,' mumbled Bony through a mouthful. 'I just don't like the feel of crisps on my fingers.'

Yasmin rolled her eyes and Arthur laughed.

'What . . . what do you reckon about this new stuff at work, then?' said Dean. 'Reckon it'll change much?'

'Not much,' replied Arthur. 'Except maybe they'll be even more bastardly. More desperate.'

'Bracket was . . . was saying that there might be some opportunities coming up.' Dean's head bobbed up and down like that of an excited chicken. 'Said they might have a proper restructure, like. I was thinking I . . . I could maybe apply for something. Not often you get such a good chance to . . . to develop.'

'You should,' said Arthur. 'You'd make a good team coach.'

'Th . . . thank you,' said Dean. 'Are you going to apply for something, Yasmin? If it comes up?'

'Maybe,' said Yasmin. 'If it gets me off the fucking phones, then yeah, too right.' She drank deeply from her wine glass. 'The only way I get through the day is by forgetting I'm even there. The way people talk to me I feel like a prostitute. It's like, how far do people go? Do they think it's OK to be so rude because they're not physically beating the seven greenest shades of shit out of you?'

'They would kick your head in if they could do it via the telephone,' said Arthur. 'As long as they can't see you and don't know you, then you're fair game.'

'You'd think people would be intelligent enough these days to realise that you don't have to be actually physical to be violent or damaging,' said Yasmin.

'They know,' said Arthur. 'They know all right.'

'W . . . will you go for any new jobs, Arthur?' asked Dean.

'Maybe,' said Arthur, after a moment. 'I don't know. I don't really know what I want. I want to work at Sellafield is what I want, but nothing ever comes up there. Nothing that I can do, anyway.'

'You see all those Sellafieldies going past on the train in the morning,' said Bony. 'They're all weird.'

'As if *you* can talk,' said Yasmin. Her eyes lingered on him.

'I'm not weird,' said Bony, though not making eye contact. He looked as if he was about to say something else, when he noticed somebody entering the pub and got distracted. The person in question was a young man, quite short and fat, with a blond thatch and big teeth and a sweaty red face. He wore a white shirt and heavily dyed blue jeans. He grinned at Bony and Bony nodded at him before standing up.

''Scuse me,' he said to the three seated around the table. 'I just need to see Ollie for a moment.' He squeezed himself out of the alcove and disappeared into the crush.

'Isn't that Tiffany's son?' asked Yasmin, frowning.

'Yeah, it is,' said Dean. 'How . . . how does Bony know him?'

Arthur peered around over both his shoulders and then leant forward before replying in a low voice.

'Acid,' he said.

Karaoke

It was karaoke night in the Vine and the pub was full. Harry was up at the bar, perched on a tall stool, his head swaying loosely to 'Do You Think I'm Sexy?' by Rod Stewart. The lights were low and the air felt brown. Lots of big bald men in striped shirts danced without moving their feet, while tall women with long blonde hair and bottomless cleavages shook their heads around, their arms up in the air. People were shouting and laughing. The woman behind the bar looked like a retired pirate with a blonde perm.

The man singing along to Rod Stewart was short, about Harry's height, with straight chestnut-coloured hair hanging down to his shoulders. The top of his head was bald, like a monk's, and as orange with fake tan as the rest of his face. The words coming out of his mouth were low and throaty and unintelligible, like the sound of coal being shovelled. He seemed to have some teeth missing, and kept tripping over his own feet. After many failed attempts, he managed to thread the cable of the microphone between his legs, and pull it to and fro. He grinned as he did so, jerking his hips forwards and backwards. He tried unbuttoning his bright pink shirt, but didn't seem to know how to do so. He still held the microphone but had momentarily stopped singing.

A young blonde girl with six-inch heels came forward as if to help him, before turning to laugh at her friends. They all joined her and danced around the karaoke singer, whose lips were pulled back in a weird kind of smile. One of the girls helped him shrug the shirt off, revealing a very round stomach, like he was going to give birth to a beach ball. His whole body was orange, and his chest and stomach were completely hairless and shiny. He dropped the microphone and started bending over, kind of dancing, but kind of just bending over. The girls dispersed, a couple of them exchanging glances as if to say, *It's getting too weird now.* The man carried on in the middle of an empty space.

Harry watched him, not smiling any more, just watching. Harry loved karaoke night in the Vine. Sometimes he got up and sang himself. Sometimes he would sing 'Dignity' by Deacon Blue. That was his favourite song to sing at karaoke night in the Vine. Not in an ironic way, either. He just liked it because nobody really noticed him and nobody really cared. His eyes were closing now; he was drooping, nearly falling off the stool.

He was suddenly aware of somebody else standing near him at the bar. A young man in a white shirt with blond hair and a red face, who was talking to him.

'All right, marra,' he was saying.

'Evening,' said Harry.

'I'm selling Viagra,' said the boy. Ollie. 'You want any?'

'What?' said Harry.

'Viagra, marra. You want any?'

'Oh!' said Harry. 'No, my wife and I have a very satis-factory relationship, thank you. We've got everything we need. Our . . . bodies are OK. We don't need . . . don't need anything extra, thank you very much. No, thank you very much.'

'Not to worry,' said Ollie. 'I can always shift a few in Gallagher's.'

'But I thought that was where young people go?' said Harry.

'Yeah,' said Ollie, 'but it still helps them out. You know how it is.'

When Harry turned back again, he was disappointed to see that the strange little topless singing man had disap-peared. He wondered if he'd temporarily drifted off. There was still music playing and people dancing. He gestured to the bartender. She looked at him uninterestedly from the other end of the bar, then slouched over towards him. He smiled at her. He was going to sing.

Before the Lighthouse Night

Arthur remembered things being OK. He remembered everything being fine, back when his dad had been working at the museum. It had been a good time for them. Harry had come back in the evenings with his head still supported by his neck, not just lolling forward like it did now. His hair had been grey but clean and swept backwards, not grey and greasy and flat. He had ironed his clothes, and they had always been fresh and fragrant. Every evening he had walked along the cliff from the museum with some kind of bounce to his gait. Sometimes, when the sun set in a hallucinatory blaze of pinks and greens, streaking the ocean with coloured ink, Harry would stand there on his way home and look out over the water like some kind of personable scientist in a far-future utopia, his shirt loose and his glasses low on his nose, his hands in his pockets. Once upon a time Harry had been a perfectly capable man. A respectable man. Standing there on the cliff experiencing some kind of joy in the view.

Rebecca used to get home later than Harry and, as a rule, Arthur and Harry would have the tea ready for her arrival. Rebecca was a manager at the Tesco supermarket. It was a good job. She was a sharp, smart woman usually dressed in a fitted navy-blue suit when out and about, with glossy shoulder-length hair and subtle, but effective make-up. She was the first person Arthur knew to acquire a mobile phone. After tea she would sit in the armchair with her knees pulled up – she always wore jeans and soft jumpers when at home – and do the crossword while half-watching the news.

Thinking about it, the house used to be pretty nice, with its clean, plain rooms and lots of warm lamps. Where were all the lamps now?

Arthur stood in the doorway to the living room and looked around. Actually the lamps were all still there. It was just that the bulbs had gone years ago, and the stands and shades had faded away into the dust and accumulated clutter of the background. Drying clothes now hung over them or they rested, broken, down alongside the skirting boards.

What had his dad done? Arthur stepped into the room but then just stood there indecisively. It felt disloyal and vindictive to ask the question, but what had Harry done?

Had he actually done anything? Did it have to be his fault? Well, no, but Arthur felt pretty sure that it had been. Yet his mother had never seemed like the kind of person who would react to something, to anything, by killing herself. Getting angry or walking out, yes. Throwing a frying pan across the kitchen, absolutely. Suicide, however, seemed too much. Maybe she did simply fall. Maybe she did fall after all.

What could his dad have done to her? The worst thing Arthur could imagine was some kind of violence, but even then, his mum would not just have left the house and jumped to her death. She would have fought back, screamed, shouted, or called the police. She had not suffered fools, or bastards, ever.

Arthur had been quite an intelligent, observant child and also quite an intelligent, observant adolescent, even if it had not been very apparent. Surely he would have spotted any signs of domestic violence. Surely he would have seen the signs if Harry had been having an affair. The thought of Harry having an affair was laughable these days, but not so much back then. He had once possessed the wiry handsomeness of Samuel Beckett or somebody, albeit with thicker glasses. But he was not the kind of man who would have had an affair. Assuming there was a typical kind of man who would have had an affair. He had not been much of a drinker then either. That had come afterwards. After the lighthouse night.

Monday Morning at Arthur's

On waking, Arthur lay in his bed and listened to the wind. It was getting light; his thin blue curtains glowed. He got up and looked out of the window. The house was at the southern end of High Road, and his room lay at the back, with a view to the west. He could see out over some scrubby grass towards a muddy footpath, beyond which the ground dropped away into sheer sandstone cliffs. It was a clear day, and the sea shone bright in the sunlight. He could see the Isle of Man outlined faintly on the horizon. Seagulls were getting blown this way and that by the wind.

Silhouetted against the shining sea, to the right of his view, he could see the defunct minehead balancing on the edge of the cliff. It was a tangle of rusted metal, an assortment of tin boxes and a big yellow wheel that had once lowered people down into the earth. After the mine closed, the minehead had been turned into a museum. His father had been the curator, until the museum had closed too.

Arthur made his way to the bathroom. A few of those bastard worms were visible around the bath; they must have surfaced during the night. He checked the cistern but, thankfully, found none. He looked at the bath and the worms and the tiles all around the bath, and chewed his lip and realised that he was shivering. He could imagine them all packed in together behind the tiles. Writhing and dividing like bacteria under a microscope. If that was the case, then they'd soon burst through the walls. But, of course, that wasn't the case. It was bacteria that did that. These were fully fledged worms, therefore different. Different things altogether.

Arthur's eyes hurt after spending all Sunday morning at Bony's along with Yasmin, the three of them playing *Mario Kart* and getting stoned, and then all Sunday afternoon on Drigg beach, the three of them squinting up at the sun and drinking tea from a flask and taking photos of the rusty remains of twentieth-century shipwrecks. It had been a warm day for September, and a marked contrast to the weather of the night before. Thinking about it, though, thinking about that Saturday and Sunday caused Arthur almost physical pain, given that it was now Monday morning.

He felt, as he felt every Monday morning, a kind of corporeal reluctance to get ready for work. It was as if the anger and disappointment and dread that would once have occupied his thoughts had seeped out to infect the rest of his body, leaving a kind of numbness in his head and an acidic unpleasantness everywhere else. He took it out on the worms, smacking some tissue paper down on top of them. He did the last couple slowly, and was faintly nauseated to find that the crushing of the creatures made a small sound, as if they were actually chitinous. The noise was like a split second of static or a little *click*. To Arthur it sounded like somebody a long way away putting the phone down. He wrinkled his nose. Everything came back to work. *Work.*

What he was most afraid of was arriving at the call centre to find the place crazily busy, with calls queuing up. That is, with irritated customers waiting to have their calls answered. Because that would result in him having to answer such calls rather than getting on with his own job of monitoring call quality. But customers could *not* be allowed to wait. Little did it matter that the main reason for them calling was that their previous calls had been dealt with incorrectly. Little did it matter that if he and his QP colleagues were allowed to get on with their job, and thus monitor enough calls and deliver enough feedback, then customer queries would get dealt with properly and then the customers wouldn't need to ring back, which would prevent the calls queuing up, which would solve the problem pre-emptively. None of that mattered. Why bother thinking long-term to fix a problem, when you can exacerbate it superbly by just reacting in the most knee-jerk and haphazard way imaginable?

Arthur started brushing his teeth. The mirror in front of him already wore a thin veneer of splattered toothpaste. Either he or his father was going to have to clean it one of these days. Well, it wouldn't be his father.

Of course, Arthur understood the panicking mentality that drove the all-hands-to-the-wrong-deck approach. Nobody wanted to piss off the customers. And besides, he was probably wrong about it all anyway. What did *he* know? In the grand scheme of the business, he was nothing. He was sure somebody up there in the upper reaches of the company – whichever company it was – must know what they were doing. They would have it all worked out.

Still, though, he didn't want to go to work. Monday mornings were always busy. There were always calls queuing on a Monday morning. Customers across the country pressing telephone receivers into their faces. All of them part of the same phantom line, and all holding each other up. All of them frustrated. All of them waiting. Waiting. If Arthur was taking calls, he tended to imagine a long queue of ghosts just beyond his desk, waiting for him to log into his telephone. He dreaded that moment. He dreaded the customers. Most of them were OK, but it only took one to ruin everything.

WHERE ARE YOU?

Yasmin felt like she still had Drigg beach sand in her eyes. Monday fucking morning, and the weekend had never even happened. She was busy trying to revert to her I'm-not-here bubble as she made her way across the buzzing floor to her desk. *I'm not here.* It was only twenty past eight and the calls were queuing already. Still, it was only a job, and she wasn't there. *I'm not here.* She had ten minutes yet before she needed to be logged in, so she turned her computer on, giving it time to boot up, and then went to the canteen to get a small plastic cup of water. Water was the only thing from the canteen you could take back to your desk.

Yasmin unlocked her desk drawers and took out an A4 pad of paper. All paper and notebooks had to be locked away between shifts, in case you'd written down any customer details that could be stolen. There had been a short-lived rule that nobody was allowed to write anything down at all, but the impracticality of that had been quickly proven. Some customers seemed to speak purely in numbers, and many of them didn't take kindly to having to repeat themselves. The original idea had been to make notes on the computer as the customer spoke, but that meant not being able to look at those notes at the same time as you worked in another computer program. And, besides, which idiot really thought that information saved on a networked computer was actually safer than information written down by hand and locked away in a drawer?

Anyway, Yasmin's pad of paper didn't have any information on it at all. It was for doodling only. It wasn't that Yasmin didn't pay attention to customers speaking on the phone, or didn't make sure to remember what they were telling her. Her doodling was completely automatic, and required none of her pretty formidable brainpower, so she was able to focus all of that on the customer at hand. About sixty per cent of the customer advisers working there doodled like this, too. Most of Yasmin's doodles ended up full of ears and mouths and wires. Pointed ears, that is, and impossibly plump lips, and thick black biro wires that snaked out all over the page. About halfway through each shift, she'd find the outer edges of her hands leaving big smudges across her desk, and see that they were covered in ink from leaning on the densely populated paper. A lot of the other customer advisers would, without thinking about it, draw ships and sea monsters.

Yasmin logged into the billing system, which was called Jupiter – for reasons nobody really understood. She accessed the call-logging system, which was named Tracker, and the system which connected the computer to the phone, which was called PhoneLink. After that, she logged into the online business encyclopaedia, which was called Edison. She next logged into the company email system, and finally, she logged into a system which was like an email program, but about a million times slower and clunkier, which was used to send details of customer queries to other departments on especially formatted templates. This system was called NOM, or Net Object Management. Yasmin considered it a particularly crap piece of software, which was unfortunate because the job it did was absolutely crucial. But, there you go. Was that surprising? Not really. She counted down the seconds on the LCD screen of her telephone, took a deep breath and logged in just as the time hit 8.30.

She immediately heard a *beep* in her earpiece, signifying a customer, and launched into her call opening.

'Good morning, you're though to Yasmin. Could I take your customer account number, please?'

'What?' said the customer. She spoke with a Received Pronunciation kind of accent, but obviously had no manners.

'Could I take your customer account number, please?' Yasmin repeated.

'Where are you? Are you an Indian?' The customer's tone was already curt.

'No,' said Yasmin.

'You don't sound English.'

'Do you have your account number there, please?'

'Tell me where you are.'

'This call centre, you mean? It's in Cumbria.'

'Where's that? Is that in England?'

'Yes. You know where Sellafield is?'

'Of course I do. Don't you start patronising me, young lady. I've read all about that terrible place.'

'Well, that's Cumbria.'

'So you're English?'

'*Yes.*'

'Oh good! I don't want to waste my time trying to talk to those Pakis you people insist on employing.'

'Please don't use that kind of language or I'll have to terminate the call.'

'I see PC's gone mad even up in the middle of nowhere.'

'Do you have your account number or not?'

'Yes! Just give me a chance to find it, if you don't mind.' The customer tutted and huffed.

After three or four calls, Yasmin started to get a feeling that she frequently experienced at work. It was the feeling that the fabric of this place was *thin*. Thinner than in other places. Part of it was down to the fact that inside the building you could really have been anywhere, because of the generic office accommodation – the bland décor, the horrible veneer-surfaced desks, the rows of humming computers. That always served to make Yasmin a little uneasy, because you weren't anchored to anything solid or meaningful. The other major reason for the 'thinness' was the nature of the work performed there. The *base-*

lessness of it. The sense of existing only at the end of a telephone. It made you feel a bit weird if you let it – if you thought about it for long enough. Yasmin always ended up thinking about the telephones. You ring somebody up, it doesn't matter where they are, right, as long as they have a phone there with them. More so if you're ringing a call centre.

The only people Yasmin and her colleagues ever really spoke to – the customers – couldn't see them, so as far as the customers were concerned they were just voices coming through the wires. They weren't living, breathing bodies in a town by the sea; they weren't anywhere. They became almost nothing but words on the end of the line, for eight hours a day. *Every fucking phone call is a kind of reduction*, she thought. *A reduction of me. The proportion of time I spend as just a voice is far too high. Every phone call tips that balance just a little bit – for me and for everybody else who works in these places.*

If you weren't lucky enough to face the windows and be able to fix your eyes on something solid – the lighthouse was Yasmin's favourite – then you could find yourself drifting in a susceptible state, and thus suffer a kind of vertiginous horror at the absence at the centre of it all. You were somewhere *in between*. Between two companies. Between two phones. *You could forget that you were here at all*, she thought. And every phone call was a kind of puncture into your head. The beep that signified a new customer was a terrible sound, and it seemed to Yasmin to be the sound of something actually penetrating space;

in its blunt, aural violence, it seemed to be indicating that a phone call was an invasion, was one place invading another. It was some kind of dart piercing the fabric. *That's why call centres are thin places*, she thought. *That's why it feels thin. Because there are thousands of little needles arriving every day from other places, thousands of little needle voices, thrusting into our heads and into our lives and into our world.* And they left holes just like pinpricks in a piece of paper. Letting the light through. Making it weak. This was something that she'd talked about with Arthur and Bony, on many hazy nights spent at the Vagabond. Arthur would always understand completely, nodding and grinning, and saying 'Yes!' at various junctures, but Bony would just look blank. But then, that was Bony.

'I've got two degrees,' said one customer who couldn't understand her bill. 'I doubt you've got any qualifications. Don't tell *me* I'm wrong.'

'You stupid fucking bint,' said another caller, who didn't seem to remember why he'd rung, or even whom he'd rung. 'Fuck you.'

The next call consisted of some kind of telephonic malfunction: it was another call adviser, assuming Yasmin was a customer, so both Yasmin and the other girl started following their scripts at the same time. A seagull flew into the window. The next call was another strange one. It was just static, really, but with a certain texture and depth that somehow made it a *landscape* of static. A difficult terrain of peaks and troughs and shadows. Somewhere in the distance there was a quiet voice – probably that of the customer – that sounded high and panicky, due to the bad line. It was slowly eclipsed by a high-pitched whistle of white noise that sounded like a train grinding to a halt. Yasmin winced and disconnected.

She looked out of the window at the lighthouse. *I'm not here*, she thought. *I'm somewhere else. I'm sitting in a tree in Lothlorien. I am discovering intelligent life on another planet. I am impressing everybody with my elegantly pointed ears. One of these days*, she thought, *I am going to develop some kind of real-world ambition. One of these days.*

DEAD WEIGHT

Artemis stood in the meeting room, his hands behind his back, and stared at the cream-coloured wall. His nose was wrinkled. The wall was covered with small blue and grey spots where Blu-Tack had either left a stain or pulled some paint off with it when removed. The wall looked dirty. It looked diseased. It looked *disgusting*. What kind of place was this? There were tatty, torn posters as well, depicting stacks of pound coins. Something to do with this year's company targets. No, *last* year's company targets. Artemis snarled and ripped one of them down.

The room was the closest thing the workplace had to a boardroom, in that it was quite spacious and contained a long table, but it also seemed to serve as something of a storage area. Three or four flipcharts – devoid of actual paper – leant against one wall, and there was an ancient acetate projector gathering dust in the corner. Boxes full of old posters were stacked up on the windowsill. Artemis screwed up the poster from the wall and shoved it into one of the boxes, not being able to see a bin anywhere in the room. He then pulled out one of the older posters. It was advertising some employee incentive, something about collecting cash from customers, and it looked as if the incentive had been themed around a contemporary blockbuster film release. Artemis wondered, idly, if Outsourcing Unlimited had paid to use the copyrighted logos, images and slogans. He doubted it. Interext never did. He looked out of the window, which faced out to the front of the building. There was a young girl sitting, smoking, on the steps leading up to the entrance. You weren't supposed to smoke down there. He thought about knocking on the window and making threatening gestures at her, but decided against it because he could see right down her top from where he stood.

There was a loud bang behind him as the door of the room flew open and smashed against the wall.

'Oops,' said Bracket, stepping through. 'Sorry. I always do that.'

'Learn to move more gracefully,' said Artemis, without turning around. 'Please.'

'Am I the first?' asked Bracket.

'Work it out,' said Artemis, finally turning around. 'There's nobody else here. You look tired.'

'I always look like this,' Bracket said, as he sat down and started playing with his tie. He thought about telling Artemis to stop being so fucking rude, but instead kept his mouth shut.

'Where are all of the others?' Artemis said.

'On their way, probably,' said Bracket.

'Should get here early,' said Artemis. 'Managers should at least be able to manage their own time.' He turned to look out of the window again.

Behind Artemis's back, Bracket shook his head and rolled his eyes.

Once all of the team managers had arrived and were seated around the table, Artemis turned away from the window to face them.

'As you are all probably aware,' he said, 'my name is Artemis Black. Interext have taken over the management of this operation at the behest of Northern Water, and they have made me responsible for it.' He thought about explaining that Interext had always owned Northern Water anyway, but didn't. They might be easily confused. 'There are going to be some radical changes, both in the way we serve our customers, and the way this place is managed. To be frank, I get the impression that bad habits have been allowed to flourish here, while good practice has been allowed to slide, simply because it's so fucking remote.'

'I don't know if—' started Sally, a relatively new team manager with long straight blonde hair, large skittish brown eyes, and a small pointed chin.

'I don't care what you don't know,' said Artemis, 'and it probably doesn't matter. You know what "I don't know" did? Pissed the bed and blamed the blanket, that's what.'

'I thought that was "thought",' Bracket said.

'Is that a joke?' Artemis snapped. He placed his fists on the table and glared at Bracket.

'No,' said Bracket, 'I just mean . . . that's what Mam used to say.'

'This is exactly the kind of bollocks that I'm talking about,' Artemis replied. '"That's what Mam used to say," for Christ's sake.' He turned again to the window, while behind his back the team managers raised their eyebrows at each other and mouthed the word 'wanker'.

Bracket cleared his throat. 'So what are we going to do?' he asked.

'You're going to deliver to me exactly what I require,' Artemis said quietly. 'I will set the standards and you will meet them. Is that understood? Before we get into the specifics, do you all understand that I cannot accept any half-measures or twatting about?'

The team managers nodded their heads and murmured assent. Bracket couldn't quite work out if they were actually overawed or just quietly contemptuous. God knows they weren't easily impressed. Their present inscrutability made him proud to be Cumbrian.

'Firstly, I want to see the call quality-assessment criteria,' Artemis said. 'Bracket, that's you, yeah?'

'Yep,' said Bracket, nodding. 'That's me.'

'We're going to go through them, you and me, and raise the game. We need cash. We need lots of cash. We need to collect cash at every opportunity, and we need to weight the quality-assessment criteria to reflect that. We also need to look at the consequences of failure. It has to matter. People have to know when they've fucked up, or when they're just not good enough. OK?'

'OK,' said Bracket.

'We also need to make sure the calls don't last too long. The shorter the calls, the more customers we speak to, the more cash-collection opportunities we have. So we need to hammer them on average handling time. Kat – is that you?'

'I'm the duty manager,' Kat said, uncertainly. Kat was short with a dark ponytail and glasses. She was pale, and had a limp.

'You watch call volumes and can see the status of all of the phones, yeah?'

'That's right.'

'Then you're doing the hammering,' Artemis said, and scratched his chin thoughtfully. 'Of course, we can't forget about C-sat.'

'C-sat?' Kat queried.

'Yes,' said Artemis, and he looked up at the ceiling. He still held one of his massive hands by his throat. 'Don't tell me you don't know what see-sat is.'

Nobody said anything.

'C-sat,' Artemis said, 'as you all know, is customer satisfaction. Customer satisfaction – or *C-sat* – is an essential measure of our performance. We can't forget about customer satisfaction.'

'So the advisers here are simultaneously pushing for payment, keeping their calls as short as possible, and trying to ensure that all the customers are satisfied?' Bracket asked.

Yes,' said Artemis. 'Don't you think they're capable? Are you telling me that they don't have the right attitude? Actually, speaking of advisers, we need to lose a few – to save money.'

'We've always focused on the . . . on the C-sat,' said Bracket. 'In the past, we've found that the shorter the call, the less likely the customer is to be satisfied, because the issue won't have been investigated thoroughly.'

'To me that implies that the advisers are not of a high enough calibre,' said Artemis, staring down at Bracket.

'They're of a *very* high calibre,' said Bracket, feeling flushed. 'But it doesn't matter how high a calibre they are if they're to be set two contradictory objectives. It just won't work.'

Artemis stared at Bracket for a moment longer. 'We'll take this offline,' he said abruptly. 'We'll park it. I want to see you after the meeting, Bracket. Just drop it for now. OK?'

Bracket nodded. Suddenly ashamed of losing his temper, he couldn't bear to make eye contact with anybody, so dropped his gaze to the table.

'Did you say something about redundancies?' Kat asked Artemis.

'Yes,' Artemis said. 'Yes, I did. There will have to be redundancies. This ship is simply carrying too much weight, and some of it is dead. We have to dump that dead weight or we will sink. It is very simple.'

'How will it be decided? And how many will have to go?'

'I will decide,' Artemis replied, 'based upon perform-ance metrics. In two months' time, the lowest-scoring twenty per cent of the workforce will be dropped.'

'Twenty per cent?' Sally repeated faintly.

'Yes,' Artemis confirmed.

Bracket didn't really want to hear any more. He found himself looking out of the window, his awareness of the meeting around him turned down to nothing. When, completely unexpectedly, the bright white sky started hurling raindrops like ball-bearings against the glass and Artemis jumped away from it and swore, Bracket reached a decision. He would just keep his mouth shut and do what he was told. He would stop caring about whether or not it worked. He would stop worrying. He would stop thinking altogether. These hours were not his, so why pretend otherwise?

THE WAVERLEY

Artemis waited at the call centre for the rain to stop before making a break for it and heading back to the hotel. The night was cold and a sharp breeze blew in from the sea, causing the yachts in the marina to chatter and clack like loosely-boned skeletons.

The Waverley Hotel was a 300-year-old building with an impressive Georgian façade that had been painted an unfortunate shade of beige. Artemis stood on the opposite side of Tangier Street and looked up at all four storeys, hands pushed deep into the pockets of his long black coat. Some of the large rectangular windows were lit up, and the place looked extraordinarily welcoming beneath the rolling waves of black cloud that broke across the dull silver of the sky above. He crossed the road and entered the lobby, barely glancing at the tall, sleek young woman on reception, and headed straight through to the bar.

The carpet in both lobby and bar was red, mostly, featuring a busy pattern of large, interlocking diamonds.

The chairs and bar stools were upholstered in red velvety stuff. The curtains were also red. The lower parts of the walls were panelled in some kind of dark wood, above which there was beige wallpaper. The bar was an almost perfectly square booth located right in the centre of the square room. The grey-haired, smartly dressed man behind the bar nodded to Artemis.

'A Midori and lemonade,' said Artemis. 'A double Midori, actually.'

The barman didn't say anything as he prepared the drink. Apart from the two of them, the room was empty. Artemis counted out his change and placed it on the bar while he waited. Once his drink was ready, he picked it up and went and sat in a corner, placing his mobile phone on the table in front of him. He drank up quickly, wishing he'd thought to ask for a stirrer. By the time his phone rang, he'd nearly finished it but the thick liqueur was still mostly lying in the bottom of the glass, not having had the chance to affect him in the slightest. They were ringing him earlier than he expected. He had planned to be secure in the privacy of his hotel room. He measured his breathing, cleared his throat, then picked up his phone and answered it.

'Artemis speaking,' he said.

'Artemis,' responded the voice at the other end of the line. The voice was distorted by faint clicks and beeps, which sounded like the noises dial-up modems make when connecting. It was an old, phlegmy voice – not just croaky but rough and animalistic. 'We believe we are communicating with the Interstice. Expect contact.'

'What exactly is required of me?'

'That is as yet unclear,' said the voice.

'Thank you,' said Artemis. But, even as he was speaking, the line had gone dead. He downed the rest of his bright green drink, swept out of the bar, through the lobby, and out of the hotel. He turned immediately right and headed north up Tangier Street, involuntarily sneering at a bingo hall, and stopped in front of a pizza place with an ugly, incongruous yellow and black façade. He ordered himself a sixteen-inch Beast Feast, then waited outside in the slight drizzle until the Turkish proprietor called him back in once it was ready. Looking further north up Tangier Street he could see the yellow glow of the Tesco petrol station staining the darkening night. Damnable little town with its wind and rain and sandstone and its shrieking seagulls! He would wake up through the night, sweating, disturbed by the note of pain in their constant cries. He would wake up to the sound of the seagulls, and the sound of the sea, and he would feel like his lonely little box of a room was perched right on a cliff edge overhanging the ocean, and was poised to drop at any moment, the rock beneath him being eroded by the waves. He would get out of bed and look out of the window, just to reassure himself, and would see seagulls wheeling against a black sky, lit up like yellow sparks by the twenty-four-hour glow of the nearby supermarket.

From the Depths

It drifted up, as if propelled by the cloud of rotten filth and blood that it had suddenly released from the thin, white, bulging skin of its underside. The brown cloud billowed outwards in murky waves. The scent of it – the stink – would inevitably draw sharks and other creatures, but the thing had nothing to fear from such scavengers. They would only be interested in the matter that it had left behind.

It was not floating at a particularly great depth, but the water beneath it was incredibly deep. It hovered there in a dark blue void. If it had possessed a human mind, it would no doubt have experienced fear at the blankness below, but it did not.

Above was a slightly paler, brighter expanse of water, the different shade indicative – the only indication – of the presence of the sun. That was the direction in which the thing moved. That was the beginning of the journey that would take it to Drigg.

Blind, pale, bulbous and hulking, the thing slowly rose up.

BAD THURSDAY

The shower sprayed water on to the tiles, washing little black worms out into the bath tub. Arthur kept having to lift his feet so that the worms could float on past them and into the plughole without touching him. He still made a point of killing any that were already visible before turning on the shower, but had resigned himself to the fact that there was an inexhaustible supply of the bastards lurking either in between or behind the tiles. It didn't help that little flakes of grout fell out, leaving sinister black holes, every time he tried giving the tiles a clean. The water would get in there and rot the walls and cause damp, no doubt thus creating the perfect environment for these creatures to live and breed in. Not only that, but these holes provided the openings from which the worms crept once the shower was turned on. The more holes there were, the more worms there would be.

Arthur was even thinking about the possibility of retiling the wall completely when he felt something tickling his foot. He looked down and saw one of the bugs clinging on to the little toe of his right foot. He shivered slightly and bent down to flick it away, but the water streaming from his fingers dislodged it, and it slipped in between his toes.

The first ripple of revulsion caused Arthur's body to quiver, but the second caused outright panic. He could feel the creature squirming against his skin, he was sure, and the shower seemed to be cooling down. He lifted his foot and shook it vigorously, but couldn't tell whether the worm was still there. He tried to bring his foot up behind him, twisting his head around to examine the sole, but found himself hopping about ridiculously on his other foot, his right knee brushing the shower curtain, and realised just how slippery the surface of the bath was. Suddenly he lost his balance and fell, smacking his elbow on the rim of the tub and hauling down the curtain as he grabbed it for support. He gave a loud cry, the shooting pains in his elbow blanking out everything else, and then his entire arm went numb. The shower head had been knocked askew and was spraying cold water out across the bathroom floor. Arthur imagined he could feel the worms moving all around him and he scrambled to his feet. Clambering out of the bath, he expected his father might come to see if he was OK.

Harry didn't come to see if he was OK.

'I was on the phone to your mum,' Harry explained, pleadingly. 'She was upset. I heard all the noise, but I couldn't just—'

'You were *not* on the phone to Mum!' Arthur shouted, slamming his mug down on the worktop. 'You know you weren't!'

'I . . . I *was*!' Harry said, and Arthur felt sickened to recognise that frail stammer from the numerous recorded calls he had listened to at work. Harry kept shaking and scratching the back of his hands. 'And . . . and anyway, I don't know what you're talking about, going on about these worms. What worms? I . . . I've never seen any!'

'The *worms*,' Arthur said, between gritted teeth. His eyes grew wet. 'I've told you about them before, Dad.'

'Son,' Harry said, looking concerned, 'I keep telling you, there are no worms in there.'

Arthur looked down. His wet hair flopped in front of his face. He was still leaning against the worktop. 'You just can't see them because you don't wear your glasses when you're in there,' he said.

'That's not the case,' Harry protested. 'I think you just imagine them.'

'No, I don't,' said Arthur. 'Go and look! Go and look at them!' He pointed upwards, at the ceiling. 'They're still in there! Go and see!'

'I've been and looked,' Harry said. 'I can't see anything.'

'But with your fucking glasses on!' Arthur yelled.

Harry lowered his head at that, and started scratching more vigorously at the backs of his hands. Red blotches had appeared on his face. It was the first time he'd ever heard Arthur swear.

'No,' Harry breathed. 'You imagine them.'

'I don't imagine them. You imagine Mum, though.'

'That's different. I've already explained. I talk to her over the telephone.'

'Put your glasses on,' Arthur insisted. 'Put your glasses on.'

'No.' Harry was shaking his head. He backed away. 'You're going to be late for work,' he said, and then he turned and left the room.

Harry had suffered poor eyesight for a very long time. For as long as Arthur could remember, his father had worn very thick glasses. At work, Harry needed all on-screen text to be written in font size twenty. Similarly, he needed all of the computer programs to be displayed at twice their normal size. If anybody passing Arthur's desk glanced over his shoulder as he checked his emails, it would be painfully obvious to them that all of the email messages were from Arthur's father, all of them asking him for help.

Arthur got to work just on time. He nodded to the new security guard on the reception desk – one of several new Interext people working shifts to cover the desk twenty-four hours a day – and then he stopped dead.

The bottom drawer of the guard's desk was open and a litre bottle of whisky was clearly visible.

Arthur looked briefly at the security guard, now deep in conversation with a courier, and continued up the stairs before the guard realised that Arthur had spotted the bottle. Arthur shook his head as he went, and grinned. It was the little things that made the days bearable.

He nodded in acknowledgement to several people as he walked past their desks, but couldn't bring himself to talk. He was relieved, in a way, to notice that Tiffany – who sat opposite him – looked pretty miserable. When she was in a good mood she would babble on excitedly about anything and everything, and today he just wasn't in the mood to feign any degree of interest.

It was only once he'd sat down that he sensed just how miserable she really was. Her bloodshot eyes were surrounded by tired, purple-looking skin, and she kept muttering to herself.

'Are you OK, Tiffany?' Arthur asked finally.

She looked up, as if only just noticing his presence, and smiled faintly before she shook her head. 'They've locked up my Ollie . . .' she explained, and for a moment her voice broke. 'And the bastards have thrown us all on to the incoming, because there are so many calls queuing.' She started crying.

'You should go home,' Arthur said. 'Go home and try to get some rest. You can't be in the right frame of mind for work.'

'I can't go home. There's no availability for leave, and they say it's not policy to give compassionate leave for this.'

Arthur didn't say anything to that. Instead he looked at the telephone on his desk and steeled himself to lift the receiver and log in. He stared at it, and stared at it.

'Oh,' Tiffany said, 'I've just remembered. I'm sorry, Arthur, but I can't cover for your dad any more. They're changing the call requirements now this Artemis feller's arrived, and Harry, bless him, doesn't do any of the things he's meant to do according to this new script. It's going to be too obvious. I reckon you're going to have to have a word with him.'

Arthur stared blankly across at her and – after a moment or two during which Tiffany wasn't sure he'd heard her – he nodded. Then he put his headset on.

Even though Arthur was busy dealing with customers himself, he was still aware of Tiffany becoming more and more panicked. She was too tired to think as quickly as the impatient customers expected of her, and too distracted to notice some of the important details of their accounts. Every customer who displayed anger or outright rudeness put her in an even worse state to deal with the next. She ended up aggravating people by saying things like, 'I'm sorry, I got that wrong,' or, 'Well, I'm buggered if I can understand this one myself.' As the day progressed, she started repeating, 'I'm sorry, please bear with me,' while she stared at her screen trying to remember what it was the customer had originally asked for.

Inevitably, her callers became more and more pissed off, until they were regularly demanding to speak to her supervisor. Even this was proving difficult, as Tiffany kept pressing the wrong button – or the right button at the wrong time – and disconnecting them. Arthur could tell when it happened, because her teary eyes widened and her hand flew to her mouth. At one point he looked up and was startled to see Artemis Black standing behind Tiffany's chair, looking down at her with a mixture of curiosity and disgust. She didn't know he was there, and Arthur hadn't noticed his arrival either. Arthur's eyes returned to his screen, then looked back, and found that Artemis had gone again as silently as he had appeared.

Later, in the canteen, Arthur overheard a conversation between Diane and a relatively new employee called Oscar. Diane was sitting with her back to him and Oscar was sitting opposite her. Behind Oscar was a small poster Blu-Tacked to the glass.

Arthur looked at the poster, while listening to Diane and Oscar talk. It read:

Bums off Seats – Control, Alt, Delete

It was one of many carrying the same message, and they were supposed to help people to remember to lock their computers while they were not at their desks. The words had been burnt into everybody's brains just through this constant exposure. By the constant repetition.

'I was late on t'dinner because I had a proper fucked-up account just,' Diane announced. 'Some right bitch screaming that she wanted to speak to Harry. He's proper messed it up, he has.'

'Who's Harry?' Oscar asked.

'He's this weird old twat. You'll soon recognise him: flaky skin, smells of meat.' Diane lowered her voice. 'Everybody says he's a paedophile. Got sacked from his last job because they found stuff on his computer. He's a fucking freak.'

'He got sacked from his last job because he had a mental breakdown,' Arthur interrupted. 'He's never been accused of paedophilia.'

'Well,' said Diane, turning to face Arthur, 'that's what people say. And I heard that's why he smells of meat. I'm just saying.'

Arthur put down his sandwich and swallowed. He stretched out his fingers and looked at them. 'You know that what you're saying is nowhere near true, but you're saying it anyway,' he said.

Diane shrugged.

'You're a spiteful, nasty little maggot,' Arthur continued. 'You're malicious and small-minded, and what you think and what you say count for nothing good. Don't you *dare* reiterate such vile, destructive *shite* about my dad.' He stood up. 'You're a fucking disgrace,' he concluded, then picked up her cardboard mug of tea and poured it all over her plate of chips.

Diane stood up and jabbed a long, sharp fingernail at Arthur's chest. She screwed up her mouth to speak just as Arthur felt a hand fall on his shoulder.

'Arthur! What the hell are you doing?'

Arthur turned to see Bracket's pale, dark-eyed, stubbly face looking at him in confusion.

'Sorry,' Arthur said, quietly. 'She was being very cruel.'

'Come with me,' Bracket said. 'Now.'

Arthur left work that day with a warning. 'One foot wrong and you're gone,' Artemis had told him. Interext wouldn't tolerate such deplorable behaviour.

He hurried along by the harbour to the Vagabond, passing elderly couples sitting on benches while eating bags of chips from Crosby's. It was a clear day, but breezy, and everybody seemed to be wearing heavy beige coats. He could tell that Old Man Easy was out and about, as he could hear music drifting across the marina. Just before he got to the pub he kicked out at a big metal sculpture of a knotted rope, one of several rising from the promenade at regular intervals. Yasmin finished half an hour after he did, and had told him she would meet him there. He was about to go inside and buy a drink when he saw Old Man Easy ambling towards him down the Sugar Tongue. He carried his knackered, fuzzy-sounding stereo in his right hand, as ever, while he murmured along to the Engelbert Humperdinck tape he was playing at full volume. He wore a pair of glasses that he'd covered in Sellotape to turn them into sunglasses. He nodded and smiled at Arthur as he passed. He gestured at his glasses with his left hand, and puffed out his already sizeable chest.

'Better than my own eyes, these are,' he declared. That

118

was what he always said. Or, at least, that was all Arthur had ever heard him say.

Arthur nodded and entered the pub.

'It's not a good time to be pissing them off,' Yasmin said, staring at her empty wine glass.

'I know,' Arthur said. 'I know, but I didn't do it on purpose.'

'What's wrong?'

'I shouted at Dad this morning.'

'Don't worry about it,' Yasmin said, and she put her hand on Arthur's arm. 'I used to argue with my parents all the time when I lived with them.'

'I'm worried about him,' Arthur said. He shook his head. 'He talks to Mum on the telephone. I shouted at him because he thinks *I'm* imagining things, and yet he talks to Mum on the telephone.'

'Maybe it's just his way of coping.'

'Maybe,' Arthur said, 'but I don't think he's coping at all.'

'How do you cope?'

'You know how I cope.' Arthur looked up at Yasmin and grinned. 'I go out during storms and look for her.'

'Oh, yeah,' Yasmin snorted. 'Well, maybe you shouldn't go pointing the finger at your dad. You're both pretty weird.'

'Thank you, Yasmin,' Arthur said.

'What is it you're imagining, anyway?'

'I'm not imagining anything! There are little worms in

the bathroom walls. They drive me mad, but Dad can't see them, at least not without his glasses.'

Yasmin pulled a face.

'I know,' Arthur said. 'It sounds disgusting.' He looked at his hands. 'Jesus fucking Christ, I want to *do* something, Yasmin.'

'What?'

'I don't know! Anything! I've read so many books about so many things, but they're only books, and I feel like I'm only scratching the surface of things.'

'Why don't you go to university?'

'But I don't know what I'd want to study.'

'What are you interested in?' Yasmin asked.

'I'm interested in everything,' Arthur said. 'Everything. But I could only study one thing at a time, really. And that would be after a few years of saving.'

'You could study one thing and then go on to another.'

'That would be very expensive,' Arthur replied. 'And I also wouldn't have time.'

'What do you mean, you wouldn't have time?'

'To fit it all in before I die. I could live another hundred years and I wouldn't understand half of what I want to understand.'

The two of them were sitting at a table by the window. Arthur looked out through the glass.

'You'll just have to accept a certain lack of understanding, then,' Yasmin said.

'Really?' asked Arthur. 'You think university is the only way?'

'Do I fuck think that. Anyway, maybe you could upload.'

'What do you mean, upload?'

'Save your consciousness to a computer and live forever. That way you could learn just as much as you want.'

'What are you on about?' Arthur asked, laughing.

'I don't really understand it,' Yasmin confessed. 'I read about it a while ago though, and it made sense at the time. My avatar would have pointed ears.'

'You do talk some bollocks.'

'Arthur,' Yasmin said, 'is Bony coming through tonight?'

'I haven't heard from him today.'

'I want to see him. Do you think he could be interested in me?'

Arthur looked at her, suddenly feeling very conscious of the expression on his face. 'Why?' he asked. 'Are you interested in him?'

Yasmin nodded.

'Bony's a bit odd when it comes to these things,' Arthur said. 'He's not really into women.'

'What?' Yasmin laughed incredulously. 'You're not telling me that Bony's gay?'

'No,' Arthur said, 'he just isn't really attracted to anybody. Anybody real, I mean. He likes you as a friend, I know that much. He thinks you're great. And don't let me put you off making a move. He just . . . his most intense feelings are for *things* . . . and fictional characters. He likes fictional characters. Especially video-game characters.'

'Wow,' Yasmin said.

'Don't tell him I told you,' Arthur said. 'He gets paranoid that people might think he's some sort of freak.'

'No,' Yasmin shook her head. 'I know people just like him online. I don't think he's a freak.'

'He's tried in the past,' Arthur continued, 'but ultimately people are just objects to him, and eventually they get tired of just being that.'

She bit her lip. 'Excuse me.' She got up and headed off in the direction of the toilet.

Arthur looked back out of the window. He wanted to get up and leave, right there and then.

Bony and the Thing

Bony set off walking down the road from the level crossing in the direction of the beach. It was a narrow, unmarked road, and was longer than it looked. Bony wasn't deceived by that, though, because he walked it frequently.

In front of him there was the road, and to the right of the road there was a tall metal fence that marked the edge of the Nuclear Decommisioning Authority site that was the Drigg low-level waste repository. To the left of the road there were green fields dotted with white sheep. And at that point where the road disappeared there was a wavy line of sand-dunes. Above it all was a bright, mottled-white sky. Bony felt like the last human being alive.

The road twisted a couple of times before ending in a small car park, usually occupied at that time of day, during the week, by the vehicles of people walking their dogs. There were no cars there at the moment, though.

Next to the car park – which wasn't really a car park, more of a lay-by – there was a huge black shed with no windows, boxed in by another high metal fence. The shed shared this enclosure with a mouldy old caravan and a pile of wood, stacked up as if for a bonfire. Bony had never seen anybody actually inside that fence, although the padlock on the gate – which Bony examined regularly – always seemed to show signs of recent use.

There was another gate, which barred the road, and it was this gate that Bony paid a visit to each day. Or, rather, it was the left-hand gatepost: a tall, wide metal pipe with a hole in it. Bony sat down with his back to the pipe, and positioned his head near the hole. The gatepost sang to him. Well, not just to him, he reflected, it could be to anybody, but he was the only one who sat and listened. The gate was located where the road and the fields terminated at a narrow stretch of sand dunes. Bony gazed along the dunes stretching to the north, the long grass on their spines rippling in the cold wind. The sky was huge. Just inland from the dunes, in that direction, the terrain was marshy – a Site of Special Scientific Interest due to the population of natterjack toads. The gatepost sang tunelessly but hauntingly; it had a deep, sad, fluting voice. Bony stood up and ran his hand over the top of it. He held himself close to it and felt the subtle resonance. He then walked through the gate, closed it behind him, and picked his way down the path towards the sand. The path also served as a run-off for water draining off the dunes, and as such it was often more of a stream than a path – a stream of water that was orangey-red, for reasons that Bony did not understand.

*

The beach was empty and the tide was out. The sky was even bigger now – a colossal wall of grey and white, rearing up beyond the sea and curving overhead. The sea itself was just a thick black line above the distant silvery expanse of flat sand. In places the level surface of the beach was interrupted by stretches of smooth stones or by large, jagged lumps of concrete. Nearer the water there rose a huge concrete cube, half buried, with a tall metal pole protruding from the top of it. This was Barnscar, and how such a small spot of land had earned its own name was a mystery to Bony, but the pole was a mark, a warning – the indicator of an area where it was easy to get caught out by the tide coming in fast. Somebody had drowned there once, hence the pole; that much he knew.

To the right of the pole, several long, thin things protruded from the sand in some sort of regular formation. He understood these to be the metal ribs of something left over from World War II. They were surrounded by gnarled, rusted panels and plates. He couldn't tell if it had once been a boat or a plane, or even a small submarine, but this was one of his favourite places to visit. Bony headed there first – the ribcage, as he thought of it – and let the desolate voices of the seagulls penetrate his awareness, take root in his consciousness.

Once he reached his goal, he could barely make out the metal frame for the colony of molluscs that encrusted it. They weren't anything new to him, however, their colonisation of the wreck being part of its attraction. He ran his hand over the skin of shells and looked around, working out which way to walk from here. He decided to head south, in the direction of Ravenglass, because the last time he had been to the beach he had walked north towards Seascale and Sellafield. The previous time it had been past midnight, and the bright lights of the power station had turned the sky above it orange and purple, drawing Bony towards it almost as if he was searching for the source of some incredible music.

After walking for about twenty minutes, occasionally stopping to investigate particularly interesting pieces of flotsam (two wooden chairs standing side by side; a red leather handbag; a giant, deflated balloon shaped like a bird), Bony approached something that he'd already noticed from a distance but had not been able to identify. Twenty or thirty gulls rose discordantly on his arrival. He had thought that maybe it was some item of bedding, or a ragged length of plastic sheeting. It wasn't either of those, though. Upon reaching it, he dropped to his knees and placed both hands on top of his head. He was completely alone there, a skinny figure amongst the millions of pebbles. He didn't cry or vomit, although he wondered if maybe he should be reacting in a more visceral fashion.

The object he'd spotted was a soft-looking expanse of uneven white flesh, about forty feet long and in places three feet thick. It was ragged around the edge, and stank like the breath of a violent, snarling dog. Bony got to his feet and walked all around it, but could not see any discernible features. He wondered for a moment if it might be some giant kind of jellyfish, but its flesh was completely opaque. There was no central bulk to it, and nothing that he could think of as a head.

He finally touched it. He stretched his hand out and touched it, wondering if it would respond in some way – if it would suck itself in like snails or slugs did. When the thing didn't react at all, Bony squeezed it gently between his fingers. It felt quite tough, like raw meat that had been left out in the sun. If it was a creature at all, then obviously it was dead. He wasn't even sure that it was a creature, but he couldn't think what else it might be.

Bony looked up at the white sky, where the seagulls were small, sharp-voiced sentries wheeling around. This lonely beach with its relics of humanity and its salt air and its weird flesh belonged to them. Bony knew that, and he also felt as if the seagulls knew that he respected them. He looked back down at this *thing*, whatever it was, and wondered if maybe something important was happening.

It had survived the relentless, grasping fingers of the tides due to being trapped within the rusty half-cage formed by the bones of another dead ship or submarine or plane, or some other machine relic of some war. Over time, of course, the thing would be tugged against the prongs, and the edges of it would be swept seawards, and it would bulge out ever more between the metal struts containing it. But for now it just rested there, encased, like an internal organ being gently squeezed in the hand of a giant.

Bony imagined it under water, that fluid environment lifting it slightly, giving it the semblance of living motion, the illusion of life.

Maybe things like this were washed up all the time, but normally swept away again by the outgoing tide. Maybe this one was only here still thanks to the fluke of it landing inside such a perfect trap. Bony could not quite believe that, though. He had spent a lot of time on this beach, so knew that things like this really did not wash up all the time. In fact, the placement of the thing felt intentional almost. Or maybe not intentional but meaningful. Like a message. Like it was supposed to be found.

Bony normally slept on his back with his arms crossed over his chest. After seeing a picture of an Egyptian mummy during his childhood, he had tried to imitate its pose and had found it surprisingly comfortable. That night, though, he could not sleep at all, in any position.

His room was a tangle of old games consoles and bookcases stuffed with small boxes, in which legions of tiny wargame figurines lay sandwiched between pieces of sponge. As well as the boxes of models, there were rulebooks for role-playing games he didn't play any more, or at least, he hadn't played for a long time. He and Arthur and Yasmin still talked occasionally about getting another game going, but he knew – as did the others, he suspected – that it was never going to happen. They were adults now. Completely.

It wasn't normal for Bony to find sleeping difficult, and

he wasn't used to the pure physical discomfort of insomnia, the hyper-sensitivity to sounds. He had to get up early, very early, to be in the box at seven, which meant that – he checked his mobile phone – he would get, at best, four and half hours' sleep. That thought did not help, of course, and a creeping panic squeezed at his heart until he had to get up and turn the light on. He then sat down on the bed, his vision blurred by the sudden brightness, and hugged himself. He might as well just not bother trying, he reflected. He yawned.

There was a positive side to it, at least, for it was a long time since he'd walked along the beach at this time of night. Or day. Whichever it was at 2.30 a.m.

The solitude was palpable. You could be on the beach throughout the day and not see anybody at all, but you knew that there were probably dog walkers strolling the paths between the dunes, just out of sight, or fishermen digging for lugworms down by the breakers, where the rocks, surf and bending light combined to make visibility difficult. Now, though, at night, with the beach lit only by stars, Bony knew without doubt that he was totally alone. It was something he could feel, in the same way that he could feel the cold coming in off the ocean. The gentle waves hissed and whispered and rustled. There was no other sound.

Bony stood motionless on the sand, a half-smile on his face as he gazed westwards out to sea. The sky above it was blue, a dark night-time blue densely peppered with stars of varying size and distance. The depth of this starscape was unlike any he had ever seen.

The Milky Way, above all, was clear and momentous, a luminous path traced through the middle of the sky that brought the spiral shape of the whole galaxy home to Bony in a more forceful manner than ever before.

Bony could hear himself laughing. His chest felt tight with a kind of hope, and his mind felt unfettered by anything worldly or dull, like it was a helium balloon trapped inside his skull that had suddenly been let free. This was true love, he reckoned, at last. He now knew what people were always going on about. It must be nice to feel such a thing for another human being, though so completely ludicrous that Bony could barely imagine it. To have such strong desire for something so similar to yourself.

He looked down from the sky and scanned the beach, before his gaze came to rest on the hulking shadow of the thing. The *Thing*. He now thought of it as having a capital T. Facing south-west, he set off towards it.

The odour was more intense than previously, and Bony reckoned that by any normal person's standards it was probably a lot more unpleasant. He didn't usually let bad smells bother him though, for as long as he knew what was causing a smell, he could tolerate it. He didn't understand those people who scowled and retched when they caught a whiff of some stench that was both explicable and harmless. Like when farmers were muck-spreading and some teenager standing on the platform at Drigg station would pull a face and mutter, 'Fucking farmers.' You know what it is, and you know it won't hurt, so shut the fuck up. All it required to tolerate just about any sensory input was a shift in perspective. That was all.

Bony reached the Thing and looked down at its mass. He kneeled in the sand and rested both hands on its tough exterior. It felt harder than it had before, like it was gradually drying out. And that smell was definitely one of decomposition. Bony ran his hands over the gnarled surface, exerting pressure here and there in order to determine the structure of it. After a short while, he stood up and fished a small metal torch from his back pocket. He swivelled the torch on and began walking around the Thing.

About halfway round, he stopped and frowned, then knelt down again. He held the torch between his thighs and felt with both hands for what he thought he'd seen. An opening? Not a tear, or anything violent, but a hooded tunnel, or something like it, edged with folded flesh.

He found it again. With a grunt, he worked one hand inside, ignoring the sudden slime and softness, and then took the torch with the other and illuminated his discovery. Yes! Although there was no denying what it felt like – a giant vagina – more than anything else it looked like an eyehole. Not quite an eye socket, because there was no bone or anything else to form a socket in the true sense of the word. Granted, the eye itself would have to be about the size of Bony's head, but that was what it looked like: an eyehole.

Did jellyfish have eyeholes? He wasn't sure. And yeah, there was always the possibility of this opening actually being what it felt like – a giant vagina – but he could nevertheless imagine it housing a large, glassy orb. And it would just look so right, so fitting, *so much like an eye*, that to entertain the idea of the aperture being anything else seemed stupid and delusional. He was not knowledgeable in marine physiology but he knew that much, at least.

Bony finally pulled his hand free and the withdrawal resulted in a loud, bubbly, squelching sound. Strings of dark matter clung to his fingers no matter how hard he tried to shake them off, and if he'd thought the odour emanating from the outside of the Thing was strong, it was nothing to that of its internal gases.

He grinned and turned the torch off, then looked back up at the stars. As he waited for his eyes to readjust, he saw ever more stars emerging as his pupils widened. Maybe the Thing wasn't from the sea at all? Maybe it was from space? Wherever, whatever, it didn't really matter. Bony loved the whole beach right then, the whole beach including the sky, if that made sense, and including the Thing too.

It would, of course, be dangerous and disgusting to put his penis inside the Thing. Bony knew that, but he still felt the need to interact somehow – to plug in. He did, after all, have a condom in his wallet. Although the prospect of sex with another human being was not one that he actually entertained, he knew that it might always be a possibility. He did not, therefore, want to get caught unprepared and thus make some kind of stupid mistake. He thought about it further, still staring up at the Milky Way, at the thickening starscape, at those even brighter points that were planets. Everything moving quietly in accordance within its own system.

Distant. Huge. Graceful. Terrifying.

Friday Night At Captain Bens

Arthur was in the Vagabond alone. Yasmin didn't really do Friday nights, and he hadn't been able to get hold of Bony. And besides, after his conversation with Yasmin the previous evening, he wasn't sure how much he wanted to see either of them.

He kept on drinking pint after pint of Darkest Ennerdale until he felt like he needed some fresh air. Upon finally leaving the pub, he had walked out on to the Lime Tongue. Out there on the harbour he could hear shouts and shrieks emanating from the centre of the little town: the wild, vicious and otherworldly sounds of hundreds of people moving erratically from one bar to another. Arthur stood there with his head down and felt the tug of those busier nightspots. The sky above the harbour and the town and the bars and the pubs, and the short-skirted good-time girls and the T-shirted skinheads and the stumbling drunks, was mostly a bulging black blanket with livid blue streaks. The sky was perpetually on the brink of breaking and raining.

Arthur made his mind up after hearing a peal of high-pitched female laughter spiking up from some part of Whitehaven that was obviously livelier than the one in which he stood. He turned and walked away from the constant clacking of the moored yachts, back on to the promenade and then into the mouth of Marlborough Street, heading back past the Vagabond. He turned left on to Swingpump Lane, which was lined by the backs of shops and takeaways, and cluttered with massive wheelie bins.

He continued up the road – which, imperceptibly, became Strand Street – and turned on to Duke Street, then left again on to Tangier Street. This end of the town was busier: small groups of people clattered up and down, shouting good-naturedly and pushing each other around. Arthur peered in through the windows of a bar called Blue, which was quite small but quite busy. Although he couldn't see them from the window, Arthur knew there were small screens arranged on the bar itself which played music videos that you could watch while you waited to get served.

He continued looking for a while, but he couldn't see anybody he recognised; he could guess where most of the people he knew would be, actually. They would all be in Captain Bens, but it just wasn't somewhere he particularly wanted to go. Still, he was tired of being on his own, so Captain Bens it was. He turned away from the windows of Blue, headed back to Duke Street, took a left, took another left, and walked up Benjamin Street towards the gaudy yellow sign that marked the entrance of the place he sought. He hesitated, wondering what he was doing, and at that moment his mobile rang.

'Hello?' he said.

'Arthur, it's Bony,' said Bony. 'Where are you? Are you in?'

'No,' said Arthur. He couldn't think of anything else to say.

'I'm on the train,' Bony said. 'I'm on my way through. I'm coming to see you. I've found something amazing.'

'OK,' said Arthur.

'So where are you?'

'I'm . . . I'm on my way to Bens.'

'Bens? Why the fuck are you going to Bens?' Bony's voice was edged with mockery.

Arthur looked around him. The pavement outside the bar was clogged with smokers. The sky above lurked threateningly.

'I don't know,' he said.

'Well, I'll see you there, anyway,' Bony said. 'Won't be long.'

He hung up.

Captain Bens was a total shithole. It was not a seedy yet atmospheric dive; it was just a total shithole. A soulless box with sticky, patterned carpets and a psychotically bland taste in pop which was played at stupefying volume. There was a dance-floor, too, above which hung a giant

136

screen. Depending on the time of day, the screen would either show sports events or music videos. When it was showing music videos, though, they were never fully synched to the actual music being played, so the general effect was to make everybody feel just a little bit more drunk.

The taps in the toilets never worked, but the sink was usually full of vomit anyway. You could often see vomit spattered around in the bar and on the dance-floor as well, because the place was always so full that it became a real struggle to get to the toilet in a hurry. Somebody Arthur had gone to school with had actually once seen a disconcertingly fat man voiding his bowels on to the floor in a darkened corner of the main room. The bouncers, apparently, had rolled him down the steps on to Benjamin Street before proceeding to break his nose and one of his legs.

This story made Arthur feel uncomfortable in lots of ways, and he hated Captain Bens. For a start, he thought it should be spelled 'Captain Ben's', with an apostrophe. That missing apostrophe always wound him up even before he got inside the door. Usually, he never set foot in the place, but tonight . . . well, it was where most of the people were. People that Arthur worked with or had gone to school with. People that he vaguely knew, which at that particular moment was better than people he didn't know at all.

Once inside, Arthur started to feel that he'd made a mistake. He immediately felt hot, and disorientated by all the loud sounds. He moved around, trying to look purposeful, like he was on his way somewhere in particular, so that nobody would realise that he was on his own. He did sometimes see people that he recognised – a best friend from primary school, a girl he'd once asked out online – but on these occasions he just nodded and smiled, and kept on pushing his way through the crowd. The sheer density of people made him feel a bit sick and after doing two full circuits of the sweaty, smelly room he just leant against the wall near the door and tried not to stare at cleavage, which he found difficult.

Bony materialised, grabbing Arthur's elbow and shaking it.

'I'm sorry,' he mouthed, and then, louder, 'I'm really sorry. I had to pick up some stuff. Now, then, let's get out of this pit.'

He made for the steps and the exit, without waiting for an answer.

Arthur shook his head and followed.

'I had to find somebody else to pick up from, now Ollie's been arrested,' Bony explained, holding a crisp near his mouth. 'He was late. That's why I was late. I'm sorry.'

'Don't worry,' Arthur replied slowly and quietly, trying not to sound drunk.

'Jesus,' Bony said, 'you're steaming.'

'I am,' Arthur said. 'Yes, I am.'

They were in the Three Tuns, which was a small, dim

pub with a jukebox full of rock. The place was frequented by men in military-style gear with long hair, and girls with lip piercings and big black boots. The bartender was extraordinarily old and short, and she sat on a very high stool behind the bar, scowling into a newspaper. There were a lot of stuffed animals attached to the walls. Some song by Metallica blared from the sound system. Arthur tried to nod his head in time as he watched Nazi Dave dancing slouchily around on his own, the swastika patches peeling from his old denim jacket. Nazi Dave was in his fifties, and was always drunk and sunburnt. He was friendly enough, supposed Arthur, but espoused ugly values. Ultimately he was a right prick.

'Why the hell were you in Bens, anyway?' Bony asked.

'I was looking for somebody.'

'Yasmin? But she hates it in there.'

'No,' Arthur said, 'not Yasmin.'

'Oh.' Bony looked confused. He pondered for a moment. 'Who, then?' he said.

'Not really anybody in particular,' Arthur replied. He was slurring badly by this point. He looked at the pint he had in front of him. It seemed like he'd been drinking it for ages but the glass still looked quite full. The beer was dark and there were bits in the bottom. 'Just, y'know . . . just felt like it.'

'Is there something wrong?' Bony inquired.

'Yasmin likes you,' said Arthur. 'But I like her.'

'Oh,' Bony said. He ate a few crisps thoughtfully – their

yellow greasy crumbs spotting his dark-grey woollen gloves – and then he pursed his lips. 'Jesus, I'm sorry, Arthur. I had no idea.'

'I told her you wouldn't be interested.'

'Well!' Bony said, and he laughed. 'Yeah, I suppose you're right.'

'I wouldn't be angry,' Arthur said. 'I would be sad if you got together, but I wouldn't be angry.'

'We won't get together,' Bony said.

'OK,' Arthur said.

Neither of them said anything further for a few minutes. Arthur just drank, and Bony just sat there. Nazi Dave turned clumsily around and around, near the bar, like a small flying insect near a river at dusk. The bartender shook her newspaper impatiently, but it couldn't be heard rustling above the Korn track from the jukebox.

Bony suddenly laid his hands flat on the table. 'I came here tonight to tell you something,' he said. 'To buy some drugs and to tell you something.'

'What is it?' Arthur asked.

'I found something on the beach,' Bony said. 'If I could buy that beach and have it all to myself, I would. I would bury myself somewhere in the middle of it, looking up at the seagulls.'

'They'd peck your eyes out.'

'Not *my* eyes,' Bony said. 'Not mine, they wouldn't. I think we have an understanding.'

'What did you find?' Arthur asked, looking up wearily.

'I don't know what it is,' Bony answered, grinning now, 'but it's huge and fleshy and mysterious. I think you'd like it.'

'It does sound like something I'd like.'

'Oh, you would. Come down tomorrow.'

'OK!' Arthur offered a wonky smile and looked momentarily excited. Then his face crumpled. 'Oh no!' he said. 'Oh shit! I'm working tomorrow! I forgot!' He put his hands over his face. Bony heard him say the words, 'I'm such a fucking *fuck-up*,' but they were muffled.

'Saturday shift?' asked Bony.

'Fucking overtime,' Arthur said, 'so I'm on the phone all day. And now I'm three fucking sheets. I forgot, Bony. Oh, *God*, what time is it?'

'It's about half eleven,' Bony said, after glancing at his watch. 'You can come down in the evening though?'

'What? Yeah, sure I can . . . I can do that.'

'I wouldn't worry about work,' Bony said. 'I mean, you're fucked now. You can't change that. May as well really go for it. You're going to be hungover whatever happens, right? Here, I'll get you another drink.'

Arthur wanted to stop him but could not marshal his thoughts quickly enough to raise an arm or shape a word. He just looked despairingly at Bony's back as Bony placed his elbows on the bar and waited for the old woman to put her newspaper down and serve him. The huge, fleshy mysterious thing was forgotten.

*

Harry was still up and about when Arthur and Bony entered the living room. He had a can in one hand and the telephone in the other.

'I'll . . . I'll call you back,' he said into the receiver upon seeing his son, and put the phone down.

'Hi, Dad,' Arthur said.

'Hi, Harry,' Bony said.

'Hello,' Harry replied. 'I was just going to bed.'

'OK, then,' said Arthur. 'Goodnight.'

Harry stood up, putting his hand against the wall to steady himself. 'Goodnight, lads,' he said, and smiled slightly, then exited the room. He left behind him some dandruff or something on the back of the chair. Arthur looked at it for a moment and then quickly brushed it away. Arthur was starting to feel ill again. The light seemed dim and overly yellow.

'You can have the sofa,' Arthur said.

'Thank you,' Bony said. He took his coat off and laid it carefully on the floor. 'Remember when we used to stay at each other's houses and watch *Karaoke Fishtank* at three in the morning, or whatever?'

'I remember,' Arthur said. 'What was the name of the fish presenter? Vince Finn, I remember.' He sat down and put his head in his hands. 'I feel terrible,' he said.

'I'll get you some water,' Bony said, and left the room.

Arthur felt blurry and uncertain of himself. He saw that something had fallen out of Bony's coat pocket: a small re-sealable plastic bag. In it were a couple of acid tabs.

'You can take one of those, if you like,' Bony said from

the doorway. Arthur looked up at him. Without really thinking about it, he opened the bag, tipped the tabs into his hand and put one of them into his mouth. He had never taken acid before.

'Shit, Arthur! I didn't mean *now*. I meant you could take one for, you know, when you're in a better mood – or not drunk, or not about to go to *bed*!' Bony put down the two glasses of water he was holding and flapped his arms around. 'That probably wasn't a good idea!'

'Oh,' Arthur said. 'Sorry. I didn't know.'

'Don't apologise,' Bony said. 'I just don't know if you'll enjoy it very much.'

'It just felt like I had to do something,' Arthur said.

'Yeah, I know,' Bony said.

'I need to go to bed,' Arthur said. The room was starting to spin now. He kept focusing on an old picture on the wall. In a dark wooden frame, it was a print of a painting of the exterior of a farmhouse. He kept focusing on it, but it kept sliding away. He remembered the first time he'd been drunk and had experienced a room spinning round him. He had been lying in bed and it had felt like he was on a fairground ride. He had thought it wonderful; it had felt *nice*.

'I know,' Bony said.

It was a good ten minutes before either of them moved or spoke. Arthur broke the silence.

'If Captain Ben was a real person, he'd be a cunt,' he said.

OVERTIME

'The room is still spinning,' Arthur said. 'Even now. Even here.'

Yasmin felt sorry for him. She didn't tend to feel sympathy for anyone who was hungover, but it wasn't like Arthur to get himself into such a state. He sat at his desk with his eyes closed, a blue biro trembling between his fingers. He wore a white shirt with a yellowing collar and ink on the cuffs, even though more casual dress was allowed on Saturdays. 'Why were you out so late?' she asked. 'Who were you with?'

'Bony,' Arthur said. 'He came through to buy some acid or something.'

'You should have told me,' Yasmin said.

'I didn't think,' Arthur said. 'Oh no . . . Yasmin. I took some of it, I think. Before I went to bed.'

'What? Why?'

'I don't know!' Arthur said.

'What happened?'

'Nothing.' Arthur tapped his teeth with the pen. 'It was very disappointing – or it would have been if I'd been hoping for anything better.'

On Saturdays far fewer call centre staff were required, so those who were present had to abandon their usual seats and sit clustered around the command centre where they were easier to oversee. This left the periphery of the massive room empty and echoey. Artemis sat up on the command centre, glowering intently at his screen like a painted gargoyle.

'At least it's dead,' Yasmin said.

'What?' Arthur asked, looking up at her over the low partition screen separating their desks.

'It's dead.' Yasmin gestured at her telephone. 'No calls. The nation must have better things to do today than ring us up.'

'Oh, right. Yeah.' Arthur held up a stress-ball shaped like a lightbulb. It looked like Pinhead from *Hellraiser* because somebody had drawn a little face on it and then stuck it full of countless straightened-out paperclips. 'Can you remember what incentive or initiative these things were handed out for?' he asked.

'Not the slightest idea. I lose track.' Yasmin said. 'I don't know why Bony takes acid. Why does he take so much acid?'

'I don't know,' Arthur said. 'But he goes out on to the beach on his own and takes it.'

'Why does he do that?'

'Because he's a massive freak,' Arthur said. 'That's why.'

Yasmin didn't pursue the line of questioning. There was a slight bitterness to Arthur's tone that made everything clear to her. She played with the cord that connected her headset to the telephone and regretted saying anything at all about how she felt. This was the seventh Saturday in a row that she'd worked.

The Landscape

There had been worms around the bath again that morning, as usual. Arthur couldn't now get them out of his head. Even here at his desk, talking to customers, he thought he could see them out of the corner of his eye, only to find that he was recoiling from nothing more than a squiggle of biro or a small fleck of dust.

Arthur didn't normally do overtime. He was often asked, as he was a particularly capable customer adviser, but he refused it so regularly that saying no felt almost like a principle. It wasn't a principle, really. He just couldn't bear to spend any more time here than was necessary. Overtime was necessary now, though, because Arthur had decided that he and his father were going to get a new bathroom. He had decided, lying awake in bed one night recently, that this would make a significant difference to their quality of life.

At about eleven o' clock on this Saturday morning, Arthur's headset beeped and he launched into his scripted call opening. There was no response, though. All he could hear was music. Not hold music or anything like that, but music being played at the other end of the telephone line. He couldn't identify it. It seemed to change from relaxing, summery classical music to some upbeat, fifties American rock with blurry, unclear vocals. And then it changed back again. The change was somehow seamless – Arthur couldn't quite pinpoint it. He didn't let it worry him, though. He just sat back and let the music keep his phone line engaged. It lasted for about five minutes before the line went abruptly dead. The silence rushed in like water, and like water it was threatening. The whole thing seemed momentarily awful, but then Arthur looked about him at his mundane environment and felt slightly less afraid, if a little sad at the end of the distraction.

Arthur was seated at Harry's usual desk. He tended to sit there when he was on the rota to work a weekend shift to prevent anybody else sitting there and noticing the flakes of skin in the keyboard, the stray hairs littering the mouse mat.

Yasmin was talking to somebody, and laughing gently. It didn't matter who Yasmin spoke to, she maintained her calmness and patience, her kindness of tone. She would sometimes have a rant about a call later on, or even a sob, but the customers would never know. Arthur wasn't sure it was good for her, really. He watched her over the top of the screen. Maybe he should ring up and ask to speak to her, then pretend to be a customer and talk to her for a long time. That might be nice. Although she'd probably recognise his voice.

Arthur took another call. As he spoke to the customer he looked through their account history and saw that Yasmin had spoken to the same customer in the past. There was a note from her on the system, date-stamped two years ago.

PTC Customer rang to set up direct debit. Explained charges scheme and possible allowances. Yasmin, Team Kansas.

This note had no bearing on the customer's current query, but Arthur kept returning to it, moving the mouse cursor back and forth over her name. He suddenly realised that one day she might leave. He imagined coming across notes like this after she'd left, and considered the impact they might have on him. Whether or not he found them would be totally random; it would depend on which customers rang up, and which of them dropped through to his telephone line. But they would be there, buried in the depths of the system like little bright stones, waiting to be found. Like clues, almost, or notes that she'd left just for him, containing some kind of message. He would have to keep a record of the reference numbers for any accounts that she'd worked on. Starting straight away. After the customer had gone, he wrote down that same account number in the back of his notebook.

The day started to get a little busier. Call volumes were

forecast according to bill dispatch dates, public holidays, time of day, previous volumes, that kind of thing, and the number of agents scheduled to work was varied accordingly. Sometimes, though, for reasons that nobody really understood, the forecasts were wrong. People up and down the country would all start ringing at the same time, as if in response to some kind of general signal. It didn't make much sense, but it happened. The only explanation Arthur could think of was some kind of deeply buried, collective consciousness. Whatever the reason, the number of calls now coming in seemed higher than expected, and customers were obliged to queue to speak to the advisers. The leisurely tone of the place gradually changed, becoming harder.

Artemis started prowling around, shouting things. 'If two per cent or more of customers hang up before getting to speak to an adviser then the company gets fined *billions* of pounds!' he shouted. 'Get the customer on, answer their questions, get them off again, then get the next one on!'

Taking one call immediately after another was stressful at the best of times. You didn't have any time to think, and it was easy to accidentally leave one screen open from the previous customer's account and thus get mixed up, or confuse this caller's surname with the last caller's. Without the opportunity to speak to real people around you, you became a creature of scripted speech and mathematics and nothing else. Coupled with the threat of an angry Artemis, it was deeply discomfiting.

Arthur started to feel weird. He started to panic that

he was disappearing. Not physically – just the part of him that was feeling weird, the part that was thinking. He was aware of his mouth moving and parts of his brain working out corrections to customers' bills, and his fingers amending addresses and adding notes to accounts, but all of those things were happening outside of his consciousness. He felt that he was trapped behind the eyes of a robot, yet with no means of communicating with it or controlling it. As far as the world was concerned, he was only a customer adviser – he was a voice on the telephone, nothing else. Yasmin and his co-workers wouldn't be aware of him, because they were all trapped inside their own automata, their minds being squeezed out of existence. Like his. The customer voices coming in through the earpiece sounded slow and soft, words stretching out like bread dough, becoming incomprehensible, monotonous, sickening. He tried to focus on what the current customer was saying. This one was talking about somebody from the call centre whom he'd spoken to previously.

'If I only knew what she was doing,' the customer said. '*She* knew what she was doing, but I didn't. She didn't do anything really to impress me, but then she didn't do anything bad either.'

Arthur unpicked this utterance in his mind, throwing away the bits of shell to reveal the point of it, the truth of it, the grain of relevance or inquiry that had prompted the customer to say it. He struggled, though, and he couldn't find anything. This was often the way with whatever the customers said. They said some words that added up to nothing, and then expected you to respond with something concrete, some kind of answer or solution to what had never properly been a question. Arthur was aware of his mouth opening as if to speak, but he didn't know what was going to come out of it. He found that he was looking at work-queues on the screen. *Yes, that's right,* he thought, *this customer's account is somehow tied up in a work-queue. That girl he's spoken to has put the account into a work-queue. We are waiting for the outcome. That's right.*

Work-queues were just that. Queues of particular tasks that needed doing. Often, the call centre staff didn't have the time or systems access to perform some necessary work on a customer account, so they sent off the task to back-office colleagues, who would then work through the jobs in the order that they had been created. The back-office colleagues were based somewhere else – Chorley maybe, or Liverpool, or Delhi, or Kuala Lumpur, or in their own homes scattered across the world. Arthur didn't really know, and he didn't really give a fuck because it didn't really matter.

The work-queues appeared vertically on screen as lists of reference numbers and explanatory comments, but they now appeared horizontally in Arthur's imagination, with all the physicality of a Heath Robinson invention, each task a little parcel, all those little parcels backing up in a tube – a horizontal tube – except they were more like clumps of staples, not parcels: clumps of staples, or milli-pedes, each bit of work forming a different segment. They got incredibly long all too quickly, growing at unmanageable speeds, coiling off into a virtual, electronic distance across the internal plains of some data bank that stretched from Whitehaven to Chorley, maybe, or to Liverpool or Delhi or Kuala Lumpur, or wherever the fuck, bits of them breaking off and getting lost or getting mixed up with other queues, all the while spinning out and bleeding confusion. *These spaces are the problem with call centres*, Arthur thought as he looked around. *Not the people who answer the phones. These eerie, empty interstices, empty of life and reason but full of lost data.*

The customer's soft words meanwhile had melted into one long, low sound – a kind of thunder that echoed around the milky, buzzing sky. The ground was made up of lurid green and purple things, like tentacles, almost. When he looked at them more closely they either looked like worms or the long, skinny arms of spindly starfish.

Arthur realised that the thunder wavering in volume was in fact made up of lots of voices broken down into component units and sounds, currently nothing more than signals on their way from one place to another. In the distance he could see a purple light that coloured the sky above it.

Arthur was still aware of his body going through the motions, sitting at his desk, talking to the customer. He was not entirely sure of his situation. He couldn't work it out. He was in two places at once, though, he knew that much.

He giggled a little bit. 'Hello?' he said. 'Where is this?'

'Don't be alarmed,' said a very faint voice, a gentle voice

that seemed to come from all directions at once. 'You are completely safe.'

'I wasn't alarmed,' Arthur said.

The voice sounded feminine, but when he thought about the sound of the voice in any detail, it started to come apart as if he hadn't heard it at all but just received the words directly into his brain.

'Head for the City,' the voice said. 'You will meet me on the way.'

Arthur was about to ask where the City was, but then looked at the purple light and saw that it was not one purple light, but many. The City.

Arthur could not recall ever having felt so excited in his entire life.

The only semi-decent explanation for these events that Arthur could come up with was that he had died. He was shocked at the warmth that flooded his consciousness when he thought of that possibility; he was dead, but the world was not over. There *was* an afterlife – a stranger existence, a more exciting existence. He was almost ecstatic at the potential. He realised that he could no longer sense his corporeal body, or the chair it sat in, or the keyboard at its fingertips.

Arthur started walking. Sometimes the ground seemed to shift beneath his feet and, as it did, it sounded like the wet susurrations of static that would occasionally whisper from the call centre telephones in place of the voice of a customer. It remained solid though – the ground, that is – in a way that Arthur didn't fully understand.

After some time spent walking – it was hard to say how long – Arthur could see a figure approaching him from the direction of the City. The City was still a long way off, but this figure was at about the halfway point. The world felt darker, but the sky was the same dirty, creamy colour that it had been when Arthur arrived. From this distance, the figure seemed very tall – a thin black line scratched into the landscape.

'I can see you now,' said the voice from the air, sounding louder than it had done previously. 'Can you see me?'

'Yes,' Arthur said. 'Yes, I can.' He felt light. The voice was definitely feminine. Not only that, it sounded almost familiar. It sounded, in as much as it sounded like anything at all, like his mother. That would make sense, right, if he was dead? You saw it all the time in films. People you loved are waiting for you when you die. That wasn't something Arthur had ever believed, but then he'd never believed in an afterlife either.

'I won't be long,' he said.

'Good,' said the voice. 'That's good.'

Arthur felt some kind of electric slap across his cheek, and screwed his eyes shut. He felt himself falling. He opened his eyes to find he was lying on the rough office carpet tiles of the call centre floor.

Yasmin was shaking his shoulder. 'Arthur?' she was saying. 'Arthur, are you OK?'

He stood up and just looked at her, mouth slack. Artemis

loomed behind her, hand pressed on chin.

'Sorry for the slap,' she said. 'Seemed to do the job, though.'

'What do you mean?'

'You were unconscious,' Yasmin said.

'Was I?' Arthur said.

'You were talking,' Artemis said suddenly, and loudly. Yasmin jumped, as if she hadn't known he was there. 'Who were you talking to, Arthur?'

'I don't know,' Arthur said, not wanting to embarrass himself.

'You said, "Where is this?" Why did you say that?'

'I was in a strange place.'

'Were you alone?'

'No.'

'Who was there with you?'

'I don't know who they were.'

Artemis nodded, looking serious. 'You should go to the doctor's,' he said. 'Just to make sure you're not a complete nut.' Then he walked off, grinning.

'Fucking acid,' Arthur murmured to Yasmin. 'I thought I was dead.'

'Oh, Arthur,' said Yasmin, and put her arms round him. 'It sounds awful.'

Arthur didn't say anything.

'Let's go to the break room,' Yasmin said. 'I think Artemis was, in his own way, offering you a breather – if not suggesting you take the rest of the day off.'

*

Arthur and Yasmin stood on the break room balcony that jutted over the car park and faced out to sea. The wind was strong here, and they were cold, but it was preferable to the crowded, noisy break room itself. Arthur was feeling scatterbrained and hollowed-out.

'I thought I was dead, but it didn't bother me too much,' he said. He pursed his lips and looked up at Yasmin. She looked back with narrowed eyes.

'What's wrong?' she asked. 'What's wrong enough for you to feel like that?'

'I don't know,' Arthur said. 'I don't know what to do with myself in the evenings. Everything feels like a bit of a waste of time.'

'Do things you enjoy,' Yasmin said. 'That's not wasting time. Even try doing the things that you enjoyed when you were a kid.'

Arthur nodded. There were other things bothering him, of course, but he didn't want to go on.

OBJECTIFICATION

That evening – after Arthur had passed out and then gone home, and Yasmin had finished work – she went back to her flat and looked out of the window at the sea, and got stoned on her own. She listened to the whole of *Oracular Spectacular* by MGMT. Just sat and listened to it. Sitting and listening to music without doing anything else was something she frequently did, but she was aware that most people stopped doing that after they emerged from adolescence. The sun was now setting and the evening had fallen still. The music was warm and slightly psyche-delic but also slightly sad. Her flat felt warm and was lit softly pink by the last of the daylight.

That day she had noticed that Paula was back at work. Paula had been away for a while and it was obvious now that she'd been off work to have breast augmentation surgery. She'd been wearing a low-cut top so that her breasts had heaved up like pale, blind, aggressive sea-creatures. They'd actually looked hard, like dead jellyfish.

Yasmin had never been a fan of breast surgery, but she wanted her ears done, so . . . well. Her ambition was no less cosmetic, no less vain, if she was honest. Breasts, ears. It was all just meat.

Some people objected on the basis of cost: if you've got that money to spare, do something beneficial with it. But where was the line? As far as Yasmin was concerned, you could say the same about make-up, or haircuts, or piercings, or new clothes, or CDs, or furniture. Where was the line? The line was probably concurrent with your skin, as far as most people were concerned. Maybe it was some deep-seated cultural anxiety rooted in religion. *Don't mess with what God gave you. God made you the way He wanted you to be.* Yasmin touched her ears. Maybe, for her, breast surgery just wasn't dramatic or obvious enough. You still looked human afterwards, if a slightly modified kind of human. That was probably it: Yasmin wanted to look non-human. Inhuman? Whatever.

Out on the horizon there was some great grey beast of a ship, one bright light like a star balancing on the prow. Maybe the future would be like life aboard an oil tanker. Everything grey, everything metal, everything floating on the surface of a new, worldwide ocean, everything lit only by vaguely pink or orange electric lights. Nothing to do with your life but work to keep the boat afloat.

What was she doing, spending all her waking hours at the call centre? What was she doing it for?

Yasmin had never known what people meant when they

said that this or that objectifies women, or men, or whoever. People *were* objects. People *were* sex objects. Everybody was a sex object and, yeah they might be something more than that, but still. They were just bodies, just objects, and that's why they got hungry, and that's why they needed roofs over their heads, and that's why they broke. Eventually people would realise this, that they were just physical objects to be manipulated and modified at will. People would eventually forget what a 'natural' body or mind was, as they augmented and reduced and stimulated and tranquilised and accentuated and implanted and removed one piece or another, and any stigma would fall away. Anyway, if there was one thing in this world that drove this home it wasn't sex, or lust, or body modification. It was work. The work culture. Work, eat, sleep. Total reduction to function. It depended on what your job was, Yasmin supposed, but if your job was something that didn't allow you to be you, then basically you would never be you. You would be body object through and through.

Bony understood, by the sound of it. What had Arthur said?

Yasmin couldn't put her finger on why, but Bony did something to her.

She realised that the CD had finished and got up to make a cup of coffee. She put the kettle on, and then she turned on her laptop and searched for Interext. She found a bland, corporate website, all white and blue and grey, kind of sleek-looking, full of photos and promo videos of smartly dressed, grinning employees who were so smooth-skinned and dead behind the eyes that they looked more like CGI constructs than the people she actually interacted with. It was terrifyingly boring. Almost nauseatingly boring.

Was something awful happening? Or had this kind of entity always existed, and always held such power? *Or,* Yasmin wondered, *am I reading too much into just a few photos?*

She studied the website for a few minutes longer, but it gave no clue to what Interext actually did. She began to feel cold and hopeless and terribly depressed.

The kettle started to boil.

The Fishing Line

It was gone midnight and Arthur was sitting on the edge of North Pier, his legs dangling over the side, his heels kicking against the ancient stonework. To his left, some steps descended into the water, hugging the inside wall. There was a small bright green plastic bucket beside him, the kind that they sell at sea-front stalls for kids to make sandcastles with. The colour of it looked subdued in the moonlight. Arthur was facing inland, so that Whitehaven lay spread out before him. Black clouds were strung out thinly across a sparsely starred night sky. Their edges shone silver. The lights of cars moved up and down the roads leading into and out of town. Occasionally people passed him, walking their dogs the length of the harbour.

In his hand, Arthur held the neon-green plastic handle of the crab-line he'd searched out earlier that day. The line itself trailed into the water lapping the wall beneath his feet. The sea was dark – or, really, he reckoned, it was black. Few things were really black but, to Arthur, water at night was one of them.

He had decided that Yasmin's advice – about doing things that you'd enjoyed as a child – was good advice.

Arthur was crab-fishing. On the end of the crab-line he'd hooked a cube of raw chicken from the plastic tray he'd bought at the 24-hour Tesco's. Then he'd gently lowered it until the line had gone slack. And since then he'd been waiting for something to scuttle across the silty ocean floor and start chewing with its overly complicated mouth parts, causing the line to tense, and prompting him to raise it quickly, before shaking the creature into the green bucket, its legs waving and claws snapping. But, so far, that hadn't happened.

Arthur remembered a crab-fishing competition from many years ago, when he'd been very young, maybe only five or six. They had been on holiday in Cornwall, and the sun was beating down, the sky clearest blue, the sea below their feet a clear turquoise. His mother had organised it, and Arthur, his father and a couple of friends had fished. He couldn't remember the friends clearly. They may even have been cousins. The seagulls had been loud and bold, and local fishing boats had gone puttering past non-stop. They'd used dry, vacuum-packed pieces of fish as bait, and the crabs had bitten eagerly. Arthur clearly remembered himself squealing as he raised them up out of the water, partly with delight but partly with fear, scared of dropping them into his lap rather than into the bucket. There had been loads of them, too. They'd filled their buckets with lively little specimens, mostly red in colour, and then finally tipped them all back into the sea. His was the same bucket he was using now.

Tonight, though, he hadn't caught a thing. Not a single nip. Maybe it was because there weren't any crabs there. This was not Cornwall, after all. Or maybe it was because crabs slept at night, although Arthur doubted that.

As Arthur watched the white nylon wire of his fishing line, he became aware of his mother observing him from somewhere behind, but he couldn't spot her anywhere when he turned around. He felt almost as if he were appearing on TV or in a film, and she was only watching him on screen. That was OK, though. That was enough. He smiled and waggled the crab-fishing line's handle, hoping that she'd notice it and remember the same holiday that he had been thinking about.

After a while he found himself specifically watching the spot where the nylon wire entered the water. He wondered how long he'd been sitting there. He even started to wonder if he'd been asleep. He'd been having a conversation with his mum about something, but he couldn't remember what. It felt like it had lasted a long time though. There was a milky glow staining the horizon to the west, and he watched its thin light waver uncertainly, as if it were cast not by a star but by a candle placed in a draught.

Something pulled suddenly on the line. Arthur sniffed, and for a moment he couldn't remember what that meant or what he had to do, but then he began furiously rotating the handle, wrapping the line back around it, standing up at the edge of the high stone wall, and smiling. A slight breeze moved his long black hair half-heartedly around his head, as his hands moved quickly and rhythmically, turning the handle this way and that so the motion remained smooth and constant. Whatever he'd caught felt quite heavy, and he wondered if it might be some kind of fish rather than one of those little orange-red crabs he'd seen people catching in Whitehaven before. He noticed that the water no longer looked completely black, but a dark and muddy army green, while the sky above was rapidly turning pale grey.

Arthur started to wonder if he'd merely caught the hook in a mass of seaweed or something, as he hadn't felt any further movement on the line since that initial jerk. He watched intently as whatever it was now broke the surface of the water. At first he thought that he'd been right – it was just an accumulation of weed and mud and molluscs, the centre of which tangle he'd accidentally snagged. It measured about a foot across, and strands of something trailed beneath it. It was only seaweed, Arthur knew, though it looked like hair. He considered just shaking it free, but that would have felt wrong.

The greenish bundle was dangling at about the level of Arthur's ankles when it suddenly moved. Arthur jumped backwards but didn't let go of the line, so the thing swayed with him, bumping into his shins. It wriggled and quivered against his jeans. He yelped, dropping the handle and moving further away. The object sat motionless again in the grey pre-dawn dimness, and Arthur still couldn't tell what it was. He didn't move either; he just stared at the thing. After a moment, it started to unfurl, seeming somehow to widen and thin out. Two ungainly claws extended themselves from either side, whereupon the weed and mud fell away to reveal that it was a crab after all – just an especially big one. One of its claws was about the size of Arthur's own hand, and the other was even larger. It looked uncomfortable, as if it were too heavy. The crab itself was a sickly green colour, like pea soup, and its shell seemed misshapen and swollen. The word that Arthur kept trying to dismiss was 'fat'. The crab was *fat*.

Arthur stared at the crab, and he knew that the crab was staring back at him. The white nylon line led from the crab-line's handle into the murky depths of the creature's machine-like mouth. It must have ingested the hook and Arthur felt sick at the thought. The crab-line and the bucket had been bought for him by his mother. He couldn't lose them. He went to grab the handle, intending to just yank the line until the crab relinquished the hook, but at the same time the crab started scuttling away, dragging the handle along with it towards the edge of the pier. It moved at an unnerving, spidery speed, but also with a sick scraping sound, as if it were dragging a considerable belly along the ground. Arthur missed the handle and stumbled forward to grab for it again. But he was already too late, and he saw the crab go plunging over the edge and the handle whipping after it. Instead of the muted splash he was expecting, though, he heard only a wet crunch. He perceived it with his stomach, rather than with his ears, and blinked nervously.

He crept forward and peered over the edge.

The tide had gone out a little, revealing the lower level of the steps built against the pier. The crab lay on its back on the bottom step, its thick little legs whirring like those of a beetle. Looking down at it in the morning gloom was like gazing down into some kind of mechanical grinder. Arthur thought about going down to try once more to retrieve the crab-line, but then the crab started groaning like a man. A tired man with a sore throat. Arthur's spine stiffened. He stood up and ran away, his old trainers slapping loudly against the pitted stone surface of the pier, the groans of the crab becoming less audible as he put some distance behind him. He imagined himself completely alone, running along the top of an endless wall which bisected an endless ocean. He had tears in his eyes, worried that he'd betrayed the memory of his mother.

The sky grew whiter. The voice of the sea was quiet and kind.

PART THREE

THE SUICIDE

Harry was woken by Arthur entering the house in the early hours. Harry didn't cope with the night-time very well; he tried to spend it drunkenly, if possible, so that there was little chance of waking up before the alarm clock went off.

This time, though, he did wake up and, once awake, there was nothing he could do about it. He lay there in the dark, surrounded by piles of clothes. After Arthur did the washing, he would hang the clothes up on radiators all around the house and then collect them and sort them. He'd pile Harry's clothes up on his bed, but Harry never put them away. He didn't even move them, just crawled under the covers and let the piles topple over. Harry tended to dump his dirty garments on the bedroom floor as well, so they were all mixed up. He didn't know how Arthur knew which ones to wash, and quailed at the thought of Arthur having to sort them by smell. At times like this he knew he had to sort himself out, do a better job, not just of being a parent but of being an independent human entity. But by the time he'd got up and gone to work and then come back from work, a quivering wreck, anything resembling resolve or pride or rationality had gone, replaced by an unintelligible mess of anger and shame and confusion and exhaustion and desperation. It wasn't that he looked at his clean washing and then decided against putting it away. It wasn't laziness. He just didn't even see the washing. He didn't see the washing up either. He didn't see the grease on the kitchen surfaces, or the limescale in the bathroom sink. Part of it, of course, was that he always removed his glasses upon entering the house, and so everything appeared pretty blurred.

Harry sat up in bed. The backs of his hands were feeling itchy and he was aware of a bad smell in the room. Through the wall, he could hear Arthur getting ready for bed. He waited for sounds of movement to stop, then quietly got up and threw on an old dressing gown, before creeping out of his room and making his way down the stairs. He was without his spectacles, so the interior of the house was indistinct.

He was hungry. In the kitchen, Harry opened and closed the cupboard doors looking for something quick to eat. The light seemed dim. In one cupboard, there was the remainder of a packet of dry spaghetti and a tin of green beans.

In the fridge there was an open packet of bacon, the edges of the meat turning dark and curling, a slimy black lettuce and an empty margarine tub. He looked into the margarine tub for a while before putting it back and closing the door. He turned around and leant against the fridge. He pinched his nose with an itchy hand and closed his eyes. He could hear it raining outside. He imagined that the curtains were open, and he was looking at the windows. At the small beads of water that impacted and burst against the outside of the glass. The way they gleamed white against the black darkness beyond. He could hear the wind rising.

His stomach now moaned like something sick. He thought about boiling some water for the spaghetti, but knew that then there would be nothing left for tea the following day unless one of them went to the supermarket, and that would mean spending money. He wasn't sure if Arthur realised it but financially things were pretty bad, although who was he kidding? Arthur would have a much better handle on the money situation than he did.

It was when he woke up during the night that Harry understood fully how close the two of them were to the brink. Yes, they both had jobs and a roof over their heads, and they would survive for as long as that remained the case, but Harry *knew*, in a way that Arthur couldn't, that aspects of their life were even softer and weaker and more unstable than they appeared. Harry was held together by nothing more substantial than his own skin, and that skin was flaking away fast.

Harry reopened the fridge door and took out the bacon. He pulled a slice out of the packet and held it there, staring at it. He looked around for the frying pan but it lay crusted with grease beneath a pile of dirty plates and cutlery. He looked back at the meat and peeled a strip off, and lowered it into his mouth. It was cold. It tasted of nothing. He chewed it and chewed it and threaded it around with his tongue, and chewed it some more, but it wouldn't break apart. It was stringy, like a piece of elastic. One end of it slipped down his throat and he gagged. He instantly spat it out into the bin, which thankfully didn't have a lid. God, Jesus. People ate raw meat, didn't they? Maybe it was a better kind of meat that they ate. Harry sighed and shuffled through into the living room, where he collapsed into his usual armchair. The room was dark and, to his feeble eyes, the air there was thick with dust. He was letting Arthur down. He knew it.

There were rumours about a wolf that drifted across the mountains surrounding Wasdale, preying on sheep and the lost. There were stories, of course, that it was something more than an ordinary wolf. A werewolf, they whispered. At one of the lock-ins held at the Vine, Pauline the barwoman had got drunk, and, curled around her vodka and Coke, swore desperately that a walker who had been staying at her sister's guesthouse had seen it halfway between one thing and another. Other people snorted and said it was not a wolf but a ragged man, just some freak, probably a paedophile or something. Harry had kept quiet at that point, not really interested whether the thing was real or not. He had been thinking, *God, Jesus, what a freedom. If only I could be some kind of wolf, I could hang up on all the snobby, patronising cunts on the phone. I could tell them all to fuck right off. I could walk tall, safe in the knowledge that my survival did not depend on the appraisal of some suited worm, some cold-eyed shark. I would be strong and powerful and I would never be hungry again. I would never have to go back to the supermarket. Oh my God. Oh my God. If I had been a good man, a real man, a wolf man, then maybe Rebecca . . . Rebecca . . . Rebecca.* Harry put his head in his hands.

Rebecca was dead in the sea. Harry had seen her standing there on the cliff, dressed in her thick white pyjamas, facing out across the ocean, the moon full and gigantic amidst a sky packed with insolent little stars staring down at her, like they were waiting for her to do it, encouraging her, almost, demanding some kind of drama to justify their attendance in such numbers. The moon had been like a monarch – some obese patriarch surrounded by sprightly, twisted little subjects all thirsty for something. For anything. Perverts!

Rebecca had turned around and seen him struggling and staggering across the sparse, tufty grass towards her. She had lost her footing and slipped and hit her head on her way down to the waves below. That was all that had happened. He had seen it himself. He had seen it himself, hadn't he?

I saw it myself, Arthur.
I swear to God.

ARTHUR AND THE THING

Arthur stood on the railway platform with his hands pressed into his pockets and his head down. It was half past one, and dry and windy. The sky was something between blue and white. On the other side of the tracks rose a green and yellow grassy bank, regularly criss-crossed with footpaths where people walked their dogs and rode their bikes. Beyond the grassy bank were some houses. Some boys and girls in their early teens were wandering along the paths, drinking and spitting. Arthur watched them surreptitiously from beneath his fringe, until the train arrived from the north. It hissed slowly down the tracks towards him and it stopped with a set of doors directly in front of him. He felt pleasure at this, but no surprise, since it seemed only right.

The doors opened, and he, amongst others, embarked. The train set off again, tentatively, and disappeared into the round black mouth of the Bransty Tunnel.

*

Bony was waiting for him at Drigg station. 'You look tired, Arthur,' was the first thing he said.

'I *am* tired,' Arthur replied. 'I don't think I slept at all last night. I am *very* tired.'

They were alone on the platform, and on their side of the railway was an inn called the Queen Victoria. The kitchen window opened on to the tiny gravelled car park separated from the platform by a low wall, and the whole place smelled appetisingly of chips. Drigg was not as windy as Whitehaven had been, but the sky looked exactly the same.

'Do we have to go to the beach?' Arthur asked. 'Can we not just go to yours for a cup of tea? Or maybe even' – he nodded towards the Vic – 'in there?'

'No!' Bony said. 'You came here to see something, so that's what we're going to do.'

'I came here because you said I should. Because—'

'I started telling you about it on Friday night, I think. But something happened, and we got distracted. You started talking about something else.'

Bony fell silent and gave a wave to Jonathan, who did Bony's job when Bony himself wasn't doing it. Jonathan had been reopening the level-crossing gates, once the train had passed through, and was now ascending the steps back up to the signal hut. Arthur thought of Jonathan, in his head, as 'Bony's replacement'. He didn't actually know his name.

Arthur and Bony started walking.

*

Continuing on down to the beach, Arthur and Bony passed the singing gatepost on the left and the fenced enclosure on the right. At this point the road turned into a sandy, stony track that ran with rivulets of red water draining down on to it from the surrounding dunes. Arthur had never understood why the water was red, usually putting it down to rust, although he acknowledged that such an amount of rust would itself require an explanation.

The dunes lay still beneath the wheeling gulls, and they rose on either side of the path, as if to frame the beach ahead. The tide was out, yet the rustling surf could be heard, even from this distance. On top of the dune to one side of the path, and immediately before the sand levelled out, there stood an old lookout hut or some such. It was a stone structure shaped like half of an oval with an open doorway in its flat side and a long, narrow, curving window – protected by a thick, gnarled metal cover on a hinge – facing it, and looking out over the beach and the sea. The little building stood resolute, silhouetted blackly against the pale, indistinctly coloured sky. It was probably from the war: World War II, or maybe even the first one. Or maybe it was even more recent than that. Who knew? Arthur would like to have known, but had never got round to looking it up.

'We have to head left,' Bony announced, once they'd emerged from the dunes. The afternoon was cool but not unpleasantly so, and Arthur felt glad of the walk after all.

'I went crab fishing last night,' he said.

'You should have called me,' Bony said.

'It was late.'

'Catch anything?'

'A weird crab, Bony. It scared me. It was all fat and had a voice like a person.' Arthur looked sideways at Bony as he spoke, expecting him to laugh or look doubtful, but instead Bony just looked like he was thinking. 'I ran away from it,' Arthur concluded.

Bony remained silent for a moment longer, then said, 'That's strange.'

'I thought maybe it was something to do with the acid. I don't think I ever want to take it again, Bony. I had an episode.'

The two of them were walking side by side, keeping to the slightly wetter, harder sand, and leaving footprints as a result. Ahead of them, in the distance, the shore curved out to the right, out to sea, ending in the massive dark bulk of Black Combe.

'There was no acid,' Bony said shortly. 'I was had.'

'What?' Arthur said, stopping.

'I was conned. No acid. It was dud.'

'Then what . . . ?' Arthur started, but stopped. He narrowed his eyes and looked down at his feet. He carried on walking.

'*What* what?'

'Nothing . . . Well, let me think, and then I'll tell you.'

'Tell me afterwards, then.'

'After what?'

'After this. We're here now, nearly. Look, you can see it.'

179

Bony pointed.

Arthur's gaze followed the direction of Bony's skinny arm and long finger, and saw something lying on the beach.

'It doesn't look all that interesting from this distance,' he said. 'It looks like plastic. Lots of big white plastic bags full of sand.'

'It is more than that,' Bony said.

As they got closer, Arthur became aware of the smell. It smelled foul and somehow warm. It smelled like faeces and sweet, rotten fish. The white mounds rose up to Arthur's head height, and he saw that it was all flesh, it was something organic. Dead, maybe, but organic. It looked soft, like dimpled, skinless fat, but when he reached out and touched it it felt tough and dried-up. For a moment he saw it as the remains of some astoundingly obese human, broken up by the waves and deposited on the shore, but it was too big and, besides, there was nothing recognisably human about it.

It was not totally white, but had pinkish cords and threads stretching over and around it – dark red protrusions that spoke of some kind of internal structure. And black spots that may have been caused by decomposition, or maybe not.

'What is it?' Arthur asked.

'I don't know,' Bony replied. 'Exciting, though, isn't it?'

'Very.' Arthur walked all around it, examining it from all angles. It was *huge*. He hadn't realised how big it was. It was also quite shapeless, and it spread out from the central mound in various twisted arrangements and contortions. In places, though, it looked flat and smooth, almost as if it had pooled there and then solidified. 'You'd think it would have attracted more attention,' Arthur remarked.

'Well, people do stop by and look at it – like we're doing right now.'

'No,' said Arthur, 'I mean . . . scientists and people. Biologists, zoologists . . . people who can work out what it is.'

'I guess that would need somebody to actually report it,' Bony said, 'and I know I certainly haven't. I think everybody just assumes that somebody else knows what it is.'

'Maybe somebody else *does* know what it is.'

'Maybe.'

'What are we going to do with it?'

'I don't know. I think we should have a think. I'm sure the answer will come to us.'

'It feels important,' Arthur said.

'I know,' Bony said. 'Let's go and sit on the stones. I've got a small bottle of Jack in my pocket.'

The afternoon wore on, and Drigg beach took on the aspect of a surrealist painting. As the sun lowered, everything turned bright pink and bright orange, the colours shining up from the wet sand as well as down from the sky. The Thing, the big dead flesh thing, looked – from this distance, this angle – like candle wax that somebody had melted and then poured slowly, allowing it to solidify. Further

181

along the beach, beyond the path and out towards the sea, the Barn Scar mast stood thinly and yet vividly against the sky, like a streak of black ink. Those rusted frames of old ships or submarines or planes, or whatever they were, grasped upwards from the sands.

The whisky – or bourbon, as Bony insisted on calling it – felt warm in Arthur's blood.

'Bony,' he said, 'I had a hallucination when I was at work on Saturday. I put it down to the acid.'

'No,' Bony said, 'I think it was only rice-paper that somebody had drawn on with a highlighter pen.' He swigged from the bottle. 'I feel ashamed.'

'It was quite extreme,' Arthur insisted. 'Are you sure about . . . about the acid?'

'I am completely sure,' Bony said.

'That person over there – see them? They look like the person from my hallucination.'

Bony squinted.

'To be fair,' Bony said, 'that looks like just about anybody. That doesn't look like any one person in particular. I don't think you are actually recognising them. I think you're just seeing another person from a distance.' He gazed at Arthur with a vaguely concerned expression. 'That's what people at a distance look like,' he said.

'I know, I know,' Arthur replied, scowling. He waved his hands around. 'I was on the phone at work, and I started to feel like I was being reduced. Like I wasn't really there. Like I was just a voice; just signals passing down the wire. The system on screen, the one we use for billing

. . . I was imagining it as being made up of physical things. And then I was there, I was walking through this landscape made of static and the dead sounds you hear when telephones are broken. I was just there. And in the distance was a city – the City – and . . . and there was this person walking towards me from a long way away.' Arthur pointed at the figure still standing just where the small waves were breaking. 'And that person over there looks just like the one I saw in that landscape.'

'I wouldn't read too much into the similarity,' Bony said, sitting forward. 'Even so, though, your vision sounds incredible.'

'But if we didn't take any acid, then what caused it?'

Bony pulled his woollen gloves from a pocket and put them on. 'I guess that's the question,' he said. 'And the other question: what is that dead thing I found?' He nodded in the direction of the pile of meat.

'Do you think one thing is connected to the other?'

Bony was silent while he thought about it.

'I doubt that very much,' he said, finally.

Once the bottle was empty, Arthur and Bony stood up and made their way back to the path. They walked unsteadily.

'Fucking rice-paper,' Bony said suddenly, looking back across the beach one last time before they headed back through the dunes. 'A disgrace.'

A REQUEST FROM HEAD OFFICE

Bracket and Sally sat in the break room. They hunched over coffee in cardboard cups, and let their gaze rest on the large TV that had been muted. The lunchtime news was on.

'Well, I just think he's very rude,' Sally said. 'We don't have bad habits. We've been doing all right. Our customer satisfaction scores were getting better. We would have got better at cash collection too, after we'd sorted out the' – she stifled a laugh – 'the C-sat.'

'Fucking C-sat.' Bracket shook his head. 'People from big companies don't half talk shite.'

'They think they're too busy to use full-length words,' Sally said.

'I think Artemis just likes to be in control,' Bracket said. 'He likes to get you on the back foot.'

'Well, I think he's a prick,' Sally said. 'If he can't manage manners, he can fuck off.' She sighed deeply and looked out of the window. 'He stresses them out, you know, the kids.'

Sally referred to her team as 'the kids', and she wasn't being derogatory. It was just because they were young: all of them sixteen or seventeen.

'Yeah,' Bracket said, 'he stresses me out too.'

'They all forget their scripting whenever he walks past. It's like . . . it's like in a film where somebody walks down a corridor and all the lights go out as they pass them. You know the kind of film I mean? It's like that. One after the other, bang-bang-bang. You can see it in their eyes: panic. It's like they think he's going to hit them if they get something wrong. Well, fuck, sometimes *I* think he's going to hit them.'

'I know what you mean,' Bracket said. 'He's threatening.'

'He's damaging.'

Bracket nodded slowly.

'Did you have a good weekend?' he asked.

'Yeah,' Sally said. 'It was OK. Didn't do much, though. Went out on Friday and went out on Saturday. Went to Mam's for dinner yesterday. It just goes by so quick. *Too* quick. How was yours?'

'It was OK,' Bracket said. 'Didn't do much.' He thought about it. He really hadn't done much. He had taken Yorkie on a couple of long walks. That was about it. Isobel had spent most of the weekend playing *Animal Crossing*. 'No,' he said, 'didn't do much at all.'

Sally sighed again and looked at her watch. 'I'd better get back,' she said. 'My ten minutes are nearly up.'

'OK. Yeah, I should get back, too.'

'See you later, Bracket!' Sally said as she stood up. She smiled brightly. 'Don't let them get you down!'

Bracket smiled back as Sally left. 'But you're new,' he said quietly, once she was too far away to hear.

On his way back to his desk, Bracket passed the command centre. It was unoccupied, and the phone on Artemis's desk was ringing. The background hum of the call centre – people speaking quietly in numbers, the occasional raised voices as advisers announced that they *would* terminate the call if the customer carried on speaking to them like that, the occasional outburst of manic laughter – receded.

Bracket looked at the phone. Normally he would answer a ringing phone on anybody's desk, without hesitating, but Artemis . . . He thought about it a moment longer, and then picked up the receiver.

'Artemis,' said a voice like stones shifting about in mud, 'contact with the Interstice has, we believe, been made. On Saturday past. Employee ID number T387561. We now have a request to make.'

'Sorry,' Bracket said, scribbling the number down on a nearby Post-it note. 'This isn't Artemi—'

A sound like a sudden hailstorm howled down the line, and somewhere within it were traces of the voice that had been speaking. It was high-pitched with rage and it sounded as if it were splitting up, disassembling, breaking down into multiple other voices. Then the line went dead. Bracket stood there with the receiver in his hand and stared at it. He scratched his stomach and put the receiver down. What a fucked-up voice! And what a wanker! Jesus, you could always leave a message, or at least say goodbye. Manners cost nothing. It was almost as if people thought that their success in a corporate environment meant that normal, everyday rules – like being polite – no longer applied. If being successful at work meant having to deal with people like—

A heavy hand landed on his shoulder.

'You do *not* answer my phone,' Artemis whispered into his ear from behind. 'You do not answer my phone. Got it?'

'Yeah,' Bracket said, 'but I was only trying to help.'

'Got it?'

'Yeah!'

Artemis removed his hand, stepped past Bracket, and up on to the command centre. 'Who was it?' he asked.

'Somebody saying that they've had contact from the Interstice or something,' Bracket replied. He nearly went on to say that whoever the Interstice were, they'd better not be some kind of consultancy firm or something, because they'd been down that road before. But the look on Artemis's reddening face discouraged him from saying anything at all. It suddenly felt to Bracket as if the wrong word or facial expression could be the end of him.

'Was that all?' Artemis whispered, bending over towards Bracket from his higher ground.

'No.' Bracket was leaning backwards. 'No, he . . . they said that it happened on Saturday, and gave an employee number. T387561.' He frowned, looking at the number he'd written down. 'Actually, I know that employee number. That's Arthur.'

'Arthur,' Artemis said, and it wasn't a question. He nodded. 'Yes, Arthur was here on Saturday. Interesting.'

'They said that they had a request to make.'

Something flickered briefly across Artemis's face. Not quite alarm or panic, but something more fundamental. A kind of fear.

'Did they give you any more details?'

'No, as soon as I said that I wasn't you, they . . . they kind of howled and hung up.'

'OK,' Artemis said. 'OK. Fuck. *Fuck*. OK, you come with me. Now.'

Artemis grabbed Bracket's arm and started dragging him along between the desks, before remembering where he was and releasing his grip. Customer advisers looked up worriedly. *For Christ's sake*, Bracket thought, *I've got work to be doing*. Reports on the quality of calls across the site. Charts showing which teams are better, which business processes result in the poorest customer service, all that bollocks. And instead . . .

Artemis led Bracket into one of the pods lining the far wall of the centre. There were two chairs in there, one behind the desk and one in front of it. It had probably recently been used for a performance review or something. Just another poor fucker, Bracket thought, having to pretend that they really gave a shit. Just another two poor fuckers, actually, if you included the manager doing the assessment.

188

'Sit,' Artemis said, gesturing to the chair in front of the desk. He himself sat down in the other chair, then moved the desk telephone so that it was directly in front of him. He looked like he was thinking hard.

Bracket didn't know what to do or what to say.

'If in future you are ever again presented with the opportunity to answer my phone, you do not do so,' Artemis said, one finger raised but without looking at Bracket. 'That is best for all concerned.'

'I understand,' Bracket said.

'It is a big *if*,' Artemis continued, looking up. He lifted the receiver.

Bracket nodded. 'We are expecting our first child,' he said.

'I know,' Artemis said. 'I wouldn't expect them to give a fuck about that, though. Besides, redundancy is not exactly what I'd be worried about, if I were you.'

Bracket tilted his head as if asking Artemis to elaborate, but Artemis did not. Instead he started dialling.

The phone was answered quickly.

'Artemis Black here,' Artemis said.

Bracket patiently watched the larger man nod and grimace and mutter acquiescence for the next five minutes, and then Artemis put the phone down. He hung his head and steepled his long fingers.

'Bracket,' Artemis said, 'you are involved now. There is nothing that can be done about that. So, you have a task to complete.'

'I have quite a lot to do,' Bracket said.

'I am not suggesting that you shouldn't do everything that you already have to do,' Artemis said. 'Your new task will, I think, have to be completed outside of office hours.'

Bracket looked at Artemis without saying anything. He thought about refusing. He even thought about walking out. 'What is it?' he asked.

'I was thinking of enlisting your services, anyway,' Artemis said, 'once I found that you were expecting.' He laughed in a strange, forced way. 'Money, right? You can't get enough overtime with a kid on the way!'

Bracket smiled uncertainly.

'Anyway,' Artemis continued, and Bracket was relieved to see the awkward smile drop from his face, 'Head Office demand your involvement, now that you know a little too much.'

'How can I know too much?' Bracket said. 'This is just work. This is just a call centre. What are you talking about?'

'There are things you don't know about Interext,' Artemis said. 'My advice to you is to just to do as you're told. There's more going on here than you might expect. You don't want to – trust me on this – you don't want to piss Head Office off.'

'Sounds like a warning.'

'Let's make it more of a threat,' Artemis said. 'Let's just say that you don't want to piss me off either, OK?'

'Or what?' Bracket was all tensed up. He knew that either way his actions now would shape the rest of his life, and he didn't like that feeling. 'The worst you can do is sack me.'

'You say that like it means nothing,' Artemis said, 'but we both know that you don't really have anywhere else to go. You've seen this town. You've seen the shops closing down. You've heard people talking about redundancies. Besides' – Artemis leant forward – 'I can actually do much worse than sack you.' He lowered his voice to a whisper. 'You don't want to know.' He sat back up.

Bracket didn't say anything. What was this? What the fuck was this?

'Can you send me Diane, please, once you get back to your team?' Artemis requested, as if the previous dialogue hadn't just happened. 'I overheard her talking to a customer in a somewhat less than appropriate manner.'

Bracket stood up.

'Just await further instructions, Bracket,' Artemis said. 'We'll let you know what we require.'

'OK,' Bracket said.

As Bracket left the pod, he pictured Isobel and their as-yet-unborn child sitting on the sofa, playing *Animal Crossing* on matching hand-held consoles. He wanted to join them, but there was something in the way.

He found Diane at her desk, resting her chin on her hand and looking out of the window. Bracket told her to go and see Artemis in the pod and then immediately felt bad, like he'd done something awful.

Later, Bracket collared Arthur at his desk.

'Arthur,' he began. 'I'm going to be busy with some extra work from Artemis. I'm going to need your help.'

'What?' Arthur looked up at Bracket and took his headset off. 'That's fine, but . . . I didn't think I was doing very well here at the moment. That stuff with Diane?'

'Well, yeah, your general demeanour could do with an overhaul but, to be honest, you're one of the strongest team members I've got. I want you to run the calibration sessions and report on the call-quality scores, OK?'

'Will I get some time to do it?'

'Well, hopefully. I don't want to make any promises, though.'

Arthur looked out of the window. 'OK,' he said, 'I guess. OK.'

'I'll email you the process maps,' Bracket said, 'so that you know what you're doing.'

Arthur didn't respond. Bracket hesitated, and then walked away. He thought he knew exactly how Arthur felt.

WITNESS

Yasmin watched as Diane slouched across the workspace floor towards the glassy walls of the pods. Diane looked like she wanted to appear nonchalant and uninterested, but she couldn't help casting several nervy glances back at her colleagues and friends.

It wasn't usual for the site manager to carry out coaching sessions or disciplinaries; these had always been the responsibility of the team managers. Maybe this was one of Artemis's new schemes. Or maybe, Yasmin thought, and more probably, Artemis was just a pervert. After all, Diane *was* quite attractive in a slovenly, fake-tanned kind of way, and tended to wear low-cut tops or leave her shirt open a little further down than necessary.

Diane glanced behind her one last time before disappearing around the side of the last pod, and presumably, entering it. Yasmin shivered, imagining Artemis as some futuristic monster hulking in his shiny lair, while Diane was . . . what? Irritating – yes. Small-minded – yes.

Casually cruel – yes. But ultimately young and naïve, and hopefully fundamentally OK deep down. She was only seventeen, in all fairness, even if she did look slightly older.

Yasmin checked the time on her phone, took her headset off, and lifted her leather jacket from the back of her chair. She put the jacket on, then checked the pockets for cigarettes and a lighter. It was cold outside – well, it was September – so she put her fingerless gloves on too. Then she made her way to the back door, which was the fire exit, and descended the stairs. She went alone. Most people went for a cigarette with other people, but Yasmin was alone.

The smoking shelter occupied a corner of the car park between the call centre and the narrow, muddy shore path that followed the beach up from Whitehaven towards Parton. It was like a bus stop with no side walls. Yasmin stood beneath it and shivered, the wind gently tugging at her hair. The car park was square, and enclosed by a tall metal fence. After a moment, the door by which Yasmin had exited the building opened and Harry emerged, blinking. He approached her.

'Good day to you, Yasmin,' he said with a lopsided smile.

'Afternoon, Harry.' Yasmin grinned.

'How are you finding the new regime?'

'It appears to be much the same as the old regime,' Yasmin said, 'apart from that it feels like people are waiting. It feels like they're waiting for something to change.'

'I'm waiting,' Harry said, glancing down. 'I'm waiting for the boot.'

'What makes you say that?'

'I don't know what I'm doing,' he replied. He looked up at Yasmin as he said it, and she was struck, not for the first time, by the clarity of his eyes. His eyes were at odds with the rest of his face, which was mottled and soft-looking, like a ripened fruit. She now just looked at his eyes. 'I find myself saying things to customers just to calm them down. I make . . . I make it all up, Yasmin. Not all of it, but . . . but you know what I mean. Or . . . or I think I know what I'm doing and then it's as if I wake up, and I'm looking at a screen full of numbers that I don't understand, and so I panic. So I tell the customer I'll look into it for them and ring them back, and I make a note in my work-queue or in my notebook and then the next time I get five minutes I'll have a look but I never get that five minutes. I never get it. Or I get the five minutes and then I can't find the notes I made. Or I ring some customer up and Sally comes over and tells me to get off the phone because we can't make outbound calls because there are so many incoming calls queuing up. I mean, Sally's a lovely girl but, but there's somebody higher up leaning on her, isn't there? There is. There's always that.'

'Do you want a cigarette, Harry?' Yasmin held the packet out towards him. 'Do you smoke?'

'Sometimes I smoke,' Harry said. 'I think I would. Yes, please. That would be lovely.'

'I wasn't sure you smoked.'

'Sometimes I smoke.'

Yasmin lit the cigarette for him.

'Thank you, Yasmin,' Harry said. 'Most generous of you.'

'A pleasure,' Yasmin said. 'Y'know. The company.'

'Yeah,' Harry said. He could not keep still. He kept shifting his feet around. 'I just don't know how to do the things that matter,' he said. 'In fact I don't know what things *do* matter. And then when I think I've got it worked out, when I think I understand this or that or the other, some . . . some fool, some cretin, some middle-class barbarian comes on – comes on the line and shouts and swears and stamps their foot and blows it all out of the water.' He took a long drag and then exhaled smoke as he spoke. 'I don't think I'm coping,' he finished.

'I know what you mean,' Yasmin said. 'I mean, you've been here longer than me, but it feels like you can either be conscientious and lose your mind, or you can not give a fuck – pardon my language – and do all right.'

'You're spot on,' Harry said. 'Spot on.'

Yasmin finished her smoke and stubbed it out on the top of the little waste bin. She then threw the stub away and folded her arms, and watched as a train pulled in from the north. 'How's Arthur?' she asked.

'Oh, he's OK. Well, you know Arthur. It's hard to tell.'

'I suppose.' Yasmin had been thinking of Arthur's small collapse even as she asked, but didn't want to mention that explicitly in case Harry didn't know about it.

'Hey,' Harry said, suddenly smiling widely, 'Arthur said that Bracket's asked him to help out a little bit with team managing and stuff. Did he tell you that? Did Arthur tell you? He's just emailed me.'

'No, he hasn't said. That's good, though!'

Yasmin remained silent while Harry finished his cigarette and disposed of it. Harry then stuck both of his hands deep into the pockets of his cheap waterproof coat and said, 'I'm so proud of him.'

Yasmin nodded. 'He's a lovely boy,' she said.

Harry looked back up at her with those eyes.

'I was worried that me being a loony might make him a loony too,' he said.

Yasmin opened her mouth to reply but couldn't think of anything to say, just as Harry turned around abruptly, his shoulders hunched, and hurried over to the door. He swiped his access card and disappeared inside.

Yasmin thought she saw him wipe his eyes once inside, but through the smoked glass it was hard to tell and, besides, her eyes were watering slightly too with the wind and the cold so it probably didn't mean anything.

She looked at her phone. She'd have to get inside, too, and plug back in. She looked up at the blank expanse of wall, then turned and looked out towards the sea. It was dark and turbulent today – the kind of seascape that could be romantic and inspiring but could also, if your moods were aligned in the wrong way, be incredibly disheartening. Yasmin realised that her present moods were aligned wrongly. The sea was indeed disheartening.

Threatening, almost. She had been thinking of texting Bony, but decided against it.

Yasmin bit her lip and wondered how Diane was getting on.

Young Eyes

Artemis studied Diane as she sat down. She was wearing loose, pale grey trousers and a tight V-necked jumper. She had huge, young eyes, but they were somehow both scared and scornful at the same time. Or rather, Artemis thought, they were scared but attempting scorn. Call centres were full of girls like Diane. They didn't want to be there but didn't really have anywhere else to go. The boys felt that way too, of course, but with them it didn't translate into the same sexy, smouldering resentfulness that turned him on so much. Or maybe it did and he just didn't realise it because he wasn't gay, but whatever.

'Diane,' Artemis began, resting his elbows on the table with his hands clasped in front of his face. 'I thought I overheard you accuse a customer of ringing us up because they had nothing better to do. I hope I misheard.'

Diane didn't reply, but her skin paled beneath the fake tan. It was like looking into a frozen pond and seeing something beneath the ice suddenly swim away. It left her face a mottled orange and white.

'Did I mishear?' Artemis pressed her.

'Y-yeah,' Diane said, and then fell silent again for a moment before continuing. 'Yeah, you misheard. This guy, right, he—'

'I misheard?' Artemis interrupted, opening his hands out. 'So what did you say?'

'I said . . . I asked him . . . I said have you not got anything better to do than ring us up and kick off? He was shouting like a proper mentaller.'

'Maybe he *was* a proper mentaller. Did you think about that?'

'No, but—'

'Was he being abusive?'

'No, but he was saying—'

'Diane,' Artemis interrupted her, holding up a finger. He looked down. 'If he wasn't being abusive, then I don't give a fuck what that customer said to you. You just deal with it, OK? No matter how angry, no matter how stupid, no matter how self-righteous or argumentative or snotty – you deal with it, OK?'

The moment Artemis uttered the word 'fuck', he spotted a change in Diane's face. A brief indication of shock, but then the stealthy appearance of some kind of grudging respect. Besides, his tone had not been unkind. He could be a very kind man when he wanted to be, he reflected.

'OK,' said Diane.

'I know it's a tough job.' Artemis smiled slightly, 'but someone's got to do it, right? Imagine you're providing these people with a service – a kind of stress relief.'

Diane nodded slowly and smiled slightly.

'What shift are you on?' Artemis asked.

'Twelve–eight,' Diane said.

'Excellent. I'll be around until eight. Come and see me once you've logged off, and I'll print you out some confrontation-management stuff. Just come and see me at my desk.'

'OK,' Diane said.

There was a silence.

'That's it, Diane,' said Artemis. 'You can go now.'

'Oh!' she said, and stood up. 'See you later.'

'Yeah,' Artemis said, 'see you later.'

He watched her arse as she left the pod. It looked more or less perfect. She was how old, sixteen or seventeen? He couldn't really tell. Seventeen, though, that's the age his daughter would've been if she hadn't died. Same age as Diane.

Perfect, more or less.

Artemis was just typing nonsense in order to look busy by the time Diane approached his desk up on the command centre. He had been watching her and noticed how she had packed her things and tidied her desk slowly. She probably wanted to be left alone with him, he reasoned; after all, he was the boss, right? Not to mention his over-whelmingly attractive physical presence. He looked towards her and smiled. She was zipping up her short black jacket. Everybody else was gone. All of the lights in the huge room were off, bar the ones above the command centre. Through the window great big pink clouds could be seen hanging over the sea.

'Just let me log out,' he said. 'I've printed off the material. I've got it in my briefcase. Shall we go for a drink?'

Diane smiled in a small, surprised way, and nodded.

'Excellent,' Artemis said. 'Excellent.'

What did he feel like now? He felt like having sex above all else. He felt like fucking. He felt like fucking *her*, to be specific. It was Diane inspiring the lust in him. Although, in fairness, it was always there, just waiting for something or somebody to awaken it. Would she go for it? He couldn't tell. She was only young, after all.

He looked at her across the table in the bar of the Waverley Hotel. He had considered taking her somewhere else – somewhere a little more lively, maybe – but that would have been too risky.

She sipped at her Midori and lemonade. 'Never had this before,' she said. ''Snice.'

'It is nice,' Artemis said. 'I'm glad you agree.'

Outside there was a strange kind of playfulness to the weather: a light breeze, a bright sky, brief spatters of rain every now and again. Diane just slowly sipped her drink.

It was almost as if she didn't know what to say.

'So,' Artemis said. 'What do you know?'

'What?'

'What do you know? What's the gossip? What goes on amongst all of you guys when you're in the break room?'

Diane shook her head. 'There's no *craic*,' she said.

'What?'

'No *craic*,' she repeated.

'You don't mean drugs? I'm telling you now there'd better fucking not be.'

Diane snorted. ''Course I don't mean fucking drugs,' she said. 'Y'know, there's no *craic*. No gossip. No news.'

'What? Oh!' Artemis threw his head back and laughed. It was only slightly put on. 'What are we? Are we Irish now?'

'We say it up here, too,' Diane said.

'Well,' Artemis said, 'I think I have a lot to learn about West Cumbria.'

'It's shite!' Diane said with fury, almost slamming her little tumbler down as she said it. 'Nowt ever fucking happens and every fucker knows each other.'

'I see,' Artemis said, and he smiled. 'Well. Nobody knows me, eh?'

'No,' Diane said. 'Nobody knows you.' She leant forward and tilted her head so that she was looking up at him with those big, big eyes. Artemis found himself trying not to look down past her neckline. She smiled. 'Where are you from?'

Artemis reclined back and thought about it.

'I'm from Manchester,' he said. 'Not originally, but that's where I've been for the past God knows how many years. Managing a call centre down there, or at least one contract – one floor in a massive building full of call centres. But let's not talk about that. It's all very boring.'

'Any family?'

'What?' he asked.

Diane sat back a little when he said that, as if she thought that she'd seen something awful, and her smile wavered. But then Artemis caught a hold of himself and Diane realised that she must have been mistaken. She laughed nervously.

'I don't have any family,' Artemis said.

Diane was very drunk before too long. She was not half as mature or experienced as she seemed to have been making out, Artemis thought, as he walked her up the stairs. No matter. Maybe he'd been misreading her.

No matter.

Once they entered his hotel room he locked the door and then, positioning himself between her and the door, he let Diane go. She looked around her. She looked confusedly at the cream-coloured walls, or coffee-coloured, or whatever the fuck they were, and at the cream-and-coffee-coloured bedclothes, and the cheap white bedside units.

'I think I want to go now,' she said.

'I think you're a bit too drunk,' he said. 'I don't think it would be safe for you to go outside now.'

'I think I'm going to be sick,' she said, then unzipped her jacket and shrugged it off.

'Into the bathroom,' Artemis said, and pointed. He pushed her towards the bathroom door and, as soon as she'd entered the smaller en-suite room, he took off his coat, jacket and shirt. He followed her into the bathroom and watched her throw up in the toilet. When she stood up again, she stared at him blankly, her mouth slack, then looked at the wall and put her hand out. Artemis took it and led her through to the bedroom.

'I'm fucked,' Diane said. 'S-steaming, like.'

'I know,' Artemis said. 'Let me take your jacket off. You're probably too warm.'

Diane nodded, despite the fact that she had already taken her jacket off. Artemis gently pushed her down on to the bed and then lifted her arms up. Artemis rolled her jumper up over her head, which flopped around like her neck had no strength in it, like she was already falling asleep. She didn't try to stop him; she was more or less unconscious. She was wearing a white push-up bra underneath, nothing else, and the bra was too small, Artemis thought. He stood back and smiled. Diane just slowly sank down on to her side and lifted her legs up on to the bed.

Once Artemis was sure that Diane was asleep, he unfastened her bra and slowly manoeuvred the straps over her shoulders and down along her arms. Her breasts were large and her nipples small and dark. He undressed completely and sat down in the small, ugly, hotel-room chair. He looked at Diane. He stared at Diane. He liked her body. He felt his arousal gathering, strengthening, swirling into him like water into a plughole, filling him up. He liked these girls: young, doe-eyed, precocious, naïve.

If Diane had opened those eyes, she would have seen him sitting there naked, somehow weirdly gaunt without his suit on, his head bald and bulbous and disproportionately large, the beakish hook of his nose a kind of counterpoint to the questing cock that reared up from his lap. Hands like talons.

Artemis liked hotel rooms, and he liked offices too. He was really *somebody* here in these bland, generic places. He was powerful. *Give me a hotel room*, he thought, *or give me an office, and I can do anything. Anything.*

THE CELEBRATION

Harry and Arthur both sat with their plates of beans on toast on their knees, watching *Come Dine with Me* on the TV. Harry was acting like there was something wrong with him, though; he was even more nervous and fidgety than normal. Arthur watched him across the living room. Harry kept putting his knife and fork down, then picking them up again and cutting off a little corner of toast and eating it, and then putting them back down.

'What is it, Dad?' Arthur asked.

'Nothing, son. Nothing.'

'OK,' Arthur said.

'Oh, son, OK! I can't hide it any more.' Harry moved his plate aside and stood up, and then waved his hands around. 'I'm so proud. I've got you something. I was going to give it to you after tea, but I can't wait.'

Arthur moved his head slightly to one side. 'Proud of me?' he said. 'What for?'

'For getting your promotion!'

'I haven't had a promotion,' Arthur said.

'Let me just . . . let me just get this for you,' Harry said. 'Wait a second.' He left the room for a moment, and came back with the scrappy old backpack that he always took to work. He sat back down on the sofa and opened the backpack, removing from it a Tesco's Finest chocolate cake of some sort.

'Oh, Dad,' Arthur said. 'You shouldn't have. It's not a real promotion, you know.'

'Of course it is! They . . . they must think you're very good! You *are* very good, son. Anyway, I just . . . I just wanted to get you something to show . . . to show you.'

'You took it from the fridge at work, didn't you, Dad?'

'Well, yes, but it wasn't easy. And, besides, that Artemis can always afford to buy himself another one, can't he?'

''Course he can.' Arthur smiled again and accepted the cake. 'Thanks, Dad, but it really isn't a big deal. They're just using me because they know I'll say yes. They just push all the work downwards. It's not like they're changing my role or anything. They're just asking me to do something they don't want to do themselves.'

'You can't dismiss it like that, son. It's good to be valued at work.'

'Valued, yeah. Not exploited, though.'

'Just . . . just to have a job at all, Arthur, is something these days. I mean, look at me. I'm not long for that place.'

'Dad, they just take advantage. I mean, they know that there aren't any other jobs going around here, so they just pile on the pressure until—'

'Arthur!' Harry almost shouted, standing up. 'You're doing well working for a respected company and at such a young age too and I am so proud and your mother is so proud as well!'

Arthur saw that his father's eyes were wet.

'Thanks, Dad,' he said. 'I really love the cake. Here, let's finish our tea and I'll cut it up.'

'No, son,' Harry said. 'It's all for you.'

Harry stood there for a moment longer, and then turned and left the room. Arthur set the cake down on the floor, next to his chair, and put his face in his hands for a little while. Then he took the cake and went upstairs and lay down on his bed. He could hear his father through the wall, talking to himself. Or talking to Arthur's dead mother, whichever. It's not like there was any difference.

Arthur went to the bathroom. He tried not to look in the bath, but he did, and there they were: the worms. He gritted his teeth and, before actually going to the toilet as he'd intended, he took some toilet roll and screwed it up and set about killing all the little bastards. He counted about fifteen. He then flushed the tissue paper away and went back to his bedroom. He'd just put a CD on when he realised that he hadn't used the toilet at all, so he went back to the bathroom. He tried, again, not to look in the bath, but he did, and again there they were: the worms. There were worms in the bath again. Arthur sat down on the toilet seat and felt his face start to tremble and the tears start to come. He chewed his lip and realised that he was shivering. He could imagine them all packed in together inside the walls. The worms, that is.

He stood up and picked up his mother's heavy glass soap dish and, holding it tightly, smashed it into the white tiles. They splintered and fell easily. They crashed into the bath, along with black grout and black worms and soft, dark lumps of tile adhesive and plaster that had gone rotten. He kept on going until he became aware of his father shouting to him through all the clattering. As Arthur felt his father's hands on his shoulders, the violent world of rancid mess and angular noise that he was in the process of creating suddenly receded into nothing. The tide inside went out in a matter of seconds; where there had been waves and motion there was now just a flat expanse of nothing. He dropped the soap dish on to the bathroom floor and it broke. He didn't hear it.

'Arthur,' Harry said. 'What are you doing?'

'These worms,' Arthur said. 'They're getting to me.'

'That soap dish was your mother's.'

'It was only a soap dish.'

'Yes,' Harry said. 'Yes, it was.'

'Don't talk about it like it's something important.'

'OK.'

'I wish I could talk to her like you do.'

Harry put his arms all the way around Arthur, and held him pretty close. Arthur could feel his father shaking.

'Dad,' Arthur said, 'sometimes I feel like some kind of freak. Sometimes I feel very different to everybody else, like there might be something wrong with me.'

By this point, the two of them were kneeling on the bathroom floor, their knees wet with water from the morning's showers. Harry was still hugging Arthur. He struggled for what felt like a long time to think of a response, but in the end he couldn't.

Later that evening, Harry called up to Arthur that he was going out. Arthur shouted a goodbye from his bedroom. Off to the Vine, probably, thought Arthur, who was lying face-down on the bed. His room was square, with just the bed and a desk and a wardrobe. The desk was a home-work desk from when he was still at school; now it was a bit too small for him. On it sat a telephone handset. The ceiling light was off and the curtains were closed, but they were thin and there was still a little brightness left in the sky outside, so the room was illuminated very slightly. Arthur felt a bit like he was in an aquarium, and the window was a tank set into a wall that he could walk up to and press his face against to see something weird floating inside. He could picture that groaning green crab hanging there in mid-air, its legs dangling like the tentacles of a jellyfish, staring back at him.

Arthur rolled over and reached across to grab the telephone handset. If his dad could talk to his mother, then he could too. But now, looking at the phone, he felt the ridiculousness of it all. He didn't even know how to begin. Or what number to dial. He put the receiver to his ear and listened – there was a scratchy wind in the distance, some kind of static, and a ticking, clicking sound that sometimes seemed close and sometimes far away. What was that? Was that due to birds sitting on telephone wires and moving around? Was that how it worked? How did it work? How did anything work? He moved the phone away from his head and went to dial a number again, but his finger just hovered over the keypad.

There was no telephone number he could possibly ring to reach his mother. His mother was dead. They had found her meaty skeleton, crawling with crabs and sandflies and strange worms, down on the beach. She had drowned, he knew. She had toppled from the cliff, breaking her skull on the way down, and then drowned in the sea. The fucking sea. So where was she whenever his father spoke to her? In heaven? Maybe the phone was just some earthly prop for a much more mystical form of communication. Or maybe his father was just a fucking nut-job.

Maybe they were both nut-jobs. It could be hereditary, couldn't it? And his father's delusions were hardly more drastic than his own recent experience with the landscape and the purple-lit city and that tall figure in the distance. Or – Arthur sat upright – maybe neither of them was delusional at all. He stood up and pulled back the curtains.

Outside, seagulls squawked and squealed as they were buffeted by the wind. They looked luminous in the darkening sky, lit up as they were by the lights of the town. The rusty, decrepit-looking wheel of Haig Pit was visible if he looked south. A dinosaur skeleton. Something massive and obsolete.

He had felt kindness in that landscape, and the voice

212

had been warm. Maybe there was something else happening. He watched a seagull, which had been suspended up in front of a silvery rift, suddenly plummet down towards the sea, disappearing behind the black edge of the cliffs where the land dropped away. Maybe his father was right. Maybe his mother was in there somewhere, on the phone. In the phone lines. In that same place, elongated and silhouetted, wading through the writhing wastes, that dark figure that never reached him. In that submarine limbo. The underwater. The sea. That's where she went, after all: the sea. That's where she was. Down there with the starfish and the thick, ground-hugging cables and the silt and the fat green crabs. And with the huge, unidentifiable, fleshy masses.

Of course! Arthur smiled slightly and became aware of his reflection in the glass of his bedroom window smiling back at him out of the darkness beyond. The Thing on the shore. There was something happening in that place, wherever it was – that landscape – that was sending winding tendrils of consequence out into the same grey-green ocean that lapped against the stone and sand of Whitehaven harbour.

Arthur turned away from the window and decided – one way or another, he would get back there. He would get back there somehow.

THE WHALES

Arthur was listening in to a call from an elderly man.

'Are you telling me my house isn't here?' he was saying in a low, husky, difficult-to-interpret voice.

'No,' the CA – a girl called Linda – was saying nervously. 'I'm just saying that it's not here. I mean I can't find it on the system.'

'What?' the old man said. 'What?'

'I can't find it on the system here,' Linda said.

'What do you mean, you can't find it on the system?' the old man said. 'Are you telling me my house doesn't exist? What do you think I'm living in, then, eh? You people! The Post Office people, as well, were trying to tell me that my house doesn't exist! Well, I said, why don't you come and have a look, eh?'

Arthur had his head in his hands, as he imagined Linda had had her head in her hands during the call. The customer was not being rude or unpleasant; the call was just typical of so many calls, so many misunderstandings, so many crossed wires, so much confusion. Sometimes there were so few points of reference shared between the customer and the CA. Especially, to be honest, with the elderly. Sometimes, if the customer were elderly, all you had to do was mention a computer or a 'system', and they would immediately lose all respect for you and adopt a weary, irritable tone that, although it was not especially offensive or upsetting, was exhausting in its own unique way.

Arthur remembered a particularly strange call from a man who was querying a very high bill. When Arthur had investigated, he found the company had the property registered as empty due to a meter reader reporting that the building looked unlived in and semi-derelict. Arthur hadn't mentioned that to the customer, of course; he had just changed the company records accordingly. But he then started to imagine an alternative town, or rather a series of alternative towns. Where had that meter reader visited? He had been to the very same address, but maybe an alternative version of it somewhere else. An *empty* version. If parallel universes existed, basically, then maybe the computer system they were using was aligned to the wrong one.

What a stupid thing to think.

Arthur lifted his head from his hands and opened his eyes, and physically recoiled at the shock of seeing the strange wastes rolling out before him. He was back in the Scape. His ears were filled with that subtle, chittery rustle created by all of those tiny, ugly things that squirmed across the ground, or that actually constituted the ground. They didn't look like they were moving when he watched them; they looked like lots of still, thin, pink or white or yellow or red wires. But he got the sense that they were writhing around just out of sight, or immediately behind him. He got the sense that other things appeared sometimes: little claws or shells or wet beaks or hair-thin tentacles. But never clearly within his field of vision.

Arthur made no attempt to move this time. He sat still in his chair with his arms flat on the desk, but the chair and the desk were made of something more of the Scape than of the world he knew – some kind of thick, twisted, shell-like material, rough like the surface of a conch.

Another sound, something else. Not the whisper of the ground or the buzz and hum of the sky, but a faint, haunting cry, an eerie whistle of some kind. A long, drawn-out sound but, unlike the constant murmurings of the environment, one with a beginning and an end. It was accompanied by the appearance of something on the horizon. Arthur felt his hair move in the wind, but actually it felt more like it was moving in water; the movement was slower and heavier. The dark shape on the horizon grew larger until it became apparent that something was moving through the sky towards him. It made that sound again: an emotional, evocative, high-pitched song.

Whatever the creature was, it was huge and it was black against the sky. It was long, with a heavy, rounded front end that tapered to nothing at the rear. It moved with a gentle undulation, like . . . like it was swimming.

Arthur recognised it only when it was nearly directly above him. It was a whale. It was about half a kilometre up, maybe. It was hard to tell. His sense of perspective was all shot, so he couldn't really tell how big it was. He realised that his mouth was hanging open, so he closed it again. The whale suddenly moaned, and the sound of it sent waves of pleasure surging all over Arthur's skin, sent bright tingles running up and down his spine. Where was he? Why was the whale in the sky? He didn't much care. The whale looked like it was moving slowly, like it was not in any kind of rush. Like it didn't care about anything.

The whale turned out to be the first of a pod. They all spoke to each other in their incredible voices. Arthur did not understand them but he felt like he understood. Their presence made his presence there OK. He sat at the desk and looked up until he became aware of a pain in his neck. Then he reached up to rub the back of his neck and found that his knuckles were banging against some kind of rough surface. He realised that he was lying on his back, on the floor. He looked up and, instead of the whales, he saw Bracket's face hovering over him, slack-eyed and frowning.

REBECCA'S LAST DAY

'What was she running away from then?' Pauline asked.

Harry – dirty, bleary Harry – raised a hand to his face and dragged it down across his wet mouth. He shrugged slightly, as best he could without lifting his elbows from the bar.

There was some kind of game on. Football. The TV screen wasn't very big for a pub and the sound was quite low, so it wasn't too intrusive, but Harry found it intrusive enough – something bright and fast-moving hovering in his peripheral vision. It was pissing him right off. He shrugged again.

'She must have been running from something,' Pauline suggested.

Her words did, of course, imply that Rebecca had been running away from Harry himself, but Pauline was saying it so brazenly that Harry couldn't tell whether or not she was aware of that implication.

'So was she running away from you, then?' Pauline said.

Harry couldn't help laughing. He should have known better. Pauline did not 'imply'. But, of course, his was not genuine happy laughter. It was something sharper and more muscular, a kind of hacking sound.

'Shall I tell you what happened?' Harry said.

Pauline rolled her eyes. 'Might be a fucking idea,' she replied. ''Sonly what I've been driving at.'

'It is . . . it is a strange thing,' Harry said. 'It was a strange thing. She was off work . . . She was off work and we woke up quite late in the morning. Rebecca seemed quite quiet, and she was often quiet but this was different, like something had happened or something was wrong. I . . . I can't explain how scared I was, Pauline, just sitting there, sitting in bed with the sun pouring in through the window, looking at her. Looking at Rebecca and not knowing what to say or do. I felt like I had to say or do something, because it just wasn't like her.'

Harry stopped speaking and sipped from his pint. There were other people in the Vine, but they were sitting at the tables or in the wide, shabby booths. Nobody else was sitting at the bar.

'Arthur was at school, so he wasn't around when we had breakfast. It was just Rebecca and me. I made scrambled eggs and really crispy bacon with croissants. I was standing in the kitchen feeling like my chest was going to burst or something because I knew that Rebecca was just sitting there at the table not doing anything and not saying anything and not even moving. That wasn't like her, Pauline. It was a lovely day, too, really bright outside.

The seagulls sounded clean and it felt like we were on holiday. We *were* on holiday. I mean, we were both off work. That was such a rare thing, too, so I couldn't understand what was wrong. She smiled at me when I sat down with the food but it was like she was forcing the smile, you know? Like she knew she should be smiling but didn't really want to. I asked her what was wrong but she just said there was nothing wrong. Then, after a few minutes of pushing her food around, she said that this was only her second day off work in a row and she felt bored. Said she didn't know what to do. I said, what do you mean? I didn't really understand.

'She said that she couldn't work out what to do. She had all day ahead of her and nothing to do. What did people do when they weren't at work? Well, I said, they relaxed or they carried on with hobbies or they spent time with each other. She nodded at that, but looked confused. She said that she couldn't do the crossword all day. No, I said, that would get boring. That's exactly it, she said.'

Harry shook his head slightly and shrugged again. Pauline gazed at him but gave nothing away. She was inscrutable. Without taking her eyes off Harry, she moved some clean glasses from the dishwasher tray into their separate compartments beneath the bar.

'She told me her heart was racing. She was just sitting there at the table and she was a very healthy woman, was Rebecca, she was always running around that supermarket and she would often go running along the cliffs. But she looked at me and said in a very quiet voice that her heart was going ten to the dozen with panic. I said, what are you panicking about? She said she didn't know but she thought it was something to do with being so bored. This thing she was saying about being bored was getting to me, Pauline, so I said, what do you mean you're bored? Is it not enough to be off work for a day and just spend it with me? Am I so boring?'

Pauline grimaced and sucked in air through her yellowing teeth.

'She just looked at me,' Harry continued, 'and then she opened her mouth but didn't say anything like she didn't know what to say. I . . . I knew what she meant, though. She meant, yes, you are boring, Harry. Yes, you are a boring man. She said, no of course you are not boring. I'm sorry, Harry, I don't know what's wrong with me. I then said, I know what's wrong with you, Rebecca. You've got some time on your hands and you don't know what to do with it. It's as simple as that. It was as simple as that, Pauline. Oh my God.'

Pauline had finished arranging the glasses now, and was just watching Harry and listening to his sputtered reminiscences. Elsewhere in the Vine people were carrying on with their own conversations, but Pauline felt reasonably sure that these were conversations that were recycled, that happened every night, that were well worn by their participants. So many conversations came round again and again, like songs on a commercial radio station. But what Harry was saying felt quite new, like he was saying something that he had never said before. It was something that Pauline had never heard before, at any rate.

'It went on for hours. Rebecca just sat around with her hand on her chest and this look in her eyes. Honestly, it was a very scary thing. She said, I have never felt like this before. I have never thought these things before. She said, what do I go to work for if I don't know what to do when I am not at work? I said, there are lots of things you could be doing. She said, like what? Is there anything really that I could be doing? I was getting sick of it, Pauline. I didn't know what she was going on about. What are you going on about, I asked, not for the first time. She looked at me and she was not just sad now, but angry as well. She said, you could at least make an effort to understand, Harry. I said, I am making an effort but, despite my best efforts, I do not understand at all. Am I supposed to just understand through some psychic power? She said, isn't that what being in a relationship is all about? We should rely less on verbal communication and more on some kind of unvocalised knowing. She was a very clever girl, was Rebecca. Oh God, I miss her, Pauline. I miss her so much. She said, the better we get to know each other the less we should have to talk. Communication, she said, communication is for people who do not understand each other. Communication is only an attempt at understanding. It demonstrates a total lack of understanding.

'I knew what she was getting at, but I didn't know what to say. It felt like a terrible moment. A truly terrible moment, like everything was changing, and changing for the worse. The house was so light on that day with all of the sun coming in. Looking back, I don't know how it was so light because it's never that light any more, even when it is sunny outside. Anyway. She said, people who understand each other do not need to talk at all. That is true understanding. I said, how do you know that? She said, it is just common sense. It is a common-sense conclusion that I have arrived at. I said, I think we have drifted off-topic. We were talking about how boring you find me. She said, for fuck's sake, Harry. For fuck's sake.'

Harry was now propping himself up by resting his forehead in his hand, his elbow resting in a puddle of old beer on the bar top. He didn't mind that. He was barely aware of it.

'The day went on,' he said. 'Rebecca started trying to occupy herself. She did the crossword, she read some of a book, she took me to bed. All within about an hour. She didn't finish anything, though. She moved from one thing to another, looking for something that would seem to her to be worthwhile, but she could not settle. Have you ever felt like that?'

Pauline did not respond at first. She didn't realise that Harry was even addressing her; thought he was merely reporting some further snippet of remembered dialogue.

'Pauline?' Harry repeated, meeting her gaze with his. 'Have . . . have you ever felt like that?'

'No, Harry,' Pauline said. 'Chance to get bored would be a fine thing.'

'I suppose there is always that,' Harry said. 'I don't

think I've ever felt like that either. There's always something to do, isn't there? Or if not that then . . . then . . .
there is always some pleasure to take, surely?'

Pauline just nodded. It was rare for Harry to be this
articulate. But then she, Pauline, was a good listener. Good
at kind of fading away and letting people more or less
talk to themselves.

'It got worse as the afternoon went on,' Harry continued.
'We went on a walk along the cliffs and it was such a
beautiful day but Rebecca was not talking and she was
not really looking at anything. She did not bother looking
at the sea or the view. She kept just walking, and looking
straight ahead or down at the ground. We got back and
watched some TV, but then she just shook her head and
said, I feel like I'm wasting so much time. I said, why?
What should you be doing? And she said there is nothing
that I should really be doing. That is what's wrong, Harry.
That is precisely what is wrong. And then she said, and
what about Arthur? She said, we have just inflicted this
same thing on him. What will he do when he is not
working, or not at school? What will he feel? He won't
feel anything, will he? He will get bored like me.

'I have to admit . . . I have to . . . I have to admit that
knocked me for six, Pauline. When she said that. Honest
to God, it knocked me for six. Why are you bringing Arthur
into this? I asked. How can I not, she said. Everything we
feel our children also will feel. Every problem we face,
our children will face. That is what makes things so terrifying. Knowing that your children will have to face them

224

too. I said, things are not terrifying, but I was starting to feel like they were. Most things are terrifying, Rebecca said, when you think about them. When you have time to think about them, most things are really very terrifying. And when you realise that your children will be terrified, too.

'I wanted to tell her that things could be wonderful and that the world was a good world to live in. But I was starting to feel despair myself. We argued for hours, about everything. About the house being a mess even though it was spotless. About how we did or didn't spend time with Arthur or let him go off wherever he wanted whenever he wanted to. We argued for hours, Pauline. In the end I came down here because it felt like whatever I said Rebecca would just get more sad and I didn't think I was helping. After . . . After a few drinks I went back, and Rebecca was in bed asleep. I watched telly for a while and then I went to bed, too, and even . . . even though I was trying to be quiet, I woke Rebecca up. She just got out of bed and left the house. I don't even know if she had been asleep, really. And then . . . and you know what happened then.'

Pauline shook her head but didn't say anything.

BLOOD ON THE MOON

'I want to be Mario,' Arthur said, animated and glassy-eyed in the warmth and warm light of the Vagabond. There was some early Tom Waits on – *Nighthawks at the Diner* – and the comforting aroma of gravy permeated the air. 'I want to be Shaun of the Dead. I want to be Frodo Baggins. I want to be able to kill evil people or monsters with total moral justification. Y'know, in order to save good people. I want a clearly delineated path. You know what? I want the world to start ending so that I can rescue people, and then they'll think me noble and worthwhile. I want to wake up and find that the world economy has totally collapsed, the government gone, nuclear war. I want to be Mario, looking for Princess Peach and rescuing her. The two of us would survive somehow.' He paused to suck in some beer. 'We would be totally OK, in the end.'

'Everybody wants the end of the world,' Bony said. 'It's many people's favourite fantasy.'

'I don't know,' Yasmin said. 'I don't think it's mine.

Millions of innocent people would die. It would be rubbish.'

'I think about that,' Arthur conceded. 'My conscience and I wrestle with the fact almost daily. Somehow, though, I don't feel much compassion for the dead. Not the dead in my fantasies, anyway.'

'Hang on, though,' Bony said. 'It's never the end of the world in the *Mario* games, is it? Why do you want to be Mario?'

'A clearly delineated path,' Arthur said. 'You know where you need to go. Might be difficult getting there, but you know where you need to go.'

'The beginning of *Super Mario Galaxy* felt a bit apocalyptic,' Yasmin remarked. 'Meteorites coming down all over the Mushroom Kingdom.'

'True,' Bony said. 'You've still got to rescue Peach though, haven't you? I love those games, but the narrative is always, at root, the same. Bowser kidnapping the princess and hiding her in his castle, and what . . . what's the subtext? Is he raping her? What's he doing with her?'

'I don't know,' Yasmin said. 'I think applying video-game conceits and structures to real life, or vice-versa, is probably a bit . . . I don't know. Kind of missing the point, isn't it?'

'You know what's good about the *Mario* games?' Arthur leant forward over the shining varnish of the table top. 'The way he can jump down a pipe and be somewhere else.'

'Well,' Bony said, 'that's just pipes, isn't it?'

'You know what I mean.' Arthur said, sitting back again. 'Another world.'

'But it's another world *already*,' Yasmin said.

'Yeah, well,' Arthur said, turning to make direct eye contact. 'I'm still jealous.'

'Drinks,' Bony said, standing up. 'Who wants what? Usual?'

Arthur and Yasmin nodded assent.

Outside, the harbour was lit by a full moon. It was a cold, clear night. Another Friday. They come round pretty fast really, but then so do Mondays.

'I've fucked up our bathroom,' Arthur informed Yasmin in a low voice. 'Don't think we'll be able to use the shower any more. I've knocked loads of tiles off the wall.'

'Why did you do that?'

'I don't know. I don't know what's wrong with me.'

'I'm sure there's nothing wrong with you.'

'I know . . . I mean, I don't mean anything serious. I just mean that recently I'm not always quite with it.'

'Maybe you're stressed out,' Yasmin said. 'People sneer about stress, but it's a real thing.'

'Yeah, maybe,' Arthur said, 'I think you're right.'

'Besides,' Yasmin said, 'look at us. Look at all of us. Who's not kind of mentally ill?'

'Yeah,' Arthur said, and laughed. 'I can't think of anybody who's not kind of mentally ill.'

Yasmin put her arm around Arthur then – they were sitting next to each other – and pulled him close. Not in any meaningful way, as far as she was concerned. Just a friendly hug.

'I've been thinking,' Bony said, when he got back to the table. 'Bowser's cock is probably as big as Princess Peach's whole body.'

'Depends on the game,' Yasmin said, and removed her arm from Arthur's shoulders to accept her drink. 'He varies in size from one to the next.'

'Hey, Yasmin,' Bony said, 'you should come and see this thing on Drigg beach.'

'Is it still there?' Arthur asked.

'Yeah, still there.'

'What is it?' Yasmin asked.

'We don't know,' Bony said. 'It's a massive jellyfish or something.'

'Like, huge,' Arthur said. 'Too big to be an actual jellyfish, but that's what it's like.'

'Maybe it is a previously undiscovered species of giant jellyfish,' Yasmin suggested.

'That would just be too good,' Bony replied. 'You'll have to come and see it.'

'I will,' Yasmin said.

'I think it's part of something else,' Arthur said. He leant forward again. He was well on his way to steaming – they all were – and his facial expressions now had a childish excitement to them. 'I saw this crab the other night, Yasmin, and it was really big and soft and green. And it had a man's voice!'

Yasmin smiled uncertainly at Arthur, flicking her eyes over towards Bony to see if this was some kind of joke they'd both cooked up. Bony looked back with a neutral expression, but then his expression was nearly always neutral, so Yasmin didn't know what to make of that.

'And,' Arthur continued, 'last Saturday, when I was on the phone – you know when I passed out, Yasmin – I was in this other place. It was like being under water. The ground was covered in these starfish things, and I could only move dead slowly.'

Yasmin was smiling with one side of her mouth, eyes bright, totally incredulous, still unsure of the source of this weirdness. Humour? Drunkenness? Stress? She wanted to laugh.

'It was like . . . It was like my mum was there,' Arthur concluded, and the room seemed to fall quiet then, for him at least, and he looked down at the table, suddenly ashamed.

Yasmin glanced back at Bony. He held her gaze but Yasmin was really not sure what he was trying to convey, if anything.

'Oh, Arthur,' she said, in the end, 'are you OK?'

'Yes,' Arthur said. 'Well, like I was saying, sometimes I feel like I'm losing it slightly, but otherwise I feel happier than I've felt in a long time.'

'That's good, then,' Yasmin said.

'It is good,' Arthur said. 'What I was going to say, though, was that Mum died in the sea, didn't she? And that . . . landscape I saw, and the crab, and the Thing on the beach, and the way Dad talks to Mum on the phone, it all . . . it all adds up to something, I'm sure of it. Even if I don't know what it is.'

'I don't know about you,' Bony said, 'but I'm feeling the urge to go outside. Let's drink up and get some fresh air.'

They sat on the low sandstone wall that ran along the edge of the promenade and sloped gently down into the calm waters of the marina's far side. It was cold but that was OK. They had coats on and they were drunk, and they were only ten metres from the Vagabond door if they suddenly started to feel chilly.

'Look,' Yasmin said, pointing up. 'Blood on the moon.'

'What?' Arthur said. 'What do you mean?'

'Never heard that before? It's just an expression for when you can see those rings around it. Those pale rings.'

'No,' Arthur said, 'I've never heard that.'

'I can't believe you've never heard that.'

There was a moment's silence.

'But then,' Arthur said, 'maybe I've led a sheltered life. I thought that teacakes were savoury things until last year. They're just bread buns.'

Yasmin laughed. Arthur felt like a retard then. Her laughter was good-natured, but, still . . . *Am I a retard?* he wondered. It wasn't a word – retard – that he'd ever say out loud, but in his head, he reasoned, it was OK. Nobody knew he was thinking it, right? Stars dusted the sky. The sky was almost pale with them. People had told him that in cities and other places you could never see as many stars as you could in West Cumbria. Arthur wasn't sure he could really exist in such places.

'There's somebody over there looking at us,' Bony said. 'Over by the Wave. He's on the far side. Look.'

Arthur looked and saw a hulking figure in black, his exposed features lit green by the Wave. He could see that the figure's face was indeed directed their way.

'Artemis,' Yasmin said.

'I saw him come through Drigg on the train,' Bony said. 'Looked like a vicious fucker.'

'He is,' Arthur said.

'Fuck,' said Yasmin, 'he's walking over here. Why is he walking over here?'

The three of them sat and watched as Artemis strode towards them like a teacher might approach a fight taking place in the playground. Yasmin and Arthur already knew that this was just the way he walked, but Bony wore a faint smile of disbelief. Who was this vicious fucker, and why was he walking like he owned the whole place?

Upon arrival, Artemis glanced cursorily at Bony and then addressed Arthur and Yasmin. 'What brings you two out here?' he asked.

His voice was civil but in a strained, unnatural way.

'Just getting some fresh air,' Yasmin said. 'Been in there.' She nodded towards the Vagabond.

'I see,' Artemis said. 'Out for a drink, were we?'

'Yeah,' Arthur said.

Artemis gazed at Arthur for what to Arthur seemed like a long time, then. He felt that in some way he was being examined or evaluated.

'Well,' Artemis said quietly, 'don't spoil yourselves.'

'What are you up to out here, anyway?' Bony slurred, breaking the silence. 'And who are you, again?'

Artemis looked at Bony. 'I know you,' he said. 'I recognise you.'

'Yeah,' Bony said. 'You saw me from the train, in Drigg, couple of weeks ago.'

'Oh yes.' Artemis was sneering slightly, despite himself. 'Drigg. Well, as Arthur and Yasmin here can confirm, I'm Artemis Black, the new manager at the Interext site. You might know it better as the Outsourcing Unlimited site.'

'I know where you mean,' Bony said. 'Doesn't really matter what it's called though, does it? Or what company runs the spot. It's always just another fucking office.'

Artemis's face froze a little bit, transforming into a hard, narrow-eyed mask.

'Just remember who you're talking to,' he said.

'What?' Bony laughed, standing up. 'What? I'm not one of your employees! You can't do anything to me. You can't *sack* me. Besides, you're not at work now. You don't have to pretend to be so into it. It's Friday night, for fuck's sake!'

'Nobody's pretending,' Artemis replied, his voice quiet again. Arthur and Yasmin watched nervously, eyes flicking to and fro.

'Anyway,' Bony said, 'you didn't answer my first question.'

'I don't have to answer any of your questions.'

'But you asked these two the same question,' Bony said,

waving his arm to indicate Yasmin and Arthur. 'Why can't I ask you?'

'They're my employees,' Artemis said.

'No,' Bony said, 'not outside of work they're not.' All trace of drunkenness was gone from his voice.

Artemis's long black coat flapped slightly in the gathering wind.

'I was just out for a walk,' he said. 'Just thought I'd go out for a walk, that's all. The hotel sometimes gets oppressive. Having said that, I'm very tired and, if it's quite all right with you, I think I'll be heading back there now.'

'OK,' Bony said. 'Well, sleep well. Have a good weekend.'

'I will,' Artemis said. He grinned mirthlessly at Bony, and then looked back at Arthur before letting his eyes rest on Yasmin for a moment. He glanced back at Bony. 'I don't think drink suits you,' he said, 'because you seem thoroughly unpleasant. That's how I'll always remember you: unpleasant. You understand?'

Bony didn't say anything. There was a set to his mouth and a glint to his eyes that neither Arthur nor Yasmin recognised.

Artemis walked away – away from the harbour, past the Vagabond, and on to Swingpump Lane. He turned right and disappeared.

'Bony,' Yasmin said. 'Wow.'

'It's as if he wants the whole town to be afraid of him,' Arthur said.

'But what is he?' Bony said. 'He is nothing.'

'I know,' Arthur said. 'It's sad.'

'A nothing person,' Bony said, 'but maybe also a vicious fucker. Keep your eye on that one.'

'He kind of reminds me of Bowser,' Arthur said. 'He's like a genuinely evil version of Bowser who actually *would* be raping Princess Peach up there in his castle.'

Bony had dropped his Nintendo Wii off at Arthur's house prior to their stint in the pub. Yasmin decided against joining the boys for a late-night gaming session, despite really wanting to, as she was working overtime in the morning, of course. So Bony and Arthur both hugged Yasmin goodnight at the door to the building she lived in, and set off walking south past the old warehouses (now flats), past the Wave, past the nice restaurants, past the burnt-out hotel, up the steep steps – up and up and up to the estate.

'I'm not sure why you find her so attractive,' Bony said.

'You wouldn't,' Arthur said.

'Yeah,' Bony said, 'I suppose. I mean, she's lovely. I don't mean she's not lovely.'

'The reason you don't find her attractive is that you're not really capable of it,' Arthur said. 'The reason lies with you, not with her.'

'You're right,' Bony said. 'You're right.'

The game they played was *Super Mario Galaxy*. Bony took control of the eponymous hero – the plumber, Mario – as he was the more sober. Arthur happily fulfilled the role of Player Two, pointing at the screen with the second controller to gather the collectibles, or firing multi-coloured projectiles at the numerous weird denizens of the various planetoids that Mario traversed.

The room the two of them were seated in was dark, apart from the glow of the TV screen. It was a mass of bright colours, and soon, to Arthur or Bony, there was no room surrounding them, and there was no darkness either. Just *Super Mario Galaxy*, in which Mario had to visit and fix one solar system and then the next on his voyage to catch Bowser – some giant, dragonish, turtle creature – and rescue Princess Peach. Each solar system was made up of tiny planets of varying incredible shapes and sizes, some close enough to each other for Mario to jump between them, using their gravitational fields to zip from one puzzle or obstacle course to the next, and all the while that incredible gulf was wheeling beneath him, the infinite universe – a dazzling black or deep-blue or kaleidoscopic sea of nebulae, always full of stars that glinted in the depths. A beautiful space. And it was always there – just beyond the edge, just one clumsy step away.

It was a strange and compelling contrast, Arthur felt: the traditionally cartoony, fantastic world of the *Mario* games, replete with all of the magic and character that was unique to that world, against a backdrop of terrifying nothingness. A game that ultimately just asked you to jump from one tiny rock to the next, with no up, no down. And there, always, that dizzying, dizzying, drop. It would kill you, if you fell.

BAD SMELL

That Saturday, at work, Harry received one of those spoof emails. One of those funny ones that people passed on to each other. This one was supposed to be a letter from the manager of a branch of Tesco's explaining to somebody why they'd been banned from the supermarket. The introduction to the email suggested that the catalogue of misdemeanours identified could be used by male shoppers as a 'to-do list' with which to alleviate the boredom of being dragged around by 'the wife' on the weekly food shop.

It wasn't very busy, so Harry checked that there was no manager lurking behind him, looking over his shoulder, and then opened the attachment. (Not that anybody would have to be looking directly over his shoulder to see what he was up to; Harry's screen resolution was set to display everything massively, so that anyone with adequate eyesight could read his screen clearly from a fair distance.) All around him was a combination of noises: the sound of the heavy rain falling against the glass and the sound of people talking quietly, tiredly, into their mouthpieces.

Harry read the letter listlessly, his lips pursed, his eyes flicking along each line in turn. He could see the bits which were supposed to be funny, but nothing elicited a laugh or even a smile. He stopped when he got to the line about leaving a trail of tomato ketchup from the feminine hygiene products to the toilet doors, feeling disproportionately depressed by that, then closed the email. He'd rather just sit and wait for the next call than read things that made him feel so unhappy in such an insidious way.

The beep.

'Good morning – um, afternoon – you're through to Harry. Sorry about that. How can I help?'

'Hi,' the customer said, male with a Lancashire accent. 'Harry, did you say?'

'Yes, that's . . . that's right.'

'Good afternoon, then, Harry.'

The man's voice was measured and yet hard. Harry knew this tone of voice. It meant the customer wanted you to know they were angry, but also wanted you to know that they were big enough not to express that anger.

'Good . . . good afternoon. Could I take your account number, please?'

'Hang on a moment, Harry. I thought you wanted to know how you can help me?'

'Yes. Yes, I do. That's right. But . . . Sorry, how can I help?'

Harry could feel himself sweating and flaking.

238

'Well, Harry. Let me tell you. I've had so much trouble with your company you wouldn't believe it, so you'd better be able to help me. Anger is not the word. Now, then, I was expecting—'

'S-sorry,' Harry said. 'Actually, could I take your account number please? It just means that I can look at the notes. If . . . if you've called about this before, then—'

'Have I called about this before? Ha!'

Harry thought the customer sounded like he was enjoying himself too much to be as angry as he claimed. Maybe, after a long enough period of anger, people stopped actually behaving angrily and just became slightly psychotic.

'No,' Harry said, 'I know you've called before. I just mean . . . I just need, um, please can I have your account number?'

'For God's sake, man! It doesn't bode well for the rest of our conversation if you're getting confused before I've even told you what's wrong! Dear me. Are you ready? My account number is seven-two-five-four-one-one-one-eight-seven-one. Get that?'

'Yes,' Harry said, and actually he had caught the number, even though the man had spoken so fast that Harry was sure he had been trying to make things difficult for him. 'Thank you. I'm just going to look at the notes, if that's . . . if that's OK.'

'Basically I've been expecting a visit from one of your people to establish whether or not my supply is shared by my neighbours. Because, if it *is*, then I might be paying

239

for *their* usage, and that would explain why my bills are so high. Would you agree?'

'Yes,' Harry said quietly, while he waited for the notes page to load on screen.

'But if we *don't* share a supply, then there must be some other problem. Anyway. *God* knows how many times I've rung about this, and *God* knows how many times I've asked for this inspection, but as yet all you've done is disappoint me.'

'I'm just . . . just looking all of this up now, Mr Planer.'

'How do you know my name?'

Harry wasn't sure if the man was being serious.

'I'm . . . I'm looking at your account,' he explained, just in case. 'It shows your name on here.'

Mr Planer did not reply.

'Well,' Harry said, 'I can see . . . I can see that you've rung up lots of times before to try and get this visit arranged.' Harry was scrolling through pages of notes relating to previous calls – one after the other, twice a week more or less, all the same issue.

'I can't tell you how many times,' Mr Planer said. 'And, every time, whoever I speak to refuses to help me.'

'I'll . . . I'll see what I can do,' Harry said, although he could already tell from the notes how this conversation would probably end. 'I can arrange for one of our contractors to call you and make an appointment. If I could just take your phone number, then—'

'Never!' Planer spat. 'I will *not* give you my phone number! You'll pass it on to *God* knows who else, and all those sales people will *never* let me go, will *never* stop ringing. I've been down this road before and, believe you me, I know where that goes and I'm not falling for it again, Harry, oh no, I'm not.'

'You . . . you don't have to give me your phone number,' Harry said, 'but our contractors will need it, if they're going to visit. They won't just accept a request from me without a phone number, because . . . because it's expensive for them to visit and then find there's nobody in or something. That's a . . . it's a wasted visit.'

'I don't *care* how much it costs your company! I'm a paying customer, damn it!'

'S-sorry, Mr . . . Mr Planer,' Harry said. His forehead was wet now and he could smell his own armpits. 'It's not quite the . . . the cost that's the issue. They just . . . they simply . . . they just can't do it without ringing you first. I can't request a visit without giving the phone number.'

'What about people who don't have phones, eh? Eh? What about them?'

'I can't . . . I can't honestly say that anybody without access to a phone has ever rung me up,' Harry said.

'I hope you're not trying to be funny with me, Harry.'

'N-no,' Harry said, confused.

'Do they have a telephone number, these contractors?'

'Yes, they do,' Harry said. 'I was . . . was just about to try and speak to them now, actually. But I should . . . I should say beforehand that their phone line is very busy, so I might not be able to get through.'

'Just sort it out,' Planer said.

'O–OK,' Harry said, and put Planer on hold while he dialled the number for the contractors.

Five minutes later Planer was still on hold, and Harry still hadn't got through to the contractors. He was on hold too, in effect, listening to some on-hold music as inane and frustrating as that to which Planer was probably listening as well. He was about to give up and return to Mr Planer, when he heard something. It sounded like a kind of rattling, metallic laugh in the distance, a long way down the wire.

Harry terminated the outgoing call as soon as he heard that sound. He mopped at his forehead with his shirt-sleeve, then took Planer off hold.

'Hello? Hello, Mr Planer?'

'Still here,' Planer said.

'Sorry . . . sorry about the wait there,' Harry said.

'You'd better have some good news for me after wasting so much of my time.'

'I . . . I'm really sorry, Mr Planer, but I wasn't able to get . . . to get, um . . . to get through to . . . to the . . . to the contractors, so I'm going to have to ask . . . to ask you again for your phone number, or . . . or we won't be able to, um, come and visit your . . . your property to . . . to . . .'

'Right,' Planer said. 'Right, then, Harry. This is what's going to happen, OK? I'm going to take your name, and then you're going to sort this out, OK? I'm going to take your name and hang up, and then you're going to get

242

back in touch with me to let me know the next steps. So, then, what's your surname, Harry?'

'Miller,' Harry said.

'Harry Miller,' Planer said. 'OK, then, Harry Miller. I'll expect a call from you within the week. And if I ever have to ring back, it'll be you I'm asking for, OK?'

'OK,' Harry said. 'But I don't have your—'

The phone went dead. Harry quickly logged out and put a damp forehead in his wet hands. He felt like he was dissolving. His brain had become totally useless. He took his headset off and placed it on the desk and he saw that he was shaking. He stood up, and saw everybody else quickly look away, and he wondered how loudly he had been wittering, stammering, blathering.

He went to the toilets and locked himself in a cubicle for a few minutes.

While Harry was away from his desk, a newish employee who was sitting nearby – Oscar – rushed over and unscrewed the small metal microphone from the end of the arm of Harry's headset. He looked furtively around him and, encouraged by the stifled laughter and witless gestures of a couple of his team-mates, stuck the mic down the back of his trousers and pushed it into the puckered aperture of his anus. He then removed it and screwed it back on to the headset arm, gave his team-mates the thumbs-up and went off to wash his hands.

*

Harry returned to his desk after composing himself, and put his headset back on. He lowered the arm so that the microphone was positioned in front of his mouth, ready for the next call, and logged back into his phone. He grimaced. He could smell shit. There was no doubt about it. Shit. He panicked, started to stand up, but stopped himself in case somehow the smell was coming from him and its source was visible on his clothing. It smelled strong, so it *must* be coming from him. He wouldn't be at all surprised if his body had humiliated him in this way. He wouldn't be surprised if, in the sweaty, flapping state he'd got into, he'd let a little bit go. He knew his arse felt damp, anyway, and had thought that was just sweat; but what if it was more than that? He realised he was vigorously shaking his head and stopped it. He looked up and saw that people nearby were staring at him and laughing. They must be able to smell it too.

Fuck's sake. Harry could feel tears rising. This was intolerable.

He shrugged his ratty little coat on and stood up and started walking quickly away from his desk. The headset caught and pulled, and he ripped it from his head.

'Fuck – fucking thing!' he said, and threw it on to the floor. Then he left the room and went down the stairs and exited the building.

It was only as he was walking past Tesco's that he realised he couldn't smell shit any more. But he didn't know what that meant.

Water was bucketing down out of the sky. Harry sloped

244

along the harbour towards home, still feeling fragmented, still feeling incoherent and brain-dead. The seagulls, with their mad shrieking, seemed to be making more sense than his own thoughts.

As he climbed the many steps up to the estate, an idea solidified in Harry's thoughts. *A hot shower.* Yes.

That's what he would do.

Realisation

Arthur was looking out of his bedroom window at the rain, jacket half on, when he heard the front door go. He frowned. Dad shouldn't be back from work this early. He listened to his father ascend the stairs and then slam the bathroom door.

'Dad?' Arthur shouted, moving out on to the green-carpeted landing. 'Are you OK? Have you come home sick?'

'Yeah,' Harry shouted back. At least, that's what it sounded like through the door. 'Fine.'

'I'm going out,' Arthur said.

'Fine,' Harry said. 'Fine. Fine. Fine.'

Arthur stretched out his arms and flattened himself against the slick, streaming exterior curve of the light-house, his cheek cold against the wetness, the water running down his neck and under the collar of his jacket.

The rain splashed down heavily, roughening the surface of the sea and dancing across the pitted stonework of the pier. The sky was a whitish-grey, not the dark sultry grey of storm clouds, just the colour of frosted grass maybe, or the colour of bone. The sea itself was the colour of bruises, a less vibrant version of the palette that had been evident in that other landscape – or, as Arthur had been thinking of it, 'the Scape'.

The Scape was not under water. Arthur realised that much now. He thought about it again, as the violent precipitation plastered him against the bright white and red of the lighthouse. He closed his eyes. He had needed to move slowly, when he was there, but that wasn't due to any resistance from water. It almost wasn't physical movement as such at all, but it was as if his mind had been floating over the green and purple surface of spidery starfish and pulsing tentacles. There had been a sky, of sorts, and the City in the distance and – despite the creatures crawling over the ground, so numerous and densely packed as to have maybe even *formed* the ground – his impression had been of a dry place. He had not been aware of having to breathe. And yet there had been a solidity to it all: a tangibility.

Arthur turned and walked to the edge of the pier and looked down at the water splashing up in the rain. The Scape was not the sea, but there was still some kind of connection; some kind of echo or reflection of one in the other.

When Arthur got home the shower was running, and he could hear the voice of his father from the bathroom. As he went upstairs, Arthur could see that the bathroom door was actually open. Steam billowed out, floating down the top few steps, and leaving moisture on the landing walls.

Harry was singing weakly. He was singing something excruciating by some terrible rock band from the eighties, but Arthur didn't know what.

'You OK, Dad?' he called, from just outside the bathroom door.

'Son?' Harry replied and the shower was suddenly turned off. 'Is that you?'

'Yeah,' Arthur said, placing his hand nervously on the door. He was aware of his pulse speeding up.

'Oh, son,' Harry said, 'it's been an awful day. Put the kettle on, eh? Must be time for . . . for Paxman.'

'It's only half past three,' Arthur said, 'and it's Saturday.'

'Well,' Harry said, 'it's still been bloody awful.'

'What's happened?'

Harry didn't reply.

'Dad,' Arthur persisted, 'I'm going to open the door. I don't think you're well.'

He waited a moment and then entered the room.

Harry was sitting in the bath, his shoulders shaking, his skin blotchy. He evidently hadn't pulled the shower curtain across, and water was everywhere. It was all over the bathroom floor, the hand-towel they used as a bathmat almost floating, the whole room sodden and miserable.

The plughole was partly blocked with loose plaster that the shower had washed away from the now exposed section of the wall, which meant that the bath itself was nearly half-full with grit and soapy water. The wall, where the tiles had been, was now black and disgusting.

The worms were there, too, of course. When he approached the bath, Arthur baulked on seeing them all wriggling in the water and clinging to his father's skin. He didn't dare look too closely at the wall itself, for fear of spotting some as-yet unseen writhing knot, evidence of some kind of habitat cluster.

After what felt like an age of hesitation, he grabbed his father under the armpits and hauled him up.

PART FOUR

ARTEMIS AT WORK

Artemis worked best when there was nobody else there. He tended to haunt the call centre through the night and on Sundays. This was a Sunday. This was the Sunday after the Saturday on which that flaky fuckwit Harry had thrown a pissy-fit and run screaming from the office. Well, he needn't think of coming back.

Artemis was going through the head count with a red pen, comparing names against call-quality scores and then cross-referencing with average handling times. He ticked people off as he went.

'Dozy cunt,' he would mutter as he did so. 'Uppity fucker. Daydreamy bastard. Egotistical twit. Intolerable bitch.'

Anybody observing might have found it curious that Artemis had such vehement personal feelings towards each and every employee who was, by his draconian standards, underperforming. The fact was that Artemis had vehement personal feelings about everybody, underperforming or not.

The vacant floor stretched away from him in all directions. Empty chairs, desktop terminals with blank screens. The place was quiet. The only sound was the terrible, interminable precipitation outside. It never seemed to end here. Of course, obviously, sometimes there would be nothing falling from the sky; it was just that Artemis always seemed to miss those rare moments.

After a time spent slashing the head count, he stood up and went for a walk around the centre: the working floor, the pods, the training rooms, the meeting rooms. In one meeting room he stared out of the east-facing windows and watched waves of white hailstones billowing across the railway platforms and the small scrappy skate park beyond them.

One thing – just one more awful thing – about this awful place was how the seasons seemed different. It could be cold in summer or hot in winter, which was confusing. The bizarre weather just kept happening. Like hailstones. What month was it, anyway? Artemis scowled and turned away.

Besides, these things didn't really matter any more.

Back at his desk, Artemis fiddled with a stack of paper and then fell idle. He had a phone call to make, and he knew it. He started breathing deeply in order not to panic. After a couple of minutes of this he picked up the phone and dialled.

His call was answered almost immediately, as expected. 'Artemis,' said the voice.

'Good afternoon,' Artemis said. 'Is all well?'

'What do you want?'

'A potential body has been identified.'

'Good. When will you start communicating with the interstitial entity directly?'

'As soon as I've worked out how.'

'Work it out, Artemis,' the voice said. It sounded like the sound of somebody whispering into his ear, but overlaid across an old vinyl recording of the same words. 'You don't get paid just to have your fun with the bodies. We have now made contact with the Interstice, but you need to open that line of communication with the entity. And keep it open.'

'No, I'm sorry. I'll be communicating as soon as I can.'

'We know what you've been doing. You can do what you want with the bodies, but don't get neglectful of the whole.'

'I won't,' Artemis said. Sweat cooled and then ran down his face. The knuckles of his right hand, which gripped the telephone receiver, shone white.

'When necessary, the operation can be moved elsewhere. An alternative location has been established.'

'What? Where?'

'No *where*, Artemis. You know better than that.'

'You're talking about the AI,' Artemis said.

'Yes.'

'The calls will be dealt with by the AI.'

'Yes.'

'By my wife.'

'By the voice of your wife. Yes.' The voice paused, and there was a sound like it was clearing some kind of throat or other. 'In short, the entire business of that site can be redirected at a moment's notice. Everything is ready.'

'Redirected to what? The recordings?'

'Yes.'

'I didn't know we were ready for this.'

'We are ready.'

'Where is the AI based?'

'What do you mean?'

'Where are the computers? Where is the server?'

'There are multiple servers, and back-up servers. The AI exists on those. More accurately, it exists between them. This is how we made contact with the Interstice itself.'

'And the customers won't know?'

'Of course not.'

Artemis nodded. He thought back to the years – no exaggeration – his wife had spent recording her voice. Going through dictionaries, recording a word at a time. Over and over again to ensure variety. To ensure it sounded authentic. Real.

The last few years of her life. Alone in that small room at Head Office. Jesus Christ.

'I'm still not entirely sure why this contingency plan is required,' Artemis said.

'There is one other thing,' the voice said. 'The increase in interstitial activity may be producing some effect elsewhere.'

'What?'

'We believe there may be something in the sea.'

'What?!' Artemis said, standing up and putting his left hand to his forehead.

But there was no answer. The line had gone dead.

Outside the hailstones grew fatter and fatter, and then just stopped.

What It Is and Stuff

The sound was a shock. Yasmin's first thought was of an insect, and she jumped in surprise and fell out of the armchair. A gigantic fucking insect trapped inside an envelope, and vibrating fit to shake all of its chitin off. But it was just somebody at the door, pressing the buzzer.

The air was thick with joss-stick smoke. Yasmin realised that she had been drowsing. That Sunday-evening crash. She was wearing a jumper way too big for her – it came down almost to her knees – and leggings, and she felt like she was sprawling and shapeless. The buzzer was still buzzing, violently. It was, to be honest, an unfamiliar sound.

'Yeah,' she said. 'Yeah, hang on.' Even though there was no way the person at the front door of her building would be able to hear her, seeing as it was two flights of stairs down. She considered going to the window to look out and see who it was, but that would only mean that whoever it was would be kept waiting for even longer. She dithered and then darted across the room to pick up the telephone-receiver-like thing mounted on the wall.

'Hello?' she said.

'Hi, Yasmin? It's Arthur.'

'Arthur? Come on up.'

'Is it open?'

'Yeah,' Yasmin said, pressing the button that unlocked the front door. 'It's open. Come on up.'

Yasmin glanced at the clock on the wall. This was the first time Arthur had visited her flat on his own. She clicked the kettle on and then went to put out the original joss-stick, while brushing some floaty hair away from her tired eyes.

'I wanted to talk to you about what I saw,' Arthur said. The two of them sat on the floor, as Yasmin only had one armchair, and each cradled a mug of tea. Something calming and ambient was playing on the stereo, but Yasmin didn't know what it was. It was a compilation CD that some ex-boyfriend had made for her, to which she had long ago lost the track listing. 'I saw another world, Yasmin.'

'What about your father?' Yasmin asked. She could not let go of the image of Harry distraught in the bath along with the worms. 'Are you sure he'll be OK?'

'He'll be all right.' Arthur nodded. 'He just needs some rest. He's been in bed since Saturday. I think he's had a cold or something, as well.'

'It sounds like he needs help.'

Arthur shifted his weight from one buttock to the other, and bobbed his head around like a little bird. 'He'll be OK,' he said.

If Arthur thought he was being subtle in his evasiveness then he was wrong, but Yasmin decided against pushing the topic.

'I wanted to talk to you about what I saw,' Arthur said again.

'The landscape?' Yasmin asked.

'Yeah,' Arthur said. He bit his lip and looked around wide-eyed, not seeing but thinking. 'I call it the Scape,' he said.

'Full of goats?' Yasmin joked, smiling.

'What?' Arthur asked, smiling back, but uncomprehendingly.

'Never mind. It was a joke, kind of.'

'Oh! Scapegoats!'

'That's it,' Yasmin said.

'Jesus, Yasmin, I'm sorry. Being friends with me must sometimes be like being friends with a child.'

'Not really,' Yasmin said.

'No goats,' Arthur continued, 'but creatures, almost. Like being under water. I once saw this thing on TV: this footage of a dead seal on the ocean floor. The footage was all speeded up, but basically it showed how the whole body, and all of the ground around it, got covered in small animals and . . . *organisms* that came to feed on it. I mean *covered*, like the whole scene was thick with tiny starfish and weird eels and long-legged crabs, all crawling all over each other and burrowing in and out of the seal and . . . It was really scary, Yasmin. It was really horrible, and, uh . . . um . . .'

Yasmin knew that when Arthur's mother's body had finally been recovered, the corpse had been picked almost entirely clean. She guessed that this was in the back of Arthur's mind as he spoke. She guessed that this was why he'd stopped, and was now wiping his eyes.

'The ground, Yasmin, it was like that. It was like the sea floor in that TV footage – moving, and alive. You know, like some of the walls in the old *Doom* games? Once you get to Hell, and the walls are supposed to be fleshy or something, and they're moving? The ground was like that.'

'Arthur,' Yasmin said, 'it sounds really pretty fucking awful.'

'It wasn't as awful as I'm making it sound,' Arthur said. 'The thing is, I want to go back.'

'What do you mean?' Yasmin said.

'Yasmin,' Arthur said, 'this is a real place I'm talking about! It's a place you can *go* to. I want to talk to you about it because you're clever, so I thought maybe we could think about what it is and stuff.'

'OK,' Yasmin said. She put her now-empty mug down and stood up. 'I'm going to put the kettle back on. I'm sorry, I didn't realise . . . I haven't been sure all this time whether or not you've been talking literally or figuratively.'

'Literally,' said Arthur. He waved his hands around. 'It's all literal.'

'Do you want tea or coffee?'

'Tea, please.'

'I'm going to have coffee,' Yasmin said. 'I need to wake myself up a bit.'

Yasmin had a laptop with a broadband connection. This was not unusual in itself, but it was something Arthur and Harry did not have, and so far Arthur had not been able to look online for anything in the way of explanation. He'd tried to get on the internet at work, but the firewalls had blocked him. And anyway, he felt like he wanted some company for it. Somebody to help him sort the helpful from the nonsense.

'It's difficult to know what to search for,' Yasmin said, fingers hovering over the keyboard, the search-engine field sitting empty in the middle of the screen. She typed 'world inside telephony system' and the search returned lots of telephony-system consultancy companies and technical websites. She searched for 'telephone limbo', and the results were equally useless. She tried 'interstitial world' which brought back dictionary websites and medical pages about interstitial cystitis, whatever that was.

They spent ages trying to find something useful. Yasmin was well aware that real research involved more than trawling the internet, but the public library wouldn't be open. Arthur paced around behind her, suggesting things to try, swinging around a cricket bat that Yasmin usually kept by the bed in case of intruders. 'Informational systems world,' he would suggest, or 'data landscape' or 'hidden reality'.

After a while, Yasmin was trying things like 'new world hidden information structures alternative reality', but still to no avail.

'I know we're not finding anything useful,' Arthur said, 'but I feel like by doing this we've kind of worked out what it is I'm trying to describe.'

'I know what you mean,' Yasmin said. 'Fucking hell, though, some of this stuff is a bit heavy for a school night.'

'Sometimes I wonder what I'd be capable of, if that place – work – didn't drain me,' Arthur said. 'Sometimes, when I'm not there, I feel almost intelligent.'

'Work guts you,' Yasmin said. 'We're all capable of great things, but work uses that capability up.'

'True,' Arthur said. By this point, he was looking out of the window at the sea.

'Speaking of work,' Yasmin said, 'we should do a bit more digging there. See what we can find out.'

HARRY'S PHONE CALLS

Harry never stopped to reflect on it, but it was strange, really, that Rebecca only rang when Arthur was out at work. If only Arthur were at home when she rang, then his son would be able to answer the phone and hear for himself that Harry was absolutely not imagining the voice. He'd passed the phone over, of course, in the past, on those occasions when Arthur came home and Harry was on the phone to Rebecca, but Arthur refused to listen. He had taken the receiver once, and spoken into it, but Rebecca had not replied; in fact, when Arthur had passed it back to Harry, the line was dead.

'It's no wonder he doesn't believe me,' Harry complained.

'Don't think I believe you,' Pauline said.

'Ooh, *I* believe you,' Tiffany said, 'but then I'm a medium.'

The Vine was never that full on a Sunday night. Harry, Tiffany and – unusually – Bracket sat at the bar. Yorkie, too, had a bar stool to himself, which – unbeknownst to anybody, he was urinating on. The worn green cushion just soaked up the liquid. Pauline stood behind the bar, leaning on it with her elbows, her mass of curly brown hair flopping forward over her red, worn face.

'You're a what?' Harry asked.

'A medium.'

'Look like a small to me,' Harry said.

'Ooh!' Tiffany said, and she started giggling. 'You awful man!'

Harry gave a watery smile, as if his flirting had been accidental. Actually, it had been accidental. Sometimes when drunk, and especially in the company of women, he just said things. Really stupid things. What a stupid fucking cretin he was.

Pauline gave an over-dramatic roll of the eyes and shook her head.

'A medium?' Bracket said. 'Really?'

'Call yourself a manager?' Tiffany said. 'Don't know the first thing about me, eh?'

'I'm sorry,' Bracket said.

Bracket was drunk. Bracket was really very drunk. He had left the house after Isobel had fallen asleep on the sofa at about six o' clock. He wondered if maybe she was depressed. Or maybe she was just perfectly content to not communicate. Maybe she was very happy. Who knew? Anyway, he'd gone out to walk the dog, and somehow ended up here, at the Vine. The haunt of real drinkers. And what's more, he was enjoying it.

'Shame that I can't just talk to any old body up there in the afterlife,' Tiffany said, 'otherwise I'd ask your Rebecca why she won't talk to young Arthur. He's a great lad, your Arthur, Harry.'

'I know,' Harry said. 'He's the greatest.'

'Good at his job, too,' Bracket said.

'I'm very proud of him,' Harry said.

'Maybe she gets too upset to talk to him,' Tiffany said.

Bracket wasn't sure what was going on. It sounded like Harry was claiming that he talked to his dead wife on the phone, and Tiffany was saying that this was OK, this was possible. He wanted to tell them that this was not possible. Maybe ghosts did exist, but not like this. Surely not like this. Other people were sitting at tables elsewhere in the pub, and were probably having conversations that actually meant something.

'What do you talk about,' Bracket asked, 'when Rebecca rings you up? What do you talk about?'

'All sorts.' Harry shrugged. 'Can be anything. She starts by asking how I am, and what I've been up to – she always asks me those things. And I always tell her I'm fine. And then I tell her about my day. And it just kind of goes on from there.'

Patent Leather

The weekly communication was issued every Monday. Arthur looked forward to it in a perverse kind of way, because it was always so badly written and so full of errors that it was almost funny. This week's was no disappointment, as he found himself reading and re-reading one sentence:

This is primarily as a result of failure against service levels and abandonment rates where performance on both over-loaded and other causes is poor.

He couldn't work out if it made sense or not; it either didn't make sense at all, or he was being very, very stupid. Probably the former. Yasmin was convinced that half of the communications, directives, initiatives, training, briefings, etcetera – anything that came from higher management – were deliberately nonsensical to confuse the front-line staff so much that blame for every conceivable failure could then be loaded on to them.

Not that this was really necessary, for senior managers seemed to face no long-term consequences for their actions. Anyway their career progression seemed to work differently. They just floated from one role to another, one company to another, like massive self-aware Zeppelins built for the higher reaches of the atmosphere. The upper echelons. It appeared to be an entirely different world up there. Of course, maybe Arthur and Yasmin and all of the other customer advisers were wrong in their perception of the way these things worked, but as yet nobody had noticed anything to suggest so.

So the communication was usually almost funny. But only ever *almost*. It was, rather, on the boundary between 'funny' and 'pathetic'.

After reading this latest communication, Arthur searched for another call to listen to and assess. The assessments were done by quota: every customer adviser had to have a certain number of their calls assessed per month. Arthur chose one by Victor. Victor was the call centre's only member of staff with a discernible foreign accent – Indian, in his case.

The call was good. Victor was good. Things only started to go a bit off-script when the customer was put on hold. Of course, what a lot of customers didn't realise was that sometimes when they thought they were on hold, the customer adviser had merely muted their mic and could hear everything the customer was saying. As could anybody listening to a recording of the call.

'Bloody call centre's in India, innit?' the customer was

saying to somebody in the background. 'I mean he's tryin'
his best, but they don't understand over there, do they?
I'm not being racist, but they don't understand our culture
or owt.'

Arthur wasn't sure what culture the customer was
talking about, or how exactly it was relevant. These things
were often said, though, and race cropped up as a topic
of conversation pretty frequently in telephone calls across
the site. 'Oh, it's nice to get somebody English for a change,'
was the usual line – the usual starting point.

On the call Arthur was now listening to, the customer
was wittering on about outsourcing and cheap labour and
strong accents when Victor un-muted the mic and spoke.

'We're actually based in the UK, sir,' he said. 'I am
English.'

There was a silence.

'Oh right,' the customer said. Then, after a long pause,
'They tell you to say that, do they? Think we can't tell?'

Victor hung up then. Justifiably too, Arthur thought,
but of course you weren't supposed to terminate a call
without warning the customer, and so Victor should be
marked down for that.

And of course, for all the customer knew, the call centre
could indeed be based in India. Could be based in fucking
Siberia, the bottom of the sea, or a network of caves in
South America. Didn't make him right about any of the
other stuff he spouted, but the truth was that there was
no way of knowing the whereabouts of the people that
you were speaking to. They could be anywhere and the

scary thing was that it didn't make the slightest difference. Their only location, in any meaningful sense of the word, was inside the networks – just rafts of signals, of ones and zeroes, drifting down the wires and emerging from the telephones of all of the customers.

Arthur raised his hands to remove his headset as soon as he heard it. That voice again. The voice he'd heard in the Scape.

'Arthur?' it said. It was now coming out of the headset, which meant that it was coming out of the phone. 'Arthur? Are you there?'

And then it seemingly wasn't coming out of the headset at all. It was in the air; it was being spoken and heard directly, as if the originator were there alongside him. Arthur took the headset off and stood up quickly and looked around.

He was alone. The call centre was empty. Not just of people, but of everything. In fact it was not a call centre at all. It was just an empty room of the same size and shape, with blank, smooth, grey walls that looked cold to the touch. The floor and the ceiling were grey, too. Everything was the same, uniform colour, apart from the light that came in through the windows, which was purple.

Arthur knew where he was. He was in the city that he'd seen: the City. He knew that for sure. He moved to a window and looked out.

The streets and the exterior walls of the other buildings were made out of the same gunship-grey substance. They were untextured and featureless, apart from the regularly spaced windows, and even the windows were not windows so much as smoothly edged apertures opening into rooms that, Arthur assumed, were identical to the one in which he stood. All of the buildings were also identical, apart from their varying heights. They were the same width, the same shape, the same design. The colours and the lines were exactly the same as those of the computer system they used to manage customers' billing accounts.

Arthur felt a strange hand crawling through his stomach.

The City was the billing system, wasn't it? For a brief moment he was fully certain that each building corresponded to a record of a building in the database. Then the moment passed, and he was certain of nothing.

Arthur gripped the windowsill. The street in front was quite narrow and, when he looked down, he saw there the same pulsating organic matter that he'd witnessed on his first visit to the Scape. So he was definitely back there again. The street was illuminated by bright orbs emitting that same purple light. They seemed to be attached to the walls of the buildings, although Arthur couldn't be sure. He looked up into the ill sky, and could see some kind of small dark speck moving far, far above.

Turning back to face the room, Arthur saw a door in the middle of the wall opposite the window. Going outside wasn't an appealing prospect, though.

'Hello?' he said.

'Arthur,' said the voice.

'Whales!' Arthur blurted, without meaning to, and

without thinking. 'Last time I was here, I saw whales!' He ran his hands over his face. He did not feel either hot or cold but his skin was coated with a layer of oily sweat.

'This is the Interstice,' the voice said. 'It is in between. It is in between various places. It is linked to the planes of your telephony systems. It is where all of the voices are when they are in between telephones. It is linked to deep waters – the place through which the Ancient Egyptians believed all waters were connected. It is linked to other places, too, Arthur, but the deep waters are where the whales come from. The whales exist both here and in their own waters. There are other things that can move from one place to the other but I, alas, cannot.'

Questions crowded Arthur's brain. 'Why whales?' he asked, panicking. He looked around the room, staring hard at every surface, trying to make sure that he was alone. For some reason, he had to keep talking. He had to keep that voice occupied.

'The great whales can do many things, Arthur.'

'What else can travel from the water?' Arthur asked. He started moving towards the door, slowly.

'There are spirits that can travel through the Interstice, from one place to another. From somewhere else into the waters.'

'Somewhere else?'

'Somewhere else. When they make it through to your world, they occupy other bodies. Bodies of things they find crawling across the bottom of the sea.'

'Who are these spirits?'

'They are the dead.'

The question Arthur had been about to ask – *Where is 'somewhere else'?* – faltered on his lips. The dead? He found himself at the top of a staircase and, again, it was made out of the same grey matter. The same gunmetal grey colour, exactly, as the screens he wandered amidst every day at work.

'Where do the dead come from?' he asked.

'The souls of the dead live beyond the borders,' the voice said. 'Not every body has a soul, of course, because some people just rot and then are gone. The souls, though – some of them find their way here.'

'Are there any here right now?' he asked.

'With you? With me? No. But in the Interstice, yes. And there is nothing to stop the stronger ones – the most recently released – from journeying through the Interstice to other places. By the telephones. The water. There is nothing to stop them but they have little motivation. They are sluggish things.'

Arthur thought about his mother. How recent was recent? Her soul must be relatively recently released, if all the souls from all of history were out there. Maybe she was still strong. Maybe she *was* ringing his dad. But then, no. Why were the dead not always telephoning?

'The souls must find some kind of host body in your world,' the voice continued. 'Some kind of shell to carry them. It is a difficult process.'

Arthur still hadn't seen anybody who might have spoken. The voice sounded like it was getting closer. And like some kind of Impressionist painting, the closer it was, the less clearly defined its composite elements were. It sounded disparate and rough, and no longer reassuring. He started to run down the steps, following each flight round right-angled corners until, after a couple of levels, he saw before him an archway leading to the outside. He barrelled through it, and stumbled to a halt on the spongy surface of the open ground.

The sky softly hissed above him: a ragged tissue of whispered static and distant, indistinct voices.

The purple light was cold, the steely colour of the surrounding buildings was forbidding, and the weird, slithery rustle beneath his feet was nauseating. Arthur did not want to be here. If this was the afterlife – an idea that now seemed less plausible than it first had – then he did not want to die. Not ever.

He slapped himself across the cheek, but without effect.

He was about halfway between one end of the street and the other end, and he didn't know which way to head. He didn't know where he was going. He only wanted to get out of the City. He'd quite liked this place the first time he was here, and the only difference really was that then he'd been out in the middle of nowhere, out in the middle of some great, empty plain. The City, though . . . the City was threatening.

He chose to head left. No sooner had he taken a few steps when he saw a figure appear at the end of the road, about two hundred metres away.

'Arthur,' it said, 'you're back.'

The voice seemed louder than he'd heard it before, and harsher; like something being played too loudly for the speakers to transmit effectively. The figure was tall, dressed all in black. It moved in a stilted manner, as if it were from an old stop-motion B-movie.

Arthur started to feel light-headed and realised that he'd stopped breathing. When he started again, he inhaled greedily, not able to absorb enough air. Where was he? Where was his body? He bent over double and put his hands on his knees. He crouched down and coughed. He just could not breathe deeply enough. When he looked up again, the figure was moving slowly towards him. He could see that its legs were bizarrely long and its torso very small. Its head appeared to be almost perfectly triangular, but with the apex pointing downwards. The purple light reflected off it cleanly, like it was dressed entirely in patent leather.

Arthur groaned and stood up. He turned around and, without fully recovering his breath, started running again. He started trying to slow his breathing: four seconds in, four seconds out. Four long, slow seconds in; four long, slow seconds out. He picked up speed.

'Why are you running, Arthur?' came the voice.

Arthur shook his head but did not reply. He did not really know why. He knew that he was scared, but not why he was scared. There was no reason to believe that the thing meant him any harm.

At the end of the street he risked a backwards glance. The thing was gaining on him, somehow, despite the fact that it moved jerkily, as if its legs were injured. Its arms were waving about like tentacles, but it was close enough for Arthur to see that they really were arms.

'Come back, Arthur,' it said.

Still, Arthur kept on running. He turned right into another street that looked exactly the same as the one he'd just left. It was longer, though, and actually had a slight curve to it. And who were all these buildings for, anyway? Was the thing behind him the only citizen of this whole place? It felt that way.

Without looking behind him, he darted left into a small alleyway. It was darker in there because there were none of those purple lights. He kept his speed up, the things coating the ground crunching slightly beneath his feet. He did not assume for a moment that he had not been seen entering the alley, so there was no point trying to move quietly just yet. He looked behind him again and saw the thing – the patent-leather thing – silhouetted at the end of the alley. Then he ran straight into the wall.

A dead end. *Oh no. Oh no. Fuck. Oh fuck.* Arthur started shaking, still lying there on the ground. He tried to stand up but his legs would not support him. He could feel his body trying to dump all the excess weight from his bowels in preparation for either fight or flight, but he kept his arse tightly clenched. Even now, even here, where there were no other people, he could not allow that. His teeth were gritted and his pale skin poured sweat. But where exactly were his bowels, his teeth and his skin? Were they all really here? It felt like they were all there with him, along with his mind, in this hell-hole.

He rolled on to his back and saw the thing was advancing. It did not have a triangular head, as he'd first thought, just a collar that rose up high behind the top of its head. Its head was actually the same shape as a human head, but, like the rest of its body, it seemed to be entirely coated – laminated almost – in patent leather. It was not actually patent leather, Arthur realised, just something that looked like it. The thing wore a cloak made of the same material, which flared down behind it almost to the ground.

Instead of a face, it had various slits and slots that looked randomly placed. Its spine, if it possessed a spine, seemed to move of its own accord, for the creature seemed to struggle to keep its torso steady. It flopped forwards and backwards constantly, as if something that should be holding it upright were broken.

Its legs were very long, but when Arthur looked carefully, that wasn't quite all – they appeared to be longer than they were because, where its groin should have been, a square section of the creature had been cut away.

Arthur pushed himself backwards until his back rested against the wall and his legs were stretched out in front of him. The creature's torso flopped forward as it bent down towards him and started to speak.

The ensuing sound was so loud that Arthur screwed up his eyes and slammed his hands into his ears. That didn't make much of a difference though, it didn't really block out the sound. Any words were unintelligible, because the sound was now just a roaring wind of distortion, a total cacophony of howls and screams and shrieks. Then it stopped.

The creature tilted its head as if awaiting some kind of response.

THE PANOPTICON

During office hours, on a weekday, everybody more or less had their own desk. Yasmin's usual one was in the group of desks between the command centre and the bank of desks in where Arthur was, and she sat with her back to him. This meant that when Artemis suddenly stood up, wide-eyed, holding his still-open laptop in both hands like a tea tray, and started bounding across the call centre floor, Yasmin at first assumed that he was heading for her. She had never before seen him move so quickly or with such urgency, and she froze up completely, terrified that she had unknowingly done something awful and was about to be punished accordingly.

It was only when Artemis sped past her that she turned around to see that Arthur had tipped sideways from his chair and landed, twitching, on the green-carpeted floor. Lots of people were standing up now, pointing and whispering and looking very concerned. Yasmin immediately made her phone 'busy', meaning that she wouldn't receive any calls coming through, and she stood up too, suddenly cold.

'Back on the phones!' Artemis bellowed, as he weaved between the desks. 'Back to your calls! It's nothing! He'll be fine!'

Upon reaching Arthur's desk, Artemis put his laptop down and went to pick him up.

The laptop was left open.

Bums off seats, Yasmin thought automatically, despite herself. *Control, Alt, Delete.* You haven't locked your laptop, Artemis.

But as soon as she'd thought it, Artemis himself seemed to remember the laptop.

'Dean!' he cried, standing up again from where Arthur lay, 'Dean, pick Arthur up and get him into one of the pods!' He then turned back to his laptop and gathered it into his arms.

'Sh-should we be moving h-him?' Dean asked, moving forward.

'Yes!' Artemis shouted right in Dean's face. 'Of course we should be moving him!'

'Oh . . . OK,' Dean said, nodding, and then bent to pick Arthur up. He got one arm under Arthur's knees and the other one under his shoulders, and then tried to stand up. But Arthur, thin as he was, must have been too heavy for Dean's equally spindly frame, and they both tipped forward, Arthur's head bouncing off the desk.

A collective gasp floated upwards from the assembled audience.

Artemis nearly dropped the laptop then, but caught it in time. He turned and put it back on the desk. When he turned back, his face was bright red.

'Dean!' Artemis was roaring now. 'You clumsy fucking spastic! Get the fuck out of the fucking way, you pale fucking bag of fucking shite!' He crouched down and hoisted Arthur up easily.

'S-sorry,' Dean said, in tears now, snot glistening around his spotty mouth.

Artemis didn't reply. He just shouldered past him and marched off with his burden in the direction of the pods.

Yasmin looked around. There were no other managers on the command centre. They all seemed to be gravitating towards the pods, from various locations all over the floor.

Yasmin quickly removed her headset and, while everybody's attention was still held by the receding figure of Artemis, sneaked over and grabbed the man's laptop. She waited until Artemis had rounded the corner, presumably to enter one of the pods, then took off after him, her fingers sweaty against the black plastic casing of the machine she held. She was banking on everybody assuming that she was taking the laptop back to Artemis – and, sure enough, nobody challenged her. She passed various managers already on their way back from the pods, who, she guessed, Artemis must have sent away.

Once she arrived amongst the glass partitions and blinds of the pods themselves, she ducked into the first unoccupied one she found and closed the door. She could hear Arthur murmuring deliriously in the adjacent pod, and

Artemis's low voice responding, but he was talking very quietly and she couldn't make out a word.

She didn't waste time trying to read the emails on his laptop. That would be too risky, she reasoned; he was bound to realise any moment that he'd left it unattended and come looking. Instead, she just forwarded to herself all the emails she could see that had come from an Interext email account and then swiftly, assuredly, deleted the same forwarded emails from the 'Sent' mailbox and, finally, from the 'Deleted' mailbox.

Artemis must have been watching Arthur, she thought. He had stood up *so quickly*. Of course, the command centre was designed that way: a raised platform on which a varying selection of managers would sit, each facing a different direction, to be able to observe the whole extent of the floor.

A panopticon, that was what it was. The point was not that managers would see everything that went on, because inevitably they would sometimes be looking at their computer screens or their notebooks, or whatever. The point was that the staff out on the floor would know that they were potentially being observed, and so would behave themselves even if there was nobody actually watching. The original Panopticon had been a prison, hadn't it, with the wardens stationed in a central office from which all of the corridors and all of the cells radiated? Yasmin wasn't sure. Couldn't totally remember. Something like that, anyway. It was the principle behind CCTV: the knowledge that you might be visible helps shape your behaviour, because there is the possibility that you are being watched and judged. It doesn't matter if nobody views the footage. It doesn't even matter if the camera is not recording. It doesn't even matter if you can't see a camera at all. You just know that it might be there and it is the potential that matters. It was like a corrupt inversion of Berkeley's Law, which was a philosophical dictum that had fascinated her during the time she spent studying for her A levels. She would still find it scrawled in her own handwriting on old textbooks and folders, again and again and again: 'To be is to be perceived.'

To be is to be perceived.

She was thinking about this, about to knock on the door of the adjacent pod and hand Artemis his (now password-protected) laptop, when she noticed – with an icy, gut-wrenching sensation in her stomach, before the onset of any cerebral reaction – the small, glassy eye of a webcam gazing at her from its mount within the plastic framing of the laptop screen. She felt horror slacken her face and, shaking, she slammed the lid of the stupid, stupid fucking computer shut and put it on the floor, then knocked on the pod door and ran back to her desk.

THE SEA NEAR DRIGG

Bony sat in his little hut and thought about one day a long time ago, when he and Arthur were pretty young, really, and Harry had still been sober and had not yet sold the fishing boat. Harry had once been a big fisherman, though you wouldn't know it now, of course.

For Harry's last birthday before Rebecca had died, she had bought him a Fishfinder, a small box with a screen that sent signals down below and told you what was under the water. Harry, Arthur and Bony were taking it out for the first time. They had first got it all set up at one side of the boat, and then motored out, gazing back at the receding shoreline, where Harry's old four-wheel drive stood sentinel on the beach. The weather was not bad, but you couldn't have said it was good either. Good fishing weather probably, but Bony did not know an awful lot about fishing.

Bony remembered the three of them watching the Fishfinder in silence. Rebecca had been dead seven months, maybe. For an hour and a half they sat still and watched it, and drifted, without a bite from the fish or a word between them. Except for the words that swam through Bony's head, at any rate; as to what swam through Harry's and Arthur's he didn't know. Every now and again, they would hear pairs of explosions from further down the coast, from Eskmeals way. Every now and again, a drop of rain would fall. Just one. Bony liked to think it was the same one, coming back round again and again to visit them. Something like a friend. Usually it would land on the skin of his right arm.

Eventually, it was Arthur who spoke. 'If there's so many fish,' he said, looking at the Fishfinder, 'why aren't they biting?'

'They're not fish on that thing,' said Harry.

'Then what's it picking up?' said Arthur.

'Weed,' said Harry.

'Then why aren't our lines getting tangled in it?' said Arthur.

'Well,' said Harry, 'it's bubbles, then.'

'The sea isn't that full of bubbles,' argued Arthur. 'It's got to be fish.'

'Then why aren't they biting?' said Harry.

'Maybe they're scared,' Bony said.

'Scared of what?' said Harry.

'The explosions,' Bony said. 'The weapons-testing.'

'No,' Harry said, 'they've been doing that for years. Makes no difference to the fish. If it made a difference, I'd know it made a difference.'

'The Fishfinder says that the depth is only two feet now, Dad,' said Arthur. 'How can it be only two feet deep when we're this far out?'

'Because it's wrong,' said Harry. 'Turn that shite off. We're moving.'

As their boat had moved through the water, the outboard motor sent short, hard tremors through the hull, the bench and Bony's body, and he thought about all those inland towns and the women in them wearing vibrating knickers or some such. And if he had looked at the shore at exactly that moment, and his line of sight were perfectly perpendicular to the shore, then the point on the shore that he was looking at was the point where that dead whale had washed up all bloated and sad when they were kids. Bony's mum had sent them all off to ride down through the dunes on their bikes, and they had all stood around it taking pictures of the patterns in the skin of the thing. Remember that? A minke whale, it was. Bony had learned that later from *National Geographic*.

He ran his hand over his head. Today was a hot Monday, and his hi-vis jacket felt heavy. It had been a while since he had heard from his mother. His parents had moved to somewhere remote – even more remote – up in Scotland, to look after his father's sick brother. They were the kind of people who liked being in the middle of nowhere.

He was half thinking about giving them a ring, his hand almost on its way to the receiver, when the phone rang.

Bony thought about it for a moment, and then answered.

'Hello?' he said.

'Bony!' Yasmin replied. 'It's happened again – to Arthur. I just thought I should let you know. I really think there's something wrong.'

'What's happened again?'

'He's collapsed. But . . . I don't know. There's more to it. I'm going to send you some emails now. I think we should meet up.'

'OK. OK, yeah, come down after work.'

'I'll be on the five-forty-whatever from Whitehaven. I'll be there just after six.'

'See you then,' Bony said.

'Thanks. Bye.' Yasmin hung up.

Bony put the phone down and sat back in his chair, running his hand over his head again. Outside his cabin, the sun beat down hard. He thought back to his night on the beach. The stars. He closed his eyes, tried not to think about what he'd done.

ESCAPE

Arthur didn't know what to say. The creature was waiting for a response, that much was obvious, but Arthur could not imagine what.

'I'm sorry,' he said.

The creature moved its gleaming visage closer to Arthur's. Behind it, the sky was stained with purple light. Then he felt something tugging at his hair, at his head, and everything went white. He was dimly aware of being carried by somebody. His first thought was his father but, no, whatever was carrying him was far too strong to be Harry.

Full consciousness found Arthur slumped in a chair in one of the pods, with the blinds down. In another chair, Artemis Black sat, observing him intently, a hint of a smile on his face. This reality was barely less threatening than the last.

'What?' Arthur said. 'What? I'm feeling really fucking . . .

really fucking tired.' He could feel something rise within him, getting close to the surface, something that would bring with it total fury.

'What did you see?' Artemis asked.

Arthur narrowed his eyes. 'You know about it?' he said.

'Yes,' Artemis said quietly, 'I know about it. I don't know what it's like, and I don't know what is there, but I know about it.'

'What is it?'

'It is the Interstice,' Artemis replied. 'It is a place. A real place.'

'What? How?'

'Now then,' Artemis said, leaning forward and placing a hand on Arthur's knee, 'you keep asking me questions, but you haven't answered mine yet. Just you answer my question, Arthur.' His fingers dug in around Arthur's kneecap. 'You answer my question now.'

'OK.' Arthur nodded. He felt sweaty and nauseated. 'I will, but let go of my leg, please.'

Artemis let go and sat back. 'Go on,' he said.

Just then there was a knock at the door.

Artemis snapped his head around to look and lifted a finger as if to caution Arthur against speaking. He stood up slowly, silently, and covered the distance to the door in one long stride. He opened it a crack, looked around, looked down, bent to pick up his laptop, then closed the door and returned to his seat, looking slightly puzzled.

'Go on,' he urged again, after sitting back down.

Arthur then started to talk about the Scape – or the

Interstice, as Artemis called it. He was hesitant, uncertain. He stammered and kept putting his hand over his eyes.

They were cut off from the entire world inside that pod. The blinds inside the glass walls were dark grey, and Arthur kept forgetting where they were. More than anything, he felt like they were both trapped in a small glass cube that was suspended high up inside a gigantic, threatening cumulonimbus cloud above some violent ocean.

Arthur told Artemis about the ground. About the sky. The sounds. The City, and the light, and the thing – the patent-leather thing.

When Arthur mentioned the creature, Artemis widened his eyes and grinned like a skull. The expression alarmed Arthur, and something spinning and whirring in the back of his head told him not to elaborate, not to tell Artemis everything. Arthur's voice faltered and he cleared his throat.

'And then I found myself in here,' he said. 'I felt something pulling at my head, and then I found myself in here.'

'Your headset?' Artemis said.

'What?'

'The thing pulling at your head. Could it have been your headset? Dean tried to pick you up and your headset came off. Or it might have been when he dropped you. Either way, do you think that was what you felt?'

'I don't know,' Arthur said. 'I don't know why you

expect me to know anything. I think you know more than I do.'

'Probably,' Artemis said. He was still grinning. The sound of the call centre was faint in the pod, but it was there, in the background: a palimpsest of sound that was all too familiar from the Scape. It was the sound of quiet voices. The sound of the sea.

'Artemis, please,' Arthur said, 'tell me what you know.'

'I can't,' Artemis replied, still grinning. In the gloom of the pod – there was no overhead light – the large man looked terrifying. Even more terrifying than usual, because of the gloom and because of the grin.

'I want to go,' Arthur said.

Artemis didn't say anything.

POTATOFICATION

Diane had rung in sick again. She was sitting, wrapped in a duvet, on the sofa of her parents' house – well, after all it was where she lived – and watching the *Saw* films boxed set. Mondays were the worst days, she reckoned. There was no desolation like Monday. It wasn't that it meant five whole days to go until the weekend – well, it wasn't just that – it was that the beginning of the working week was like a hammer slamming into your brain. Like a hammer that somehow communicated the awful message that all you were doing, really, was waiting now for those two days off at the end of it. You hated getting up early to go to work. You hated being at work. You hated having to go to bed in order to get up to go to work. You got through it all by looking forward to the weekend; that was the *only* way you got through it. Was that really worthwhile at all? Was that as good as life was going to get?

On a Friday you could forget about it, because Fridays were intensely joyful. That was just it, though: troughs and peaks. Long troughs, short peaks. If Diane let herself think about it, the weekends seemed hysterical. Short and desperate and hysterical. It was the same for everybody else, she knew – it wasn't just her, but that made it worse. Was it right to emotionally yo-yo in that way, and not even acknowledge the swings? Was it good for your heart?

That night with Artemis had not been the first time she'd got drunk with a man and ended up regretting it. It was the first time, though, that she'd got drunk with a boss and woken up in the cold blue light of an early coastal morning, in his empty hotel room, with her face and breasts encrusted with his semen. She was assuming it was his. It was a fair assumption. He had left her and gone. To work, she thought.

She had showered to the tortured cries of a seagull echoing through the small extractor fan of the en-suite bathroom, dried herself, dressed herself, and then left the hotel room. Afterwards, she had thought that maybe she should have searched his belongings; looked for something that she could somehow have used to take some kind of revenge on him for being such a horrible fucking bastard. But, at the time, such a thought had never entered her fuzzy, teary, pissed-off, hung-in-shame head. She just rushed down the red-carpeted stairs, past the reception desk, breaking into a slight run, and straight out of the front door.

She hadn't gone into work since, and had been off for nearly a week now. Another two days and she'd need a doctor's note.

Could she report him? She didn't actually know. It wasn't really illegal, what he'd done. Or was it? Was it some kind of rape? On the other hand, as much as she hated it, she didn't want to lose her job. It wasn't like they were thick on the ground hereabouts. She was checking the Nuclear Decommissioning Authority website for jobs at Sellafield daily, but she already knew that they had a massive waiting list. As if she'd ever get a job there anyway. You probably needed A levels or something. She'd take the risk and resign, but she knew her parents wanted her out of the house, and that would be even less feasible with no job.

Diane lived on the Orgill estate in Egremont. Egremont was a small town to the south of Whitehaven, built around an iron-ore mine, and Orgill was a housing estate much like any other. The houses were grey, though they'd once been white. There were children's playgrounds there, where Diane and her friends had frequently sat on the swings through the night with cider and cigarettes. Then they'd all left school and got jobs, and that, for some reason, had been the end of everything.

There was something else at the call centre that scared Diane: not just the tedious passing of time, the waiting for the weekend, the wishing your life away, but something else. You had to have worked there for a period of time before you could see it, and it *was* related to the days, weeks, months, and years passing you by. But it was also something else, and Diane thought of it as 'potatofication'.

Everybody who had started at the call centre at the same time seemed to potatofy at the same rate. They would get gradually paler, gradually heavier, gradually less well-defined. Every group of new starters – fresh, fit, attractive, lively – would eventually all put on weight and slacken around the eyes and mouth, start to look bored, start to move more slowly. Yeah, it was probably to do with being stuck at a desk all day, but it was also to do with the mental fatigue from the conversational gymnastics you spent eight hours a day performing. It left you worn out, come the evening, left you craving takeaways and shitty films.

Were all call centres like this? Sometimes it felt like *everybody* worked in a call centre. When Diane looked at job vacancies located in the cities, all of the job titles were different but they all sounded the same; when you got right down to it, so many of them looked like jobs where you spent all day either ringing people up or answering the phone. Were people potatofying all over the country? Diane had actually had nightmares where she was walking through an office space in which all the chairs were occupied by white, pasty lumps with uneven and mottled skin, rather than by people. As if the entire purpose of the place were to turn people into potatoes, as if it were some kind of giant potato farm. As if the employees were merely objects – or even the product.

Diane knew that when she went back to work – which she would have to do, tomorrow or the day after – she would become transfixed once more by the shape of people.

The waddle of girls who had once been svelte, their bulky arses, their flat hair. The sagging jowls of men who'd arrived there with sharp, vibrant features. The total breakdown of some of them – like that freak, Harry. He could probably still have been semi-respectable if he'd worked somewhere else.

Diane curled in on herself and pulled the duvet tighter. She had been hoping that the *Saw* films – *Saw III*, she was on now – would distract her somewhat. But they weren't. She was still feeling pretty scared.

DISTRESS

'I think I'm going to be sick,' Arthur said. 'Please, Artemis, let me go to the toilets.'

'We need to talk about this some more,' Artemis replied. 'Maybe when you're not feeling so weak.'

'Yeah,' Arthur agreed. 'Maybe. I don't care. Yes, please.' He could feel everything in him start to contract, and his vision was paling, as it did whenever he had not eaten enough. His skin was getting clammy in a way that evoked memories of drunken vomiting.

'Go on, then,' Artemis said, with the hint of a sneer in his voice. 'And then go home. You're no good to me like this.'

Arthur got up and scrambled out of the pod without another word. Artemis listened as he ran from the pods area, his footsteps receding into the background murmur of the work floor.

'Pathetic,' he said quietly. 'Absolutely pathetic.'

*

Thankfully, Yasmin wasn't at her desk as Arthur ran past it, his hand clasped over his mouth. She must have gone to get a drink or something. He didn't really want to talk to anybody or see anybody, or have to explain anything. Various people did turn in their seats to watch him go, of course, any such drama being magnified by an urgent desire to relieve the daily tedium, but as long as nobody shouted his name or put their hand out to stop him, then he was OK with that.

Nobody did try to stop him. Clearly, everybody could tell that he really needed to get to the toilets.

He didn't quite make it to a cubicle, and instead threw up in one of the sinks. It was a raw, violent thing, loud and convulsive. He felt as if his body were trying to burst him open to expel something, but his throat and his mouth weren't big enough. After a few minutes the violent feeling subsided; it had merely been the sensation of his body and muscles contracting. It left him feeling ragged and rough. He paused, head bowed, over the sink for a short while, getting his breath back, and then turned on both taps to rinse the mess away. He even scooped the bigger bits out of the plughole with his fingers and threw them in the bin. Arthur wasn't really squeamish about vomit, since he'd cleared his father's sick from the sink numerous times on mornings after the karaoke nights at the Vine.

After cleaning up, Arthur looked into the mirror and inhaled sharply. He staggered backwards and coughed. Then he moved forward again, getting right up close to

298

the mirror, and stared, horrified and almost on the verge of tears, into the glass.

The white of his left eye was turning red, the red clouding up from the bottom. Blood – he assumed it was blood – was creeping across the white of his eye like night over the surface of the Earth. What was this? What was happening to him?

The toilet door opened and Johnny entered. He was approaching Arthur from the right, so Arthur just turned his head slightly to the left to hide his red eye, and hoped that Johnny wouldn't look in the mirror.

'Just bin on the phone ter bloody India!' Johnny said, shaking his head as he launched straight into his gripe. His big moustache twitched. 'Oh, it wis a struggle. He bloody spoke like an outboard motor. Bloody *put-put-put-put-put*. Couldn't mek out a bloody word!'

Arthur didn't say anything.

'Y'is alreet, lad?' Johnny asked, moving closer.

'Yep,' Arthur said, nodding. 'Yes, thanks. Just . . . think I'm going to go home. Feel a bit sick.'

'Gone pale as a fish,' Johnny said. 'Git yersel away.'

'Yeah,' Arthur said, 'I will. Thanks, Johnny.'

'Nae bother, lad,' Johnny said. He disappeared into a cubicle. They were the kind of cubicles composed of just panels of wood in a metal frame, not really self-contained or at all private. Johnny evidently didn't mind, though. The moment the sound of his defecation started, Arthur knew he had to leave or he was going to be sick again.

Sometimes dehumanisation was so normal, so common-place, that you didn't really notice it.

The feel of the cool breeze on Arthur's face was immediately pleasurable. It seemed to blow the sweat and the clamminess away, drying him out and bringing him round from what had been – although he hadn't really realised it – a less than fully conscious state. He stumbled, head down, along North Shore Road, away from the hulking white shed of the call centre. Then, as he passed the Tesco's car park, the harbour opened out before him. There was only one place he could go to really get his head back, and it wasn't home – it wasn't home to his father, who was having a rest day and was probably already drunk, or trying to heat up some baked beans and burning them, or shivering and crying in his bed, or deluding himself that he was talking on the phone to . . .

To his wife, Arthur's mother. That was the one place Arthur could go. To the end of the pier. Jesus Christ, why wasn't it his mother there in the Scape? Why, instead, was it that fucking horrible *thing*?

Arthur stopped walking. How could he accuse his dad of deluding himself, now that Arthur had seen what he'd seen and been where he'd been? Surely there was a possibility that his dad wasn't as deluded as Arthur had always thought. Still though, he didn't feel up to having that conversation just yet. He fixed his gaze on the lighthouse, gleaming white out there above the navy blue water, and narrowed his eyes. He looked out over the sea. Clouds reared up over the horizon. They were so big that they looked much closer than they actually were. The sun was behind them, so that their edges were shining yellow, but their mass was an intensely dark, matt grey. Out there, below the clouds, the surface of the sea looked black. How was the lighthouse so bright when those clouds were in the way of the sun? Arthur had long ago stopped trying to work out the passage of light near the sea, though. It never really did what you would expect it to.

The pier was relatively busy with people fishing, from young teenagers through to very old-looking men who seemed incredibly fit for their age. Or maybe they weren't that old. Maybe they just looked old because they sat out in every kind of weather all the time. Anyway, on his way out to the lighthouse, Arthur passed numerous people and groups of people who sat dangling their legs off the edge of the pier. It wasn't very warm but it wasn't wet either, and the wind wasn't powerful enough to pose any kind of risk – not unless you were a child or a waif and risked standing too close to the drop – so it was a pretty good day for fishing. Yeah, once upon a time Harry would have been out here, too, but not any more.

People were smoking and drinking and eating. Arthur knew that after they were all gone, a fair amount of their rubbish would be left behind. The seagulls loved it, especially the gory remnants left by those who had killed and gutted their catches on the spot. The scavenging birds peppered the sky.

God it was beautiful if you let yourself feel it.

Arthur kept his head bowed because he didn't want anybody to see his blood-red eye. He had been thinking about it, the eye, and had calmed down a little bit. He had seen something like it before on Facebook at Bony's house. Somebody had posted a picture of herself with a red eye like his, adding a comment about how she'd got so drunk that she'd been sick – violently enough to burst a blood vessel in one eye. That was it, then – a burst blood vessel. That was all it was. Like a nosebleed, but inside the eyeball. Nothing to worry about.

A wave of nausea rolled over him, and he stood still until it passed.

It discoloured your eye, but then eventually it went away. That's what had happened to the girl on Facebook, anyway. No permanent damage.

Arthur hadn't ventured out here since that night with the crab. He found himself thinking about it and the way it had moaned.

Reaching the lighthouse, he extended the palms of both hands against it and stretched himself. He was aware of probably looking like some sort of freak; he would probably always look like some kind of freak. He didn't have the energy right then to worry too much about how other people must perceive him. He wondered if he would ever have that kind of energy again. This was probably how people became strange and lonely and troubled. Through preoccupation.

Well of course it fucking was. That went without saying,

didn't it? Arthur shook his head. He couldn't tell whether such thoughts were blatantly obvious or totally nonsensical. Somewhere in between had to be insight; he doubted very much that he was achieving insight, though.

The wind was bringing those clouds closer, quite quickly.

He needed to stop thinking for a while. He just needed to be somewhere and not think. He turned away from the lighthouse and went to sit on the edge of the pier, away from the west-facing wall over which the fishermen leant. He sat at the very tip of the pier, where there was no wall, facing north. In fact, he was almost facing the call centre, which was still all too visible, even at this remove. Maybe that was because it was white: a great, big, white, barn-like structure against a slope of brown and yellow grass.

Arthur looked away from the call centre and down towards the water lapping at the stone beneath him. The movement of the liquid was hypnotic. The way something natural could possess such a regular rhythm was fascinating. Incredible. Arthur watched it, and watched it. If he let it, it would draw him in; physically draw his body forward. The lure of the sea. He had always acknowledged that as something real, something dangerous. Well, since his mum had thrown herself into it, anyway.

Something moved beneath him. Not the water, but something else, something not part of the rhythm of the water. It was this dissonance that made it visible. Because, when he looked for it, looked for the thing that was moving but was not the water, he couldn't see it. It was the movement he had seen, not the thing itself. He frowned and maintained his focus. He was peering through the surface of the water now, since whatever had moved must have been beneath it.

Minutes passed. A few of the fishermen pointed at the approaching clouds and started reeling in, disassembling their rods. The seagulls above wheeled and laughed.

There! There it was again! Arthur opened his mouth slightly and leant forward a little more. Whatever it was, it was clinging to the stonework of the pier, moving along it, or maybe . . . maybe even *up* the wall itself. Its colour was barely distinguishable from the colour of the depths in which it crept.

It reached up and broke the surface.

The crab! It was that fucking crab again. Or . . . no, it was a similar crab but it was different. It was bigger. Or was it even a crab?

Had that other thing, the other night, been a crab?

This thing was bigger than the kind of crab you found in British waters, and it didn't look like it had enough legs to be a crab, anyway. And it moved in the wrong way. It maybe moved more like an octopus or something, as if its limbs were arms instead of legs – as if it were pulling itself along with arms, not walking with legs – but these limbs, these arms, were jointed and hard-looking, not like the tentacles of a cephalopod. And how many limbs were there? Four? No, five. With those massive crab-like claws, which it was using to climb steadily, dextrously, intelligently. *Five* limbs? What the fuck kind of number was that? Maybe it had lost one. Jesus Christ. It was only moving

304

slowly but it was fucking disgusting. Its head was more prominent than that of a crab. It protruded, rounded and bulbous, from the centre, whereas the head or face of a crab was, of course, a small, well-protected thing tucked away on the side of the body. Could this be the same creature he'd seen previously? That had looked more like a crab, whereas this . . . it was about the size of a child, for a start, a three- or four-year-old child.

It was dark green and slimy-looking. Its body appeared to be mostly a kind of hub for the limbs and a . . . a socket, almost, for the face. The face itself seemed to be looking directly up at Arthur. He was still sitting on the edge, legs dangling, bent over at the waist, looking straight down at the crab thing, and it seemed to be looking right back up, as if it were conscious of him. It moved in a horribly deliberate way.

It moaned – with the same weary, almost bored sound that Arthur remembered from that moonlit night when he'd last been out here. It was the deep sigh of a depressive. The throaty gasp of a heavy smoker suddenly shocked or winded. Then it made a sound like coughing, but it wasn't coughing. It was a sharp, regular, hacking sound.

Arthur's head was swimming. It was all he could do to prevent himself from pitching forward face-first into the creature, and into the sea. It was only when its front claw, the largest, tentatively nudged his foot that Arthur wailed. He scrambled backwards, his heels kicking against the stone, and rose to his feet.

He looked around him. All of the fishermen had gone.

Those oppressive clouds were now more or less overhead. Even as he looked up, the first few drops of rain hit his skin like they'd been spat. These were raindrops falling from a great height. A *phenomenal* height.

When he looked back, the horrendous being was now perched just on the edge of the pier. Its eyes were visible. They were far too large. It was not a natural thing. It was too much. It was too wrong.

Arthur turned around, and as he did so, he saw that there was another one. Another of the massive bastards. Not directly behind him, but just to his left, as he stood with his back to the first. As if it had climbed up the side of the pier that had been to his right when he was sitting down. It was easily distinguishable from the first, having only one claw, but it was slightly larger. It didn't look injured, though. Just . . . different. It was as if, whatever species of thing these were, every specimen of it could be different. As if they hadn't all evolved to turn out the same.

Arthur ran towards the second one and booted it square in its horribly over-active mouth. It rattled backwards, squealing, and over the side, splashing into the water beneath. From behind him the first of the monsters made that sickening coughing sound, and Arthur could hear it running towards him. He ran in the same direction, and found, thankfully, that he was faster.

Why was there nobody else around?

Once he'd put some distance between him and his nightmarish pursuer, Arthur turned. He thought about it and then went back – started running back towards it. Because it had been visible for longer, and he had longer to think about it, he felt much more squeamish than he did with the other one. He'd had longer to let the revulsion in his body build up until he almost felt like he was going to stop running completely. But no, he reached the thing and kicked it hard, the sharp toe of his work shoe crunching into the space between its two – *panicked?!* – eyes. The crab, or whatever it was, flipped over, and . . . and, God, that mind-fucking *sound*, the *voice*, that hellish fucking *voice*. It babbled, the thing babbled. It was like . . . it wasn't like the sound any animal makes. It was like it was talking, like a human, but in another language. Arthur didn't attempt to understand, though. He just closed his eyes and stamped. He held his arms up high for some reason, and he kept his eyes closed and his mouth tightly shut as well, just in case some kind of fluid escaped and splattered on to his face. All the while, the thing spoke. Arthur carried on stamping, though. He could feel its legs clawing, twitching and spasming against his own.

Once he thought it had stopped moving, he opened his eyes and looked up at the sky. The rain was torrential, but he hadn't noticed it develop from those first few drops. It was the kind of rain that's so heavy you can't hear much else. Arthur had previously been able to hear the creature, but that was it. Now the only sound was the rain. He looked down at what he'd done.

Really, the underside of the thing was not remarkable. It did look like the underbelly of a crab, albeit a very large one. Pale green with lots of chitin connecting and inter-locking. The size of it made Arthur shudder and look away again for a while. It was like a huge dead hand lying there, palm facing upwards.

Arthur knew that he should turn it over and try to establish what the creature was. Try to establish that it was, in fact, just a large crab. But he couldn't. He couldn't bring himself to prove that there was nothing wrong, just in case there *was* something wrong.

What the fuck was wrong with him? The Scape, then his red eye, and now – now this. And what was he doing out here, anyway – trying to somehow find some peace with his mum? She was dead.

He was as bad as his dad. He was turning into his dad.

The rain was roaring now. The sound was aggressive and muscular.

Arthur used his foot to push the now dead thing towards the edge of the pier, its ugly limbs snagging in the pitted stone surface. His shirt and lightweight coat stuck to his skinny frame. Finally, eventually, he gave the monster one last shove, and it slumped over the edge.

There was one person he now needed to talk to before anybody else: his father.

It was only when he was nearly home, walking along the road where he lived, in fact, that he started to wonder if any of those creatures had emerged from the sea while he wasn't around. If so, where had they gone?

Or . . . were they only drawn to him?

THE EMAILS

Yasmin got on the train at Whitehaven in a metallic, cloud-warped sunlight. The train plunged into the Bransty Tunnel immediately after the Whitehaven station platform, and by the time it shot out the other end the rain was torrential.

As usual, when it stopped at Sellafield, the train filled up with noisy commuters chatting and laughing. *Maybe I could get a job at Sellafield*, Yasmin thought. *I really don't know what else to do.*

She was the only person to get off the train at Drigg. As soon as she did so she was soaked. The sky above was black. She ran from the platform out on to the small road, and then continued down the middle of it – there were no cars – and away from the railway, away from the level crossing, heading towards Bony's house. Trust her to be wearing such a flimsy dress on a day like this. It was dark blue, mind, with a pattern of tiny red and yellow flowers, so she didn't look indecent, but still. The long, lightweight white cardigan she wore above it was as protective as tissue paper now. She hammered on Bony's door until he answered, which he didn't do nearly quickly enough.

'Yasmin?' he said, frowning at her. 'You OK? Something wrong?'

'It's raining!'

Bony looked up at the sky, and then all around. 'So it is,' he said, and stepped back to let her in. 'Hope you didn't get too wet.'

They sat in Bony's living room, which – compared to other rooms in his house – was quite sparse. There was a sofa, a small coffee table, a big TV on a stand crammed with various consoles, and some shelves full of video-game boxes, DVDs and books. The floor was bare wood, without carpet or rugs. The walls were white. The windows were huge, with French doors leading on to a small patio at the rear, but there was so little light outside now that the blinds were drawn and the lights turned on. Yasmin knew that Bony was weirdly anal about keeping this room tidy; whenever they visited him, he would pick up any rubbish or empty mugs and take them through to the kitchen immediately, rather than wait to clear everything up later, in one go.

They each soon had a steaming mug sitting on the coffee table, and the room felt warm and safe. Yasmin felt she could just rest here, if she let herself – just sit back and rest. It was a restful place.

'These emails,' Bony began.

'Yes.'

310

'I haven't read them yet, but how did you send them to me?'

'I sent them from Artemis's own laptop to my personal email address. Then I used my phone to forward them to you.'

'Oh, right.' Bony nodded. 'And Arthur's OK?'

'I don't know,' Yasmin said. 'I don't even know where he is.'

'They'll have made sure he's OK, though, if they took him away?'

'You would think so, wouldn't you?' Yasmin said. She looked at Bony with eyes wide.

'Well, I would think so, yeah.'

'I tried to ring his mobile, but couldn't get through,' Yasmin said. 'Otherwise I'd have told him where we are.'

'Let's ring his home number now, before anything else,' Bony said. 'We can speak to him or leave a message.'

Bony reached for his mobile, which lay on the coffee table, and dialled one of the only two numbers he knew by heart. He put the phone on loudspeaker and then held it to his ear. It rang for about half a minute, before there was a click and somebody answered.

'Rebecca?' said a small, fearful voice. 'Is that you?'

Bony and Yasmin looked at each other and winced.

'Harry,' Bony said. 'Hi, it's—'

But Harry had already hung up.

'Harry's phone calls are something to do with all of this,' Yasmin said, 'but I can't work it out.'

'With all of what?' Bony asked. 'Arthur passing out?'

'Yeah.' Yasmin bit her lip. 'Bony, Arthur came round the other night . . . God, it was only last night. Anyway, he came round to talk about that vision he'd had.'

'Oh, right,' Bony said. He nodded. 'Did he tell you he fancies you?'

'*What?*' Yasmin exclaimed.

'What?' Bony said, jumping at her sudden sharp tone and looking behind him. 'You mean he didn't?'

'No! And I'm sure he doesn't.'

'Well, he does and I thought he would have said something. I would have thought that's why he came round.'

'Can we stay on topic, please?'

'Yeah, sure. Sorry . . . I just. Well, I think it's better that you know, anyway.'

'I can't believe you just told me that,' Yasmin shook her head. 'Something like that's probably a big deal for Arthur.'

'So you do believe me, then?'

'Shut up!'

'To be honest I think it's hard to know what's a big deal for Arthur, and what's not. He's hard to work out.'

'He's not the only one.'

'Yeah,' Bony nodded. 'That's true.'

'Anyway.'

'Anyway.'

'I think Arthur's really found something out. I'm starting to believe him.'

'Shall I put some music on?'

'Will you *listen* to me, you big, fucking . . . *prick*?' Yasmin shouted, throwing her hands up in the air and tensing her fingers into claws.

Bony eyed her quite calmly. 'I *am* listening,' he said, 'but I'm going to put some music on. For some reason I'm starting to feel a bit nervous, and some music will help diffuse that nervousness. I'm sorry if it looked like I wasn't listening.' He stood up and went over to the TV, which he turned on. 'Please,' he said, looking back at Yasmin. 'I'm sorry. Carry on with what you were telling me.' He knelt down and found a CD, which he slid into one of the consoles.

'Well, as I was saying, Arthur came round the other night – last night – and we were talking about his vision, and . . . what's this?'

'It's the Lady Gaga album,' Bony said. '*Fame Monster.*'

'Oh, Bony,' Yasmin laughed, 'you are such a freak.'

'It's been said,' Bony said, grinning at her.

'The gist of it was, I think, that Arthur believes there is a landscape – some kind of landscape – in the telephone system. Not actually *inside* the system, because he kept talking about an interstice, like . . . like when you ring somebody up, their voice isn't where they are, and yet they are not where you are, but you are both communicating somewhere . . . somewhere else, somewhere in between. In that place, that somewhere else – that's where he's talking about.'

'In the wires,' Bony suggested.

'I'm not sure.'

'Well, that's where the voices are.'

'Maybe, then.'

'But you can't fit a whole other world inside the wires. What's he on about?'

'I don't know if I'm explaining it very well.'

Yasmin and Bony were both standing now, although neither had been aware of getting up.

'You know how it is when you're at work, and you start to forget where you are?' Yasmin said. 'You even start to forget that you're there at all, that you have a physical presence. You become this thing that only exists in the phone call. And then there's this *space* – there has to be, if you think about it – that all of these telephones access, where all of those signals exist.'

'I'm not sure,' Bony said. 'I still think he might be losing it.'

'Really?'

Bony looked at her very seriously. 'Don't you?' he asked. 'I mean, look at Harry.'

Yasmin didn't say anything. Instead, she sat back down. Neither of them spoke for a moment.

Then Yasmin clicked her fingers and stood up again. 'Bill Viola!' she exclaimed.

'The artist?'

'You're full of surprises, Bony,' Yasmin said. 'Yeah, the artist. He talked, in an interview, about another world – something to do with shared spaces, empty spaces, blank spaces. Something to do with there being no horizon.'

'Something to do with perception, too,' Bony said.

'Something to do with . . . like *The Matrix*, you know? The world as we know it is created by our perception of it, but it might actually be very different.'

'Yes! So, what if Arthur just saw, for want of a better word, this Scape – that's what he calls it – through some other input?'

'Through the phone?' Bony looked puzzled for a moment, and then laughed. 'He saw it through his ears!'

Yasmin laughed at that, too, and then grimaced. 'Oh, I don't know,' she said.

They fell into silence again, and both sat back down.

'Let's have a look at these emails,' Bony said, after they spent a short time finishing off their now cooling coffee.

Bony left the room and returned with his laptop, dragging a power cable behind him.

'I've just remembered something,' he said, as he plugged the machine in. 'Talking about Bill Viola reminded me. Nu.'

'What?'

'Nu. It's from Ancient Egyptian mythology: Nu or Nun.' He pronounced the word as 'noon'. 'It's an abyss or a void, a place with no horizons. It surrounded the whole of existence, and you could access it in places where there were no edges. If you were deep underwater, say, and everything all around you looked the same, or if you were in a cave and there was absolutely no light, you could find yourself in the abyss. Nu itself was a deity; the abyss was a being. The same abyss that Aleister Crowley used to claim he could communicate with, or summon from.'

Yasmin still gripped her mug tightly, despite it now being empty. 'Bony, that's really interesting,' she said.

'Well, of course,' Bony said. 'Would you expect anything less?'

'How do you know all this stuff?'

'I read a lot,' Bony said, again.

Yasmin didn't quite believe him, but she didn't press it. 'So . . . what about this Nu?' she asked, instead.

'It sounds almost like the place you're talking about,' Bony said. 'A kind of nowhere place. Like a shared void that connects everything. I mean, I'm not an expert or anything, so maybe I've got their mythology totally wrong, but that sounds right.'

'Arthur said it was like being under water, as well,' Yasmin said. 'He did say that.'

'Here.' Bony pointed at the screen. 'The emails.'

'Scroll down,' Yasmin said. 'Go to the first one.'

From: central.office@interext.com
To: artemis.black@interext.com
Sent: 13.09.10 at 14:56
Subject: Subject

Artemis,

Since I had my call answered by somebody else last time I rang, I will ring no more. Ring me if necessary – you know that only I can possibly answer if you ring me – but I will only email you from now on.

316

I want you to know that I am disappointed in your negligence. We trust you to show us that you can do the job required of you. If not, we will have to remove you. I know that you understand.

In short, we have had a response from the Interstice. As discussed, we used the AI to elicit the response. She probed ceaselessly and Eleanor would have been proud.

We know now that there is an intelligence there. An intelligence with the power to interact with and disrupt telecommunications. You may have experienced some disruptions at that centre of yours. If not, you undoubtedly will.

Now that we have established the presence of an entity, you need to establish a channel of communication. You already know of the subject. He is key. Use him.

Central.

Bony and Yasmin looked at each other.

'There,' she said. 'The Interstice, it's real.'

'Who's Eleanor?' Bony asked.

Yasmin shook her head. 'I don't know.'

'There are loads of these emails,' Bony said, scrolling upwards. 'Most of them are about call volumes and customer-service levels. Normal stuff, I'm guessing.'

'Yeah,' Yasmin said, 'that's all the shite we get smacked around the head with every day. Reduce your handling time, increase the number of calls you take, increase your call-quality scores, increase customer satisfaction, increase the amount of cash you collect, all that bollocks. And . . . who do you think the *subject* is? Arthur?'

'Must be,' Bony said.

'What's this, though?' Bony pointed to another email.

From: central.office@interext.com
To: artemis.black@interext.com
Sent: 24.09.10 at 11:32
Subject: Diane

Artemis,

If you must have your way with the bodies, then please be more discreet. Even we, from our remote location, could surmise your intentions and the subsequent course of events. Remember, you are in a small town now.

Central.

Yasmin felt like her core temperature was plummeting. She'd known how Artemis had summoned Diane to the pods, but . . . but she hadn't actually seen Diane since that same day, now she thought about it. And *bodies*?

'They keep mentioning the AI too,' Bony said. 'I mean, I know what AI is, but I don't know what they're talking about here, in this other e-mail. "Re-routing to the AI".'

'They're talking about re-routing calls,' Yasmin said. 'Re-routing calls away from the call centre and to the AI.

So it must be an automated system. You know how some-times you can ring a company and you go through lots of pre-recorded options? And sometimes you press buttons to choose different options, or sometimes you actually speak and it manages to pick up on what you're saying?'

'But customers would notice that,' Bony said.

'They would,' Yasmin said, 'unless it was a genuinely powerful system. And I'm sure it's possible to have a system like that. You hear about things called call analytics, where the system can identify the mood of the customer through their tone of voice, never mind what words they're actu-ally using. And they can compare the words used by the customer against records of hundreds of thousands of sentences, and thus match them up and then give the appropriate response. It's not genuine AI, but . . . Those are only the commercially available systems used by normal companies. A company the size of Interext, if it has its own research and development people, and enough money . . . I don't see why they couldn't build something powerful enough, and with enough pre-recordings to sound sufficiently varied.'

'Then why would Interext employ so many people?' Bony asked.

'Maybe the systems are new. Maybe they haven't been used before. In fact . . .' Yasmin nodded, scrolling back down through the emails until she found the one she wanted. She nodded towards the laptop screen. 'Yeah, here. It says something about only re-routing a few calls at a time to test it.'

'Then they're going to sack you all? Close the site down?'

Yasmin looked at Bony. 'I imagine they will, if they don't really need us. Unless they need us for something else.'

'I'm wondering what they need Arthur for,' Bony said.

'Bony,' Yasmin said, 'there's something I should probably tell you. Artemis's laptop – the one I forwarded these emails from – had a webcam fitted in the casing.'

'For video-conferencing?'

'Well, yeah, but . . . what if somebody was watching me?'

'Were you able to see if there were any webcam programmes open?'

'I didn't look.'

'It's probably nothing to worry about.'

'Bony,' Yasmin gestured towards the screen, 'these people sound really, really scary.'

'It does all sound pretty heavy,' Bony said, 'but I still wouldn't worry about that.'

Yasmin nodded and fiddled with her hair. 'I know,' she said. 'I know.'

'There's more to read,' Bony said.

'I know.'

'Artemis asking what they're doing it for. Why they're trying to contact this entity. Central Office doesn't really seem to answer him, though.'

'"We need to ensure that we remain leader of the pack in terms of service-level delivery and shareholder return,"' Yasmin read out loud. '"This project is the cornerstone of a long-term strategy."'

'Doesn't tell you much, does it?' Bony said.

'Not really,' Yasmin said. 'Bony, for fuck's sake, do you have anything to drink?'

'I've got wine,' Bony said, 'and I've got weed.'

'Can I stay here tonight?' Yasmin said. 'Please? I'm not going to work tomorrow. I'm going to ring in sick.'

'Of course you can,' Bony said. 'Um, yeah.' He nodded, and then smiled and left the room. After a moment he reappeared. 'You do want some wine, right?' he said.

'Yes,' Yasmin said. 'Yeah, if that's OK.'

THE WORMS

Harry was pacing around in the kitchen when Arthur returned home. He was muttering to himself and it was evidently one of his not-so-good days. Arthur removed his sopping shoes by the front door.

'Dad?' Arthur said as he came through, puddling water behind him. 'You OK?'

'Hi, son,' Harry said. 'Yeah, yeah I'm OK, thank you. How are you?'

'I've had a pretty bad day, Dad,' Arthur said carefully. 'I'm going to make a cup of tea. Do you want one?'

'Oh, yes please, Arthur,' Harry said, still pacing.

'Dad,' Arthur said, as he moved forward and put his hands on Harry's shoulders. The man stank of alcohol. 'Go and sit down. I'll bring it through.'

'Yes, yes, of course,' Harry said. 'I'll go and sit down. Wait, wh-what's happened to your eye?'

'It's nothing,' Arthur said. 'I was . . . I sneezed too hard and it, uh, it burst a blood vessel. It sometimes happens to people. It's OK.'

'Are you sure? It l-looks terrible.'

'I'm sure,' Arthur said. 'You go and sit down.'

Harry nodded warily and headed off to the living room. He shuffled there, really, in his ancient slippers. Sometimes it was like living with a geriatric. He was ageing prematurely, what with the alcohol and the stress and the . . . well, the mental problems, Arthur reflected. That was what they were, though – *mental conditions*, maybe, was a better way of putting it.

Arthur put the kettle on and looked around the kitchen. It was pretty repulsive. Everything was grease-flecked, dirty dishes were stacked up on every surface, the sink was full of filthy water, the lino was covered in crumbs. And . . . no. Arthur peered more closely at the sink.

One of those worms – here, in the kitchen. Not *today*. I mean not ever, ideally, but *please* not today. It wriggled its way vigorously along the back of the sink, as if it were having a really good time.

Arthur waited for the kettle to boil and then poured a little of the steaming water over the worm. The water ran all along the side of the sink and spilled over the edge of the worktop, cascading to the floor and scalding his feet through his worn old socks.

'Oh fuck!' he yelled at the ceiling. 'You fucking *prick*!'

'Arthur?'

'It's all right, Dad!' Arthur shouted. 'I'm all right!'

*

Eventually they were both seated in the living room. Harry had already closed the curtains, but Arthur didn't reopen them. It was, after all, pretty dark outside for the time of day.

'Dad, I need to talk to you,' Arthur said.

'OK,' Harry said.

'I think I've been seeing things.'

'Really, son?' Harry sat forward. 'What kind of things? Do . . . do you mean the worms?'

'No, Dad, not the worms. Those are real. I mean at work. I've been . . . a couple of times now, I've . . .' Arthur realised that he was almost tying his fingers into knots. This was hard, harder than he'd expected, and he didn't really know why.

Or maybe it was because he couldn't remember the last time he'd actually needed his father. Arthur just sat there in silence for a moment once he realised that. He hadn't needed his father in any meaningful sense for years. He'd only really needed his contribution of money for the rent, since it tended to be Arthur who looked after that kind of thing now. He hadn't really needed Harry's advice, or his company, or his opinion, or his reassurance, or his approval. Certainly not his approval. And didn't everybody want the approval of their parents? Harry needed Arthur, maybe, and Arthur was more than happy to help Harry get by, but really, Harry was a burden. In a sense, he just took and took. He didn't mean to do so, but he did.

'Son?' Harry said.

'Yeah,' Arthur said, wiping his eyes. 'I, uh . . . at work, a couple of times now, I've kind of passed out, and, um, seen things . . . Seen another place.'

'R-really?'

Arthur glanced up, saw Harry looked surprised, but not too worried.

'Yeah, and I wanted to tell you. And I just want . . . I don't know, I just . . .'

Arthur really broke down then. He slapped his hands on to his face and sobbed. Harry merely looked on, sitting slightly forward with his hands on his knees, trembling.

'Son?' he said, finally.

Arthur just shook his head. He couldn't speak. How hard could it be, really, to say that too many things were happening and you didn't understand enough? But it was hard. It was really difficult.

'There *is* a place, Arthur,' Harry said. 'That's where your mum is.'

It took a while for the words to get through to Arthur but, once they did, he uncovered his face and looked up at his dad.

'What?' he said. 'Do you mean like, um, the afterlife? Or do you mean something else?'

'I mean s-something else,' Harry said. 'Some*where* else. I talk to her on the phone, see, and I know she's gone from us, I know that, but she does still exist and that place . . . that place where she is, that's the place I mean.'

Arthur thought about his mother existing in the place he'd seen. That didn't seem quite right, but who was he

325

now to doubt it? And it couldn't just be due to some hereditary illness, not if Artemis believed in this place, too.
Artemis had acted like he was even expecting something
like this. That aside, though, the thought of his mother
being in such a place was not a pleasant one.

'I never believed you,' Arthur said.

'I know,' Harry said.

'I don't know what's happening, Dad,' Arthur said.
'Artemis seems to know about this other place too.'

'S-strange,' Harry said.

'And, Dad,' Arthur said, 'I don't think I want Mum to
be in that place, if that's where she is. It's not a good
place – the place I've seen.'

'Sh-she always says that she's happy,' Harry said. 'She
always sounds happy.'

'Maybe we're talking about different places,' Arthur said.
'We could be talking about different places.'

'I suppose so,' Harry said, looking thoughtful.

'There's something else,' Arthur said.

'What?' Harry laughed and reached over, put his
hand on Arthur's knee. 'Some. . . something even more
weird?'

'Ha,' Arthur said. He actually said the word 'ha' while
attempting a smile, and he realised that that was something his mum used to do. 'Something *as* weird maybe,
yeah. I was on the pier before.'

'You still go out on the pier?'

'Yeah. Yeah, I do. And I saw these things come out of
the water, out of the sea. Like big crabs, but they weren't

crabs. I kicked them back in, but . . . it wasn't the first time, and I don't think it will be the last.'

Harry just remained silent and nodded.

'I think they want me for something,' Arthur said.

Harry continued nodding. His face looked weird, like he was trying to keep it impassive or something, but he only succeeded in making it look strained.

'Arthur,' Harry said, 'have . . . have you thought about seeing a doctor, maybe?'

'You don't believe me?'

'It s-sounds like you're under a lot of pressure. Maybe with your promotion and everything, you—'

'I haven't been promoted!' Arthur shouted, standing up. 'I haven't had a fucking promotion! I don't even know what I'm doing at work! I just have more to do! I have to listen to more calls from more idiots, I have to tell more people how badly they've failed. I now have to tell people – people doing the *same job as me* – that they're doing it wrong. I . . . I just hate it all!'

'Son,' Harry said, 'y-you should be grateful to have a job at the moment. There are people who would kill for a steady job, with overtime. And I can tell you, when I was unemployed things were so difficult. Your mum was so worried all of the time. I don't know if you remember, but—'

'Of course I fucking remember,' Arthur spat.

'P-please don't swear, Arthur,' Harry said.

'Then please don't try and tell me how fucking lucky I am!' Arthur shouted – screamed, really. His face was red and taut, his whole body shaking. 'I should be *grateful*? Grateful for that shitty job working for that brainless fucking monster? Grateful for this house with its rotten bathroom and walls full of fucking *worms*? And a stinking, useless fucking *alcoholic* dad who I have to think about all of the fucking time, because he can't fucking look after himself, let alone me?'

'I've . . . I'm sorry,' Harry said. 'I'm just—'

'You're just a fucking *mess*!' Arthur waved his hands around as he yelled, trying to expel all the pent-up physical energy without actually hitting his father.

In the silence that followed his last utterance, he jumped over to the wall and punched that instead. His fist made a hole, from which he then pulled it, ragged and bleeding. He noticed that his hand was damp, even aside from the blood. That meant there was moisture inside the wall. He turned his hand over and saw a little worm curled around the tip of his finger. He pressed it against the wall – an undamaged part of the wall – leaving a small brown smear. He turned around.

'How did Mum die, Dad?'

'I don't r-really w-want to talk any more,' Harry said.

'Tell me.'

'You know how,' Harry said. 'Sh-she fell off the cliff and drowned in the sea.'

'No, she didn't.'

Harry shifted in his seat. 'What do you mean?' he said.

'She jumped, didn't she? She killed herself.'

'N-no!' Harry shouted, standing up too. 'She *fell*! She *fell*!'

'Why are you lying?' Arthur said.

'I-I-I-I'm *not* lying!'

Arthur stood there and stared at his father for a long time, without saying anything. Harry was rigid, vibrating, tears in his eyes, spittle on his lower lip.

Arthur nodded. 'Well, then, you're just wrong,' he said, quietly. 'Mum threw herself off that cliff, Dad. I could see from the window. I understand that maybe you've convinced yourself that it was some kind of accident, but it wasn't. It was her intention to die, and that was what she did.'

'Then w-why does she ring me up, then?' Harry asked, jerking his head up and trying to look defiant. 'Hm? Tell me that.'

'I don't know where to start,' Arthur said. 'Literally, I do not know where to start.'

He looked at his father for a moment longer, feeling baleful and ashamed, and then left the room, left the house, disappeared back out into the rain and the wash of seagull sounds, and into the new streets and the old streets.

Harry collapsed, folding in on himself, a poor shell-like substitute for a man, falling back down into the sofa on which he now spent far too much of his life, a sad husk confused in a dark room, because he'd thought it was quite a good question. Confusion was not all he felt, but it was certainly one of the things that he felt.

Why did she ring him up?

She must still love him. She *must* still love him. That was the only thing that made sense.

AT THE MUSEUM

Harry used to work in the Haig Pit museum, before it closed down. That was the museum on the cliff just to the south of Whitehaven, next to the big rusted wheel. Old Man Easy had worked there too. Harry himself had managed the place while Old Man Easy – known as Roger back then – had been a museum attendant. They had been good friends.

The museum consisted of only two rooms: one was full of displays of photographs, the other full of lumps of coal. Those things were still there behind the locked doors, beneath the rusting wheel, the turning sky. Roger always used to be a big reader; he used to read a newspaper while the fascinated tourists learned about different types of coal or the coal trade, or looked at photographs of the harbour when it was covered in rail tracks and black dust. He would read the paper and then later, over a cup of tea, he would talk seriously with Harry about the pleasures of hard physical work and jobs in manufacturing – in

331

making things. He would speculate about the death of industry, and how Great Britain would become a 'service nation'.

'I don't know what the kids are going to do for work,' he'd say.

PART FIVE

Yasmin Makes a Move

Yasmin stood at the French doors, looking up at the sky. It was early in the morning but still dark. The rain had stopped hours ago and the clouds had scurried off, leaving the sky open to the stars. The difference in light pollution between here, Drigg, and even a little town like Whitehaven was astonishing. Yasmin stood there looking up at the sky for about fifteen minutes. Maybe she was still drunk or stoned. Maybe not. She didn't know.

Bony was asleep on the sofa. Before going to sleep on the sofa, he had changed the sheets on his bed and made it ready for Yasmin and, as far as he knew, that's where Yasmin was – sleeping in his bed. That's where she'd been when he lay down on the sofa, anyway.

What time was it? About four o' clock. The early hours of Tuesday morning. There was no way Yasmin would get to work today. Well, there were ways, obviously, but she would not attempt any of them. It wasn't like she ever usually rang in sick, so she didn't feel too bad.

Who was she kidding? She didn't feel bad at all. She felt more honest and true and virtuous than she did on those mornings when she hauled her reluctant body to the call centre, every cell in her body rebelling and getting heavier with misery the closer she got. Was that over-stating it? Actually, no, she didn't think it was. And here, now, on this morning, pre-dawn, she felt very hopeful, almost as if success were nothing at all to do with going to work. That was a naïve and futile feeling to hold on to, she realised, but she held on to it anyway.

She turned to look at Bony, lying there asleep. He was buried beneath a double duvet, piled up like a mountain on the narrow sofa. The duvet was white and it seemed to glow. Bony's head stuck out from underneath it, like the duvet had fallen out of space and squashed his body. His breathing was slow but shallow, and he seemed very peaceful.

Yasmin sat down carefully on the edge of the sofa, at the very end, so as not to wake Bony up. He shifted in his sleep, obviously quite a light sleeper. She reached under the cover and put her hand on his shin. He woke up then and sat straight up, in a way that seemed totally unnatural to Yasmin, before landing all tensed and wary on the floor. His eyes were wide and the whites of his eyes showed clearly all the way around. The duvet was gone, whipped across the room. He was wearing just his boxer shorts.

'Yasmin?' Bony whispered. 'Is that you?'

'Yeah,' Yasmin said. 'Jesus, Bony, I'm sorry. I didn't mean to wake you up.'

'What were you doing?'

'Well . . .' Yasmin began, her hands clasped together in her lap. She was wearing dark green satin pyjamas, with a sleeveless top. Her pale arms shone. 'Oh, well, I suppose I did mean to wake you. I wanted . . . I just wanted to touch you. I thought maybe we could sleep together. Just sleep . . . or, I don't know. Why don't you come back to your bed with me?'

'No!' Bony said, yelped almost. 'Yasmin, what are you saying?'

Yasmin didn't know what to say.

Bony seemed to relax a little bit, then stood up fully. He was still uneasy, though – Yasmin could tell that by his posture and expression. Bony usually looked totally serene, but not right now.

'I understand if you don't want to,' Yasmin said. 'I'm sorry. I don't know how to explain what I want.'

'You don't have to,' Bony said.

'No!' Yasmin said. 'I mean, I don't just want to have sex with you. I think you're a great person, Bony. You're not like anybody I've ever met before. I love how you don't care whether or not anybody knows you. And you know so much without having to keep showing people what you know.'

'I think maybe you're still drunk,' Bony said.

'I might be,' Yasmin said. 'But I feel these things when I'm sober too.'

'Oh, Yasmin,' Bony said. He sat back down on the sofa, not quite next to her. 'I don't think I'm good boyfriend material. I'm a very strange person.'

'In what way?'

'I cannot invest in any kind of relationship,' Bony said. 'Not really. I feel a lot, but I've never felt a lot more for one person than any other person, or felt more than I do for things, like – just the world in general. I mean, I feel intensely positive about most people, but I feel the same for most things too.'

'Arthur told me you don't find people sexually attractive,' Yasmin said.

'Did he?' Bony laughed. 'That's not really true. I do. I find most people very sexually attractive. But I don't have sexual relationships with people, because I can't pretend to commit. Or they realise that I like trees or machines just as much. I just – I see sex as just objects responding to other objects. And I think that's OK. There's nothing wrong with objects. I see our minds as objects, parts of the body, that's all. The relationships between these objects are complicated – more so than with magnets or thermometers, for example – but, still, that is how sex appears to me.'

'So you don't . . . you don't do it?'

'I avoid sex at all times.'

'So that you don't upset people?'

'More or less.'

Yasmin nodded. 'I think I understand.'

'But you don't feel the same?' Bony said.

'No,' Yasmin said. 'No, I don't.'

The two of them sat there in silence for a while.

'I feel emotions for you,' Yasmin said.

'I think sex would be an especially bad idea, then,' Bony said.

'You were thinking about it?'

'Yes.'

'I don't think it would be a bad idea at all,' Yasmin said. 'Not now that you've explained yourself.'

Bony looked directly at Yasmin. 'So it would not upset you that all the time I would be thinking of you as just a load of interlocking systems that I am manipulating?'

'That's how you think of me anyway, though, right?'

'Yes,' Bony nodded. 'I think of all people that way all of the time. And there's something else I should tell you,' he said. 'I use objects . . . I mean, non-human objects. I like to . . . oh God I can't explain it.'

'Like sex toys?'

'No. Like . . . well, kind of, but more than that. Everything is connected, Yasmin. Everything is one big network. Things I come across: unusual textures, unusual vibrations. Like the railway line. Or like . . . like the thing on the beach. Everything is part of the same system, inter-locking. I try to plug in.'

Yasmin narrowed her eyes and breathed in. 'You fucked the thing on the beach?'

'Yes.'

'Did you use a condom?'

'Yes. There was no contact between my skin and that thing.'

'That's OK, then,' Yasmin said, breathing out again.

'What? Really?'

'Yes,' Yasmin said. 'Why wouldn't it be?'

'It's the kind of thing that might disgust normal people with normal emotions,' Bony said.

'It is disgusting,' Yasmin said. 'It is weird and disgusting, but it's not *wrong* in any way I can really put my finger on. It doesn't point to any kind of moral deficiency.'

'Some people would claim that's exactly what it points to.'

'I suppose some people would,' Yasmin said. 'But I'd say that they're wrong.'

'It's good to be able to tell somebody about these things,' Bony said.

'Bony,' Yasmin said, 'you are one of the best people I know.'

'OK.' Bony nodded. 'So basically,' he said, 'I don't really differentiate between people and things in a lot of ways.'

Yasmin nodded. 'Work makes me feel like a thing,' she said. 'Work makes me feel like a baked potato or something, just waiting to be eaten.'

Bony laughed at that.

They stood up and left the room. On the horizon, the stars started to fade away as the sun rose, although of course the sun wasn't rising. It was just becoming visible there, in that part of the world.

THE STREETS OF WHITEHAVEN

Arthur wandered around the town in a state of almost total blankness, his hands in his pockets, his head down. He was cold. It was a cold night.

He found a bar called Sydney's. He remembered going there when he was younger, about sixteen, although it had been a different place then; it had been called Shadows, and was a rock club. It had always seemed empty when it was Shadows. Arthur remembered sitting there on a chair at a low table in a corner, probably with Bony, and watching Paedophile Ted slowly headbanging, alone, in the middle of the too-bright dance-floor, a cart-wheel interwoven with fairy-lights suspended above him, and his long blond hair moving around like seaweed. Maybe he wasn't slowly headbanging at all, maybe Arthur was just remembering it all in slow motion. Paedophile Ted was called Paedophile Ted because he was aged twenty-four but was going out with a fourteen-year-old girl. Although that would have been ten years ago, so maybe he wasn't a paedophile any more. Maybe he was with the same girl, and she was now twenty-four and he was thirty-four. Or maybe he had kept going after the young ones, and he was in prison now. Who knew? Whatever had happened to Paedophile Ted and his denim jacket and his long blond hair and his lumpy, scarred, acne-ravaged face?

Arthur hadn't been back to Shadows – or Sydney's, as it was now called – since that night. In ten years, he hadn't been there. He stood outside for a moment, wondering how he'd ended up here in this dark little back alley off New Street in the first place, because he hadn't consciously decided to walk here. It had happened by accident. And then entered the bar.

There was no dance-floor any more. There was just a long bar, and a load of booths. It was all leather and cocktails now. Quite nice, really, in its way, Arthur thought, but not what it used to be. Did that matter? Maybe it didn't matter. It was dead there, but then it was a Monday night, and what time was it, anyway? How long had he been out walking?

It was nine o' clock and they were still serving. Arthur sat at the bar and looked up at the lights. They had chandeliers now, but the chandeliers were enclosed in plastic cylinders. Why was that? It looked a bit stupid. He ordered a cocktail, after checking that you could pay by card. He couldn't afford it – all of his money in the bank was already spoken for, earmarked for bills – but that had never stopped anybody before, had it? It had never stopped Dad in the Vine. Besides, Arthur wasn't sure if he'd ever tasted a proper cocktail before, and that seemed just abnormal for somebody of his age. The cocktail he'd chosen was a Long Island Iced Tea because that, he thought, sounded quite sophisticated. It would be nice to be sophisticated.

What else could he remember from all those years ago? He remembered Bony staying over one night and being so drunk that Arthur had propped his friend's head over a biscuit tin in case he was sick. He remembered how once, at Bony's house, he and Yasmin and Bony had been sunbathing – it was a fantastically hot summer's day – when the three of them were disturbed, to their incredulous joy, by an ice-cream van turning up from nowhere. It had been playing 'Stairway to Heaven'.

By the time they threw him out of Sydney's, Arthur could barely walk. 'Maybe all people are wrapped in an impenetrable membrane,' he was mumbling, 'that prevents genuine emotional interaction.' In his mind he was picturing a second skin that mapped itself to the contours of the human body, including the interior surfaces of all of the orifices, and through which another human being could never, ever pass.

Yasmin! That was who he wanted to see. Yasmin was kind and he felt like he loved her, which was maybe the same thing as loving her. Who knew? He slowly made his way down to Lowther Street and turned right, occasionally having to push himself away from the wall. It was a bright night; the moon and the stars were out. Arthur was a stooping, stumbling silhouette. Oh, he was a right fucking mess.

Lowther Street took him up to the harbour. There he looked briefly at the dark water of the marina, which made him uneasy, and then turned abruptly left and headed for the building in which Yasmin lived. All of the lights were off, but then it was late; so what did he expect? She was probably in bed, but still, she wouldn't mind being woken up by a friend. A friend in need.

Arthur raised his finger to the buzzer and then leant on it with all his weight. He heard the sound of it from her flat up above. Like an insect or something. It went on for a long time. He released the buzzer and waited. That must have woken her up. Must have.

He pressed the buzzer again.

Still no answer.

He heard the ocean lapping at the man-made shore behind him and pressed the buzzer again, feeling more urgency now. Still no answer.

He turned around, but could see nothing untoward. The Wave was lit tonight, and the swans bobbed in the water, heads tucked under their wings, lit up either blue or green, depending on where they were positioned in relation to the neon strips of the sculpture.

The boats moored nearby rattled and clacked and jangled, their rigging starting to sing as a breeze picked up.

Arthur could not bear to remain there near the sea any more. Yasmin was definitely not answering the door. She must be sleeping very deeply. What time was it now? He didn't know. He staggered away from her building, and made an attempt to run along past the Vagabond – now closed – to Strand Street. He turned left, then right back on to Lowther Street, and ran clumsily until he came to Michael Moon's bookshop, where he stopped and put his hands on his knees, and threw up. *That won't do my red eye any good*, he thought.

Michael Moon's bookshop. The shopfront was a rich blue with the words 'OLD BOOKS, MAPS & PRINTS' painted in a yellowy cream. Arthur wiped his mouth and peered through the window at all the local history books and curling maps. It was a wonderful shop, closed now obviously, it being whatever time it was in the middle of the night. Arthur hadn't been inside it for years, not since his mother had last taken him there. And where was she, anyway? Why was she dead? Why had she jumped?

Of course he could never know. A couple of boy racers flew past in their little cars and, still gazing in through the window of that little shop, he realised the truth. *He could never know.* He would never know – that was what it meant. That was what her jumping meant. She was dead, she was gone, and with her had gone the explanation. Anything but an explanation direct from her would be speculation and nothing more.

Arthur turned around and crossed the road. He didn't check for traffic, but there wasn't any, so he made it safely to the other side. He opened the gate into the tiny little bit of parkland that surrounded the old church building between Church Street and Queen Street. He lay down on his back, on the cool green grass beneath a young tree, and tried to sleep.

BRACKET'S DEVELOPMENT OPPORTUNITY

Usually Isobel got up and went to work before Bracket, but for some reason Artemis had rung Bracket's mobile late the previous night, waking both Bracket and Isobel up, and requested – demanded – that Bracket turn in for work at 6 a.m.

'Sorry,' Bracket had replied. 'It's a bit short notice, isn't it?'

'Don't you need this job?' Artemis had said.

'Artemis,' Bracket had protested, 'you can't just make threats like that. I could go to the union. You're talking about unfair dismissal.' He wasn't in the union, of course, but hoped that Artemis wouldn't call his bluff.

'You can go to the police, for all I care,' Artemis said. 'I'm not sure you understand who or what you're dealing with here. Come in tomorrow and I'll explain in more depth.'

Bracket had opened his mouth to reply, but just then

Artemis had hung up. Isobel was now sitting up in bed, too.

'Who was that?' she said.

'Artemis,' Bracket said. 'He wants me in at six tomorrow.'

'He shouldn't be ringing you at this time,' Isobel said. 'He shouldn't want you in at that time tomorrow, either. You're not going, are you?'

'Yeah,' Bracket said, after a moment, 'I'm going.'

He then didn't sleep at all.

And now here he was, spooning soggy cereal into his mouth at the kitchen table at half past five in the morning, the room bathed in the dim orange glow of the street-lamp outside. He'd left the light switched off because his eyes felt so sensitive; his whole being felt sensitive at this time of day.

'Hey!'

Bracket nearly jumped out of his seat. He turned to see Isobel standing, swaying, in the kitchen doorway.

'Please stop being so noisy,' she said tiredly, her eyes still more or less closed. She was clearly still half asleep. 'You're banging your spoon about on the bowl.'

'What?' Bracket said. 'I'm sorry. Yeah, I'm sorry. I'll be quiet, I promise.'

'No, I'm sorry,' Isobel said, and shook her head. 'I just didn't sleep, because I was worrying.'

'I know,' Bracket said. 'You go back to sleep. I'll be quiet now.'

'Sorry,' Isobel murmured once more, then she turned

and melted into the darkness of the hallway. Bracket listened to her footsteps as she ascended the staircase.

Tuesday. Fucking Tuesday.

The call centre was empty of staff save for Artemis himself, who was seated on the command centre and tapping away feverishly at his laptop. Bracket slowly approached him through the maze of desks, uncertain whether or not Artemis realised he was there. He noticed a piece of A4 paper taped to the screen on Oscar's desk. The sheet of paper was almost filled with just one word, in capital letters thick and black, made up of many heavy, repeated biro strokes:

BREATHE

This was unexpected because Oscar came across as such a snide little bastard – not the type to let the job get to him. But, Bracket supposed, customer service could be a great leveller.

'Bracket!' Artemis said, without looking away from his screen. 'You're here!' His voice was stern and deep and loud, and he made the statement sound like an imperative, somehow.

'I'm here,' Bracket said. 'Yeah. I'm here.' He felt slightly sick, probably because he hadn't had enough sleep.

'I'm ready to tell you more about what we need to do,' Artemis said. He looked over towards Bracket, who was still standing amongst the desks, looking a little lost. 'About your development opportunity.'

'My development opportunity?' Bracket said. 'What's that?'

'An opportunity for you to develop,' Artemis said. 'An opportunity for you to progress your career. To take your career to the next level within the Interext hierarchy. Within the structure.'

'A promotion?' Bracket almost felt a little hopeful.

'No!' Artemis said firmly, and laughed. 'Not a promotion! A development opportunity! It means you get to experience the superior role without committing to it.'

'O-K,' said Bracket. He waited for Artemis to elaborate, but after a moment it became apparent that no further elaboration would be forthcoming.

'Are you coming up here or not?' Artemis's gesture indicated the command centre.

'Yeah, sure,' Bracket said, hurrying forward. 'Look, Artemis, I'm still not certain I understand.'

'All right!' Artemis threw both hands up in the air, feigning exaggerated exasperation. He swivelled around on his chair to face Bracket, who now stood beside him on the command centre platform. 'I'll be honest with you. A development opportunity is where you're given extra responsibilities, but your pay – and everything else, really – remains the same. But, truly, it does stand you in good stead for when jobs at the higher level become available.'

'So . . . if I take on a development opportunity, and then a role that matches my new responsibilities becomes available, would I automatically get that new role?'

'What? No, you'd still have to apply for it.'

'Then . . .' Bracket frowned and shook his head. 'I'm not sure I want this development opportunity, really. Doesn't sound that great.'

'This is how companies work these days,' Artemis agreed. 'It's standard industry practice. You'd still have to apply for the job, but if you don't take on these development opportunities, then you may as well not bother.'

Bracket nodded. *What a world of shite*, he was thinking.

'You know how we identify employees who might be suitable for a development opportunity?' Artemis asked.

'How?'

'We identify a *need*,' Artemis said. 'We identify employees who desperately *need* their job.'

'Doesn't everybody?' Bracket said. He shifted uncomfortably.

'Well, they do, but everybody also has a moral or ethical line drawn in the sand over which they will not step unless circumstances prove exceptional. So we look for people in those exceptional circumstances.'

'I see,' Bracket said. 'OK.'

Artemis grinned.

'I'm not going to pretend that you're going to like your new role, Bracket,' he said.

'I could say no,' Bracket suggested.

'Will you?'

Bracket sat down. 'You still haven't told me what my development opportunity is,' he said.

'I need to start at the beginning,' Artemis explained. 'We will get on to the specifics of your role all in due course. Also, I need to remind you of the confidentiality clause you signed when you first started working here.'

'OK,' Bracket said. 'But that was for Outsourcing Unlimited. Not for Interext.'

'Yeah,' Artemis said, 'but it's all transferred over. Don't worry about it.'

'OK,' Bracket said. He felt like he was becoming an 'OK' machine.

'So. You signed a confidentiality agreement, and what I'm about to tell you cannot be disclosed. It's covered by the terms of that agreement, understand?'

'OK, yes, I understand.'

Outside the sun shone brightly. There were no clouds in the sky, as if they had all rained themselves out of existence last night. It was a cold day, though. Cold and hard like a stone plucked from the seabed.

'A good few years ago, Interext embarked upon a very large project,' Artemis said, as he leant back and entwined his fingers behind his head. 'Do you want a drink, by the way? You look fucked.'

'A coffee, maybe,' Bracket said. 'But the canteen won't be open yet.'

'Go and get one from the machine,' Artemis said.

Bracket went and fetched one from the machine. *OK*, he was saying in his head. *OK. OK. OK.*

Artemis then explained that Interext had spent years developing an advanced call-analytics system. This was not the very large project that Artemis actually wanted to talk about; in fact this was a separate project, but one which was to play a key part in the greater project.

'It is fucking amazing,' Artemis said, gesturing extravagantly. 'You wouldn't know – you *would not know* – that you were talking to a programme and not to an actual human being. It's like science fiction but it's not, Bracket. It's loaded with so many pre-recordings that every time you ring up you get the words spoken differently, in a slightly different tone. And what is being said is different every time because it depends on what the caller, what the customer says in the first place. In essence, it's AI. It's clever stuff. But it works.'

'Then why aren't Interext using it?' Bracket asked.

'We will,' Artemis said. 'We're just a bit ahead of our time. It's all a bit sensitive, because all the subsequent redundancies wouldn't do our corporate responsibility profile any good. To be honest – you know me – I couldn't give a fuck about the workers – no offence – but that wouldn't be my decision ultimately. And, besides, it needs testing.'

'OK,' Bracket said, uncertainly. It sounded fascinating. It genuinely *did* sound fascinating, Bracket had to admit. But alarming, too, for all the obvious reasons.

'My wife was involved,' Artemis continued. 'She was the project lead, but she was . . . what would you say?'

Bracket didn't know what you would say. He widened his eyes and tried to think of a suitable response, but Artemis was now looking upwards, thinking hard, as if grasping there for an answer to what was, Bracket now realised, actually a rhetorical question. The room – seeming especially massive when there was practically nobody in it – hummed with the electric sleep of hundreds of dormant computers, their power cables and connective wires alive with power and energy and information and yet totally immobile.

'What would you say?' Artemis repeated, with an expression almost of wonder, one that Bracket had never witnessed before.

Artemis seemed to finally settle on something. 'You would probably say that she was not afraid to get her hands dirty, or something equally as inane. That sounds a bit too tawdry, but you see what I mean. Towards the end of the project, she herself contributed her voice. She recorded herself speaking. She spent hours of every day for months – for years, Bracket – recording her voice for this project.'

'I didn't know you were married,' Bracket said, but he was already thinking how Artemis's wife must have been trying to get away from him. Either that or she was obsessed in some way. But, then, a lot of highly successful business people are successful only because they are totally obsessed.

'Well,' Artemis said, 'Eleanor is dead now. She died in hospital shortly after giving birth to our daughter.'

'I'm sorry,' Bracket said. 'God, I totally put my foot in it. I'm really sorry. That must have been awful.'

'Yes,' Artemis said. 'It was awful. You might find it hard to believe, but we had a very loving relationship.'

'So . . . you have a daughter?'

'Bracket,' Artemis said, firmly, 'stop asking questions. Our daughter was stillborn.'

Bracket didn't say anything to that. He just swallowed, and then swallowed again.

'Eleanor spent most of her last year alive in that one little room, making all those recordings,' Artemis continued. 'She spent the final months of her pregnancy on that project. She didn't spend any of her time with me. She didn't spend it resting. She spent it here. Not here in Whitehaven, but *here*, at work, do you see?'

Bracket nodded.

'This work is so very important,' Artemis insisted. He was now leaning forward, his face closer to Bracket's face. He grinned mirthlessly. 'Do you see?' he repeated.

'Yes,' Bracket said, 'I see.'

'Good,' Artemis leant back. 'I loved her very much, Bracket.'

'Of course,' Bracket said.

Artemis pinched the bridge of his nose. 'We're drifting off topic,' he declared. 'Where were we?'

'We—'

'Ah, yes, the voice! The system's voice, it is my wife's voice. It is female. This is important.'

'OK,' said Bracket.

'We'll come back to that, though. The other project – the big one – relies upon it.'

'OK.'

'So, there is the AI. Then there is something else: the Interstice. Now, the Interstice is a place.'

'Yes!' Bracket said. 'When I answered your phone that time, that's what they said! "We have made contact with the Interstice," or something like that.'

'It is actually a place,' Artemis continued, as if Bracket hadn't spoken, 'but it is very hard to reach. You can't travel there by everyday means. Being there is about perception. It is about total faith.'

'Faith' was not a word you usually heard thrown around the office environment. Bracket wasn't sure what to make of it, how to take it. He felt uncertain. He looked uncertain, too.

'Wait,' Bracket said. 'How do *you* know about the Interstice, if you can't know about it without perceiving it?'

'You can simply *know* about it,' Artemis said. 'People have known about it for centuries – for thousands of years. And people have been there, too. But to open up a channel of communication, or an actual reliable route in or out – those things have never been done, as far as we know. So, we need to access the Interstice, and we need to communicate with that intelligence, that entity. We have made contact with it – we had the AI calling out through the telephone network in order to attract its attention – but we now need somebody that can report back.'

'Me.'

'No, not you. The subject was identified years ago.'

'What? Who?'

'Harry.'

'Harry! How? What do you mean?'

Artemis frowned. 'Harry has been receiving phone calls,' Artemis said, 'from his dead wife.'

'No,' Bracket replied. 'I don't actually believe that. Now I think you're making things up.'

'Bracket, you pillock,' Artemis said, 'of course they're not really from his dead wife. They're from the AI. We're not using it commercially, but it's been dialling him for ages. We know whenever he's not at work, see, and it just rings him in accordance with his shift patterns.'

'Why Harry?'

'We were looking out for somebody susceptible,' Artemis said. 'We were waiting for an employee to suffer a bereavement.'

'But Harry didn't even work for Interext then!' Bracket exclaimed. 'He would have been working for Outsourcing Unlimited.'

'He was not working directly for Interext, no, but ultimately he was. Many, many people work for Interext, without knowing it. That's just the way the world has gone.'

'So the AI is ringing Harry up in order to . . . what? I don't get it.'

'In order to trick him into believing in the Interstice,' Artemis said.

'Why? Why do you have to trick anybody into believing in it, if it's real?'

'Do you believe in it?' Artemis asked.

Bracket thought about that.

'You see?' Artemis said. 'It's the same for me also. It

357

sounds too fantastic. I can't sit at the end of a phone line and just imagine the place, and then *be* there. The plan was for Harry to believe in it, and for it to happen to him. It didn't happen to him, though.' Artemis rubbed his eyes. 'It happened to Arthur instead. The entity came for Arthur, somehow. Arthur was sitting at Harry's desk on that day. The implication is that the awareness runs both ways, which is ultimately good, but it resulted in the entity trying to make contact through Harry's phone, and reaching Arthur instead. We think.'

'You think?'

'We are not dealing with an exact science here, Bracket,' Artemis replied, 'as I'm sure you appreciate. We are operating at the limits . . . no, we are operating beyond the limits of our understanding.'

'I think I get that,' Bracket said. 'I still don't know what you need me to do, though.'

'You need to know all this, just in case. If I for some reason have to go, Bracket, then you will be responsible for this shithole. You will get sent all of the briefing packs in that eventuality, of course, but by then . . . well, you might appreciate the little understanding I've just given you before things get to that stage, shall we say.'

'I can't believe what you've done,' Bracket said. 'It's horrible.'

Artemis looked at Bracket and frowned. 'Please,' he said, 'let's not get sentimental.'

HARRY IN A STATE

Pauline would always open the doors of the Vine to Harry. He was a good customer for a start, spending an obscene proportion of his wages – and maybe even his son's wages – inside. But, more than that, he was a kind of friend. A friend purely out of familiarity, if that made any sense. So, however early he rolled in, Harry was welcome.

This time he had turned up within official opening hours, arriving at about nine o'clock on Monday night. Now it was nine o'clock on Tuesday morning and he was still here. Pauline herself was asleep, her head resting on the bar. Harry was not actually asleep, but he was not really conscious either. Not in the true sense of the word. He swayed around on top of the bar stool like he was dancing slowly, even though there was no music playing.

Apart from Pauline and Harry, the bar was empty. The

room was dark, too, apart from the stripes of light that made it through the cracks in the blinds. They didn't illuminate anything, though. They just hung there, in the dust-filled air, like solid things.

LATE

Arthur showed up for work at about eleven o' clock. It wasn't like him to be late, but then it wasn't like him to have slept outdoors like a tramp. He was wearing yesterday's clothes, as well.

Bracket accosted him as he walked across the call centre floor.

'Hey!' Bracket shouted, 'Arthur!'

Arthur pretended not to hear him, but was forced to turn around when Bracket grabbed him by the shoulder.

'What?' Arthur said.

'Jesus Christ,' Bracket said, jerking backwards. 'What happened to your eye?'

'I was badly sick,' Arthur said. 'Look, I know I'm late. I just want to get started, OK? I'll make the time up at the end of my shift.'

'Yeah, OK.' Bracket nodded. 'God, are you alright?'

'I barely know what I'm doing here,' Arthur said. 'I haven't really slept.'

'Well,' Bracket said, 'if you need to, go and have a sit-down in the break room.'

Arthur looked down at the smaller man for a moment, and then nodded. 'Thanks,' he said. He turned away and continued to his desk.

Bracket watched him go. He had wanted to tell Arthur to go home and get some real, actual rest – to go home and not worry about this stupid, stupid job.

Go home and stay safe.

Bracket couldn't stop thinking about Artemis losing his baby. Of course, the possibility of something going wrong with his and Isobel's baby was a fear that never stopped throbbing away unpleasantly at the back of his head, but up until now he had, by and large, been able to dismiss it as some kind of natural paranoia. It was something that he assumed every prospective parent must feel. But this – what had happened to Artemis – made that eventuality seem much closer, much more likely, for some reason.

Something else that Bracket hadn't really considered before was what if the baby grew up to be a total bastard? What if the baby grew up to be like Artemis? What were Artemis's parents like? Bracket didn't think he'd ever met such an absolute wanker before, and so hadn't worried unduly about his child growing up to become one. But now . . . now things were different.

At night, when neither he nor Isobel were sleeping that well, he would be assailed by sweaty panics and dreadful fantasies in which their child grew up miserable and bitter and became the kind of man or woman who could only wear suits and spent all night at the office because they had nothing to go home for and ended up getting a prostitute habit and dying lonely or angry or both. He worried that, despite their best efforts and intentions, their child would become some kind of monster. For some reason, he envisaged the baby as something with green rotten eyes and skin slick with algae. Something that would grow up to feel just as at home slithering around in silt as it would all cleaned up and masked and slithering around some boardroom somewhere.

It might help if Isobel would talk more about what she was feeling. But she didn't really. They spoke less and less, as if ever-longer periods of their lives were being spent with some kind of 'mute' button on. Isobel did not seem angry or unhappy; just completely content within a self-contained world. She and the baby. The bump. Bracket sometimes touched the bump – the sensation of movement within was thrilling – but he always felt like he was intruding on something private when he did so.

After about half an hour of listening to calls, Arthur felt his eyelids increasingly difficult to control; they kept closing of their own accord, and not really opening again unless he really concentrated on them. Time for a coffee, maybe? Definitely.

The coffee from the vending machine came in a small yellow plastic cup and smelled like stale cigarettes. Arthur really wanted one of the full-size proper coffees from the canteen – a cappuccino or something equally as exotic – but they were more expensive, and ... well, how much money had he spent on cocktails last night? He felt sick just thinking about it.

He stood by the vending machine and looked out of the window while waiting for his drink. Outside, the day was bright and hard-edged; the sea was sparkling and difficult to look at. Everything looked old and shabby in that unforgiving light. Seagulls made sounds that felt like scabs itching on his consciousness. He had another full day of total shit to look forward to, more or less. And his dad ... where was his dad?

Where was Yasmin, for that matter? It wasn't her rest day today, Arthur was pretty sure. He took his actually quite manky-looking coffee from the vending machine and stuck his head through the break room door to double-check her desk. No, she wasn't there. Then where was she? She never rang in sick. Yasmin wasn't that kind of person.

When Arthur returned to the vending machine for his change, which he'd forgotten, Diane was already standing there. She looked at him, quite expressionless, and extended her open hand, which held thirty pence.

'This yours?' she asked.

'Yes,' Arthur said. 'Thank you.'

'What happened to your eye? Burst a blood vessel?'

'Yeah.'

'I did that once. Through being sick.'

'Yeah,' Arthur said, 'that's how I did it, too.'

Diane smiled faintly.

'I'm sorry about the other day,' Arthur said. 'I don't normally get angry.'

'Yeah, right.' Diane laughed briefly. She looked around, and then at Arthur. 'I'm sorry for what I said about your dad,' she said.

'That's OK,' Arthur said.

'I've been off work for a while,' she said.

'Are you OK?'

'I've just been ringing in sick.'

'Oh, right,' Arthur said.

Diane looked like she wanted to say something else; her eyes kept darting around and her mouth was sad. She didn't, though. She just looked up – she had such big eyes, Arthur thought – and smiled briefly, then left him standing there.

Arthur spent the whole of his shift half expecting to be pulled back into the Scape. He didn't know how he felt when the time to log out rolled around and it still hadn't happened. Last time he'd been there, though, he'd been scared for his life. What did it mean, then, that he now felt as disappointed as he was relieved?

Probably nothing good; it probably meant that he was suicidal. Was that what it meant?

Arthur slipped his biro in his coat pocket and left the building.

BODY

Artemis was alone in the call centre. Well, alone apart from the security people manning the desk downstairs.

Artemis felt like a god when he was in these places: flatpack, templated environments designed for function and little else. Supermarkets, offices, generic hotel rooms – bland places where you could be anybody. Out there on the harbour or in the dank little pubs, he felt uneasy and threatened, but *here* he felt that same power that he'd felt when Diane lay, passed out and naked, on his hotel-room bed. He could do anything here, too, and the anonymity of the location protected him. Not only that, but he felt like he could draw on some kind of power that was not accessible to him elsewhere. He was physically stronger and more agile when he was plugged into that sad network of vacant conferencing centres, business parks, industrial estates, motorway rest stops, etcetera. And call centres.

Diane was one of many, many young women he'd taken off to hotel rooms. Even here, in Whitehaven, there had already been several. Most of them – four or five – were customer advisers at the call centre. The youngest, prettiest, most insecure, least experienced in terms of employee rights or, indeed, in any of the ways of the world. Of course, there had been that checkout girl from Tesco's, as well. Where were they now? At home probably, sleeping, or watching *Dirty Dancing* or some other crap girl film from the eighties. Feeling a deep sense of unease, most likely, and wondering what they'd done, or what they'd had done to them, and trying to work out whether or not it mattered.

The bodies – Artemis liked to have his fun with those bodies.

He checked his emails. Somebody called Sally – he couldn't remember who that was – had sent him an email about some 'mass confusion' that many of the managers were apparently feeling. She finished her message with a paragraph that sounded quite critical.

I wouldn't want to be responsible for calling a series of unnecessary meetings, thereby initiating a low-level radioactive hum of useless talk. But I do want to know what's going on. I do want to instigate some kind of meaningful discussion.

Artemis would have to have a word with her. Not only because of the unacceptably negative insinuation that there was a lot of meaningless talk going on, but also because of the overly extravagant language used. Where did she think she was? Some kind of university?

There *was* a lot of meaningless talk going on, of course, but that was all part of it. Part of the boondoggle. Talking about talking about meetings about planning meetings about planning for projects about talking to people who talk to people about other people. It was a whole meta-economy. Meaningless talk was fine, especially given what would happen in the end.

It was as Artemis was about to start replying that the phone rang. That is, *a* phone rang. Artemis stood up.

Identifying a ringing telephone is normally quite easy, but not in a room full of hundreds of telephones. Especially when you realise that they all have different settings; they all ring at different volumes and tones. *Stupid damn telephones*, Artemis thought as he paced around, looking for the offender. Why can't they all sound as uniform as they look? If the sound is quiet, how do you know whether it's a quiet-sounding phone or just a phone that's further away?

He did find it, eventually.

It was Harry's telephone.

He didn't answer it. He just watched it for a while.

Maybe this was it. Maybe this was the entity trying to communicate.

The telephone didn't stop ringing.

Eventually he reached out his hand and picked up the receiver.

He heard distant sounds: something scratching against a distant wall, the wind resonating through a faraway chimney. The sea. He frowned.

The sounds grew louder and louder. Was there a voice in there, too? Somewhere in there, there *was* a voice.

The sounds merged, dispersed, merged again. They were flattening out, somehow sketching and defining the boundaries of some kind of surface, some kind of plain. The static rose and fell like hills, like peaks and troughs, like waves, but he saw them as solid. He could envisage them as solid.

He saw the writhing plain. He saw the dead sky. He turned around and he saw the walls of the City rearing up in front of him like some kind of solid, smooth, grey sludge. Between him and the walls there was a figure – a tall, spindly figure dressed in shiny black leather. Next to the tall figure there were two other creatures, possessing something like human torsos with no legs, but three or four arms too many, which they used like legs. They looked up at him with big protruding eyes, and hissed and groaned and spat.

The tall figure moved awkwardly towards him, every step looking painful and uncoordinated. It was talking but Artemis couldn't tell what it was saying. It was repeating itself – saying the same thing, or making the same sound, over and over again.

'Ohdiee,' it was saying. 'Ohdi. Ohdie. Ohhdee.'

Artemis stepped backwards. He knew what it wanted. Body, it was saying. *Body*. It wanted a body.

Artemis wrenched the receiver away from his ear and clapped it back down into its cradle.

He knew what he needed to do.

Come and Meet Me

Arthur woke up to the sound of the telephone ringing. It was night-time again. He felt like it was always night-time, because all the time spent at work just didn't count. The phone was ringing away like a bastard. Arthur swore into his pillow and punched the mattress, but the ringing wouldn't stop.

He heard Harry banging around in the next room.

'Just coming,' Harry was saying. 'Just coming.'

Arthur lifted his head from the pillow and listened as Harry slipped and stumbled down the stairs. In Arthur's mind he saw his father, hunched and muttering, descending through unlit space. Eventually he reached the telephone, or at least he must have reached the telephone, because the ringing stopped, and Harry said, 'Hello?'

Arthur waited.

'Rebecca? Is that you?'

He could only hear his father's side of the conversation,

of course, broken up by silences when whoever was on the other end – or, rather, whoever his father thought was on the other end – was speaking.

'Rebecca? Are you OK? What's wrong? . . . What? . . . What? . . . Really?'

Silence.

'I'll come and meet you now. Just stay there. You'll be OK. I'll help you. I'll bring you back. Oh my God, Rebecca, it's been so long. It will be so good to see you. Stay there. See you soon. OK, bye.'

Arthur was sitting up by now. He got out of bed and went to open his bedroom door and shout down to his father. But, even before he got there, he heard the front door slam. He ran out on to the landing and down the stairs to the front door, opened it and looked out.

His father was running away, running along the street. He turned off between two houses, towards the steps that led down to the harbour, and disappeared.

Arthur went back inside, took the stairs three at a time, and got himself dressed.

A REQUEST FROM THE INTERSTICE

Artemis stood at the windows at the southern end of the building and looked out over the harbour. You couldn't make out individual figures when it was dark, but he knew that Harry would be there, or on his way. Excited, hopeful, deluded. It felt strange to be here witnessing the culmination of a plan that had first been kicked off years and years ago. It felt strange to have shaped somebody's life subtly, for once, rather than by using threats or violence or sex.

Most of the lights in the huge room were now off, with just a couple still on, right in the middle above the command centre. And, of course, the red LEDs that gleamed from monitors and computers all over the place.

Artemis used his mobile to ring the security desk downstairs, advising the night-watchmen to let Harry in as soon as he arrived.

*

Artemis himself met Harry at the top of the stairs. He had arrived wearing bedroom slippers, a pair of boxers, and a horribly stained old dressing-gown. Arthur was with him, his forehead creased, his hunched stance suggesting shame and embarrassment.

'You smell of alcohol,' Artemis said to Harry.

'Where is she?' Harry asked. He was looking around eagerly, like a dog expecting a biscuit. 'Where's Rebecca?'

'Come this way,' Artemis said, steeling himself, then gingerly put a bulky arm around Harry's shoulders. He manoeuvred the smaller man through the double doors leading to the call centre floor.

Arthur followed.

'Is she in here?' Harry asked.

'Kind of,' Artemis said, pushing Harry forward now. 'She is kind of in here, yes.' He turned and closed the door behind them. He made eye contact with Arthur then, and grinned.

'Where is she?' Harry asked, turning around and staring up at Artemis. 'I can't see her.'

Artemis looked down into Harry's excited and blood-shot and yellowing eyes, huge and moist behind his thick spectacles. The man was a total mess. He shouldn't even be employed. He wasn't capable of work. Well, he *was* on the to-be-sacked list, although maybe that wouldn't be necessary, in the end.

'What were you going to do?' Artemis asked. 'What would you actually have done if you'd found her here?

How did you imagine it would happen?' He folded his arms. 'What state would her body have been in?'

Harry looked at him for a moment, not comprehending. Then he blew up.

'*Where is she?*' he screamed, fists clenched and arms held rigid down by his sides, the dressing-gown flapping open, spit flying from his chapped lips and brown teeth. '*Where the fuck is she?*'

Artemis frowned slightly, and then back-handed Harry across the face in a movement too quick for Harry or Arthur to see it coming, let alone have time to react to it. Harry's glasses flew off and smashed against the wall, and he went down straight away. He himself would have said that he hit the floor 'like a sack of spuds'. He crawled forward and tried to stand up, using a desk as support, but just then his legs failed him.

'Oh my God,' he was saying, quietly. Blood flecked from his mouth. His eyes were half closed.

Artemis looked at Arthur, who had clapped one hand over his mouth and was staring at the scene with one white eye and one red one.

'Nothing to say?' Artemis asked him.

Arthur took his hand away from his mouth. 'Dad?' he ventured.

Harry didn't reply.

Arthur looked up at Artemis, while Artemis looked back and waited for Arthur to do something. But it looked like Arthur did not know what to do.

Artemis grinned again. 'What are you going to do, Arthur?'

After another long moment, Arthur hesitantly stepped forward and aimed a slow kick at Artemis. But it was nothing – just a pathetic, ineffectual gesture. Artemis side-stepped it easily and, with one long arm, grabbed Arthur's shoulder. With the other he punched him hard in the face. Arthur's head snapped backwards, blood spraying from his nose. He would have fallen if it were not for the grip Artemis maintained on his shoulder. Arthur swayed, eyelids fluttering.

Artemis punched him again, in the stomach this time, and let him drop. He then hauled Harry to his feet and dragged him, at speed, across the call centre floor. Harry had to half-run not to be pulled off his feet again. His legs felt weak. Artemis dragged him over to Harry's own desk, where he just stood, looking dazed.

'What do you want?' Harry asked.

Artemis pushed him down into the chair. 'Put your headset on,' he said.

'What? Why?'

'Put your fucking headset on,' Artemis snarled.

'What for?'

Artemis slammed both hands down on the desk and spoke very calmly right into Harry's face. 'So that they don't find you floating in the fucking harbour with your bowels turned inside out,' he said. 'Just do it. Do it for me. Do it for your boss. Come on, Harry. Just fucking do it.'

Harry picked up the headset and put it on. Artemis grabbed his head and forced it into the desk, knocking him out. Then he turned back to Arthur.

Arthur was getting to his feet a few desks back, one hand covering his face. Even in that dim light, and at that distance, Artemis could see that the boy was losing copious amounts of blood. Arthur staggered towards him. What exactly was he now planning to do? Was he going to attack again? Artemis almost laughed at the prospect. The boy must not really know what he was doing.

Once Arthur was within range Artemis drove his fist into his face again, his knuckles cracking the bridge of Arthur's nose and one cheekbone. This time Arthur did fall to the floor, but Artemis pulled him up by the hair and, in much the same way as he had done with Harry, smashed his head into the nearest desk. Arthur went completely limp in his grip. Fearing he had used too much force, Artemis held Arthur's mouth to his ear and could detect breathing. So that was OK. He would be no use dead, after all. Artemis placed Arthur into a seat next to Harry's, and slipped a headset on to his head, too.

Artemis strode over to the command centre and gave his keyboard a few quick taps. He then took Harry's and Arthur's employee IDs from the database and used them to log both their phones into the network remotely. He next set the two phones up to receive calls. Of course, there were never very many calls coming through at this time of night, but there were always a few. Nocturnal call volumes would surprise most people, and Artemis liked to wonder who they were. Wrong numbers? Lonely insomniacs? Psychopaths? People from other time zones?

Sometimes he listened in to these calls from some airy distance, and marvelled at the almost alien voices of those confused human beings at night.

The plan was not for Harry or Arthur to receive these calls, though – especially now that they were unconscious. They were here for their own unique connections to the Interstice. Well, Arthur was, at least; Harry had been a pretty effective way of luring him here. And Harry would come in useful, anyway. Artemis was pretty sure of that.

FACE TO FACE

Arthur heard the beep. It carried the impact of a hammer blow. He knew what he would see when he opened his eyes, so he didn't want to open them at all. But eventually he had to, because he was lying on his back, and he could feel unpleasant things moving beneath him. And, sure enough, there it was – that sky above him the colour and texture of rotten milk, and hung so *low*, like it was always hovering just out of reach. It swirled and fizzed with long-gone conversations and with those sounds he recognised from being constantly on the phone at work, waiting for incoming calls. Those distant murmurings, like the wind sighing through tall grass a very long way off. He had always known, deep down, that he was listening to the sounds of an actual place.

He heard something behind him crunch loudly, and he turned around. The shiny man-thing stood over him. Whatever it was, it loomed up, silhouetted against the weird sky, looking tall and willowy and strong. It hissed and burbled like a cat with a cut throat. It bent over and reached down with a hand encased in the same smooth, gleaming black material as the rest of it. The hand was long and thin, with five pointed fingers – although whether the fingers themselves were pointed, or just the veneer covering them, Arthur didn't know. Or maybe the veneer was part of the thing itself. But none of that mattered now.

What mattered now were the sharp fingers at his throat, feeling tacky like rubber; the asymmetrical face suddenly just inches away from his own; the whirring sounds coming from within it and the glinting of something like metal through the slots. Those were the things that mattered. The inexorable movement; the drawing together; the inevitable meeting of their faces; the digging and pulling and kneading of the cold hands on his throat; the quickening chatter and grinding and clicking and flashing from within the darkness of the head of the thing that faced him.

Things started to emerge from that head. Whether organic or mechanical, Arthur couldn't be sure. They were penetrating his face before he could tell.

HEADSET

As Arthur's body nearly spasmed right out of the chair, Artemis clapped his hands together. Harry jerked his head up from the desk and looked around blearily.

'Excellent!' Artemis cried. 'Looks like we have contact.'

Arthur was clearly having a seizure. Black fluid started running down the sides of his head from both earpieces of the headset – black fluid with an oily sheen.

Harry sat up, shook his head.

'Harry,' Artemis warned, 'don't you fucking dare touch anything. Harry . . . no!'

But he did not get down from the command centre quickly enough. Harry's fingers had curled tightly around the headset and, although it felt unnaturally reluctant to be detached from Arthur's head, he finally succeeded in yanking the thing away, resulting in a sudden and eerie stillness falling over Arthur's body. Harry looked at the headset there in his own hand and grinned triumphantly.

But Artemis was upon him. He plucked the headset

from Harry's grasp easily, and since Arthur was no longer exhibiting any obvious signs of life, he fastened it to Harry's head instead, knocking off the one that had already been there. The transition had started, but it had not yet finished. There was still a chance that the process could be completed with a different person connected to the Interstice. Artemis hoped so, anyway, as he didn't really want to have to report any kind of failure back to management.

Now it was Harry who was suffering the seizure. It was Harry whose face was contorted, whose ears were being filled with that otherworldly substance, whose eyes were rolling, whose teeth were clashing. He screamed and the sound was ragged and high-pitched. His body jerked and twisted, and he screamed again. Artemis was grateful that the call centre was surrounded by nothing but empty car parks.

CHOICE

Arthur was not dead. He was not even unconscious. He felt violated, though, to such an extent that his mind had diminished into nothing but a tiny, lost spark of sentience struggling to illuminate the cavernous body in which it found itself. The thought of opening his eyes or mouth, or reacting in any way to any of the things he could dimly hear, just did not occur to him. His ears felt wet and leaky, and so he wasn't sure that he could hear properly anyway. He felt like something had physically been trying to creep into his ear canals.

As he noticed or felt one thing, he found himself noticing and feeling other, related things. He felt like an office block in which the lights in a series of adjacent rooms were being turned on, one after the other.

He could hear his dad screaming and he knew he should do something about it. He knew he should help in some way. But he knew, as well, that he would fail. In the same way that his dad had failed to save his mum. His dad had let her die, right? His dad knew how it was to be power-less to help. He would understand.

Arthur attempted to move some part of his body, any part, and wasn't sure if he succeeded or not. He didn't reckon he was thinking straight; all of his frames of refer-ence seemed shot. What was it he had just been thinking about his dad? He couldn't remember. It was as if he'd just forgotten a dream he'd been having. Maybe that was what had happened. Maybe he was just waking up.

But who was that screaming?

Arthur's eyelids fluttered and then stilled, and then fluttered again.

THE MOUTHPIECE

After a few more tortured seconds, Harry's body slumped into the seat, all the tension gone out of it. He had unintentionally shrugged his dressing gown off and sprawled there nearly naked.

'I am here,' he said, although his voice was not his own reedy voice; it was something diffuse and unearthly, made intelligible by the human vocal cords thrumming within Harry's throat. 'I have this body now, and I am here.'

'Welcome,' Artemis said, grinning. 'Welcome to our world.'

Without prior warning, Harry's body jerked up out of the seat, so that he was standing. The wire to the headset was stretched out to its full length. He looked around and then took a couple of steps towards Artemis, who remained completely motionless, still grinning.

The headset fell off, Harry's body having taken one step too many away from the telephone to which it was connected. He fell.

'Lesson learned, I think,' Artemis said. 'You won't be trying that again.'

He picked Harry up as if he were nothing, and dumped him back into the seat. He then picked up the headset, now dripping and trailing something lank and black, like slimy wet seaweed. He stood behind Harry and, once more, clamped it to his head.

'I need a body,' said the voice emanating immediately from Harry's mouth.

'You have a body,' Artemis said.

'Why can't I then move?'

'You are connected to the telephone,' Artemis said, 'by a wire.'

'This is not enough.'

'You are not here for your own reasons,' Artemis said. 'You are here because we want you here.'

'I am not here at all.'

If it weren't for the very slight motion of his chest as he breathed, Harry would have appeared dead.

After a long silence, Artemis spoke again. 'We want you to help us,' he said.

'I do not just help you people.'

'You have been asked before?'

'Many times.'

Artemis nodded, his forehead creasing. 'Well,' he said, 'no matter. If you do not just help us people, what does it take?'

Silence. Then, 'A body.'

'We have given you a body.'

'You have given me a mouthpiece,' the voice replied, with a rasping sneer. 'I require a sacrifice.'

'I didn't think a sacrifice was expected,' Artemis said. 'I am quite sure this is only a Priority 2 negotiation.'

'You and your organisation are pitifully ignorant about me, Artemis,' the voice said. 'You have no understanding of what I require or what I desire. You only have a rudimentary understanding of what I can offer you or of what I am capable. Do not attempt to bully me.'

'Well, then,' Artemis said, 'if you really need a sacrifice, you can kill him.' He gestured impatiently at Harry's prone form. 'Take what we've given you. And then what? You will . . . you will accept the offering and, in return, help us?'

'Yes. But I cannot kill it – not from here. *You* must kill it.'

'OK,' Artemis said, 'no problem.' He stood up.

'But what is it that you want in return? What is the assistance that you require?'

'Disruption,' Artemis said. 'We want you to disrupt and disturb all the telephony networks of other centres, other outsourcers, other corporations.'

'That is all?'

'Yes,' Artemis said, 'for now.'

'That is nothing. That is pathetic.'

'Then . . . wait.' Artemis pointed at Harry's body, which he felt was watching him. The eyes now had a cold, remote gleam to them that didn't seem right, and Artemis couldn't work out which light source they were reflecting. 'If we can communicate like this, and what we are asking

387

you to do is so trivial, why do you need a sacrifice?'

Silence, or almost silence. There was a kind of breathing sound – waves, or maybe static.

The moment stretched out.

'Oh, Artemis,' Harry's mouth said. There was a strange, new tone to the voice – a wistfulness. 'I have not set foot in your world for such an age,' the voice continued. 'Not since Crowley came to the pyramids and called me through. And only then for mere minutes of your time.'

'You want . . . you want to be summoned?' Artemis asked. He laughed. 'Well, then, that would require a sacrifice, yes. Although I myself am not authorised, you understand, for any Priority 1 negotiations. And even if I was . . . what do you take me for?' Artemis laughed again, more loudly this time. 'You must think I'm a fucking idiot!'

'I know what you want, Artemis.'

'I've got everything I want,' Artemis said. 'Or I can soon get it.'

'You can't get Eleanor back, can you?'

Artemis felt his head jerk back as if he'd been slapped. He stared into Harry's black, shining eyes. He took a breath, as if he were about to speak, but then released it. He took another breath, a deeper one.

'What the fuck did you just say?' he asked. 'What the fuck are you talking about, you slippery fucking bastard?'

'Or what about Lisa? Yes, maybe Lisa. Maybe that is a more persuasive prospect.'

'What are you talking about?' Artemis gritted his teeth. 'What do you mean?'

'I can bring one of them here,' the voice said. 'I can bring one of them through for you, if you'll bring *me*. Or even both of them, if you do enough.'

'I don't believe you,' Artemis said. 'Why should I believe you?'

'Because I know their names,' the voice said. 'I know how they died, how old they were. They are not far from me now, Artemis. Beyond the edges of the Interstice are the fields of the dead, and I can go there. I can go there and bring them back.'

Artemis didn't respond. His jaws were still clenched, his eyes shining.

'They could be with you forever.'

'Yes, then!' Artemis said quickly, nodding vigorously. 'Do it. Let's do it.'

'You must abide by the rituals.'

'But . . . but I don't *know* the rituals!'

'I can guide you. But you will need something with which to draw the circle. And you will need blood.'

Artemis scrabbled for some whiteboard markers lying on a nearby desk. They were no good, though; they wouldn't show up on the carpet. *Think.* Chalk? But, no, no fucker used blackboards these days. *Think.* He reflected on a question he himself always asked when he was interviewing people. 'Can you give an example of when you have had to think creatively in order to solve a problem?' Brilliant fucking question. Always resulted in a momentarily blank face and a stupid, incoherent answer. From most people, anyway.

He had it.

He darted off to the nearest meeting room and tore down the projector screen, which he then dragged back towards Harry's body. He unrolled the screen and put it on the floor, and then wheeled Harry's chair into the middle of it. He weighted down the corners of the screen with other seats. The whiteboard markers would do the job now.

'I will instruct you,' the voice said. 'This feels like a thin place. In these places, these . . . telephone centres, the walls are weaker. It will be a simple ritual, but I still need the circle. I still need the blood.'

Artemis did not respond straight away. For a moment the only sounds were the background humming and, like something heard from a long way away, the wind and the rain. Then the voice issued again from Harry's mouth, and Artemis knelt down to follow its instructions.

He drew a circle, the circumference of which intersected the three points of a triangle. He drew more triangles in the space remaining between the sides of the original triangle and the circle. He kept drawing and drawing and drawing, shuffling around on the projector screen, as the voice instructed him.

By the time he had finished, his knees were aching. He stood up. 'Is that the circle done?' he asked.

'Nearly,' the voice said. 'But first the blood. Once the throat is cut, I will not be able to speak. So listen carefully, Artemis. You must cut the throat and then let the body bleed to death. You must cup some of the blood and let the rest flow. With the cupped blood, you must then complete the circle.'

The voice went on to describe the last few symbols and amendments that Artemis had to add, after Harry was dead. Once Artemis had the process clear in his head, he stepped forward and, with a pair of scissors he'd pulled from his suit jacket pocket, he slashed Harry's throat. The blood came slowly at first, so he did it again in the other direction. It came faster after that, sputtering and streaming from the two rough-edged wounds. It looked black in the darkness, as it ran down Harry's scrawny, shivering body, soaked into the padding of the chair, dripped from his fingers, pooled on the projector screen, obscuring various intricacies of the circle. Apart from the small, wet dripping noises the blood made, and the faint sound of the sea outside, there was silence.

STRANGE WEATHER

Bony looked out of Yasmin's flat window. He was wearing only some loose, drawstring pyjama bottoms. The evening was peculiarly hot, the sea was heaving, and thick clouds were rushing in to make the night darker yet. He could look up at the side of them, as if they were moving in as some kind of front, and they just went up and up and up, a solid wall of gunmetal grey.

'You seen the weather?' he asked Yasmin

Yasmin slipped her arms around his waist from behind, and pulled him towards her. She was wearing a soft blue vest top and matching loose trousers. She looked out over his shoulder. 'It looks wrong,' she said. 'It looks weird.'

'And the sea, as well,' Bony said. 'The sea looks a bit . . . a bit full.'

Yasmin didn't reply at first. Bony could almost feel her frowning, though – something in the set of her jaw against his neck. After a moment, she said, 'I know what you mean. It seems quite high against the harbour wall. And . . . and what's that?' She pointed out towards the water.

Bony couldn't see what she was indicating, and he absently scratched at the bare skin of his chest while scanning the sea. 'What?' he asked, finally.

'Over there, the turbulence. See?'

'Oh, yes!' Bony said. 'The white water?'

'Yeah.'

'It's growing,' Bony said. 'Spreading out.'

'Yeah, it is.'

'A shoal of fish?'

'I don't know,' Yasmin said. 'I don't like it.'

Bony looked down along the promenade. Anybody straying on to the harbour would stop momentarily to stare at the burgeoning waves and the curiously solid sky, then hurry away, heads lowered. 'Nobody else likes it either,' he observed.

'I feel strange,' Yasmin said. 'It's clammy. Electric.'

Bony nodded. He chewed the inside of his lower lip and ran a hand over his scalp. 'I feel like something is coming,' he said. 'Do we know where Arthur is?'

'I'll try ringing him,' Yasmin said. 'Wait a moment.'

Yasmin moved away from Bony and the window. She picked up her phone and dialled Arthur's number.

'No answer,' she said, after a short while.

'Yasmin,' Bony turned around. 'We have to go to the call centre. Those emails about the Interstice – the sea – and now Arthur not being at home. Whatever it is, it's happening, and I can't think where else it would occur.'

Yasmin thought for a moment, then nodded. She stood up, moved out into the hallway, and returned with the cricket bat. 'We're taking this,' she said.

'OK,' Bony said.

Yasmin put the bat on the table. 'Come on, then,' she said. 'Let's get dressed.'

THIN PLACES

At first Arthur thought Harry must have wet himself or something. He was staring at his dad sitting there in one of those swivelling office chairs, and saw some kind of liquid was running down off the seat and dripping all over the floor. There was a big white something under the chair and the liquid kept spattering on to it. It was actually the recurrent sound that Arthur became aware of first. His field of vision seemed quite narrow, and all he was aware of seeing was his dad.

He was sitting somewhere behind his dad, looking at the back of his dad's chair, at the back of his dad's head.

He realised that it was dark. He tried to move his head, but felt the slightest movement opening up a well of pain right in the middle of his forehead. Why were they here at work when it was so obviously night-time, anyway? There was nobody around, apart from the two of them and Artemis, who was standing over by the window, looking towards the sea.

It was obvious that there was something very wrong.

Arthur focused back on his dad and felt like his eyes were fully open now, like his vision was nearly fully restored.

Blood . . .

Blood running everywhere.

Arthur tried to get out of his own chair, but his muscles were unresponsive, and it felt like any effort to move prompted his brain to try and tear itself open inside his skull. The waves of pain forced him to close his eyes, and nearly sent vomit cascading from his mouth.

After a moment he settled for just keeping his eyes open.

There were words and diagrams scribbled on the projector screen rolled out beneath Harry's chair. Arthur could not quite make them out in the poor light, especially now that his aching eyes were full of tears. From his seated position, the whole display looked like a cross between the clichéd Satanist paraphernalia from horror films or tabloid newspaper stories, and some kind of corporate diagram like an organisational chart or a process map or a training requirements hierarchy or an elaborate sales report. But maybe that was just because of the present location – the call centre – with the rows of desks, the computers, the telephones. Or even the smart suit that Artemis wore.

Arthur sensed an opportunity to try something while Artemis had his back turned, but his mind and body were still not talking to each other properly. He did manage to get his limbs twitching, but all he achieved through that was to fall out of his chair.

Artemis immediately turned back around.

'Arthur!' Artemis said, grinning. 'So good of you to join us. Observe. There are some places in which certain people can draw upon certain energies.'

Artemis seemed drunk or otherwise intoxicated. He was gesturing expansively with his arms, and there was a sheen of sweat, or something like it, across his face. He seemed to want to talk, but Arthur just lay helpless on the floor, repeatedly trying to claw his way back to the vertical, and repeatedly failing.

'This is one of those places for people like me,' Artemis continued. 'I am at my strongest and most powerful when in anonymous rooms. In generic places. When we come to work in a place like this, we are not just entering one building, we are entering all of these buildings. You are no longer just you when you come here, Arthur. You are also every miserable little fucker who has ever worked here; who has ever been in any of these interchangeable, indistinguishable places, because you too are then interchangeable, indistinguishable, insignificant. You become the piss in the river, the spit in the sea.'

'What are you doing?' Arthur attempted to say, but the words sounded limp and malformed to his ears.

Artemis grinned.

'Did I hit you hard, Arthur?' he asked. 'As I was saying, I develop a peculiar strength in these places. I would apologise if I had not meant to damage you. I *did* mean to damage you, though, so there will be no apology forthcoming. Everything is intentional. You know what? I am quite enjoying myself here. I have never believed in any of this ritualistic shit, Arthur. I did not believe it was important. But now that I am engaging with it, it feels . . . I don't know, but it feels right. It's quite good fun. I always thought it was unnecessary. I always thought that the combination of the sacrifice with a person like me and a . . . *thin* place like this would be enough. Apparently not, though. You know what I mean by a thin place, right?'

Arthur found himself nodding. Yasmin had talked to him about her feeling that the call centre was thin, or weak; as if it had a weak fabric somehow; as if reality here were soft, wormy, worm-*eaten*; as if reality here sagged like a rotten floorboard. Arthur was not sure if his eyes were closed or open, but all he could see now with his eyes, or his mind's eye or whatever, was some kind of room with floorboards. And there was one floorboard that was loose, that was falling apart, and beneath it, through the cracks, he could see black water slapping upwards, and shining with an unearthly light. That water was the world that waited. And this place, this thin place, was the crumbling plane through which it glistened.

'Is he dead?' Arthur croaked, nodding in Harry's direction.

'What?' Artemis wheeled back to face the boy. 'Think there might be something wrong with your head, my good man! Your speech is terribly slurred. Suffered any potentially concussive or traumatic blows to the head recently?'

'Is he really dead?' Arthur tried again.

'Is he *dead*?' Artemis laughed, brandishing a whiteboard marker. 'Of course he's *dead*, you little cretin! Or, rather, as good as dead. Did you see all of the blood that came out of him? See that big cut in his neck? He's a dead man sitting, Arthur. I don't know how long it takes to bleed to death, but it must be nearly done by now. Which reminds me.'

Artemis clapped his hands together and strode off towards the water-cooler by the wall, where he took a couple of the small plastic cups from the dispenser. He brought them back and then, one after the other, he pressed them to the wound in Harry's neck and filled them with his blood. He placed both cups on one of the desks.

It was already dark in the call centre, but, it suddenly grew darker. Arthur could hear something too, a sound that he recognised. But no. Not here. The sound was in the wrong place. It was that whispering, rustling susurration from the Scape, or from the Interstice, as that thing had called it. It was faint, and it rose and fell, but it was there, and it was growing louder. It looked like Artemis could hear it too, judging by the way he cocked his head.

Another noise, closer to hand and more immediate: a wet, spitting sound from the desk. Arthur managed to swivel his eyes around to identify the source, and saw that the earpiece of that particular desk's headset appeared to have ejaculated some kind of black, slimy substance across the cheap veneer. Then the same sound again, from slightly further away: an irregular kind of liquid pulsing. Now the same from all over. Arthur could see the foul, oily stuff squirting out of all of the headsets within his field of vision, and hear it happening elsewhere. There was a rotten stench to it, too, and the smell brought back, forcefully, a sightless memory – a memory of something liquid trying to worm its way into his ear. He slowly lifted his hand to the side of his head and felt the same stuff encrusted all over it.

It was starting to pool on the desktops now, and spilling over the edges. It dripped at first, and then ran steadily. Arthur rolled slightly to avoid it, but not quickly enough, and it was running from the surrounding desks as well, pooling on the carpet tiles. There was very little light to see under the desks, but it looked like whatever it was was transforming the whole office into a dank, fetid organic environment. The flow showed no sign of slowing. And that sound of static was growing louder and louder. It was the sound of a giant tide approaching an unfamiliar shore. It was the sound of alien waves slowly breaking, high above a dead, empty beach, and then crashing to the ground in a gradual explosion of white noise and strange new life. Artemis remained quite still, biting his lip, his eyes wide.

With a grunt and a jerk, Harry's body started shaking. Arthur's heart beat faster as he watched his dad's arms and head tremble. The bones and tendons of Harry's hands shone white due to the intensity with which he was gripping the chair arms, but every other part of his body seemed to be in spasm. There seemed to be some kind of life left, something that was expressing itself through inarticulate gasps and sobs and gurgles, and random, sporadic movement.

The sound from the Scape was now roaring in Arthur's ears. And there was something else: undercutting the sickly smell of the dark liquid still bubbling from the headsets, there was the sharp new scent of the sea. Arthur crawled forward on his elbows, trying to hold his head above the now sodden carpet tiles, heading for his dad. Artemis had turned back to the window and was staring out with his hands pressed against the glass. His mouth was wide open. Whatever he was looking at, it wasn't Harry.

Something landed on the floor in front of Arthur with a heavy, wet squelch, stopping his progress. At first it looked just like a clot of some sort, a congealed lump of matter, but then Arthur saw that it was moving, and it was pulsating slightly. He shouted out in disgust and recoiled, only to see and hear and feel more of the same stuff raining down from the desks ranged above him.

There were ropes and knots and clusters of thin worms, all of different lengths, writhing frantically as if trying to untie themselves from each other. There were hair-thin, eel-long things, and tiny ones, like staples, that Arthur was sure had somehow got there from his bathroom, and all kinds of worms in between. He splayed his fingers and saw that his skin was dotted with the little ones, as if they'd been there in the rank liquid all along, and he screamed out loud. He felt those living dollops landing on his back, on his legs, on his head. Without even consciously trying to stand, he suddenly found himself on his feet, clawing at his clothes and hair. He could not keep his eyes open for long, but when he did so, he saw that every desk was now thick with wriggling creatures, all of them slopping around in some kind of blind frenzy.

At the rear of the desks, through the same holes that the computer cables came through, familiar pink and red and white and yellow tentacle-type things protruded, some of them thicker than the worms, some of them similarly slender, and waving around like seaweed under water. There were other things too: chitinous, clawed things, poking and snapping but seemingly – given an apparent inability to escape their neighbouring organisms – bound to the same root flesh, whatever that might be. In that brief moment of seeing, Arthur got the impression that these things were extending, curling around each other, creeping along any surface they found.

He also noticed Harry's body shuddering violently in his seat on top of the projector screen. And beyond that, heavy rain hammering into the windows. And beyond that . . . that was when Arthur closed his eyes.

The sea had been white with a turbulence just beyond the outer harbour wall. That was what had Artemis's attention, even despite Arthur's screams. What was it? What was causing that? But things had started dropping from Arthur's fringe on to his face, and his eyes had snapped shut before he could get the fuller picture.

Harry was screaming through the slit in his throat, or trying to.

When Arthur opened his eyes again, Artemis was standing directly in front of him, bending forward to look directly into his face. Their faces were just a few centimetres apart, and Artemis was not smiling.

'I don't know what you are trying to do,' Artemis said.

'Trying to stop you,' Arthur said. 'Trying to help my dad.'

Things were crawling around their feet, and they could barely hear each other above the static, which was now loud enough for distant voices to be heard in it.

Artemis pushed Arthur back against a desk, and then further back, forcing him down on to it so that he was lying across it. Arthur tried to struggle free but found that he could do nothing – Artemis was too strong. Things moved beneath him. He could feel them squirming vigorously. Artemis punched him in the head, and lights flashed inside his skull. His mouth and his eyes hung open and Artemis grabbed a handful of the worms and ground them into his face. They dropped on to his tongue, and then into the back of his throat. Arthur felt them under his eyelids. He coughed and gagged. He felt things wrapping themselves around his arms and legs and throat. The things felt like cords of hair. He managed to turn his head to the side before he threw up.

He realised that Artemis was no longer holding him, but he still could not move.

Matter slimed wetly between his cheek and the surface of the desk. With his head on its side, though, he could see Artemis moving back towards Harry's body. He forced himself to keep his eyes open and watch.

Artemis bent down over Harry and peered into his face. He thumbed open his eyelids. Harry's body had stopped its shaking and it looked like he really was dead. Artemis turned back to the cups of blood and lifted one of them. He knelt down towards the circle that he'd drawn, which, Arthur noticed, had remained free of the filth that was still slowly deepening across the whole of the rest of the call centre floor. The room had become thick with the static hiss and the sound of lively slithering. The air smelled both sulphurous and salty.

Artemis dipped his fingers in the blood and started to mark the circle precisely, delicately, carefully.

The hissing intensified.

SECURITY

Light shone from the revolving door at the front of the building. As Bony and Yasmin approached it, they could see that the two security men were standing at the bottom of the stairs, looking up, looking worried.

'What do you reckon?' Bony asked. 'Shall we just walk in like we're visitors?'

'You can't do that,' Yasmin said. 'This time of night, the doors'll be electronically locked.'

'Right then,' Bony said. He hefted the bat nervously. 'Right, then, we'll knock, shall we?'

'We could try knocking.'

'Can we knock, really?'

'I don't know.' Yasmin grimaced.

'I'm going to try knocking before anything else,' Bony said.

'OK,' Yasmin nodded. 'OK, yeah, let's knock.'

The two of them walked up to the door, conscious that they would now be visible to the security guards if the guards turned away from whatever was drawing their attention towards the stairs. Bony propped the cricket bat against the wall just to the right of the door, well out of sight, and tapped sharply on the glass. The security guards instantly turned around, saw Yasmin and Bony, and looked at each other uneasily. They both wore black trousers and jumpers. One of them – tall with thinning grey hair, and a neat grey beard – came up to the door, pressed a button on the inside, and hauled the door open.

'What is it?' he asked, eyes narrowed.

'We need to use your phone, please,' Yasmin said quickly. 'We think we just witnessed a mugging.'

'You think?' the guard replied. 'What do you mean?'

'We *did* just witness a mugging,' Yasmin said. 'We need to call the police, and maybe even an ambulance.'

The guard looked back towards his bulky, red-haired colleague, who shrugged uncomfortably, then shook his head. A strange sound could be heard inside the building, coming from upstairs. It was like the sound of a wave breaking, but held indefinitely and prolonged artificially.

'Sorry,' the guard said.

'For fuck's sake,' Bony said, 'come on! We heard somebody screaming out there past the railway tracks. We need a telephone or—'

'Look,' the guard cut in, 'if you know what's good for you, you'll both fuck right off right now. All right? Both of you. You, lass, and your lanky, skull-faced, bastard friend. OK? You don't want to come in here. Mike here is a dab hand with his fists, if you know what I mean, right? And

406

you're trying our patience now.' As if for confirmation, he looked back towards Mike, who was still standing at the foot of the stairs. Mike nodded, and the grey-haired guard turned back to face Yasmin and Bony. 'Push us any more and he will not go easy on—'

The end of the cricket bat was in his face before he could finish his sentence. His words were choked off by his teeth being smashed inwards. He crumpled, mumbling.

'Jesus Christ!' Yasmin said. 'Fucking hell.'

'I know,' Bony said. 'Oh God, I'm sorry. I didn't . . . I don't know.' He put his free hand over his mouth and stood there in the doorway, still clutching the cricket bat in his right hand.

Mike stared down at his floored colleague with suddenly saucer-like eyes, and his mouth open. Then he looked up at Bony and drew a fairly pathetic-looking night stick. He nervously licked his lips.

Bony darted forward and ploughed the bat into Mike's stomach, and then, as he doubled over, brought it down on the back of the man's head. There was an awful cracking sound and blood oozed from the point of impact. Mike hit the floor face-first.

'Oh no,' Bony said, 'I feel sick. I'm going to be sick. Oh no.'

Yasmin was pale and shaking. 'Bony,' she whispered. 'Christ, Bony.'

'I know,' Bony said. 'I'm sorry.'

Yasmin took his free hand. 'You had to do it,' she said. 'There's something awful happening here.'

Bony nodded.

'Come on,' Yasmin said. 'We need to get upstairs.'

Yasmin led the way, and the two of them ascended the staircase, the fuzzy noise getting louder as they did so. At the top, they saw something black and sticky oozing out from underneath the door leading on to the call centre floor. 'I think we've done the right thing,' Yasmin murmured.

'I hope so,' Bony said.

Yasmin pushed open the door – letting a frantic, insectile noise escape – but it was difficult, as if there was something lying on the floor behind it. She jumped backwards as a wedge of thick, wormy sludge squeezed its way out. She glanced back at Bony, her nose wrinkling. She then leant forward to push the door open again, before putting her head through the gap and peering around. She shifted backwards and let the door close.

She shook her head. 'I definitely think we've done the right thing,' she said. 'I can't tell you what's happening in there.'

'What do you mean?'

'Bony,' Yasmin's eyes began filling up, 'I think I'm really scared.'

'If you're scared, then I'm scared too,' Bony said, and nudged the door slightly open with the cricket bat. 'What's inside there?'

'I don't know what it is, but everything is covered in crap and worms.' She gestured at the few worms that made it through the open door. 'I don't know what's happened, or where they've come from, but we've got to go in. This must be where it's happening – whatever it is that's causing that out there in the sea.'

'OK,' Bony said. 'OK.' He nodded. He swallowed. He looked at Yasmin. 'Right, then,' he said, 'let's go.'

Yasmin nodded in response. She pushed at the door again, putting all of her modest weight behind one shoulder, and, with a deep breath, stepped through on to the call centre floor.

The place was barely recognisable as a call centre any more. It looked more like close-up, time-lapse footage of parasites feasting on the insides of some marine corpse. Brightly coloured fleshy things were crawling through a bed of dead, rotten fluids. Human-sized tendrils and tubers and tubes undulated slowly from the backs of desks where telephones had been, and thin-limbed, starfish-type things crept around like giant spiders. Purple, sinuous, arm-thick creatures slid through the murk. Moisture was dripping from the ceiling now, but Yasmin did not look up to see what its source was. She looked back to make sure that Bony was with her, then slowly, unsteadily, started picking her way through the writhing tangle towards where she could hear a voice, a voice she recognised, raised above the static sound that seemed to be just hanging there in the air like a mist.

Artemis.

Yasmin could not work out what he was saying. It sounded almost as if he were speaking in some other language. She could see him now, kneeling on something white that looked supernaturally bright against the gloom filling the room. In the middle of the white space was a body in a chair.

Bony was suddenly passing her by, cricket bat raised, as he jumped from one desk to the next to avoid the sucking muck on the floor. Yasmin found herself running too, suddenly desperate to reach that small, barren island of cleanliness on which Artemis knelt. She could feel things moving in her hair, in her shoes, inside her clothes. She ran and ran.

'Artemis!' she heard Bony shout.

Artemis looked up and around. In one hand he was holding a small white cup, the kind of thing you'd fetch a vending-machine coffee in. In that one moment, Artemis looked peculiarly pathetic, cup in hand, suit dirty and dishevelled, a look of total incomprehension on his face, while he knelt at the feet of what . . . a corpse? Was that a dead body? Who was that?

Harry?

Bony swung the bat all the way around his body before it connected with the side of Artemis's head. The cup dropped from the man's hand and spilled blood all over the pristine surface in front of him. His head suddenly bent way too far over to one side, and there was a sound like a snail being trodden on, but amplified.

Everything around them seemed to spasm and tighten and coil back in on itself, as if it suffered the same pain as Artemis. The sound of static quietened noticeably. Artemis began to crawl forward on his hands and knees, but Bony hit him again and his hands flew out from beneath him. Bony struck him once more on the head.

Through the windows beyond, Yasmin could see the boiling sea. Her brain, her heart, her stomach went cold, then hot, then cold. No. *No*. What was that out there? What the fuck was that in the sea? She rushed forward, past Bony and Artemis, and pressed her face and hands to the glass. She stared for a long moment, then turned around and stared at the remains of the ritual that Artemis had been engaged in. She ran forward and tipped Harry's chair out of the circle, pushed the chair over, and then threw herself on to the circle and used smears of the not-yet-dried blood to obliterate the symbols that Artemis had been drawing. She was panting and desperate. Part of her was still at the window, looking out over the sea.

Artemis lay motionless, face down in the creeping life, but Bony was still beating at him, his face now a mask, streaked with blood and the black stuff.

'Yasmin,' said a voice. It sounded like whoever was speaking was speaking with their mouth full.

She couldn't see who had spoken. 'Hello?' Yasmin said, standing up. She realised suddenly that tears were pouring from her eyes, and that she was shaking all over.

'Here, Yasmin,' said the voice. 'Here, on the desk.'

After a moment Yasmin saw. There was not much to see. Just a few pale inches of skin, and a vaguely human shape beneath a coat of filth and wriggling worms.

'It's Arthur,' the shape said, and a gobbet of wriggling creatures was spat out along with the words.

'Oh no,' Yasmin gasped. 'Oh my God, Arthur.' She started moving towards him, distractedly brushing things off her own body as she did so. But then she halted. 'Arthur,' she said. 'I'm sorry. I'll be back . . . Just wait a moment.'

She looked back at the circle on the projector screen and saw, with satisfaction, that the organic substance that had taken over the rest of the space was now flowing into the circle as well. And, unless her senses were totally fucked, things now seemed to be moving a little less vigorously. Things were slowing down, maybe even somehow receding.

Yasmin made her way back to the window and stared out of it for a moment before nodding briefly to herself and returning to Arthur. She started to scrape matted clumps from his body, starting with his head.

'What was it?' Arthur asked. 'Where did you go?'

'Nothing,' Yasmin said, her voice subdued and faltering, even to her own ears. 'I went nowhere.'

'These things are letting go of me,' Arthur croaked. His voice, too, was weak, and his words seemed strangely formed, as if he were just remembering how to talk. 'The . . . things . . . that were holding me are letting go. They're relaxing a bit. I can move again. Thank you, Yasmin. I can move.'

He pivoted around, swinging his legs down from the surface of the desk. He swayed on his feet, till Yasmin grabbed hold of his shoulders. 'OK?' she inquired.

'Yeah,' he said. 'Thank you, Yasmin.'

'We need to go now,' she said.

'Bony!' Arthur shouted – or, rather, tried to shout. It was a strange sound but Bony appeared to hear it. He was just standing over Artemis's body, staring down at it, but now looked up and seemed to stretch, almost as if he had just woken up. As he turned around, he looked lost and confused, and sick. He had dropped the cricket bat.

'Come on, Bony,' Yasmin said.

Bony merely nodded. It was difficult to differentiate him from the hellish backdrop against which he stood.

ON AND OFF

Reaching the bottom of the stairs, Arthur ducked behind the security desk.

Bony, following, grasped the handle of the cricket bat and looked around warily. 'Where are the guards?' he asked.

'They're not here,' Yasmin said. 'They must have recovered and run off. They maybe weren't even knocked out. People are tough.'

'Recovered?' Bony mused, quietly. 'You think?'

Arthur pulled open the drawers of the security desk, one after the other, until he found the bottle of whisky that he had spotted previously. Unscrewing the cap, he sprinkled it liberally around the foyer, before hurling the bottle itself at the stacks of boxes containing printer paper stored beneath the stairs. Bony did the rest with his lighter.

The flames spread quickly.

*

Yasmin and Bony watched the fire take hold, having unthinkingly put their arms around each other. Arthur looked blankly at the smoke. The black smoke. He could see, over to the south, the green eye of the lighthouse. It blinked on, and off, and on, and off, and on, and off, and on.

Yasmin did not tell either of them what she had seen from the window. She did not tell them how the disturbance in the sea had spread, so that the ocean was jumping and spitting and boiling and had turned white from the harbour out to the horizon. She did not tell them about seeing a red cast to the thick, heavy clouds that had already gathered. Nor did she tell them that she had seen the torso of a massively tall figure rising up from the immense waves that broke against the harbour wall beside the lighthouse. A vivid humanoid silhouette, spindle thin, from which the red light gleamed as if its surface were reflective, its unpleasantly flexible arms terminating in claw-like hands with fingers that seemingly tapered into needles.

It had wrapped one hand around the lighthouse, and with the other it had pointed at her.

When she had returned to the window, after spoiling Artemis's ritual, she had seen the huge thing staggering backwards, a mass of writhing tentacles having erupted from its face, and then slipping back beneath the surface of the sea.

*

She looked over at the lighthouse again, following the direction of Arthur's gaze. The green light shone regularly. *On*, and then *off*, and then *on*.

The Thing on the Shore

Most species of whale will sink when they die. They are heavy creatures of great density. Some, though, contain enough blubber to remain afloat, so when dead, they stay near the surface of the ocean, moving with the currents of the water in which they are suspended.

Like any other living creature, when a whale dies it starts to decompose and fill up with gas. Those whale carcasses that float thus become rotund, Zeppelin-like affairs, over time – balloons of skin and blubber inflated with gas and liquid matter, their skeletons lost and concealed somewhere deep within.

Eventually the skin ruptures, so the skeleton and rotten internal organs drift away from the outer layers of the whale, sinking as they drift, to be eventually eaten by sharks and other sea-creatures. The skin, however, buoyed by the collagen of the blubber, bobs to the top of the ocean, and can stay there indefinitely. Normally the blubber floats there until, weathered and twisted and turned inside out by the ceaseless battering of the waves, it washes up on a lonely beach as something unidentifiable and mysterious. It usually causes excitement – whenever this happens, people assume they have discovered something fantastic, something unusual, something new. But it is just part of the process of death; just a physical product of the physical process of something dying – something beautiful dying in the depths of our world and briefly disturbing the surface.

WORK

Arthur rested his forehead on the desk. Seven more hours. Seven more fucking hours. Seven more frustratingly difficult, stressful, boring, confusing, draining, depressing, *identical* fucking hours. And then what? Bony and Yasmin would be out, but they would be together, and that whole relationship made Arthur feel uncomfortable. Maybe it was just jealousy, but he couldn't shake the impression that Yasmin's self-esteem was floundering, no, *plummeting* in the face of Bony's bewildering attentions.

Outside, it was raining. Inside, the air was busy with a thousand passive-aggressive responses, questions and excessively polite explanations. Like people constantly digging holes and filling them back in again. Trying to serve horrible customers using systems that didn't work, following processes that didn't make sense, based on policies the origins of which everybody had forgotten. When anybody asked for help, they found out that very few people really understood anything at all, but despite that, everybody kept on trying.

Lack of conscientiousness was not the problem. People were so conscientious. People were so conscientious that they did not sleep at night; instead they squirmed around in their beds with battleship-coloured numbers and screens flashing through their heads. They answered their home phones with their script. They wept in the mornings from thinking about that one particular customer who they knew they couldn't help. Maybe everybody was just pathetic, right? Arthur didn't know. He really didn't know. What he did know was that everybody was grey-faced and heavy-lidded and, he imagined, thinking desperately about coffee or chocolate or TV.

The fire had been treated as arson. Harry was widely held responsible; the general consensus was that he'd got drunk, then gone postal. The remains of two people – including Harry – had been recovered, according to the TV news. The guards had not been reported as missing, but nor had they reappeared.

There were plenty of people on hand to say, 'Yeah, always did think that Harry was a bit weird.'

Nobody said anything about Artemis, though.

Arthur knew that more had been found up there on the first floor of the call centre than was ever reported afterwards in the news. But, yeah, Interext had been pretty thorough. Somehow they had ensured that nothing really changed. That was the real kick in the teeth. The refurb had taken all of two months. During that time all of the calls had simply been re-routed to another centre some-where slightly further inland – another Interext-owned building that simply sat empty in case of emergencies like this. A contingency plan.

Bracket, the new site manager, had arranged for the staff to be bussed out daily, so, other than his compassionate leave, Arthur hadn't even had any time off. Jesus Christ. Maybe this was how they were punishing him – they'd just stuck him back in this loop. Get up, go to work, go home, eat, sleep, wake up in the middle of the night, go to the lighthouse, watch the water, think about it, decide against it, go home, sleep, get up, go to work. Then repeat. It was unbearable.

He felt physically sick at the thought of a fully operational, fully stocked call centre just sitting there, just sitting somewhere else completely empty for more or less all the time – *all the fucking time, just in case.* A mirror image of this call centre, but with everything switched off. Rows of empty desks, blank monitors, clean white-boards, vacant chairs, dark meeting rooms, pristine carpets.

Everything but the bodies.

That was the place he thought about at night, while looking down into the sea. That empty building. Just waiting. Waiting for them all. He couldn't bear it. If ever there was something, a symbol that said, 'There is nothing you can do', it was that empty building.

That night, he decided, sitting there, cheek pressed to the veneer of the desk. He would do it that night. Out there, beneath the green eye of the lighthouse, maybe after just one last look back at the lit bedroom window of Yasmin's flat. He would wind a rusted length of chain from Drigg beach around his legs, and then fall. It wasn't like he'd be going somewhere that he'd never been before.

ACKNOWLEDGEMENTS

As ever, limitless thanks to Beth. And also to my family. Thank you to Nick Royle for being such a good friend and agent. Thanks to Charlotte and Richard at Quercus, and of course Peter Lavery, for all of the advice. Thanks to everybody else who has helped.